Between Mothers and Daughters

BETWEEN MOTHERS & DAUGHTERS

STORIES ACROSS A GENERATION

Edited and with an Introduction
by Susan Koppelman

The
FEMINIST PRESS
at The City University of New York

Library of Congress Cataloging in Publication Data
Main entry under title:

Between mothers and daughters.

1. Mothers and daughters—Fiction.   2. Short stories,
American—Women authors.   3. Women—Fiction.
I. Koppelman, Susan.
PS648.M59B48   1985   813'.01'089287   84-13562
ISBN 0-935312-26-9 (pbk.)

Permission acknowledgments begin on page 295.

Cover design by Lea Smith
Cover art: *The Banjo Player* by Mary Cassatt. Reproduced courtesy of
the Virginia Museum of Fine Arts, Richmond, VA
Text design by Lea Smith
Typeset by Monotype Composition Co., Inc., Baltimore, MD
Manufactured by Banta Co., Manasha, WI

This publication is made possible, in part, by public funds from the
New York State Council on the Arts.

This book is dedicated to

Frances Bollotin
Koppelman

my mother and my friend

sine qua non

Song of Purification

Our Mother who created us
from a single drop of blood
from her holy womb,
Our mother, who gave us this design
of body,
these protected parts,
this internal architecture,
Our mother who enabled us
to cunningly feed and nourish,
to be the cavern of life,
Oh mother, who has protected us
with hair, with lashes, in the pits
of the arm and womb,
Our mother, who made us as womankind,
we act with your strength
and in your dignity,
We are protected and unprotected,
like you and unlike you,
each of us different in her faith,
her coloring, the shape of her body,
each of us alike in our structure.
Oh, mother, rejoice with us
in this meeting of your daughters!

E.M. Broner

Contents

Preface

This book is the product of ten years of research on short stories written by women in the continental United States or territories that later became states. Late in 1972 I became a member of the English department committee at Bowling Green State University whose purpose it was to decide whether all sophomore introduction-to-literature courses should use the same textbooks and, if so, which ones. Publishers' representatives eagerly supplied us with many books for our consideration, both multigeneric and single genre, both thematically organized and historical, both national and international. I was responsible for examining, analyzing, and reporting on all the short story anthologies.

I received some half dozen short story collections to consider. Amazingly enough, they were almost interchangeable. They had almost all the same authors, the same stories. Even the same typefaces and page sizes: all unending sameness. It seemed as if the editors of short story anthologies did all their research in other anthologies instead of in the pages of the periodicals that publish short stories and in the collected stories of various writers already anthologized.

Whatever was wrong with one anthology was wrong with all of them. It has always seemed to me that anthologies should reflect the conflicting, idiosyncratic, individualized, although educated and informed, vision of its editor or editors. Compiling a collection of stories is personal work; it reflects the strengths and weaknesses, the preferences for different orders of excellence, the unique funny bone, the limitations, advantages, and special interests of the editor. But it was clear that there was only one product in only slightly different packages on the market. Editors of collections blamed it on the publishers. Booksellers blamed it on the teachers. Teachers believed themselves powerless.

An analysis of the tables of contents revealed all the statistical

dimensions of the collections: The first noticeable fact was that
there were about seven male writers included for every one woman
writer. Only the same few women writers were included in the
collections that included women. This created the impression that
there were far fewer women writing than men. Next I looked for
writers of color. There wasn't a single woman of color except
Diane Oliver, already tragically dead at an early age. She was
included in only one collection, and that was the oldest. Three
black men were included once each in three different anthologies.
James Baldwin was the only homosexual writer included in any of
the volumes.

I began to compare the original publication dates of the stories
with each other and with the publication dates of the anthologies
themselves. Almost all the stories by women had been published
within ten years of the publication date of the anthology. Here
and there was a story by Edith Wharton, Katherine Mansfield, or
Willa Cather, and in collections that began with stories from the
early nineteenth century, there was usually a story by Sarah Orne
Jewett or Mary E. Wilkins Freeman—but never both. These "old"
stories by women appeared in anthologies that contained more
than twenty-two stories and were compiled to be historically
representative.

Not only were women and writers of color underrepresented,
they were misrepresented as well. They were misrepresented
thematically, chronologically, and numerically. Women began writing much earlier both in time and in terms of the development of
the short story genre than selections suggest: more women have
written more stories than we yet know. Many, if not most, of the
stories written by women in the nineteenth century were published
in periodicals directed toward female audiences. Those periodicals
have still not yet been indexed or searched thoroughly for lost
literature. Additionally, the themes that women have most typically
and frequently addressed in their writing have not been represented
in anthologies.

Curious about whether this pattern also appeared in the short
story collections I had read in high school and college, or that I
had found in used bookstores for personal reading, I examined
next the books on my own bookshelves. I reread stories by Mary
McCarthy, Jean Stafford, Dorothy Canfield Fisher, Hortense Cal-

isher, and Shirley Jackson. They were as good as the writers in the contemporary anthologies: Joyce Carol Oates, Flannery O'-Connor, Eudora Welty, Katherine Anne Porter. The earlier writers had not diminished in their power to move and impress me; they had merely disappeared from the anthologies. They were old women, discarded with the same cavalier carelessness with which old women, old workers, are discarded by our society.

Next I looked into the books that had belonged to my mother and her five sisters, all avid readers, in the 1920s and 1930s. When my aunts moved from Cleveland, all their books were stored in our basement. There I found Dorothy Parker, Katharine Brush, Zona Gale, Fannie Hurst, Edna Ferber, Thyra Samter Winslow— still as powerful as they had been when I had first encountered them as a young girl.

Further research in anthologies published as far back as the 1880s revealed the patterns that still prevail: women, ethnic and racial minority, working-class, and explicitly homosexual writers have been underrepresented, misrepresented, and replaced rather than supplemented by current writers. When these writers have been included at all, they have been presented as practitioners of "minor" forms. Only the very earliest collections of stories from the *Atlantic Monthly* and *Lippincott's Magazine* in the late 1860s included equal numbers of male and female authors, all of whom, however, were white.

Yet a careful study of the history of the short story genre clearly reveals that women writers predominated in the early years of its development, not only creating the majority of stories written between 1830 and 1880, but also editing many of the periodicals in which they appeared. And, of course, the majority of those reading these stories written by women and published in periodicals and annuals edited by women were women and girls.

However, because each decade's women writers were replaced rather than supplemented by the women writers of the next decade, readers have been denied a historical perspective on women's fiction and, by extension, on United States fiction.

I began to look for women writers whose work had never been collected in anthologies, using specialized bibliographies and literary histories to track them down. Reading general histories of minority communities, I discovered the names of writers considered by their own historians to be part of their particular literary history. The research was an act of faith growing from a belief that all kinds of women had told their stories and that with time, hard work, and the help of sister scholars, they would be found. I committed myself to compiling an anthology of short stories that would recapture women's multi-racial, multi-ethnic, multi-regional stories—our literary history—the other half of the history of the development of the short story genre in the United States. I was excited to find how many other women had been writing: women of color; immigrant women; women whose politics were radical, whose religious ideas were unconventional; and women who weren't enough interested in men to make male characters central to the lives of the women in their stories. And once again I was struck by the fact that the stories included in standard anthologies did not deal with the themes and issues and types of characters most typical of women's stories.

One meets in the work of women writers certain themes that are explored again and again, embellished, analyzed, debated, celebrated, agonized over, viewed in general and in the abstract, and particularized in minute detail, focused on through one eye and then through the other. Some of these themes explore the dynamics of relationships between and among women: the some-times supportive, sometimes insensitive, sometimes competitive, often intimate ones between sisters; the intense and often trans-forming ones between friends; the role-modeling by, and loving respect for, aging women; the free, usually precarious, often idiosyncratic lives of women who never marry; the painful, socially revealing relationships between women who are involved with the same man; and the theme explored in this collection: the emo-tionally laden, social-burden-bearing relationships between mothers and daughters.

Acknowledgments

Literary scholars with special knowledge about the writers of these stories have generously enriched this volume by sharing information and sources with me. I would like to thank the following: Gary Sue Goodman for Caroline Healey Dall; Carol Farley Kessler for Elizabeth Stuart Phelps; Josephine Donovan, Emily Toth, Helen Eisen, Susan Allen Toth, and Nancy Walker for Alice Brown and Mary E. Wilkins Freeman; Jeanne O'Grady Ryan, Barbara Grier, Amy Baldwin, and Judith Schwarz for Helen Hull; Beverly Seaton for Helen Reimensnyder Martin; Janet Sharistanian and Emily Toth for Tess Slesinger; Timothy Murray and Beryl H. Manne of the Washington University Library's Special Collections and Deborah G. Lambert for Fannie Hurst; Elizabeth Schultz for Hisaye Yamamoto; and Joanna Russ for James Tiptree, Jr.

Additionally, a group of mothers and daughters of various ages, backgrounds, and perspectives, working sometimes as teams and sometimes individually, read between thirty and sixty mother-daughter stories each, to help decide which would be best in this collection. They discussed the stories with each other and with me in person, in letters, and during long-distance telephone calls. I want to thank Judith Arcana, author of *Our Mothers' Daughters* (Berkeley: Shameless Hussy Press, 1979), Gail Mills and Lisa Mills Merkle, Edith and Marilyn Probe, Hilary and Nikki Salk, Gail Robbins, Jamie-Lynn Richardson, Naomi and Eve Kane, Joanna Russ, Dorothy Ann Chase, and Nancy Hinkebein for sharing their ideas and feelings about the stories and the relationships between mothers and daughters.

Many of the authors of these stories have been active in helping shape the volume. They have been extraordinarily openhearted and I want to thank them for making the work on this volume such a rich experience. Joanna Russ, Ann Allen

Shockley, and Tillie Olsen, all old friends, have been, as always, supportive of my work and generous in their participation. New friendships with Alice Sheldon, Hisaye Yamamoto DeSoto, Guadalupe Valdes, and Arny Christine Straayer make this project already the most rewarding of my work life.

Finally, I want to express my gratitude to those who form my personal support network, who have, in all the most practical ways, expressed their belief in the value of this work and their benevolence toward me: Emily Toth, Joanna Russ, Cathy Davidson, and David Elliott. Further, I am indebted to Lois Neville; Allison King; Tom, Tim, and Matt Douglas; Jack Finn; and Mr. and Mrs. Catz for generous help when it was most needed. My husband, Dennis Mills, and my son, Edward Nathan Koppelman Cornillon, have made sacrifices of their convenience, their time, and their justified expectations over and over again. Words desert me when I try to express my continuing amazement and joy at Dennis's consistent support of my work and loving participation in the partnership that is our marriage. It is often said that family members can't teach each other things; disproving that is the most fun part of our family life. Nathan helped me conquer my technology anxiety and taught me to use his word processor. It has transformed my work life, and I am forever grateful. Now that I've made a book for Grandma, I agree with him that it's time he and I made a book for each other about mothers and sons.

Introduction

Women who write fiction write stories about mothers and daughters. Often, a woman writer's first published story is about the relationship between a mother and a daughter. Nor do women writers abandon this subject as they grow in their craft and their lives. They return to the literary contemplation and portrayal of mothers and daughters again and again throughout their careers. Women of every race, ethnicity, religion, region, and historical period write stories about mothers and daughters, and the similarities among the stories are greater than the differences because what we share as women, at least in terms of this primary relationship, is more than whatever else divides us. Stories about mothers and daughters seem like different facets of one great universal story that includes not only all the stories we have, but all those still lost and all those yet to be written.

When story makers and story audiences explore a particular subject repeatedly over a long period of time, that subject gains what contemporary theologians describe as the "sacred dimension."[1] Sacred dimensions provide perspectives on reality and help shape and give focus to life. Reading important stories about a subject that is important in our own lives and discovering how important that subject has been in the lives of other women helps us identify our connections with the women who have lived before us and the women with whom we share the present.

The eighteen stories in this collection were chosen from almost one hundred written by women living in the United States between 1830 and 1980.[2] The sacred relationship between mothers and daughters is clear not only from the multitude of stories on the subject, but from the passion, intensity, and the ritualized interactions that characterize them. The stories in this collection share that passion and intensity, they capture those rituals, and they represent a wide variety of approaches to this sacred subject.

Mothers and Daughters Up Against the Patriarchy

The most common mother-daughter story describes the patriarchal harvest of the nubile daughter with or without her mother's protest or resistance. Whether through the force of law, the promise of luxury, or the simple guarantee of survival, this reaping of the daughters is always accompanied by overtones of economic exchange. And always the intent of the proposed exchange is clear: sex for protection, sex for food, sex for survival. The male sense of entitlement turns on the contemporary vestiges of the *droit du seigneur,* the legal right of the feudal lord to rape the female serfs on his estate. Hebrew, Greek, and Roman slave owners enjoyed the legal sexual plunder of female slaves, as did white southern United States slave owners, as in "Annie Gray: A Tale," the first story in this collection. The *droit du seigneur* has metamorphosed into sexual harassment at work and at school. At home, it is most blatant in the incestuous rape of daughters by their fathers or by men who stand in the place of fathers.

Such a threat leads to tragedy in "Old Woman Magoun." In that story, the grandmother, who has been conditioned to act not only as nurturer and care-provider, but as guardian of her grand-daughter's chastity, is forced to realize that she cannot protect the girl any longer. Indeed, she cannot protect herself. At the command of the patriarchy, the mother figure is expected to change from guardian of chastity to panderer and pimp. She is expected to seduce her charge to the will of their mutual master, to "turn her out." Refusal of the father's demand to make the girl available invites retribution and punishment, from something as active as the invocation of the law to compel compliance, as in "Old Woman Magoun," to something as passive as the withdrawal of proffered financial help, as in "Recuerdo."

What are the mother's feelings? What are her choices? How

will the daughters respond? These questions are raised repeatedly in the stories in this collection, sometimes with grimness and despair, as in "Old Woman Magoun," "Oats for the Woman," and "Recuerdo," sometimes with subtle conspiratorial humor, as in "The Women Men Don't See," and sometimes with the passion of the mother's compelling desire to ensure her daughter's freedom, as in "Seventeen Syllables."

In some stories, the mothers see no hope of escaping or even of surviving if they defy the patriarchy; therefore, they seek the least painful accommodation to reality for their daughters, themselves, and the community of women with whom they identify their interests. Many mothers and mother-surrogates advise manipulative compliance as in "A Marriage of Persuasion" and "The Lawd Don't Like Ugly." In the matriarchal world in which loyalty between mother and daughter comes first, as in "The Women Men Don't See," the daughter who betrays their mutual best interests because of personal preferences or illusions about romantic love would be no heroine, but simply squeamish, self-indulgent, and selfish, as she is seen by her mother in "A Marriage of Persuasion."

Where there is no true freedom, there can be no true love. Mothers know that, especially mothers who are the victims of multiple oppressions. Daughters, feeling the first stirrings of the flesh in their early adolescence, and befuddled by the myth of romantic love, often do not. Because the choice between loyalty to oneself and loyalty to a beloved is not one a free person should have to make, and because the daughters do not yet understand that in the patriarchy women are not free persons, they often resent their mothers for whatever choices are urged on them (as in "A Marriage of Persuasion," "Seventeen Syllables," and "Recuerdo").

The young women don't yet understand that their mothers aren't the ones forcing them to choose between love and autonomy, between self-possession and economic survival. Heterosexual girls don't want to believe their mother's warnings about men and women's lot in the patriarchy. They want to be able to trust those whom they find sexually attractive. They are unwilling to adopt an attitude or accede to knowledge that would make it impossible to trust the object(s) of their desire. They instinctively understand that sexual interaction with an untrust-worthy, dangerous, and/or exploitive partner inhibits healthy sexual functioning. It is natural for them to wish to protect their sexuality.[3] Although this sexual motif runs through many of the stories, it is clearest in "Seventeen Syllables."

When the daughters become women and learn to understand more of the world, mothers and daughters tend to become co-conspirators, as in "The Women Men Don't See," rather than adversaries, as in "A Marriage of Persuasion." In "Seventeen Syllables," the narrator moves from rejecting her mother's vision to understanding and accepting it, but only after the passage of many years and her mother's death. In "Mother to Dinner," the conflict between a daughter's loyalty to her mother and her desire for her husband is still a raw wound.

How can a mother teach her daughter to survive? Sacrifice of the self may be the price of survival for a woman in the patriarchy. Mothers are supposed to teach their girl babies, as they have learned from their own mothers, to sell themselves ("A Marriage of Persuasion," "The Lawd Don't Like Ugly"), to submit ("Old Woman Magoun"), to bargain with their bodies for subsistence ("Recuerdo"), to embrace the men who have exploited their mothers ("Oats for the Woman"), and to service and serve their masters ("Annie Gray: A Tale"). Daughters often hate their mothers for bearing them female into a world that will not tolerate a woman's survival intact—and for collaborating or seeming to collaborate in breaking their daughters to the will of the patriarchy. But when women become mothers themselves, they understand the fear and the love, the ignorance and the hope that drive mothers to bind their daughters' feet, to submit them to clitoridectomies, to encourage addiction to diet pills, or to advocate intellectual self-castration. They also understand better the ways in which their mothers did protest and try to warn and protect them. And they learn something about the cost to a mother of even trying to protect her daughters, as in "Oats for the Woman."

The major factor determining the nature and extent of the conflict between mother and daughter, and between them and the patriarchy, is the age at which the daughter begins to be beset by patriarchal demands for sexual performance. "Old

Woman Magoun," "Oats for the Woman," "Recuerdo," and "The Lawd Don't Like Ugly" are variations on this subject.

"Old Woman Magoun" tells of life in white New England when child custody law blatantly favored the father and when a man's ownership of his children was undisguised. Fifty-seven years later, "Recuerdo" describes a world in which nothing has changed for women, though it deals with Mexican-American culture, a different natural environment, a different religious tradition, and a different cultural patina—but the "Recuerdo" tale is very familiar: Can a female custodian of a female child protect the girl from the depredations of those who own them both? Can the mothers overcome their powerlessness, interrupt the short-circuiting of their love, and stop the rape of those they have nurtured?

Both "Oats for the Woman" and "Recuerdo" have strong implications of incest. The mother is forced to confront the sacrifice of her daughter to the same man who sexually abused her. Only in "The Lawd Don't Like Ugly" does the mother figure attempt to give her surrogate daughter psychological tools to protect her from the impact of the sacrifice—as inescapable for the black girl as it is for the white girl, the Jewish girl, and the Mexican-American girl. The black mother in "The Lawd Don't Like Ugly," recognizing the apparent inevitability of the harvest of the daughters by the masters of the world, tries to help her surrogate daughter choose the least offensive of the predators, the one likely to inflict the least damage, to offer the most protection, and to prove the least divisive of the relationship between the mother and the daughter. But the choices are limited to those who offer themselves or can be enticed, and the choices can never be made with any certainty.

The Quest for Identity

Stories about women's quests for identity are usually written from the perspective of daughters (a perspective every woman retains, even after she has become a mother herself). The daughter wants to define either her own identity or that of the

woman she has known only as "mother." In some stories, such
as "I Stand Here Ironing," a mother assesses her own sense of
identity.

Stories about daughters who search for and joyfully find their
identity in community with their mothers and the world of
women to which their mothers belong have been ignored by
literary historians and critics until recently. However, daughters
often discover or create their identities through union and
identification with their mothers and the world of women, as in
"The Way of Peace." In that story, Lucy Ann achieves union
with the world, the ways, and the place in the order of things
of her mother by assuming her mother's identity while simultaneously asserting her own. As she does so, she faces down the
power of "brotherly love," or benevolent patriarchy. Lucy Ann
doesn't wish a place for herself in their world, especially not the
place reserved for her: the visiting old maid aunt. She doesn't
wish to be identified in terms of secondary biological roles. If
she must accept a biologically determined label, it will be the
most primary in her life: the daughter of her mother.

The daughter may also discover or create her own identity by
separating from her mother in one of three ways. In modern
times, a daughter most often leaves home when she marries a
man of her choice, as Anna wishes to do in "A Marriage of
Persuasion." This story espouses the romantic idea that identity
is achieved through separation from the mother and the identification of personal romantic/sexual preferences, the choosing
of a father for her children. Such an understanding of how to
achieve identity not only forces a woman into biological roles,
but it almost forces separation from the community of women.
The daughter is propelled by marriage into isolation from the
private language and priorities of the women's culture she has
lived in until marriage. Such is the experience of the narrator
of "Mother to Dinner."

The romantic illusion that a woman can "find herself" in
isolation from her community has been dangerous for women.
It tricks a young woman into abandoning the world that has
nurtured her. Identity and the community of women have been
transformed into competitive ideas in "A Marriage of Persuasion." Anna believes that she will be injured in her search for

identity if she cannot live in accord with her personal romantic/ sexual preferences. Because Anna's point of view dominates the story, the world of the mothers is drawn without sympathy or love. Nevertheless, Anna gives in to the needs of that world. Does she have any other choice?

The daughter may also separate from her mother by leaving home to pursue a goal that she and her mother have agreed is right for her, as in "Mrs. Gladfelter's Revolt." Mrs. Gladfelter loves her daughter "with a passionate devotion" and perceives her as the repository of "the poetry and romance of her life." This maternal passion for the daughter represents yet another aspect of the search for identity: a mother transfers to her daughter those elements of her own self that she most treasures. What she hadn't the opportunity to cherish or the foresight to protect in herself, she finds the courage to defend in and for her beloved daughter. This represents a transfer of the portion of women's identity that is communal and historical. In that transfer, the mother has a renewed sense of self. The mother becomes an active participant in history and the daughter becomes an active recipient of a matriarchal tradition.

The third way that a daughter may separate from her mother is by apprenticing herself to an adult other than her mother as a model for the kind of adult woman she wishes to become, as in "The Fire."[4] Cynthia has embraced a vision of adult womanhood lived in accordance with values and goals different from her mother's. The daughter who separates herself from her mother in this way is rejecting either her mother, her mother's way of life, or both.

Dee has also separated from her mother by apprenticing herself in another world. "Everyday Use" is unusual, not only because the mother tells the story, but because the two daughters, sisters, search for their identity in different ways. One daughter's sense of identity is rooted in the maternal past; the other daughter's sense of identity hinges on her strong self-esteem. Dee thinks she has found her "roots" by leaving home, but her roots and even the name she has rejected come from the women's community she has dismissed. Dee's mother seems to consider Dee's search for identity outside the circle of the women's community to have been a farce and a failure—but, ironically, entirely in keeping with Dee's character, or identity. Mama's analysis and assessment of Dee's search has enabled her to understand and value more acutely her other daughter's search for identity in family history and women's community. Her newly found and expressed regard for Maggie sparks Maggie's self-esteem.

Thamré's revelation in "Old Mother Goose" is that she can reject her mother's way of life while accepting and loving her mother. She can include in her expanded and enriched sense of identity a sense of herself as the loving daughter of a loving mother.

If the search for identity is undertaken in the direction of the daughter's roots in the world of women, then the relationship between the mother and the daughter is portrayed as "comic," i.e., as tending towards the preservation and enhancement of their relationship and/or the community of women to which they both belong. If the direction of the quest takes the daughter away from the mother, their relationship is portrayed as "tragic," i.e., as suffering from chronic failed intentions, failed communications, alienation, and separation.

Another kind of quest story tells of the daughter's search for understanding of the nature and identity of the woman who is her mother. The daughter wants to know who her mother is, instead of how she functions as a mother. Most of these quest stories take place soon after the death of the mother. The setting for these stories is sometimes the time of preparation preceding the burial. But more often the stories are set after the formal mourning period has ended and the daughter must go through her mother's personal effects. In the process of sorting, the daughter begins to think about her mother as a woman apart from her role as "mother." She seeks evidence of continuity in the life of the dead woman who was once a little girl, a daughter, herself. It is often the little things the daughter finds that her mother has stored and treasured that reflect continuity and reveal cherished memories. Another setting for such stories is the death watch that the daughter keeps for her mother. Often the mother wanders in and out of consciousness, in and out of the present. And for the first time, the daughter hears bits and pieces of her mother's life that have nothing to do with her mothering life, as in "Annie Gray: A Tale."

Only after the mother approaches death or after she has died does the daughter feel safe wondering about this woman who has given life to her. Now she can consider her mother's dreams, ambitions, sexuality, disappointments, and vices without fear of consequences to herself or to their relationship. If she discovers, for instance, that her own birth had been unwelcome and inconvenient, perhaps even destructive in her mother's life, she needn't worry about how to continue a relationship with a woman to whom her very life has been a threat or a disappointment. "Autobiography of My Mother" is unique in this sense: A daughter examines these aspects of her mother's life as a woman, including the impact of her own birth on her mother's life, while her mother is still alive.

Occasional Stories

Some of the stories about relationships between mothers and daughters were written for special holiday issues of magazines, most often women's magazines, where they would have been read in a context of recipes for festive foods and patterns for gala clothes. Many literary artists have scorned such occasional literature because it calls upon writers to respond to stimuli for literary production other than their own imaginations and creative impulses. Poet laureates, whose job requires them to compose poetry commemorating special state occasions, such as military victories, bicentennials, and coronations, have often been ridiculed as literary hacks. And yet some of the most stunning and lasting poems have been elegies and odes, just as some of the most stirring music in the world's repertoire has been composed for specific military, religious, and patriotic occasions.

As functional art, occasional literature is often assumed to be trite and sentimental. But when an entire literary genre is dismissed by the arbiters of literary taste, something other than literary judgment is responsible. Many genres (historical romances, Gothics, and occasional stories) have been dismissed as trivial: these are all genres in which women have been the primary creators and audiences.[5] Although men have also written

occasional stories, women writers have been primarily responsible
for this genre's evolution as an art form.

Many occasional stories written by women commemorate
holidays connected to events in nature, such as harvest, the
winter solstice, and the vernal equinox. Overtly connected to
the contemporary holidays that modern religions have assigned
to those ancient natural celebrations, these stories are rich with
covert allusions to the ancient meanings of the natural events.

Two stories in this collection are occasional stories. "Old
Mother Goose" appeared first as a Christmas story; "The Way
of Peace" is a Thanksgiving story. The seamless connection
between private life and public event makes these two stories
among the finest examples of this form of literature. However,
because of the custom of reprinting stories without complete
information about their original publication, readers have generally been denied the information necessary to make clear the
occasional nature of many stories.

The transition from contemporary religious occasion to ancient
woman-oriented occasion is clear in "Old Mother Goose." The
story represents an appropriation of Christian myth. The disgraceful mother, Old Nell, who has conceived and given birth
to her daughter out of wedlock, first looks to a male deity for
justification and forgiveness when she says, "If God be for me,
my girl won't be against me!" By the end of the story, once their
reunion has been accomplished and their relationship transformed, Old Nell, dying, asks, "If my girl was for me . . . could
He be against me . . . ?" She feels her salvation has been accomplished. She has been, as it were, born again—through the love
and sacrifice of her daughter.

Life-Cycle Events

Besides the public occasions discussed above, there are private
occasions in all lives about which there is also a rich occasional
literature.

The impulse to create rituals is a basic component of human
psychology and spirituality. Those ritual traditions most rich,
varied, and deeply affecting celebrate occasions in the lives of

individuals, such as birth, death, mating, and the assumption of adult responsibility in a community. In most societies, the rituals for these life-cycle events are different for males and females.

Rituals celebrating or commemorating the special life-cyle events of women have survived from pre-literate societies, although almost entirely in vestigial forms.[6] These rituals are tied to biological events, such as menarche and child-birth, and are connected to fertility, reproduction, and the presumption of heterosexuality.[7]

The rituals that have grown up to honor special events in women's lives are preserved in women's short stories. The ritual occasions in a relationship between mother and daughter are regularly captured for all time in these stories, and women's ritual celebrations and commemorations share common elements and patterns.

Among several life-cycle events frequently memorialized in mother-daughter stories, menarche is especially important. This physical event is accompanied by the growth of the daughter's own sexuality. Mothers in these stories respond to their daughters' physical development with an often desperate attempt to make them understand what it means to be a woman in a man's world. The mother may try to warn her daughter about what life is like for women by revealing her own life history. The mothers' stories in "Annie Gray: A Tale" and "Seventeen Syllables" are intended as cautionary tales.

The occasion of the onset of puberty has been most thoroughly explored by minority women writers. These stories tend to be resolved with the daughter accepting her mother or mother-surrogate's advice and vision, as in "The Lawd Don't Like Ugly." The mystification and mythology that cloud the understanding of life for majority-culture women often lead to resolutions in which the daughter and the mother or mother-surrogate become alienated in life, as in "A Marriage of Persuasion," or separated by death, as in "Old Woman Magoun."

Other biological events commemorated in life-cycle stories are deaths of mothers, as in "Annie Gray: A Tale," and "The Way of Peace," and birthdays, as in "A Birthday Remembered."

Biological milestones are not the only life-cycle events portrayed in these stories. Among the journeys and choices celebrated and commemorated in the life-cycle stories are the separations and reunions of mothers and daughters. "Mrs. Gladfelter's Revolt" takes its shape from the preparations for and eventual separation of a mother and daughter, while "Old Mother Goose" and "High Heels" are structured around reunions and the healing of a rift between mother and daughter. When the reunion is coupled with the restoration of the relationship, the air of ceremony is heavy, portentous. When the reunion does not accomplish reunification but merely underlines the distance between the women, as in "Everyday Use," the ceremony is observed in the breech.

Every turning point in the life of a mother or daughter precipitates a crisis in their relationship, and mothers and daughters engage in a pattern of interaction and communication on these occasions that is shared across time, space, and cultural heritage with other mothers and daughters. Because this pattern is so familiar to women readers, the writer has great latitude for using the most subtle forms of artistic literary innuendo and ellipsis. But for these suggestive art forms to be available to an artist who wishes to communicate seriously with an audience, the artist must know that she shares a culture with all its nuances and idioms and perspectives with an audience. She must be able to write to her own community, not to foreigners, who would require explanations, analogies, and simplifications. Women writing for an audience of women are inferential and notational—and we can piece together women's shared culture from the ceremonies we decipher in these short stories.

The Pause

A women's holiday may be celebratory, (such as the celebration of a happy reunion or a birthday) or a holiday may be commemorative (such as a *yahrzeit*—a Jewish anniversary of a death—or a funeral). Whether celebratory or commemorative, these holidays have much in common: neither the mother nor the daughter accomplishes any domestic maintenance or administration. They pause in the business of life and concentrate their attention only on each other.

These pauses in the dailiness of life have a special character of their own. A ritual has evolved and the performance of that ritual provides the structural framework for many mother-daughter stories that focus on life-cycle events. The ritual has three phases.

The first phase of the ritual calls for a recitation of the relationship between the mother and the daughter. In these first brief exchanges they remind each other of what has taken place in their collective past. For instance, Tobie reminds Aunt El in "A Birthday Remembered" that "I never forget your birthday" and "You *know* what I like!" And in "High Heels," the rapprochement between the mother and daughter, each filled with fear and guilt about the other, begins with the daughter, who blurts out, "Hey, remember the candy kisses you gave me? . . . Remember the matching red blouses?" These remarks are allusive and elliptical, but for readers for whom this type of communication is a cultural given, such remarks resonate with meaning. This shared recounting of herstory acknowledges and reinforces the bond between mother and daughter.[8]

The second stage in the ritual is the assessment of the relationship. The women ask themselves how or why something happened that didn't work, that put distance between them, that alienated them from one another. It is during these sometimes silent ruminations that the reader learns all she needs to know to follow the action into the future. This phase ends with the rendering of a judgment on the past.

The third and final phase of the ritual is the projection into the future of the relationship. In the act of making this projection about the future course of the relationship—and the projection grows out of the judgment made on their past—commitment to the continuation of the relationship is implicit. The commitment may be indicated in various ways: subtly, as in the statement, "Next time we get together, the strawberries will be in season," or in as complex and definitive a manner as Thamré's final short speech to her audience, "If you will *excuse* me, I will leave you now, and take my mother home."

The Disgraceful Mother

"Disgraceful mother" stories portray unconventional mothers and their daughters' struggles to resolve their feelings about their mothers and about themselves as the daughters of such women. Aspects of their character and behavior that violate narrow partriarchal rules for women cause mothers to be labelled "disgraceful." The daughters do not write stories about their mothers' failures to fulfill themselves as artists or intellectuals or athletes or spiritual or political leaders. They write about their mothers' failures to be sexually conventional and circumspect,[9] about their mothers' depressive withdrawals from "normal" functioning, about the drunkenness or drug addiction that renders their mothers slovenly, unpredictable, or "unladylike," and about the poverty and hard physical labor that have left their mothers frazzled, bedraggled, and impatient. Daughters are shamed by these mothers who don't conform to social ideals. In fact, some stories tell of daughters' resentment of their mothers' failures to fulfill conventional female roles, while disregarding the mothers' successes as artists or professionals.

If the daughter learns to separate herself from her mother's "sins," to reject whatever guilt she has assumed or has had to live with in a society that has inflicted guilt upon her, she may turn her back on her mother and make a separate life for herself. Or she may try to understand her mother on her mother's own terms. She may realize she can love an imperfect woman simply because that woman is her mother.[10]

Mid-nineteenth-century temperance tracts include drunken mother stories, although many more describe drunken fathers. From the 1890s until Prohibition, drug-addicted mother stories reflect that period in women's history when doctors routinely prescribed opium-based elixers for women's menstrual cramps, depressions, and general restiveness—and turned thousands of healthy women into addicts. During Prohibition, drunken mothers began to appear in stories about middle- and upper-middle-class women. The daughters appear more passive and victimized in these stories than they did in the temperance stories, which usually portrayed families from the lower socio-economic levels with daughters taking heroic action on behalf of the disabled parent.

During the first thirty years of the twentieth century, stories began to appear about mothers who were sexually suspect—who led sexually unconventional lives. And starting in the 1960s, we begin to find stories about mothers who are mad, insane—mothers whose emotional functioning has gone "wrong." Today, "disgraceful" mothers in short stories may be addicts or alcoholics, mentally ill or sexual outlaws; all are presented as "problems" to be solved by overburdened and ambivalent daughters.

"Old Mother Goose" is the grandmother of all the "disgraceful mother" stories. It provides the pattern for all the rest. "Old Mother Goose" portrays the most disgraceful of all mothers: drunk, drug-addicted, and not only promiscuous, but a one-time prostitute. She is ugly, dirty, unkempt, and stupid—as low as a woman can sink. And her daughter has become all the best that a woman can be: pure, disciplined, beautiful, well-groomed, tastefully dressed, and brilliantly talented (as a performer of male composers' creations—the only ladylike kind of brilliance permissible). "Old Mother Goose" is about a lady and a tramp, about a beautiful princess and an ugly witch. When there is a contradiction between the ideal of motherhood projected by the society and the daughter's perception of her own mother, the daughter must find some way to explain and live with the discrepancy between the ideal and the real. At stake is not only love and respect for her mother, but love and respect for herself. Thamré has rejected the woman who is her mother and embraced an ideal, mourning its absence in her childhood and projecting that image as a goal for herself. In the course of the story, she comes to embrace the woman who is her mother, freeing herself to create a life that is authentic instead of imitative. Quite often, the passage from rejection to acceptance of her mother is for the daughter the passage from emotionally dependent childhood to autonomous adulthood.

Women have written many stories about disgraceful mothers, about mothers whose every breath, every action, embarrasses their daughters and represents a violation of the ideal mother image—whether that image is of the woman whose price is far above the rubies of Biblical tradition, the image of the pure virgin/madonna from Christian tradition, or the floor-scrubbing, dirty collar-ring defeating, loving-from-the-oven mother of secular commercial tradition. Most of these stories end with a reconciliation between mother and daughter, if not in life, at least in the daughter's heart. The daughters grow to understand that, for their own psychological health and spiritual wholeness, they must acknowledge their mothers' separateness and their own innocence of guilt by association with her "disgrace." In "Old Mother Goose," guilt by association is replaced with respect by association. This fairy-tale-like resolution presents yet another pattern for the transformation of mother-daughter relationships.

Surrogate Mothers

In some stories women other than biological mothers are central. These women come to mothering in various ways and for various reasons, but the element of choice in their accession to the responsibility for the care of daughters is always clear, as it often is not in stories about biologically related mothers and daughters. That these women—grandmothers, stepmothers, older friends—choose to act as mothers and that we recognize their behavior as mothering behavior raises important questions about the nature and meaning of motherhood. Is the *mother* the biological parent of the child, or the woman who brings her up? That question, which has been an element around which conflict whirls in many television dramas, doesn't seem to engage the imagination of women who write short stories for women readers. None of the surrogate mothers represented in this collection wonders for a moment whether she is more the "real" mother than the biological mother. She simply relates to the younger female in ways that we immediately recognize as "mothering." Is the mother the one who shapes the girl to the demands of the repressive patriarchal culture, as does the mother in "The Fire," or is she the one who helps the girl see ways to remain self-possessed, to achieve independence, and to find a way to name herself, as does the surrogate mother in that story? Is the mother the one who nourishes the body or the one who feeds the soul? Does the mother teach the arts of deception or the art of self-expression? Which is Queenie learning in "The Lawd Don't Like Ugly?" And which art is the art of survival?

There are three more stories that deal with the relationship between girls and mother-substitutes, or surrogate mothers: "Old Woman Magoun," about a grandmother, and "Oats for the Woman" and "A Birthday Remembered," about step-mothers.

As Meridel Le Sueur has suggested in her short story, "Biography of My Daughter,"[11] we are all mothers of all women younger than ourselves.[12] Hers is a political utopian suggestion, arising out of a socialist perspective and strong solidarity with working-class women across the generations. Her suggestion is echoed in many utopian works by women, such as Joanna Russ's novel, *The Female Man* and Marge Piercy's *Woman on the Edge of Time*,[13] in which society has been organized so no two human beings are ever forced into each other's company or into economic or psychological dependence on another human being for any reason, including the biological relationship of parent and child. In these utopian blueprints for a better future, the relationships between mothers and daughters are casual, less intense because less stressed, and affectionate, but not passionate, as they are in so many of the mother-daughter stories in this collection. The biological link, divorced from economic consid-erations, is never romanticized.

But in the patriarchy, none of the conditions of the utopian worlds prevail. People are forced into parental relationships; relationships are tense, and the biological links are often ro-manticized. So why do the step-mothers in "Oats for the Woman" and "A Birthday Remembered" willingly choose to be mothers to girls they haven't given birth to? The two women enter into mothering for different reasons. In the Hurst story, it is the promise of financial security, kindness, and safety that puts Hattie in a position to mother Effie; in "A Birthday Remem-bered," love draws Ellen into Tobie's life. But it is important to realize that these two women embrace their mothering roles.

Motherhood is the socio-political condition of all adult females mandated by the patriarchy, and it seems that when a woman enters a marriage in which there are already children—at least in the stories I have found—they embrace them. They know how to be mothers; they know about nurturance and intelligent caring. Margaret Mead has described a Melanesian culture in which each member is responsible, in a caring, parental way, for each younger member of the community.[14] No one is without a nurturer, and none is without the responsibility to nurture. Meridel Le Sueur suggests that the social structuring of human responsibility in this way is a tactic for the oppressed to achieve a revolution. Her radical vision has been shared by women writing about nurturant relationships between women, and that vision is reflected in the surrogate-mother stories in this collection.

Multiple Oppressions

Women who are the victims of multiple oppressions have fewer illusions about love, romance, and the benevolence of male culture than women who are only the victims of sexism. The higher the class of a woman and the more privilege she has inherited by virtue of her skin color or group membership, the more likely she is to be sentimental about the potential for emotionally honest and mutually rewarding relationships between women and men. However, women who are the victims of multiple oppressions are much less naive. The more powerless the woman, the less attempt men make to disguise the nature of their expectations and demands. In "A Marriage of Persuasion," Anna is under the illusion of the myth of romantic love, the myth that there is a possible right man to whom she will desire to submit herself as an act of love. And she does not question that compliance, yielding, deference, and submission are appropriate postures for a woman toward a man. Anna believes that love means assuming that posture willingly. Her mother knows better, but has only been forced to that knowledge by recent poverty. And she hasn't brought up her daughters to know that.

In contrast, the mother in "Recuerdo" has known since her own girlhood that there isn't much difference for a woman between what is expected from her by a man she loves and is loved by, and from a man who wants to buy sexual and domestic services from her. She does know, however, that the financial benefits may differ from one arrangement, one man, to another. And, like the surrogate mother in "The Lawd Don't Like Ugly," she supports her daughter's entrance into a liaison with a man most likely to provide her with material security and safety, if not happiness. In both stories, as well as in "Oats for the Woman," the men being compared with each other, potential lovers with potential buyers, belong to the same oppressed groups to which the women belong.

"Annie Gray: A Tale" offers a contrast between a noble man of the oppressed enslaved people and a careless white man. But the story, a deathbed confession, serves more as an indictment of slavery than it does of the patriarchy. In most stories by minority women, the writers are at pains to present minority men as superior to men of the oppressor group. If the minority men aren't all good, they are at least better, less oppressive, less victimizing, less dehumanizing of the minority women than are the men who belong to the oppressor group. But the stories by minority women that portray mothers and daughters confronting the patriarchy make no real distinctions between men of the oppressor and oppressed groups. All men have access to more power and wealth than do minority women.

The largest number of mother-daughter stories have been written by Jewish women—a great many of them testaments of love and witnesses to a culture that the daughters were nurtured by, but are leaving behind. Jewish women writers have also provided the greatest number of "disgraceful mother" stories, stories about drug addicted and alcoholic mothers, stories about manic-depressive and schizophrenic mothers, stories about daughter-exploiters. Black women have begun to write these stories, too, and, most recently, Chicana and Puerto Ricana writers have published some "disgraceful mother" stories. All of these stories portray not only daughters coping with their mothers' "sins," their mothers' failures to conform, but also upwardly mobile daughters exploring the guilt they feel for rejecting the cultures their mothers have spent their lives sustaining and maintaining.

Black women's culture is particularly characterized by mother love. The book dedications of black female critics and editors, the short stories by black women writers, and the lyrics sung by the "girl" groups on the Motown label attest to a combination of love and gratitude to the women credited with teaching their daughters about life and helping them dream and achieve lives inaccessible to their mothers.[15] If communication seems more honest between minority mothers and daughters, the threats to their survival are great, and there isn't much room for inefficient hypocrisy and euphemism.[16] Growing up with a clear vision of the way things are may be traumatic when reality is terrible, but no one has been able to determine whether that trauma is more or less damaging than the trauma of growing up in ignorance and suffering brutal disillusionment. Whose psyche will survive with fewer disabling scars and more self-love: Queenie of "The Lawd Don't Like Ugly" or Anna of "A Marriage of Persuasion?"

Conclusion

The nature of motherhood is complex and as often obscured by sentimentality as by bitterness and pain. Mothers and daughters are often alienated from each other. Daughters feel anger for many reasons: because they see their mothers pressuring them to conform to society's expectations of girls and women, or because they find their mothers paying too little attention to those expectations and offering scant emotional support to daughters attempting to conform. Mothers grow angry at daughters either because daughters don't fulfill their expectations or because their daughters expect too much of them. Such anger and its resulting alienation grow not primarily from clashes between unique personalities and temperaments but rather from the external and internalized social pressures to relate and accept responsibilities to and for each other in terms of the culturally defined roles of mother and daughter. Indeed, the relationship between mothers and daughters, formalized further by such other factors as class, religion, race, and ethnicity, may conceal and inhibit those unique selves. However, most mothers and daughters try to make the best of things; they pitch in with a good will to take care of what must be cared for in the best way they know. Usually that has meant reproducing in the daughters' lives an experience very much like the mothers'.

In the last decade, because of the most recent wave of the women's liberation movement, the relationship between mothers and daughters had come under increasing, frequent, intense, and passionate examination.[17] Women are reclaiming women's lives and women's flesh. Not only are women saying, "Keep your hands and your laws off my body," and "My body, my self—I have the right to feel pleasure and to know strength," but also "I lay claim to the bond of flesh—and all that means—between myself and the woman who was first in my life, and the women in whose lives I have been first." Mothers and daughters are reclaiming each other, not by embracing the roles they have been so long girdled by, but by embracing the unique person each finds the other. Thus, we now have a great surge of books and panels, study groups and therapy groups, lectures and classes on the subject of the mother-daughter relationship.

But long before this recent activity began, women had been writing short stories about this special relationship. While not denying or ignoring the differences among us, we read these stories to find what we share, what binds us together, and how other women have learned to transcend the rules and the roles, to learn that mothers and daughters can be sisters. There are literally hundreds of mother-daughter stories. These eighteen were chosen from nearly a hundred of the very best.

NOTES

1. In *Diving Deep and Surfacing: Women Writers on Spiritual Quest* (Boston: Beacon Press, 1980), Carol P. Christ has defined the sacred dimension as that "which orient(s) a person to the ... great powers that establish the reality of their world. These powers ... are the boundaries against which life is played out, the forces against which a person must contend, or the currents in whose rhythms she must learn to swim. They sometimes provide revelation when the self is at a loss. ... They may provide a (potent) sense of meaning and value. ... They may ground a person in powers of being that enable her to challenge conventional values or expected roles" (p. 3).

2. An extremely useful international bibliography, listing more stories about mothers and daughters, as well as treatments of this relationship by social scientists, literary critics, and others appears in *The Lost Tradition: Mothers and Daughters in Literature,* ed. Cathy N. Davidson and E.M. Broner (New York: Frederick Ungar Pub. Co., 1980). The bibliographers, Ann M. Moore, Gail M. Rudenstein, and Carol Farley Kessler, refer to their 500 + item compilation as a "Preliminary Bibliography."

3. A mother's support of a daughter's lesbian sexuality may encourage healthy sexual functioning for her daughter and allow her daughter to pay attention to her mother's experience in and knowledge about the patriarchy.

4. Quest stories, or searches for identity, are common in traditional male literature. In these stories, a boy about to become a man explores how that transition can be accomplished, what act he must perform, what name he is to be known by, who he will be as a man separate from all other men. Often an older man will accompany him on his quest, serving as a kind, wise teacher, making suggestions, pointing out directions, and warning of dangers. But the boy must commit an important act or achieve an important goal on his own. By that act (e.g., killing a bear or a dragon or an alien invader, losing his virginity, stealing another man's emblem of power) or that achievement (earning the title of Dr., or Green Beret, or All American, or Knight of the Round Table), he comes to be, generally, a man, and, specifically, his own man.

Occasionally, women write stories in which women quest after identity in these traditional male ways, as if it were something to wrest from life, rather than something to grow into, to learn to know, and to tend and nurture. Such stories often center on a girl with a sense of vocation which, if followed, will take her far from the women's world in which she has been raised and where she has been expected to spend her life.

5. A longer discussion of the ways in which women's genres, women writers, and the tastes of predominantly female audiences have been discounted appears in *How to Suppress Women's Writing,* by Joanna Russ (Austin: University of Texas Press, 1983).

6. These survivals are usually at the level of superstitious behavior. Superstitions represent the rote remnants of systems of belief whose substance has been lost through repressions or dispersal of the members of the culture who shared that system of thought. For a discussion of the process of the development of superstitious behavior as the result of repression, see *The Secret Jews,* by Joachim Prinz (New York: Random House, 1973). For a discussion of vestigial menarche rituals, see *The*

Curse: A Cultural History of Menstruation, by Janice Delaney, Mary Jane Lupton, and Emily Toth (New York: E.P. Dutton and Co., 1976).

7. Women in the contemporary feminist spirituality movement are recreating and creating rituals for contemporary women's lives. The attention they have brought to this basic ritual-making, occasion-marking component of women's psychology and spirituality has inspired a new vision through which to filter our understanding of women's creative artifacts. The ritual elements of women's work and lives are now more visible whether we look at women's quilts, women's cooking, women's conversation, or women's writing.

8. The first part of the pause ritual is like the first part of a consciousness-raising group meeting, during which women tell each other parts of the stories of their lives, providing the data for the analysis of the patriarchy upon which the theory for feminist revolution is built.

9. The meaning of sexual non-conformity varies greatly over time. At the beginning of this century, it often meant simply that the mother was divorced. In later decades it often referred to an extra-marital liaison, condemned no matter how dreadful the marriage nor how abusive, irresponsible, or absent the husband. In some stories written since the 1960s, mothers have been prostitutes. I have found no stories in which a mother is perceived as disgraceful by her daughter because the mother is a lesbian. There are, however, several stories in which, as in "A Birthday Remembered," a lesbian mother or mother-surrogate worries that her daughter might think she is disgraceful. The worry is always unfounded.

In nineteenth-century "disgraceful mother" stories, sexual non-conformity never appears as the single "sin." Non-compliance with expected sexual behavior is always part of a general portrayal of disgrace, and among the other "sins" there is always at least one form of substance abuse.

10. Christian versions of this story have strong parallels with the myth of redemption; Jewish women writers' stories rely on the perspectives of the social sciences, turning variously to psychology, sociology, history, and political science to understand a world that includes drunken, promiscuous mothers and broken-hearted, humiliated daughters.

11. Originally published in *American Mercury*, January 1935; reprinted in *Salute to Spring* (New York: International Publishers, 1940, 1977, 1980).

12. Many of my friends and colleagues (most of us are in our thirties, forties, and fifties) complain that many younger women want mothers,

rather than friends or lovers or colleagues. We are offended by the endless demand for nurturing. And yet we want nurturing, too. But we want relationships in which nurturance is reciprocal. In our friendships, we reciprocate—carefully—and negotiate nurturance, as well as jokes, gossip, and household hints as we share in the search and the struggle for peace and social justice.

In our experience, the fantasy most common among women about surrogate mothers is not the wicked, threatening, jealous stepmother. The real fantasy is the fairy godmother who can and will make all your dreams come true. I think we are always vulnerable to the attractions of a woman who will mother us, and we often make demands for mothering on women in positions of apparent authority. One of the real problems that women who teach in higher education have to deal with is the expectation by their students, male and female, that they will be "motherly." Such expectations are not harbored about male professors who, therefore, have more time for research and other "professional" activities, and whose evaluations by students don't reflect those disappointed expectations. This need and demand for mothering behavior, or nurturance, from older women by younger women has been documented in numerous studies by various social scientists.

I am no less guilty of wanting endless mothering. This emotional neediness is not only a burden put on older women by younger women, but it represents a kind of ageist, stereotypical thinking. My mother once said to me, with justified exasperation, "Susan, now that you are working so hard to liberate women from oppression, will you please liberate me from your need for my approval!" I'm trying, Mommy.

13. A Bantam Book, New York, 1975, and a Fawcett Crest Book, New York, 1976.

14. I know that there is now a vast Mead revisionism underway, but whether or not her descriptions were less or more accurate than those of other anthropologists in the field, the cultural constructs she reported on are important and have entered our culture at the deepest levels. They are part of our intellectual history and, in some cases, they have fueled our utopian dreams.

15. In an interview for *Something About the Author*, Alice Walker tells about three important gifts her mother gave her, each one delivering a message about her mother's hopes for her and her support of Walker's dreams for herself. "The second gift was a suitcase, a high school graduation gift, as nice as anyone in Eatonton had ever had. That suitcase gave me permission to travel and part of the joy in going very far from home was the message of that suitcase. Just a year later I was in Russia and Eastern Europe."

16. Candelaria Silva commented on this straight talk between mothers and daughters who are women of color. In her review of *This Bridge Called My Back: Writings by Radical Women of Color* (Boston: Persephone Press, 1981; reissued by Kitchen Table Press, New York, 1984), in the *New Women's Times Feminist Review* 22, July/August, 1982, she writes: "Some of our common colored stuff is that: most of us have seen more death than white feminist/females ever encounter—just growing up. Many of us had mommas, grandmommas, aunts and other women tell us directly and not-so-directly, that our 'pussy was a commodity.' Most of us grew up knowing we would *have* to work."

17. The article that has most influenced my thinking about the mother-daughter relationship is "The Impact of the Nazi Occupation of Poland on the Jewish Mother-Child Relationship," by Renee Fodor, *YIVO Annual of Jewish Social Science*, 1956–1957, vol. 11. This article was brought to my attention by my friend, Barry Mehler, about seven years ago. I am grateful to him for the article and for many fine discussions.

I have read the article repeatedly and it haunts me. I am overwhelmed by analogies between the situation of those Jewish mothers of sons and daughters, and the situation of mothers and daughters in the patriarchy, but after much thought and many discussions with friends, I decided not to draw those analogies in this essay because of the danger of seeming to trivialize the experience of those who suffered through the attempted genocide of world Jewry.

Caroline W. Healey Dall

Annie Gray: A Tale
1848

"Annie Gray: A Tale" was written by Caroline W. Healey Dall (1822–1912) as a contribution to the 1848 volume of The Liberty Bell, *the first abolitionist literary annual, published by the Massachusetts Anti-Slavery Society from 1839 to 1853 in order to raise funds for the fight against slavery. Attributed to "The Friends of Freedom,"* The Liberty Bell *was actually edited by Maria Weston Chapman and included work by such important anti-slavery activists as Frederick Douglass and Lydia Maria Child.*

This story is similar in structure and style to many published between 1825 and 1865 in the popular gift books and annuals that dominated the literary marketplace. These stories exhibit features of such personal genres as diaries, letters, and memoirs, and such formal genres as essays and sermons. Additionally, these early stories by women echo the oral tradition, as do the early stories of other minority or oppressed cultural groups when their members begin to practice the literary arts as they have been defined by the dominant culture. This rootedness in oral tradition accounts for the recurrent use of the framing device of a story within a story.

Caroline Healey Dall, whose contributions have been overlooked until recently, was a significant figure in her own time. Her biographer, Gary Sue Goodman, feminist historian and literary critic, summarizes her achievements:

> Dall was internationally known during her lifetime as an abolitionist, social reformer, feminist leader, and prolific author. She published over thirty books and hundreds of articles in which she analyzed diverse topics, from Egyptian history to contemporary scientific controversies. A pioneer in the organized Woman's Rights

Movement, Dall co-edited the first feminist newspaper in
America, *The Una*, and wrote scholarly studies of women's
history, literature, education, legal rights, and work. She
also founded or sustained numerous progressive organizations, including an early daycare school for working
women's infants, vocational schools for women, and the
American Social Science Association, a primary catalyst of
social reform after the Civil War.

*Dall left an immense collection of manuscripts, including daily journals
written from her adolescence until her death. This remarkably detailed and frank
record allows us to reconstruct aspects of women's experience that time and
reticence have generally buried. She included many facts, explanations, and
emotional reactions that required euphemism, fictionalization, or silence in her
public writing. From adolescence, Dall confronted patriarchal myths about
woman's nature and women's roles with naked truths about real women's lives.
She exposed common abuses fostered by women's economic dependence and
political powerlessness. But her father's tyranny, her mother's madness, and the
failure of her own marriage remained family secrets.*

*Dall's vocational choice is often attributed to her father's teaching. Mark
Healey, a wealthy Boston merchant and Unitarian liberal, taught her to read,
sent her to private schools, hired governesses and tutors, and bought her expensive
lyceum lecture tickets. He taught her that she had a responsibility to develop her
talents, to test all conventions by reason and conscience, and to discard the
superstitious dogmas that hindered the social march toward perfection. Noting
her facility for impromptu storytelling, her father even encouraged her to become
"a literary woman." "To his patience, prudence, and daily teaching," Dall
recalled, "I owe most of what I am, especially the self-control which has prevented
me from becoming the victim of ill-health."*

*Yet Dall's manuscripts reveal more complex causes for her feminism and her
powerful drive for self-expression through writing. It seems that her father's
unusually active role in her education was not chosen for feminist reasons, but
to compensate for her mother's invalidism. After almost dying during her
daughter's birth, Caroline Foster Healey endured nine more pregnancies during
the next sixteen years. Her temperament became erratic: she was often reclusive,
depressed, suspicious, hostile, and brooding. Dall later understood her mother's
eccentricity as "melancholia" and forgave her that she was "never a mother to
me" during her childbearing years. But as a child she felt abandoned, unloved,
and deprived of the perfect nurturing sympathy of the ideal mother depicted by
her contemporaries.*

*Although liberal, Mark Healey still expected his first-born child to cultivate
the feminine qualities prescribed by society—the "true womanhood" that historian
Barbara Welter has identified as "purity, piety, submissiveness, and domesticity."*

Mr. Healey demanded that Caroline assume her mother's household responsibilities while simultaneously continuing to study and to write; yet he removed her from school prematurely for failing to improve her opportunities. He judged her by perfectionist standards, criticized her harshly, and praised her rarely. He had no empathy for her struggles with heavy, often conflicting duties. He also prevented her from seeking other sympathy or guidance by forbidding her to speak of her mother's symptoms to anyone.

Annie Gray's death-bed confession has an element of fantasy for Dall, whose mother never confided the reasons for her depression and insanity. "Annie Gray: A Tale" not only illustrates the injustice of slavery, but also depicts women's sexual vulnerability, shame, and enforced secrecy. Rape, forced marriages, and unwanted pregnancies were taboo topics; even for an outspoken feminist, it was far easier to portray a woman as a victim of slavery or a "victim of ill-health," than as a victim of male lust and tyranny within the patriarchal family.

> "His rest, his labor, pastime, strength and health,
> Were only portions of his master's wealth;—
> His love—O name not love—while men can doom
> The fruit of love, to Slavery from the womb."—MONTGOMERY.

> "And what man seeing this,
> And having human feelings, does not blush,
> And hang his head to think himself a man?"—COWPER.

On the finely macadamized road which leads from La Prairie to Montreal, a number of low stone cottages attract, by the quaintness of their aspect, the attention of the traveller. They seem to link America to the Old World, and prove that some few of her sons, at least, retained a love for its elder cities. As one saunters along this road at night-fall, while the red sun still lingers in the west, many things conspire to remind him that he has passed the "line of the States;" first of all, the broad, low houses,—built of stone, and floored with clay,—with overhanging attics, without casements, protected only by large wooden shutters, until the season becomes severe; then, the crowds of foreign-looking inmates, the lazy and untidy thronging the doors in antique costume, or smoking under the stoop in bed-gowns of blue calico, quilted petticoats of white, stout shoes, and broad straw hats,—the men wearing closely fitting provincial caps, decorated with tassels of red or blue, according to the character of their ancestral blood. The active still lingered amid the harvest, even at the late autumn season in which our tale commences, fully bedecked with pipes and petticoats. But many a happy circle, in a more fortunate interior, glistens with true English tidiness. The white-washed walls betray a love of cleanliness; which the trim children, the baby with its wide cap-border of snowy lace, clustering about the frugal board,—so tempting in its niceness to the tired passer-by—only confirm. A little further on, one detects many peculiarities, significant of the mixed races which inhabit the land, and the absence of district schools. The baker has painted over his door a most unnatural sheaf of wheat, and two crusty looking loaves, while the ale-house rejoices in a rough board, which, swinging to and fro, tempts its poor victim to a freshly tapped barrel, and a foaming glass.

Glad to find himself on ground which, if not wholly free, is certainly released from the fetters which bind his own soil, the American hardly remarks the many signs of slavery to sloth, to drinking, and the pipe, which painfully surround him. The sunny landscape, enlivened by groups of gaily dressed women, in the field, a thing unseen at home, cheats him into pleasant thoughts.

About a mile from La Prairie, he passes, on the right, a huge stone farm-house, of the olden sort. The eaves run back to the ground; heavy casements and broad shutters protect it from the winter winds. The enclosure seems neatly kept, and just above the ancient well-sweep, on which the large slow-growing lichens have kept a faithful tally of years, stands the stone crucifix. Beautiful symbol of a faith that he despises, it lifts itself up, with broad arms, to the height of twenty feet, enclosing in its bosom a time-worn shield—once a beautiful medallion—recording the sufferings of our Lord. It was a fair superstition, he thinks, which thus united the living spring and the Rock of Ages; and while he bows his head, and the now vanishing sun sends mellow gleams of light through oak and sumach and broad shadowy maples, suggesting pleasant dreams of the stained windows of those "prayers built into stone"—the once seen cathedrals of his father-land,—the vespers that his childhood whispered at his mother's knee, hallow afresh his heart and memory.

It was about four years ago that a traveller found himself aroused from such dreams by the coarse voice of a woman, who, as she closed the door of a small cottage on the other side of the dusty way, looked in at the window, saying, in French, "If your mother is'nt better by the midnight, Matty, you must come for me." We have always hated eaves-droppers, and have no desire to invest any such with the dignity of a hero. Our traveller was no philanthropist, but he was still young enough to be curious; and he crossed the road, to the cottage, towards which these words had been directed; and, sheltered by a wide shutter, the projecting hedge, and deepening twilight, he gazed directly in. A neater room than ordinary met his view; and there was something tasteful in the arrangement of the white muslin curtains, about a bed which stood near the window, that at once directed his attention to "Matty's mother." A female, whose light olive skin, rendered uncommonly transparent by illness, contrasted painfully with large voluptuous eyes, and glossy curls of extreme length, lay stretched upon the white pillow. As he gazed, a sweet but startling voice said to the girl who bent over it,— "Matty, open the shutters, that I may once more see the fading light." The girl approached him, and with a vehemence which brought the prominent Roman features of the stranger into some danger, threw back the shutter, and turned again to the bedside. Rapid as her movements were, the traveller read in features very unlike her mother's, (a plain but animated countenance and a somewhat awkward frame,) the history of a heart and head such as he had seldom met in one like her, indisputably of African blood.

What was it in the face of the girl, in the voice of the mother, that startled him with by-gone memories? But he came here to listen. "Matty," said the invalid, with a faltering voice, "I have always told you, that, at the last hour, you should know your mother's entire history. I have no longer the right to keep it back. It has been, alas! simply from the fear of agitating you with its horrors, that the communication has been so long delayed. Matty, your mother was a Slave!"

"I guessed it, mother," said the girl, "I guessed it, when I saw you rise from your sick bed, with kindling eyes, to shelter a poor fugitive."

"I would have laid down my life for her," said the invalid

earnestly; "but listen, for my breath is short. I was born on a retired plantation in Westmoreland county, Virginia, within a short distance of the spot where the great Washington first saw the light. My mother I never knew. For the offence of giving me birth, she was exiled from her home. My father, it was said, was the favorite son of the old lady whom I remember as my first mistress. Mrs. Elsie Gray was wealthy, generous, and aristocratic. Her property, at her death, which occurred when I was about six years old, chiefly devolved upon my father; but for a reason which I can easily guess, she did not choose to entrust *me* to his care. I was bright, and, Matty,—I hope that there is no harm in saying it now,—I was very beautiful. I had become a favorite; and to her only other grand-child and namesake, a girl about my own age, I was consigned, in an affectionate letter. I saw that letter many years afterwards, and I cannot forget that the old lady entreated her dear Elsie to shield me from what she termed the *dangers* that had menaced my mother; and to keep me, through life, carefully by her side. It was owing, however, to the indolence of my new mistress, who resided in the city of Georgetown, rather than to the old lady's recommendation, that I received an excellent education. I was expected to amuse and occupy my young mistress; and when she was too wilful to study, I learned her tasks and taught them to her by various devices. I slept on a trundle-bed at her side—she could never bear me out of her sight—and as we grew older I read aloud to her, while she was seated at her embroidery, or pursued the quiet occupations of her station. My father died soon after Madam Gray, and the estate passed into the hands of Elsie's parents. For a number of years, we passed our summers in Westmoreland; and groups of gay friends often accompanied us. These were our most precious years of unfolding womanhood; they were spent in reading, in light employments, and the joyous relaxations suiting our age. Rapidly as Elsie had unfolded in beauty, and many as were her admirers, there were not wanting those among them who had dared to whisper that I was the lovelier; and I knew that it was true. You cannot conceive, dear Matty, all that I suffered at such hours. In the city, I was always in attendance on my mistress, unless, indeed, at the private festival,—but it was always with her hat or shawl hanging on my arm, and in a position which betokened my dependence; but in lonely Westmoreland such distinctions were not possible. In our rural festivities all depended upon my wit, my taste, and above all, *my activity*. I was in constant requisition; and so cultivated was my mind, and so fair my face,—for one of African blood,—that twice, dear Matty, I listened to words of affection from one who fancied himself my equal, and answered them with these few words,—'I am a Slave.' The first time, I can truly say, the words gave me no pain, save that which followed in the consciousness of my unprotected position,—of the impossibility of my ever marrying, in a manner that would satisfy at once myself and others. But painful as these thoughts were, they were soon banished by Elsie's affectionate care, and her childish promises, that her home should always be mine. I had been named for a great-aunt of Elsie's, and was familiarly known as Annie Gray.

"It is the custom of some Slaveholders to give their own surnames to their Slaves, and where we were known, this excited no surprise; but in Westmoreland it occasioned awkward mistakes. Among the summers that we passed there, the last two will ever remain impressed upon my mind. They were the last before my Elsie was married. There went with us, at these times, but two friends. One was a gay and dissipated man, named Meredith—my future master; the other, a distant connexion of Elsie's, from the North,—one who had been abroad, who had seen Wilberforce and Clarkson, who was the pupil of Channing. Until he came among us I knew little of Slavery,—but he expounded it; he set it before us in its true light; he pleaded against it; and in our hours of leisure he read to us from the books which he most valued. Under his influence my mind and heart expanded; a great change worked itself within me; I interested myself in the other Slaves; I tried to teach them; I talked to them of freedom, when now, for the first time, I understood it. My mistress liked to listen to him, for he was handsome and eloquent; and Meredith delighted to 'cut him up' for her amusement. He could not but feel my quiet sympathy; and though few were the words exchanged between us, we well understood each other. I never thought of loving *him*,—for I felt that I was not his mate; but he,—he met me at the table, at the fireside, and on the green sward. He little dreamt of what I knew.

"I have told you, that the first time I confessed my situation to one thus deceived, it gave me little pain; but the second,—I thank God that he did not require me to inflict all I then suffered, on myself!—the words came from Elsie's lips. It was at the close of our second summer, together,—a few weeks before Elsie's marriage. We were about returning to the city, and had gone in playful pilgrimage to the spot where Washington was born. Elsie gathered fig-leaves from a few venerable stumps, as we sat gazing at the lonely chimney which marks the site of his early home. Arthur rallied her on her inconsistency, spoke of the Slaves, and of the great beauty and distinguished ability of some. 'With all your chivalry,' exclaimed Elsie, 'I do not believe that you have ever guessed our Annie to be a Slave!'

"I sat at some distance, and my back was turned; but I could hear the husky voice, with which he asked, 'But she is surely your cousin, Elsie?'

" 'Ask Meredith,' was her only reply.

" 'No,' said Meredith, 'we do not believe that old story; she is only a Slave. To be sure Elsie's mother thinks that the old lady intended to free her, but she died before her letter was finished. So much the better for us. The said letter is the greatest gem in the old lady's casket.'

" 'But you,—surely *you* will emancipate her?' urged Arthur, turning to Elsie.

" 'That will be as Meredith says;' she answered, laughing.

"I heard their retreating footsteps, but I did not know all that I endured until some hours after, when I found Arthur bathing my forehead in spring-water, and read, in his pale face, his apprehensions for me. He staid but a moment after I was restored, and it was to utter, in a voice which he vainly strove to render steady, these few words,—'Find that letter, see if what they have told me is true,—then, fly with the rising sun. You know your route.' He pointed to the north, dropped a purse at my feet, and was gone.

"Often had I held within my hand, as I replaced Elsie's jewels, the precious letter of whose character I was so ignorant. This night, ere I retired, I did not hesitate to conceal it in my bosom.

I knew that Elsie had not looked at it for many years. I saw that the paper was rudely and *freshly* torn, but I was not prepared for the loving words I found within. I no longer doubted that freedom should have been mine, and I believed that Meredith stood between me and it. A Slave, then, I must ever be. I never saw Arthur again. In the morning Elsie learned that he had gone; and I pined in silence, for I knew too little of the world to follow his advice. I doubted not that the letter which had been so carelessly kept had contained either an express provision for my freedom, or a declaration of intentions equivalent to this. Why Meredith had destroyed it, I was too soon to know. Often I wandered alone over the beautiful heights, and under the warm sunshine gazed down upon the blue Potomac, the broad and fruitful vineyards of the Jesuits, and the rose-encircled dwellings of our friends; and, while my heart swelled, and my mind aspired, I asked of God—if I alone were created in vain!

"Elsie was married. Up to this time my duties had been nominal, but we now removed to a place of Meredith's, called Northwood, in South Carolina. Here I was entrusted with the duties of a housekeeper, and expected to confine myself to them. If I appeared at table, it was only to carve or to make tea; and when, a short time after, Meredith persecuted me with his dishonorable addresses, I no longer wondered that Elsie was dispirited, indifferent, and every way unlike her former self. Meredith threatened to be revenged upon me for my severity, and he kept his word. He knew that he was in my power; and soon after the birth of his first child, while Elsie was too feeble to dispute his will, he insisted on my marriage. God grant, dear Matty, that you may never know the agony I experienced at this prospect; I, whose heart was full of the absent Arthur,—who would rather have died than have brought a Slave into the world, and who could look for no union which would not bind me to ignorance, brutality, or irreligious coarseness! God had mercy upon me, however. I was united by Meredith's command, and the aid of a clergyman, (may Heaven have mercy on him also,) to one of the upper field-hands. With a malice well worthy of him, Meredith had, as he thought, selected one of the coarsest and least desirable men on the estate; but I soon learned to estimate a noble nature in my husband. He devoted himself to

books, and in about a fortnight mastered the alphabet. I did not
conceal from him the state of my own feelings, and I successfully
strove to indoctrinate him into Arthur's sentiments. At the end
of six weeks he disappeared, leaving me no clue as to his object,
or the direction he had taken. But I did not misunderstand him.
I knew that he was a free man, a hired hand, and that he was
too proud of his wife to wish her to continue a Slave. The light
in my eye filled Meredith with rage. For the first time I was
whipped,—not severely,—for Elsie interceded for me with tears,
and I could not tell what I did not know. I was then closely
catechized as to the condition in which I had been left; and
when I declared that I had no prospect of becoming a mother,
I was told that if nothing was heard from my husband by the
close of another six weeks, I must prepare myself again to be a
wife. Distasteful as my marriage had been, my husband's noble-
ness toward me had entirely won my regard, and this declaration
threw me into despair. Had I been a quarter Slave, I should
have made my escape; but brought up in luxury with Elsie, I
must have died ere I reached a free State. A few days of agony
converted my despair into a fever on the brain. How long it
lasted, I know not, but I was dragged from my bed to the altar;
and, Matty, can you believe me—the same clergyman united me
again to my master's steward! I felt all the profanation of the
rite, but I was both too feeble and too bewildered to resist.

I would speak of this man with all respect, for he was your
father, Matty; but he was both coarse in manner, and brutal in
mind. He did not imitate the forbearance of my first husband;
and in a few months, I became conscious of your existence.
Since my marriage, Elsie had never dared to meet my eye; but
she now sent me some delicate clothing for my unborn babe, by
the woman who had charge of her own. I melted into tears; and
to this, I believe, I owe the preservation of my reason. In the
afternoon of this day a pedlar approached the plantation; and
while he rested at the door of my cottage, the Slaves crowded
about him. As they made their gay selections of trinkets and
beads, he threw a significant glance at me, saying,—'Here is a
box of soap, which you will like better.' Unwarned as I was, God
alone could have inspired me with the presence of mind to
conceal it, until his departure. It contained a message from my

absent husband, and filled me with conflicting emotions. It enclosed five hundred dollars, which I was to leave in a farewell letter to Elsie, as the price of my body, and then, if I chose, I might fly with the still untouched sum which Arthur had left me, or join him and his fortunes at a short distance from the plantation. I could not love my second husband, but was it not my duty to remain with him until I could give him his unborn child? I debated, until I remembered that this child would be a Slave,—perhaps a daughter,—and horror-struck at the thought, I hurried my preparations for my departure. I left a letter full of tenderness and reproaches for Elsie. I took with me her last gift, and rejoined my preserver. Under sufferings and fatigues, which accelerated your birth, we escaped to this place, where we have lived ever since.

"In your infancy, dear Matty, you so resembled your father, that I could not bear to look at you; and it was then, that I was fully made to realize how far your adopted father's heart exceeded mine in holiness. 'Annie,' he said, 'if this soul must be born, you ought to be thankful that it was born to you, and not to another,—born a free woman, and not a Slave.' And from him, I learnt to love you, as you have always deserved."

The girl's breast heaved. Tears had been raining from her eyes,—she clasped her hands, and lifting them toward heaven, let loose her smothered ire in these words—"O God! let me pursue them to their death!"

"Matty," said her mother, mournfully, "that is the prayer of a Slave. I expect from you the prayer of one whom Christ has made free."

At this moment a tall, sad-looking Negro, with a noble expression, entered the room. He bent and kissed the wife's forehead, and laid his hand on the head of the child. "Be what *he* has been and is," said the wife in a clear and loving tone, as she gazed into his face, "and I doubt not, Matty, we shall know each other in heaven!"

In the darkness of the night the traveller walked away, but the tears were fast rolling over his cheeks. By the light which streamed from a neighboring window, he looked at and kissed a dried flower, which he took from his pocket-book. "She is but thirty now," he said aloud, "and she was but fifteen when she spoke to me those bitter words! *I was her first suitor.*"

Two days afterwards, an humble funeral proceeded from the little cottage, to the English burial-ground; and at night-fall, the father and daughter might have been seen in the deserted room, reading, from one Bible, words which illuminated their countenances with divine trust.

The main incidents of the above story are given as facts which came to the author's personal knowledge. She believes the strongest argument against this vile institution, to be a frank statement of its actual results—its revolting but inevitable facts.

Susan Pettigru King Bowen

A Marriage of Persuasion
1857

Upon receiving and reading a copy of Busy Moments of an Idle Woman *(1854), published under the pen name "An Idle Woman," James Louis Pettigru, a South Carolina lawyer, wrote to his daughter, Susan Pettigru King (1824–1875),*

> You have burst upon me as an author almost as surpris-
> ingly as Miss Burney did on her unsuspicious parent. . . .
> I have no doubt you will receive a great deal of praise, for
> the dialogue is witty and sparkling, and the descriptions
> circumstantial and striking. I dare say that if you were to
> take to study, you might, in time, attain to the deliniation
> of the passions and rise to the walk in which Miss Austen
> is admired.

King Bowen followed this collection of five stories with her only novel, the semi-autobiographical Lily *(1855); a novella and two short stories published in one volume under the title* Sylvia's World, *and* Crimes Which the Law Does Not Reach *(1859); another novella,* Gerald Gray's Wife *(1864); and, four years later, a single, uncollected story in* Harper's Magazine, *"My Debut."*

Her work is remarkable for its realism in a period characterized by sentimentality. In a 1903 essay surveying fiction in his home state of South Carolina, Ludwig Lewisohn praises her as "a woman of clear and vigorous spirit, eagerly ready amidst a somewhat narrow social life, to think for herself and not afraid to put her thought on record . . . she deserves praise." She was described by George Wauchope in his 1910 book, The Writers of South Carolina *as "the most distinguished woman novelist of ante-bellum South Carolina." In Lily, through the voice of her heroine, King Bowen expressed her own commitment to literary realism: "If we undertake to write novels . . . heroes and heroines of the present day must act like men and women of the present day, or else they are mere Marionettes." Her distaste for literary sentimentalism was matched by her disdain for the ideal of white Southern womanhood; she found both vapid and dishonest. Critic J.R. Scafidel concludes her 1975 essay in* South Carolina Women Writers *with the assessment that "King as a psychological realist very clearly belongs to the group of writers that includes William Dean Howells and Henry James."*

Today, Susan Pettigru King Bowen has all but disappeared, with the exception of an occasional footnote in histories of the Reconstruction. Her work has been out of print for over a century. Her literary reputation seems to have been obscured by responses to her later activities that left her with no champions.

Although her father was opposed to secession, he commanded such respect from South Carolina's Confederate aristocracy that he was given the job of codifying the state laws during the war in order to keep him and his family out of financial trouble. Susan's husband, Henry King, son of her father's law partner and junior member of the firm, enlisted on the Confederate side and was killed in 1862. However, one writer reports that she had left the marriage before his death and gone to work in the Republican administration in Washington, D.C. It was perhaps there that she met her second husband, Christopher Columbus Bowen, who moved to Charleston after the war. He represented South Carolina in Congress from 1868 to 1871 and thereafter served as Sheriff for Charleston County, a position of considerable power. After his marriage to Susan, he stood trial for bigamy. One historian reports that he was acquitted; another that he was convicted and served time in prison. In all the varying descriptions of Bowen's political and legal machinations, it is clear that his wife supported him in every way. She even published a weekly newspaper in which she exposed whatever skeletons she knew about in the closets of her husband's political enemies, thereby making herself a figure wholly inimical to Charlestonian society. Historians of the Reconstruction period treat Christopher Columbus Bowen as a dishonest and murderous villain. Her association with him, which represented an alliance not only with a man repellent to the society of her early youth, but also with a cause seen as wholly antagonistic to the world that had nurtured her, contributed to her expulsion from history.

As a writer, King Bowen deserves more attention than she has received. Her work seems to be informed by the bitter irony of a Cassandra who sees but cannot avert pain and danger. Her female characters view with a pitiless clarity the inequities and inadequacies of their circumstances. They have the courage to speak of what and how they see, but they lack the ability to take the kind of action that might lead to change. Their understanding of their own reality leaves them with few and painful choices between being vulnerable (and inevitably victimized) or heartless (and dead inside); between stifling conformity or self-defeating and isolating rebellion. Critic Rose F. Kavo writes that "the vision of young, trusting girls destroyed or embittered through their experiences with men haunts her novels."

"A Marriage of Persuasion," from Crimes Which the Law Does Not Reach, *was first published under the pen name Anne Marion Green in 1857 in Russell's Magazine, the preeminent literary monthly in antebellum Charleston, one of the chief cultural centers of the South. John Russell (whose bookstore had long been the main gathering place for the intellectual elite of the era), William Gilmore Simms, Henry Timrod, and editor Paul Hamilton Hayne were all involved in the magazine's six-volume lifetime. Susan Pettigru King Bowen was its chief supplier of fiction.*

"And so you refused him?"

"Yes, mamma."

"Without one word of hope?"

"Not one."

"Harshly? rudely?"

"I trust not. Finally and positively, I certainly did."

"Anna! I can't forgive you."

"My dear mamma, what have I done?"

"What have you done? Refused an excellent man; one whom any mother would be proud to see as her daughter's husband. Sent from the house the best friend I have—deprived us of our mainstay and support—insulted him—and—destroyed the great hope of my life!" The tears streamed from Mrs. Mansfield's eyes. She drew away her hand from her daughter's clasp, and tried to leave the room. Anna detained her.

"Dearest mother! you cannot be more grieved than I am. Mr. Gordon is a very worthy man—he has been a kind friend to us in adversity—he is, I believe, truly sincere in his love for me, and I regret very deeply that it should have brought us to this pass. I have not wounded him further than I could help, I assure you. He will return to visit us in his usual way, after a while; indeed, I hope to see so little change in our intercourse, that I would have spared you the annoyance of knowing this, had he not expressly desired that I should tell you."

"Ah, he is a forgiving and generous creature; a true Christian. Such a man as that to be so treated!"

Anna was silent.

"Anna," resumed her mother, with sudden energy, after a moment's pause, "do you love any one else? have you formed some absurd attachment which interferes with Mr. Gordon's undeniable claim to your affections?"

Miss Mansfield's noble and expressive face was calmly lifted to her mother's heated and excited gaze.

"No, mamma," she simply answered.

"Then, *why* can't you marry Mr. Gordon, and make me happy?"

"Because," and Anna's voice was firm, decided and honest. "Because I do not love him, and to marry him would make me very unhappy."

"Selfish as ever!" ejaculated Mrs. Mansfield. "Will you tell me what you dislike in him?" she pursued.

"I did not say I disliked Mr. Gordon, mamma."

"What you don't like, then? Why you don't love him?"

Anna smiled faintly. "Dear mamma! is there not a great difference between liking and being in love?"

"You are trifling with me most disrespectfully. Is it not enough that I should suffer this disappointment at your hands, and can you not spare me this beating about the bush? I wish a plain answer to a plain question. Is there anything about Mr. Gordon especially disagreeable to you? If so, what is it?"

"Nothing especially disagreeable, as a friend—as a man whom one sees three or four times a week; but as a husband, several things."

"May I, as only your mother—of course a very insignificant creature to wish or have your confidence—ask these several things?"

"In the first place, then, his appearance is not attractive to me."

"Gracious heaven!" cried Mrs. Mansfield, starting up; "do I live to hear my daughter express such a sentiment! His appearance! Do you not know that to think of such an objection is—the—the—very reverse of modest? Where have you got such ideas? To a truly virtuous woman, what are a man's looks? I might expect such an objection from a girl of low mind and vicious ideas, but not from Anna Mansfield. So this is your reason for not marrying an excellent, kind"——

"Not my only one, mamma," Anna interrupted gently; "it is one of them, but not the greatest. I named it first because it is, I think, very important; and I cannot see the impropriety which strikes you." A slight blush rose to her cheek, as she continued, "I should not like to engage myself to pass my life with a man whose attentions would be repulsive to me, if he had the right to take my hand—or—excuse me, mamma, I don't like to say any more on this point;" and then as the color deepened, she added in a lower voice, "You saw Frederick yesterday put his arm around Maria's waist, as he lifted her from the saddle; and, not caring for the presence of you, his aunt, and us, his cousins, he—a bridegroom of three months—he kissed her pretty blooming cheek, and drew her close to him. She blushed, and said, 'don't, Fred,' but evidently was not displeased. Now, could I endure?—Oh, mamma, pray don't talk about it. It makes me ill. I have named one of the smallest, and at the same time one of the greatest objections. Why dwell upon a difference of opinion, in many essential cases—a total want of congeniality—sympathy—taste, when this trivial reason (provided he possessed the others) is in itself so strong? Dear mamma, don't be angry— don't be disappointed. You would not wish to make me truly miserable? Perhaps in a year or two, Sally may be Mr. Gordon's choice; and Sally may take him as her beau ideal. Why do you want to get rid of me so soon?"

"Ah, my dear," said Mrs. Mansfield, "you know how poor we are now. Here I am with you four girls, and an income not much larger than in your dear father's time I spent upon my own dress. Is it wonderful that I long to see you settled? Heaven knows that I am not one of those mercenary mothers who would give their children to any man with money. No, indeed. I would not be so wicked. But when a gentleman like Norman Gordon— an honorable, trustworthy, generous creature—wishes to become my son, do you wonder that I should desire it too? I knew his father before him—I knew his mother—all good people; it is good blood, my child—the best dependence in the world. You are nearly twenty years old, and there are three younger than you; how can I help being anxious? And I who know what 'love-

matches' are—how many a girl goes to her ruin by that foolish
idea; marrying some boy in haste, and repenting at leisure—
children—no money—bills to pay—oh! my dear Anna, where is
the love then?"

"Mamma, am I making or thinking of making any such match?"

"But you may do it. I want to save you from this. I have a
horror of these romantic 'love-matches.' "

"Did you not love my father, mamma?" Anna asked, in a low
voice.

"Of course I did. All women should love their husbands. All
proper, well-regulated women do love their husbands."

"And yet you wish me to marry without love!"

"Love comes after marriage—every woman with good principles loves her husband. She makes the best of her bargain.
Life is a lottery, and if you draw a prize or a blank, you must
accept it as it is and be satisfied. Then, when a woman has sworn,
in the face of God and man, 'to love, honor and obey' her
husband, how can she reconcile herself to not doing it?"

"But, if she should not? if she finds it impossible? Oh, think
of that, mamma. Think of vowing solemnly in the face of
heaven—and breaking one's oath! Swearing to love, where you
feel indifference—promising to honor, where you see little to
respect—and vowing to obey, where your reason tells you there
is no judgment to make obedience possible! Taking upon your
shoulders, *for life*, a burden you cannot bear, and which it is a
crime to struggle under, or to cast aside!"

"You know nothing about it, Anna," Mrs. Mansfield said
impatiently; "it is not proper for a young girl to think and speak
in this wild way. Your mother is here to guide and direct you.
No good ever comes of a child arguing and setting herself up
in this manner, to teach those older and wiser than herself. The
Bible says, 'Honor thy father and thy mother'—it don't say,
'dispute with them.' I tell you what I heard from *my* mother,
and what every right-minded person knows. 'Make a good choice
in life; marry, and love will come afterward.' Love comes with
the—never mind. I will not say any more now. I hope sincerely
you have been careful of poor Norman's feelings. But you are
not apt to do that. You have lacerated mine enough, Heaven
knows."

"Oh, mamma! when—how?"

"In this business. When it would be so easy for you to make us all happy, and you prefer your own notions, and willfully act up to them."

A flush of transient anger and indignation swept gustily over Miss Mansfield's face; but she conquered the emotion, and playfully taking a volume from a book-stand near, said, with perfect good humor, and meaningly, "May I read 'Clarissa Harlowe,' mamma?"

"No, put it down, Anna, and don't bother me with any further nonsense."

The daughter obediently withdrew, glad to escape so painful and so disagreeable an interview.

But although this was the first, it was by no means the last of such conversations. Every day the subject was renewed, but gradually Mrs. Mansfield changed her tactics. She no longer scolded or insisted; her reproaches were silent looks of misery—pathetic appeals to heaven "to grant her patience under her afflictions." She was very affectionate to her daughter—heart-rendingly so. Anna was called upon constantly to notice what a tender parent she was distressing. Each necessary privation in their reduced household (the father's honorable failure and death had brought them from affluence to comparative poverty,) was prologued and epilogued by sighs and suggestions. "If only Anna could"—and then a sudden pause and deep respiration.

"My own dear child," Mrs. Mansfield would sometimes say; "how I wish you had a new dress. That brown silk is very shabby; but we cannot, with our limited means, buy another, and yet I saw Jane Berryman sneering at it, with her flounced skirts spreading a mile behind her."

"Indeed, mamma, I don't care for Jane Berryman's sneers. It is very good of you to be anxious about it, but *I* think the old brown very becoming."

The next day a rich plaid silk, glossy and fresh, lay upon Anna's bed. "I could not stand it, my dear," said Mrs. Mansfield. "I must do without a new cloak this winter. A mother would rather starve with cold than see her daughter less handsomely dressed than she ought to be. Nothing is a sacrifice to *me,* for *you,* Anna."

In vain poor Anna protested and tried to return the silk, and exchange it for the very necessary cloak, whose purchase was now impossible. Mrs. Mansfield positively forbade her, and the thin black shawl which covered the widow's last year's bombazine was worn with a prolonged shiver, whenever Anna was near enough to hear and see.

Mr. Gordon soon returned to pay his usual visits—to offer his usual attentions—to make his usual presents, at stated times, of things which could permissibly be tendered. The visits Mrs. Mansfield received with great delight—the attentions were allowed; but the first basket of winter produce which arrived from Mr. Gordon's farm, she requested decidedly should be the last.

Clara, the youngest girl, a child of seven, cried lustily because her mamma said "These will be the last potatoes we shall ever eat." From the solemnity of the tone, the little thing fancied that potatoes—a very important item in her daily consumption—were tabooed forever. She desisted when she found that it was only the potatoes from the Gordon farm that fell under the restriction.

Day by day, week after week, this persecution continued. It was the unceasing drop of water that "stayed not itself" for a single instant. In despair, Anna went to consult an aunt, whose opinion she highly valued—whose principles were undoubted—an exemplary wife and mother, and a kind friend always to her niece. Anna recited her woes. "What must I do to escape this torment, my dear Aunt Mary? I feel and know my duty to mamma, I trust; but this life is wearing me out."

Aunt Mary smiled.

"And you don't like Mr. Gordon, dear?"

"I now detest him."

"Oh, for shame! How can you say so? Indeed, my child, I cannot but agree with your mother. This is an excellent match; and it seems to me that if you have no positive objection against his character and standing, you ought to reconsider Mr. Gordon's proposal."

"But, don't you understand that I don't in the least care for the man, except as an ordinary acquaintance. He is well enough as he is; but, do you too advocate a marriage made on such a foundation?"

"Anna! a love-match makes no marriage of love."

"*Voilà une chanson dont je connais l'air!*" said Anna, smiling bitterly in her turn. "You will all force me to marry this man, actually to get rid of him."

"Well, you could not do a better thing, I think?"

Anna returned home disconsolately; returned to the same wearying, petty, incessant, pin pricks, unencouraged by a single word. With all her affection for her mother, she could not but see her weakness in most cases; but on her aunt's judgment she relied, and what had been the result of the interview?—a decided approval of Mrs. Mansfield's wishes.

Let those who blame Anna Mansfield for her next step, pray to be kept from the same pit-fall. This is a mere sketch; but an outline to which all who choose may fill up the hints given. Those who believe that *they* would have been steadfast to the end, will have my admiration, if, when their day of trial comes, they hold firmly to the right; but—as we look around, have we not cause to think that there are many Mrs. Mansfields, and, alas! many Annas?

There came an evening, at length, when on Miss Mansfield's finger shone a great diamond, which dazzled tiny Clara's eyes and made her uncognizant of the tears in her sister's, as she asked wonderingly, "Where did you get such a beau-ti-ful ring?"

Mrs. Mansfield triumphantly said, "That is a secret, Clara."

"No secret for you, my little darling," Anna answered very low and gravely. "Mr. Gordon gave it to me as a pledge that I am to marry him."

"Do you love him, Annie?" Clara said, swallowing her surprise, with great, open, childish eyes.

"Don't ask foolish questions, Clara," her mother cried angrily. But the tears now rolled down the elder sister's white cheek, and she held the little girl close to her bosom, as she whispered, "you shall come and live with me, my own, and when you marry, I will not need, if God helps me, to ask *you* that question."

The day came—hurried on—and Anna Mansfield was Mrs. Norman Gordon. She was the owner of houses and lands—gold and silver—a perjured conscience and a bleeding heart. Very fine possessions were they, truly, and very proud Mrs. Mansfield was and is, of the hand she had in this righteous barter.

I see Mrs. Gordon frequently; she is very pale and cold, and kind. She has no children—Clara does live with her. Mr. Gordon is not happy, evidently; he has nothing to complain of in his wife. She is scrupulously polite to him, but there is not an atom of sympathy between them. He is prejudiced, uncultivated; and now that he has her, is terribly afraid of being ruled by her. It is a joyless household, and a very rich one. I watch Mrs. Mansfield's greedy gaze lighten broader and broader as the blaze of plate—the measured footfall of a train of servants—the luxurious profusion of their constant service, are spread out before her. She treads the "velvet pile" of carpets with a happy step, and adores her daughter's noble brow, when she sees shimmering upon it—reflecting a thousand lights—the mass of brilliants that binds, in its costly clasp, the struggling thoughts of what was once Anna Mansfield.

So we leave them. What of the end of all this? Is this grand automaton really dead, or does a heart, young and still untouched, lurk—strong, free and dangerous—in that quiet, unmoved and stately figure?

Elizabeth Stuart Phelps

Old Mother Goose
1873

First published in The Independent *on January 2, 1873, "Old Mother Goose," one of the earliest "disgraceful mother" stories, is also an occasional story, written for the Christmas issue of a publication for which Elizabeth Stuart Phelps (1844–1911) had already written a series of essays on women's issues in 1871. The story was included six years later in one of Phelps's volumes of short stories,* Sealed Orders. *It was written when Phelps, at age twenty-nine, was already a famous and successful writer.* The Gates Ajar *(1868), her first novel, had become a best-seller on two continents—a success that changed her life.*

Elizabeth Stuart Phelps was the daughter of a writer. Her mother, Elizabeth Wooster Stuart Phelps (1815–1852), wrote six books in fewer years, three of which were published before her death at age thirty-seven. Her last three books, one a collection of short stories titled The Last Leaf from Sunny Side, *were published posthumously. She had been the daughter of a minister who taught sacred literature at Andover Theological Seminary and an invalid mother. A writer from an early age, she signed her work "H. Trusta," an anagram of her real name, a device used by her daughter in "Old Mother Goose." A Christian conversion experience at age nineteen led her to renounce nonreligious writing. She soon became profoundly ill with a number of painful physical symptoms and depression, all of which receded when she began again to write secular fiction. Nevertheless, for the rest of her brief life, she was the victim of periodic bouts of depression. At age twenty-seven she married Austin Phelps, a minister at a Boston church. She had already learned how much she enjoyed life in Boston when she left Andover for school.*

When, six years later, her husband began to teach at the divinity school in

Andover, she was unhappy to return to the life her mother had lived. At the time of the move from Boston, where her mother was happy, to Andover, Mary Gray Phelps, their first child, was four years old. When her mother died four years later, Mary, choosing to take her mother's name, became Elizabeth Stuart Phelps. Less than two years after his wife's death, Austin Phelps married his dead wife's tubercular sister, who died within eighteen months. A third wife added two more sons to the family.

Like her mother, Elizabeth Stuart Phelps became a writer. But unlike her mother and grandmother, she chose for many years to live an independent literary life. Then, at age forty-seven, having been ill since the publication of her brilliant novel, The Story of Avis *(1877), the story of a talented painter whose artistic life is destroyed by marriage, she married a young writer, a man seventeen years younger than she, the son of an old friend. The marriage was a failure and she died alone.*

When she wrote "Old Mother Goose," however, she was a single woman, still committed to an independent, self-directed, literary life, unimpeded by the demands of nineteenth-century wife- and motherhood.

Peg Mathers, Old Mother Goose, combines all the characteristics of the disgraceful mother: she is sexually promiscuous; uses drugs and alcohol; and is dirty, poor, and publically wretched. She is also, perhaps, mad. In the enormous number of "disgraceful mother" stories that have since been written, there are none guilty of so many kinds of disgrace. Her daughter has, on the other hand, all the graces. Her transformation from her mother's daughter to her pure, successful, adored self is as much a fairy tale as is Heathcliff's sudden acquisition of wealth and triumphant return to Wuthering Heights. Thamré has come to seek out her disgraceful mother, to come to some sort of terms with her past. She has volunteered to set up and fund a charity to offer impersonal succor to such wretched women as her own mother. Finally she is forced to confront her mother, face to face, in the only community that knows their shared history.

In most "disgraceful mother" stories, the mother remains unchanged throughout; the daughter, however, is radically transformed from hatred and shame of her mother and profound unease about her own independent female nature, to some expression of acceptance, understanding, and forgiveness. The daughter's transformation invests, and causes the community to invest, the unchanged mother with respectability. Surely it is no coincidence that this story of a mother reclaimed and redeemed by her daughter was written, published, and read in the Christmas season—the time of year when the occasional story is told about a sanctified child believed by many to have been his mother's—and all Christians'—savior.

When Thamrè consented to sing for the citizens of Havermash, last year, nobody was more surprised than the citizens of Havermash themselves.

It was characteristic of Havermash to have attempted it. Nothing is too good for Havermashers. Were St. Cecilia prima donna for a season, it would appear to them quite natural to seek her services. Have they not a brown-stone post-office and a senator, a street railway and a county jail, a local newspaper, an author (the public need scarcely be reminded of the "Havermash Hand-Organ: a Tale of Love and Poverty"), and a shoe and leather trade? Transcending all, is not their city charter two years old?

When the Happy Home Handel Association, headed by little Joe Havermash (grandson of the original shoe and leather man, whose wooden cobbler's shop occupied the site of the present post-office in 1793), took upon itself the performance of an "oratorio" last Christmas eve, "We will have Thamrè," said Joe, serenely.

Still, when Joe came home from Boston, breathless and radiant, one night early in the season, with Thamrè's tiny contract (she wrote it on a card, he said, with her glove on, just in going out, and the card was as sweet now—see!—as the glove, and the glove had just the smell of one English violet, no more) to sing in the stone post-office at eight o'clock on Christmas eve, on such and such conditions (simple enough), and for such and such remuneration,—*that* was the astonishing part of it,—even Havermash was off its guard enough to be surprised.

"She'll come," said Joe. "I supposed she would. I meant she should. But the terms are *astounding.* I was prepared to offer her twice that. I'd pay a big slice of it out of my own pocket to get her here. There's no trouble about terms. Did you see what Max offered her? Do you know what she's getting a night in New York? Do you know what she asked us? Five hundred dollars, sir! Only five hundred dollars. Think of it, sir! But the conditions are the most curious thing. She scorns to take so little, maybe. I don't know. All I know is, every dollar of it is to go to old women who haven't lived as they'd ought to in this town. 'For the relief of the aged women of Havermash, who, having in their youth led questionable lives, are left friendless, needy, and perhaps repentant in their declining years.' That's the wording of the agreement. I signed it myself in her little red morocco notebook. Most curious thing all round! It's my opinion, sir, it *takes* a woman to get up an uncommon piece of work like that."

Last Christmas eve fell in Havermash wild and windy. The gusts fought furiously with each other at corners, and under fences, and over the bleak spaces in which the new little city abounded, and through which it straggled painfully away into the open country. Where the snow lay, it lay in tints of dead, sharp blue, cold as steel beneath the chilly light; where it was blown away, the dust flew fine and hard like powder. Overhead, too, there hung only shades of steel. One long, low line of corrosive red, however, had eaten its way through against the western hill-country, and looked like rust or blood upon a mighty coat of mail.

So, at least, Miss Thamrè fancied, shivering a little in her folded furs, as she watched from the car window the swooping of the night upon the bleak, outlying lands and approaching twinkle of the town.

It was a cheerless night for the prima donna to be in Havermash. Joe had been saying so all day. She thought so, it would seem, when he handed her from the cars. She scarcely spoke to him, nodding only, looking hither and thither about her, through the shriek and smoke, with that keen, baffling glance of hers, which all the world so well remembers. Joe felt rather proud of this. *He* knew what the eccentricities of genius were; was glad of a chance to show himself at ease with them. Had she bidden him stand on his head while she found her trunk, or sit on a barrel in the draught and wait for her to compose an *aria*, he would have obeyed her sweetly, thinking all the while how it would sound, told to his grandchildren on winter nights.

Half Havermash was at the station. All Havermash remembers that. It was with difficulty that Joe could get her to her carriage quietly, as befitted, to his fancy, the conduct of a lady's welcome.

"I did not expect to see so *many* people," said Miss Thamrè, in her pretty, accented, appealing way. "What are they here for?"

"I'm sure I don't know," said Joe, with a puzzled air, "unless they're here to see me."

This amused the lady, and she laughed,—a little genial laugh, which bubbled over to the ears of the people pressing nearest to her in the crowd.

"She laughs as well as she sings," said a member of the Happy Home Handel Association.

"She has the eye of a gazelle and the smile of a Sphinx," said the Author, and took out his note-book to "do" her for a religious weekly.

"She travels alone," said a mother of four daughters. (She had, indeed, come to Havermash quite alone, with neither chaperone nor maid.)

"She can wear silver seal and not look green," said a brunette, in black and garnet.

"She sees everything within a mile of her," said Joe to himself, as he held the hem of her dress back reverently from the carriage-wheels.

It would seem that she saw far and distinctly, for half within her carriage door she paused and said abruptly:—

"What is that? Let me see what that is!"

An old woman was pushing her way through the reluctant crowd; a very miserable old woman, splashed with mud. She had a blanket shawl over her head, and her unhealthy yellow gray hair blew out from under it, over her face before the wind.

A crowd of villainous urchins followed, pelting her with slush and snow, and volleys of that shrill, coarse boys' cry (one of the most pitiful sounds on earth) by which the presence of a sacred mystery or a sorrowful sin is indicated, not alone in Havermash.

"Old Mother Goose! Old Mother Goose! Hi, yi! there! Mother Goosey's out buyin' Christmas stockins for her dar-ter! Old Mother Goo-oo-ose!"

Everybody knew how old Mother Goose hated the boys (and with good reason, poor soul!); but nobody had ever seen her offer them violence before that night.

In a minute she had grown suddenly livid and awful to see, rearing her lank figure to its full height against the steel and blood-colored background of the sky, where a sudden gap in the crowd had left her alone.

"You stop *that!*" she fiercely cried; and dealt with a few bad blows to right and left before she was interfered with.

Annoyed beyond measure, Joe entreated Miss Thamrè to let him take her from the scene. She hesitated, lingered, turned after a moment's thought, and sank upon the carriage seat.

"You did not tell me who it was," she said imperiously; "I asked you. I like to be answered when I ask a question. I never *saw* such a miserable old woman!"

"One of your prospective beneficiaries, madam," said Joe, humbly. "A wretched old creature. The boys call her Old Mother Goose. Do not distress yourself about her. It is no sight for you."

"You say the boys call her—I never *heard* such a poor, sad name! Has she no other name, Mr. Havermash? Oh! *there* she is again."

A sudden turn of the carriage had brought them sharply upon the miserable sight once more. Old Mother Goose was sitting stupidly in the slush beside the hack-stands. Her shawl was off, and her gray hair had fallen raggedly upon her shoulders; her teeth chattered with chill and rage; there were drops of blood about her on the snow; a few of the more undaunted spirits among the boys still hovered near her, avenging themselves for their recent defeat by furtive attempts to purloin her drabbled shawl; and a savage expression of his country's intention to preserve virtuous order, in the garb of the police, stood threatening poor Old Mother Goose with the terrors of the law.

It was a sorry sight. A sorry sight Miss Thamrè seemed to find it. She leaned forward to the window. Joe could not prevent her; she would see it all. The silver shine of her fur wrappings glittered through the dusk, as she moved; one tiny gloved and fur-bound hand hung over the window's edge; a faint sweetness, like the soul of an English violet, stirred as she stirred, and stole out upon the frosty air.

"There!" cried the old woman, mouthing a hideous oath, "there's the lady! I'll see her yet, in spite of ye!"

Old Mother Goose staggered up from the mud, staring dully; but the silver-gray picture framed in the carriage window flashed by her in an instant. For an instant only the two women looked each other in the eye.

Miss Thamrè turned white about the chin. Her hand rose to her eyes instinctively, covered them, and fell. It must have been such a miserable contrasting of life's chances to her young and happy fancy!

"I've seen enough," she said. "Never mind!"

"Her name," said Joe, thinking to divert her from the immediate disturbance of the sight, "is Peg, I believe,—Peg Mathers. You see the boys got it Old Mathers, then Old Mother, so Old Mother Goose, I suppose; and quite ingenious, too, I think, poor creature!"

Miss Thamrè made no reply. Quite weary of the subject, she wrapped herself back into the carriage corner, and, asking only how long a ride it was, drew a little silver veil she wore across her face and said no more. Quite weary still she seemed when Joe gave her his arm at the hotel steps (she had refused to accept his or any other private hospitality in the place); and very wearily she gave him to understand that she preferred to be alone till the hour of her appearance before the Havermash public should arrive.

Joe stumbled upon Old Mother Goose again, in running briskly down the hotel steps.

She was wandering in a maudlin, aimless way up and down the sidewalk at the building's front. Her shawl was gone, and her gray head was bare to the wind, which was now as sharp as high.

"What! *you* again?" said Joe. "What are you doing here, Peg? I was ashamed of you to-night, Peg! The people had come out to see a famous lady, and you must get to fighting with the boys and frighten her. You disgraced the town. Better go home, or you'll be in more mischief. Come!"

"I'm out hunting for my shawl, Mr. Havermash," said the old woman, after a moment's sly hesitation. "I've lost my shawl. Them boys took it, curse on 'em! I'd go to see the famous lady, if I had my shawl."

"Better go home; better go home!" repeated Joe. "*She* doesn't want to see *you*, Peg."

"Don't she, Mr. Havermash?"

Old Mother Goose laughed (or did she cry? She was always doing one or the other. What did it matter which?), nodding upward at the windows of the prima donna's parlors, where against the drawn shades a slight, tall shadow passed and repassed now and then, faintly, like a figure in a dream.

"Don't she? Well, I don't know as she does. How warm she looks! She must be warm in them fur tippets that she wears; don't you think she must? I like to see a famous lady well as other folks, when I have my shawl. Mr. Havermash!"

"Well, well, well!" Joe stopped impatiently in hurrying away.

"Would you rather I'd go home and say my prayers than fight the boys? I hate the boys!"

"Prayers, Peg? *Do* you say your prayers? What prayers do you say, Peg? Come!"

Mr. Havermash lingered, entertained in his own despite—thinking he would tell Miss Thamrè this; it might amuse her.

"I say my prayers," said Old Mother Goose, beating her white hair back from her face at a blow, as if she could give it pain. "I've said 'em this many years. I say: 'When the Devil forgets the world, may God remind him of the boys!' I don't feel so about girls, Mr. Havermash. Maybe, if I hadn't had one once myself, I should. My girl ran away from me. She ran away on a Christmas eve, thirteen years ago. Did ye ever see my girl? Mr. Havermash!"

But Joe was gone. He looked back once in running up the street (he was late to supper now; his wife waited to know if Miss Thamrè would receive a call from her, and would scold a bit,—women will, it can't be helped),—he looked back across his shoulder, and saw that Old Mother Goose was still hunting for her shawl beneath the glittering, curtained windows, where a shadow passed and repassed, high above her head, like the shadow of a figure in a dream.

Thamrè took no supper. It was six o'clock when she entered into her parlors and shut her doors about her. It was five minutes before eight when Mr. Havermash called to conduct her to the concert hall in the second story of the brown-stone post-office. It is quite evident, I think, that, in all the passage of the somewhat remarkable drama into which her appearance in Havermash resolved itself, no act can have equaled in intensity that comprised within those two solitary hours. Yet positively all that is known of it, even at this distant day, is that Miss Thamrè took no supper. Every boarder in the hotel knew that in half an hour. Loiterers and lion-hunters beneath the windows where the nervous shadow passed, picked it up, as loiterers and lion-hunters will. Even Old Mother Goose knew it—coming in to ask the hotel clerk if he had seen her shawl, and being for her trouble roughly shown the door.

Miss Thamrè, curtained and locked in Havermash's grand suite of rooms (of which the town is not unjustly proud, it may be said; in which the senator is always accommodated on election days; in which a Harvard professor and a Boston alderman have been known to spend a night; in which the President himself once took a private lunch, in traveling to the mountains), spent, we say, two hours alone. In all her life, perhaps, the lady never spent two hours less alone. For a year the public fancy has been a self-invited guest at the threshold of those hours. It is with reluctance that one's most reverent imagination follows the general curiosity across their sacred edge; and yet it is with something of the same inner propulsion which forces a dreamer on the seashore to keep the eyes upon the struggles of a little gala-boat wrecked by a mortal leak in calm waters on a sunny day.

One sees, in spite of one's self, the lady's soft small hands close violently on the turning key; the silver furs shine under the chandeliers as they fall, tossed hither and hither, to the floor; the little veil torn from the fine, refined, sweet face; the setness of the features and that pallor of hers about the chin.

One knows that she will pace just so across the long, un-homelike splendor of the gaudy rooms; that she will fold her hands behind her, one into the other knotted fast; that she will lift them now and then, and rub them fiercely, as if she found them in a deathly chill; that her hair will fall, perhaps, in her sharp, regardless motions, and hang about her face; that her head is bent; and that her eyes will follow that great green tulip on the Brussels carpet, from pattern to pattern, patiently, seeing only that, as the shadow of her on the curtain passes and repasses, telling only what a shadow can.

One listens, as she listens to the voices of the people passing on the pavement far below; one wonders, as she wonders what they say; if they speak of her, if they would speak of her tomorrow; and what it would happen they would say, should to-morrow bring forth what to-morrow might.

One hears, for she must hear, a Christmas carol chanted flatly by some young people in the street; the bustle of a hundred Christmas seekers coming homeward, with laden arms and empty pockets, from the little shops; one notices that she draws the shade, to see if holly is hanging in the windows, as it used to hang in Havermash, all up and down the street, by five o'clock,—and if she remembers how many times she has stolen out away in her clean hood, with some care that no one else need follow, shaming her, to see the holly herself and hear the carols sung, like happier little girls—how can one but seem to remember too? And when the church-bells ring out for Christmas prayers, melting through the obdurate mail of the welded clouds, till they seem to melt a star through, as still and clear as God's voice melting through a wrung, defiant heart,—if her set face quivers a little, can one prevent one's own from quivering as well?

Perhaps the church-bells ring in a vision with them, to the barred and curtained glitter of Miss Thamrè's rooms. Perhaps, by sheer contrast, her fancy finds the wretched creature whom she saw to-day, seated with the mud and blood about her, shut in from all the world with her, they two alone together in the dreadful, shining place.

Perhaps she seems to herself to escape it, fleeing with her eyes to the dimmest corner of the room. Perhaps she forces herself to face it, turning sharply back, and lifting her head superbly, as Thamrè can (the shadow on the curtain lifts its head just so, as a passer in the street can see). Perhaps she reasons with it, hotly, on this wise, as she walks:—

"I did not think, in coming to Havermash, you would strike across my way like this!"

"Heaven knows what restless fancy forced me here, Would to Heaven I had never come!"

"For thirteen years I have wondered what it would be like to look upon your face again. How *could* I know it would be like what it is,—so miserable, so neglected, so alone!"

Perhaps she argues sternly, now and then:—

"I have never left you to suffer, at the worst. You can not starve. The first ten-dollar bill I ever earned I sent to you. If you are too imbecile to watch the post, am I to blame? If you will have opium or rum for it, am I to blame? I've done my duty by your shameful motherhood, if ever wretched daughter did! What would you have, what will you have besides?"

Perhaps she droops and pleads at moments like a little child:—

"I have fought so hard, mother, for my name and fame! You gave me such a load of shame and ignorance and squalor to shake off! It has been such a long and bitter work! Let me be for a *little* while now, mother, *do!* Sometime before you die I'll search you out; but not just yet—*just* yet!"

Perhaps she falls to sobbing, as women will. Perhaps she flings her beautiful arms out, and slides with her face upon the stifling scarlet cushions of a little sofa, where she tossed her veil. Perhaps, in kneeling there, the bleeding, gray-haired figure stalks her by, and the quieter companionship of a troop of passive and exhausted thoughts will occupy her place.

It may be that she will think about a certain Christmas eve, windy and wild like this, and with a sky of steel and red almost like this. She thought of it in seeing the sunset from the window of the cars, remembering how a streak of red light crept into the attic corner, to help her while she packed a little bundle of her ragged clothes, thirteen years ago to-night.

It may be that she remembers counting the holly wreaths to keep her wits together as she fled, guiltily and sobbing for terror at the thing that she was doing, through the happy little town; that she saw crosses of myrtle and tuberoses in Mr. Havermash's drawing-room windows as she went by, and how grand they looked; and that a butcher's wife she knew was hanging blue tissue-paper roses in her sitting-room as she climbed the depot steps. She can even recall the butcher's name,—Jack Hash,—Mrs. Jack Hash; as well as a hot and hungry wonder that filled the soul of the desolate child that night, whether she should ever live to be as safe and clean and respectable as Mrs. Jack Hash, and how she would garland her sitting-room with blue tissue-roses on Christmas, if she did!

It may be that her fancy, being wearied, dwells more minutely upon the half comical, wholly pathetic irrelevance of these things than upon the swift and feverish history of the crowded interval between their occurrence and the fact that Helène Thamrè is kneeling in the Havermash hotel parlor, to-night, fighting all the devils that can haunt a beautiful and gifted woman's soul for her poor, old, shameful mother's sake.

Her battles for bread in factories and workshops, when first she cast herself, a little girl of fifteen bitter winters, upon the perilous chances of the world; worse contests, such as the outcast child of old Peg Mathers might not escape, being unfriended and despairing as the child had been; her desperate taxation of her only power, at last,—the voice which Heaven gave her, pure and sweet as its own summer mornings; the songs which she sang at street-corners before the twilight fell; the windows of happy people under which she chanted mournfully; the first solo which they gave her at a mission school into which she chanced; the friends who heard it, and into whose hearts God put it to stretch down their hands and draw her straightway into Paradise; her studies and struggles since in foreign lands; the death of the master who had trained her, and the falling of his great mantle upon her bewildered name,—these details, perhaps, float but mistily before her mind.

Sharp, distinct, pursuing, cruel, a single question begins to imprison her tortured thoughts. It took shapes as vague as smoke, clouds, fogs, dreams, at first; it looms as clear-cut and gigantic as a pyramid before her now.

If all the world should know next year, next week, to-morrow, at once and forever, what she knows?

If Havermash should learn, suppose, to-night, that little Nell Mathers, the unfathered and forgotten child of the creature at whose gray hairs the boys hoot on the streets, is all there is of Helène Thamrè (the very letters of the shameful name transposed to make the beautiful, false image), what would Havermash, falling at her feet this instant, do the next?

Perhaps to the woman's inner sense neither Havermash nor the world may matter much, indeed. She has kept, through deadly peril, soul and body pure as light. Not a sheltered wife, singing "Greenville" to her babies, vacant of ambitions and innocent of noisier powers, can show a hand or heart or name more spotless than her own. And now to dye them deep in the old, old, hateful shame! One must have *been* little Nell Mathers and have become Thamrè, I fancy, to measure this recoil.

Perhaps it seems to her more monstrous and impossible as the thought grows more familiar to her. Perhaps a certain hardness begins to creep across the pallor of her face; or it may be only that she has wound her fallen hair back from it, and exposed the carved exactness and composure of her features. It may be that she will argue to herself again, forgetting that the gray-haired vision left her long ago:—

"I could never make you happy, if I did. It would always, always be a curse to both of us. What have you ever done for me, that you should demand a right so cruel? You have no right, I say; you have no right!"

"And, if you speak, indeed, why, who believes you? What can your ravings do against Thamrè's denial, poor old mother!"

Perhaps she muses, half aloud: "You need a shawl, I see. You shall have a bright, warm shawl on Christmas Day. It is better for you than a daughter. Oh! a thousand times!"

Perhaps she laughs—as Thamrè does not often laugh—most bitterly; and that Joe Havermash, knocking at her door, hears, or thinks he hears, the sound, before she flashes on him, tall, serene, resplendent, in full dress and full spirit for the evening.

The Happy Home Handel Association were satisfied with the reception given by Havermash to their rendering of the oratorio of the Messiah last Christmas eve. On settees, in the aisles, on the window-sills, in the corridors, on the stairs, Havermash overflowed the brown-stone post-office.

Since the incorporation of the city (which is the Christian era of Havermash, and from which everything dates accordingly) nothing approaching such an audience had been collected for the most popular of purposes. Even Signor Blitz could not have eaten swords or played base ball with uncracked eggs before a quarter of the spectators; and the New England philosopher, it is well known, reads his lectures in Havermash to three hundred people.

In this triumph the Happy Home Handel Association felt compelled to own that Thamrè had her share, which for the H. H. H. A. was owning a great deal. When little Joe bowed the prima donna upon the somewhat uncertain (green cambric) stage, the East Havermash "orchestra" led off in a burst of

applause, which threatened to shake the post-office to its foundation stone, and which fired even the leader's dignity of Joe's
rotund person to ill-concealed enthusiasm. Even Mrs. Joe,
gorgeous upon the front settee, in the opera dress that (it was
well known) she wore in Boston, despite the ache of a secret
chagrin that Miss Thamrè had received no callers, reflected the
general pride and pleasure to the very links of her great gold
necklace and the tiniest wrinkle of her rose-colored gloves. Even
Mrs. Jack Hash, on her camp-stool, by the second left, though
disposed by nature and training to be critical of anything headed
by a Havermash, applauded softly with the feathered tip of her
silver-paper fan upon the frill of her brown poplin upper skirt.
Never had there been anything like it known in Havermash.

Like a bird, like a snow-flake, like a moonbeam, like a fancy,
like nothing that the brown-stone post-office was accustomed
to, Thamrè stole upon the stage. She stood for an instant poised,
fluttering, as if half her mind were made to fly, then fell into
her unapproachable repose, and at her leisure looked the great
audience over, shooting it here and there with her nervous
glance.

The packed house drew and held its breath. Women thought
swiftly: Silver-gray satin, up to the throat and down to the hands.
No jewelry, and a live white lily on her wrist! Young men saw
her through a mist, and half turned their eyes away, as if they
had seen a Madonna folded in a morning cloud. Reporters
pondered, twirling a moustache end, pencil held suspended:
Such severity is the superbest affectation, my lady! but it tells,
as straight as a carrier-dove. Before she had opened her lips,
Thamrè had conquered Havermash.

Conscious of this in an instant's flash, Thamrè grew uncon-
scious of it in another. For an instant every detail in her house
was in her grasp, even to Mrs. Jack Hash on the camp-stool and
the critical attitude of the silver-paper fan; even to old Mother
Goose, half fading into the shadow of the distance, quarreling
with a doorkeeper about her ticket. The next she cast her
audience from her like a racer casting his cloak to the wind. Her
face settled; her wonderful eyes dilated; the hand with the lily
on it closed over the other like a seal; the soul of the music
entered into her, incorporate. She grew as sacred as her theme.

"That little country house," said a critic present, who had heard her before her best houses in the great world, "was on the knees of its heart that night. She never sung like that before, nor ever will again; nor any other artist, it is my belief. She minded the jerks of that orchestra and the flats of the Havermash *prime donne* no more than she did the whistling of the wind about the post-office windows. She rendered the text like an angel sent from heaven for the purpose. When she lifted that hand with the flower on it (she did it only in the chorus, 'Surely, he hath borne our griefs,' and in the tenor, 'Behold, and see,' and at one other time) I could think of nothing but

'In the beauty of the lilies
Christ was born across the sea.'

Couldn't get it out of my head. I meant she should have been *encored*, when it was all over, to give us that itself; but for what happened, you know."

Did I say she grew as sacred as her theme? It might almost be said that its holy Personality environed and enveloped her. Reverent souls that listened to her that well-remembered night felt as if the Man of Sorrows confided to her the burden of his heart, as if he stooped to acquaint her with his grief, as if the travail of his soul fell upon her, and that with his satisfaction she was satisfied.

The sacred drama was unfolding to its solemn close, the wildness of the wind without was hushed, the Christmas stars were out, when Thamrè glided into her last solo,—that palpitating, proud, triumphant thing, in which the soul of Divine Love avenges itself against the ingenuity of human despair:—

"If God be for us, who can be against us?
Who can be against us?
Who shall lay anything to the charge
Of God's elect?
It is God that justifieth.
Who is he that condemneth?
It is Christ that died."

It was at this point that the interruption came.

Shrill and sharp into the thrill of the singer's liquid, clinging notes a quick cry cut:—

"Let me see her! Let me touch her! I can't abear it any longer! Let me see my girl!" and, forcing her way like a stream of lava through the packed and startled aisles, hot, wild, pallid, and horrible, Old Mother Goose leaped, before a hand could stay her, on the stage.

"I can't stand it any longer, Nell! It seems to craze my head! I knew you from the time I heard you laughing to the depot. I didn't mean to shame ye before so many folks, and I tried to find my shawl. They said you wouldn't want to see your poor old mother, Nelly dear. But I can't abear to hear you sing. Nell, why, Nell, you stand up like the Almighty Dead to do it!"

The shock of the shrill words and their cessation brought the house to its feet. Then came the uproar.

"Shame!" "Police!" "Order!" "Take her out!" "Arrest the hag!" "Protect the lady!" And after that the astonishment and the silence of death.

High above the wavering, peering mass, clear to the apprehension of every eye in the house, appeared a lily-bound, authoritative hand. It motioned once and dropped—as the snow drops over a grave.

By those who sat nearest her it was said that the flower trembled on the lady's wrist a little; for the rest, she stood sculptured like a statue, towering about the piteous figure at her feet. Her voice, when she spoke,—for she spoke in the passing of a thought,—rang out to the remotest corner of the galleries, slipping even then, however, into Thamrè's girlish, uneven tones.

"If you *please*, do not disturb the woman at this moment. She is a very *old* woman. Let us hear what she has to say. Her hair is gray. Let us not be *rough* or *hasty* till we have *thought* of what she says."

Old Mother Goose rose from the floor, where she had fallen, half-abashed, perhaps half-dazed at that which she had done.

"I've got nothing more to say." She fumbled foolishly in the air to wrap the shawl which she had lost about her lean and tattered shoulders. "I've said as this famous lady is my daughter, that was Nell Mathers, and remembered by many folks in

Havermash thirteen year ago. I wouldn't have shamed her quite
so much if I'd only found my shawl. It's cold, too, without a
shawl. I'll go out now, and you can sing your piece through,
Nelly, without the plague of me. I wouldn't have told on you, I
think, but for the music and the crazy feeling that I had. It's
most too bad, Nelly, to spoil the piece. I'll go right out."

She turned, stepped off, and staggered feebly, turning her
bleared eyes back to feast upon the silent, shining figure, on
whose wrist the lily glittered cruelly, as only lilies can.

"What a pretty sating gown you've got, my dear!" she said.

Mr. Havermash could bear it no longer. He took Old Mother
Goose by the sleeve, hurrying up, saying: "Come, come!"

"The woman is drunk, Miss Thamrè. She shall not be allowed
to insult you any more like this. In the kindness of your heart,
you make a mistake, I think, if you will pardon me. See! she is
quite beside herself. Something is due to the audience. This
disturbance should not continue. Come, Peg, come!"

But Thamrè shook her head. She had grown now deadly
pale,—at least so Joe thought, letting go the woman's arm, his
own face changing color sharply, the baton in his fat, white-
gloved hand beginning to shake.

"If you please, Mr. Havermash, I should like to know—the
people will *pardon* me a moment, I am sure—I should like to
know if this poor old creature has anything *more* to say."

"Nothing more," said Old Mother Goose, shaking her gray
head, "but this, maybe, Nelly dear. I says to myself, when I sits
and hears you singing,—I says, when you sang them words: 'If
God be for me, my girl won't be against me! My girl can't be
against me!'—over and over with the music, Nelly, so I did! If
God be for me, how *can* my girl be against me?"

It was said that, when Helène Thamrè stretched down her
lily-guarded hand, and, lifting the lean, uncleanly fingers of Old
Mother Goose, pressed them, after a moment's thought, gently
and slowly to her heart, she heard the sudden break of sobs in
the breathless house; and, pausing to listen to the sound, flushed
fitfully like a child surprised, and smiled.

"Ladies and gentlemen,"—her great eyes stabbed the audience
through and through; she lifted the old woman's hand, that all
might see,—"I am *sorry* that your entertainment should be

disturbed. If you will *excuse* me, I will leave you now, and take my mother home."

Home? What home was there for Old Mother Goose and her outcast child in Thamrè's hotel parlors, on that or any other night? What home was there for Thamrè in the God-forsaken cellar whence the woman of the town had crawled? Apparently, the lady had not thought of this. Joe found her standing serenely as an angel when he came into the stifling little green room. She was still smiling. She had buttoned her silver furs about the old woman's shrunken throat.

"This will be warmer than your shawl, mother, don't you see?" he heard her say. "The boys shall never bother you in this, poor old mother! There!"

Mrs. Havermash came with her husband. The Boston opera-cloak was in disorder; her rose-colored gloves were wet and spotted.

"Miss Thamrè," said Joe, "may I make you acquainted with my wife? We would not urge upon you again the acceptance of a hospitality which has been already so decidedly refused; but perhaps, considering the state of your mother's health, we can make you more comfortable now at our home than you can be elsewhere. If you will do Mrs. Havermash and myself the favor to return with us—and her—in our own carriage to-night"—

Joe's grandfather, as has been said, cobbled shoes in a wooden shop; and even Mrs. Joe to-day will drink with her spoon in her tea-cup, you will notice, if you chance to sit beside her at a supper. But show me bluer blood, if it please you, than shall flow in the veins of him and his, to preserve the existence of this most cultivated instinct and the memory of this most knightly deed.

All the world knows how Thamrè suddenly and mysteriously disappeared a year ago from public and professional life. All the world has mourned, wondered, gossiped, caught at the wings of rumors, lost them, and so mourned again at this event.

All the world does not know with what a curious development of pride in and loyalty to the personality of little Nell Mathers, Havermash has struggled, till struggle has become useless, to enforce a reticence upon the subject of Thamrè's movements and their motives.

To a few friends, familiar with her private history for the past year, its results have seemed to crown its cost, I think. At least, she herself, having proved them so, has contrived to radiate upon us the light of her own content.

"You do not know the life," she said, at the outset, shaking her beautiful, determined head, "if you would ask me to return to it while my mother lives. Even my name will not bear the scorch of hers. The world is so hard on women! Do not urge me. Let me take my way. Perhaps God and I together can make her poor old hand as white as yours or mine before she dies."

Perhaps they did. It is known that when Old Mother Goose lay dying in her daughter's quiet house in Havermash, one frosty night, not many weeks ago, and after she had fallen, as they thought, past speech or recognition, she raised herself upon her pillow, and, stretching her hands, said slowly:—

"Nell! why, Nell! It is Christ that died! If my girl was for me, Nell, *could* He be against me, do you think?"

And further it is only known that Thamrè will sing this season in the oratorio of the Messiah on Christmas eve.

Alice Brown

The Way of Peace
1898

Alice Brown (1856–1948), a New Englander who became one of the most acclaimed short story writers in the United States during the peak years of her literary career, has been lost to readers for many decades. Although her brilliant stories were identified as among the best of those labeled "local color," she wrote during the years of declining interest in literary regionalism. Despite inclusion in a few fine collections of "local color fiction," she has presented difficulties for literary historians. Although her best were written in the early twentieth century, her stories seem to belong to the nineteenth century because of their style and their focus on women of middle age and older who had lived the first half of their lives during the nineteenth century in rural settings that remained stable despite urban industrialization. For these women, life did not change significantly when the new century began.

Brown published 17 novels, 4 volumes of plays, 3 of poetry, and 4 miscellaneous volumes of criticism, personal essays, and works for children during her career, which began in the early 1890s and continued for close to half a century. But it is the 115 stories collected in 8 volumes that justify claims for her of literary greatness. She is the inheritor of the literary tradition of Catharine Maria Sedgwick, Lydia Maria Child, Harriet Beecher Stowe, and the "regionalists" who befriended her and welcomed her as their youngest colleague.

Many of Alice Brown's stories focus on women in community and in communication with each other, very often across the generations. She depicts young women in willing discipleship to their mothers, grandmothers, or other chosen mentors in those generations. It is a spiritual discipleship in peace, grace, and joy. The greatest love in the lives of these women, the most significant "other," is often a woman of an older generation. And, of course, the model couple in that scheme is that of mother and daughter. She wrote about a world in which women were free to love each other, uninhibited by the new Freudian theories that had begun to reach the consciousness of the educated and artistic. Alice Brown was familiar with these ideas; however, her mothers and daughters live with, delight in, and love each other despite them.

Alice Brown never married and left little information about her family or her girlhood on a farm in New Hampshire. She spent her professional literary life as a respected member of a community of creative women, including Annie Fields, Sarah Orne Jewett, Mary E. Wilkins Freeman, Elizabeth Stuart Phelps, Harriet Prescott Spofford, and Helen Hunt Jackson. The Irish Catholic poet, Louise Imogen Guiney, was a central figure in Alice Brown's life. After a first trip together to England in 1886, the two women founded the Women's Rest Tour Association "to encourage other women to take their vacations as they had, with pack and stick, in foreign lands." It was Guiney's influence that led Brown in her later years to enter into serious study of Catholicism, although she never converted.

"The Way of Peace" was published in the Thanksgiving issue of Outlook *(November 19, 1898) under the pseudonym Martin Redfield (later to be used in Brown's 1912 novel,* My Love and I, *as the name of a character who, according to Brown's biographer, Dorothea Walker, "prostitutes his art in a conflict between idealism and materialism"). It lifts the occasional story far above the limitations and conventions of the genre. A story of love and death, devotion and transcendence, "The Way of Peace" was included in Brown's second collection of stories,* Tiverton Tales *(1899).*

The story is one in which many of the mother-daughter categories converge. Not only is there the obvious commemoration of a major life cycle event—the death of Lucy Ann Cummings's mother—and Lucy Ann's subsequent quest for an identity adequate to her altered circumstances, but there is also the gentle, loving, but nevertheless firm and persistent confrontation with the patriarchy in the persons of her brothers Eliza and John, who "would be good to her ... always had been ... were men-folks, and doubtless ... knew best."

Although Alice Brown was never affiliated with any segment of the women's movement, her commitment to personal integrity in her own life and in the lives of her fictional characters led to frequent depictions of females who grow from complacent acceptance to active control of their destinies. Additionally, Brown's work contains frequent celebrations of the natural world and of the life of the spirit, both of which have been identified as characteristics commonly found in women's writing. In "The Way of Peace," the affirmation of the connection between this world and the next—to which Lucy Ann's mother has departed— is the tonic chord on which this virtuoso piece ends.

All eight volumes of Brown's short stories have been reprinted in recent years. The other seven are: Meadow-Grass: Tales of New England Life *(1895),* High Noon *(1904),* The County Road *(1906),* Country Neighbors

(1910), Vanishing Points *(1913),* The Flying Teuton *(1918), and* Homespun and Gold *(1920).*

It was two weeks after her mother's funeral when Lucy Ann Cummings sat down and considered. The web of a lifelong service and devotion still clung about her, but she was bereft of the creature for whom it had been spun. Now she was quite alone, save for her two brothers and the cousins who lived in other townships, and they all had homes of their own. Lucy Ann sat still, and thought about her life. Brother Ezra and brother John would be good to her. They always had been. Their solicitude redoubled with her need, and they had even insisted on leaving Annabel, John's daughter, to keep her company after the funeral. Lucy Ann thought longingly of the healing which lay in the very loneliness of her little house; but she yielded, with a patient sigh. John and Ezra were men-folks, and doubtless they knew best.

A little more than a week had gone when school "took up," rather earlier than had been intended, and Annabel went away in haste, to teach. Then Lucy Ann drew her first long breath. She had resisted many a kindly office from her niece, with the crafty innocence of the gentle who can only parry and never thrust. When Annabel wanted to help in packing away grandma's things, aunt Lucy agreed, half-heartedly, and then deferred the task from day to day. In reality, Lucy Ann never meant to pack them away at all. She could not imagine her home without them; but that, Annabel would not understand, and her aunt pushed aside the moment, reasoning that something is pretty sure to happen if you put things off long enough. And something did; Annabel went away. It was then that Lucy Ann took a brief draught of the cup of peace.

Long before her mother's death, when they both knew how inevitably it was coming, Lucy Ann had, one day, a little shock of surprise. She was standing before the glass, coiling her crisp gray hair, and thinking over and over the words the doctor had used, the night before, when he told her how near the end might be. Her delicate face fell into deeper lines. Her mouth dropped a little at the corners; her faded brown eyes were hot with tears, and stopping to wipe them, she caught sight of herself in the glass.

"Why," she said aloud, "I look jest like mother!"

And so she did, save that it was the mother of five years ago, before disease had corroded the dear face, and patience wrought its tracery there.

"Well," she continued, smiling a little at the poverty of her state, "I shall be a real comfort to me when mother's gone!"

Now that her moment of solitude had struck, grief came also. It glided in, and sat down by her, to go forth no more, save perhaps under its other guise of a patient hope. She rocked back and forth in her chair, and moaned a little to herself.

"Oh, I never can bear it!" she said pathetically, under her breath. "I never can bear it in the world!"

The tokens of illness were all put away. Her mother's bedroom lay cold in an unsmiling order. The ticking of the clock emphasized the inexorable silence of the house. Once Lucy Ann thought she heard a little rustle and stir. It seemed the most natural thing in the world, coming from the bedroom, where one movement of the clothes had always been enough to summon her with flying feet. She caught her breath, and held it, to listen. She was ready, undisturbed, for any sign. But a great fly buzzed drowsily on the pane, and the fire crackled with accentuated life. She was quite alone. She put her hand to her heart, in that gesture of grief which is so entirely natural when we feel the stab of destiny; and then she went wanly into the sitting-room, looking about her for some pretense of duty to solace her poor mind. There again she caught sight of herself in the glass.

"Oh, my!" breathed Lucy Ann. Low as they were, the words held a fullness of joy.

Her face had been aging through these days of grief; it had grown more and more like her mother's. She felt as if a hand had been stretched out to her, holding a gift, and at that moment something told her how to make the gift enduring. Running over to the little table where her mother's work-basket stood, as it had been, undisturbed, she took out a pair of scissors, and went back to the glass. There she let down her thick gray hair, parted it carefully on the sides, and cut off lock after lock about her face. She looked a caricature of her sober self. But she was well used to curling hair like this, drawing its crisp silver into shining rings; and she stood patiently before the glass and coaxed her own locks into just such fashion as had framed the older face. It was done, and Lucy Ann looked at herself with a smile all suffused by love and longing. She was not herself any more; she had gone back a generation, and chosen a warmer niche. She could have kissed her face in the glass, it was so like that other dearer one. She did finger the little curls, with a reminiscent passion, not daring to think of the darkness where the others had been shut; and, at that instant, she felt very rich. The change suggested a more faithful portraiture, and she went up into the spare room and looked through the closet where her mother's clothes had been hanging so long, untouched. Selecting a purple thibet, with a little white sprig, she slipped off her own dress, and stepped into it. She crossed a muslin kerchief on her breast, and pinned it with the cameo her mother had been used to wear. It was impossible to look at herself in the doing; but when the deed was over, she went again to the glass and stood there, held by a wonder beyond her will. She had resurrected the creature she loved; this was an enduring portrait, perpetuating, in her own life, another life as well.

"I'll pack away my own clo'es to-morrer," said Lucy Ann to herself. "Them are the ones to be put aside."

She went downstairs, hushed and tremulous, and seated herself again, her thin hands crossed upon her lap; and there she stayed, in a pleasant dream, not of the future, and not even of the past, but face to face with a recognition of wonderful possibilities. She had dreaded her loneliness with the ache that is despair; but she was not lonely any more. She had been allowed to set up a little model of the tabernacle where she had worshiped; and, having that, she ceased to be afraid. To sit there, clothed in such sweet familiarity of line and likeness, had tightened her grasp upon the things that are. She did not seem to herself altogether alive, nor was her mother dead. They had been fused, by some wonderful alchemy; and instead of being worlds apart, they were at one. So, John Cummings, her brother, stepping briskly in, after tying his horse at the gate, came upon her unawares, and started, with a hoarse, thick cry. It was in the dusk of evening; and, seeing her outline against the window, he stepped back against the wall and leaned there a moment, grasping at the casing with one hand. "Good God!" he breathed, at last, "I thought 't was mother!"

Lucy Ann rose, and went forward to meet him.

"Then it's true," said she. "I'm so pleased. Seems as if I could git along, if I could look a little mite like her."

John stood staring at her, frowning in his bewilderment.

"What have you done to yourself?" he asked. "Put on her clo'es?"

"Yes," said Lucy Ann, "but that ain't all. I guess I do resemble mother, though we ain't any of us had much time to think about it. Well, I *am* pleased. I took out that daguerreotype she had, down Saltash way, though it don't favor her as she was at the end. But if I can take a glimpse of myself in the glass, now and then, mebbe I can git along."

They sat down together in the dark, and mused over old memories. John had always understood Lucy Ann better than the rest. When she gave up Simeon Bascom to stay at home with her mother, he never pitied her much; he knew she had chosen the path she loved. The other day, even, some one had wondered that she could have heard the funeral service so unmoved; but he, seeing how her face had seemed to fade and wither at every word, guessed what pain was at her heart. So, though his wife had sent him over to ask how Lucy Ann was getting on, he really found out very little, and felt how painfully dumb he must be when he got home. Lucy Ann was pretty well, he thought he might say. She'd got to looking a good deal like mother.

They took their "blindman's holiday," Lucy Ann once in a while putting a stick on the leaping blaze, and, when John questioned her, giving a low-toned reply. Even her voice had changed. It might have come from that bedroom, in one of the pauses between hours of pain, and neither would have been surprised.

"What makes you burn beech?" asked John, when a shower of sparks came crackling at them.

"I don't know," she answered. "Seems kind o' nat'ral. Some of it got into the last cord we bought, an' one night it snapped out, an' most burnt up mother's nightgown an' cap while I was warmin' 'em. We had a real time of it. She scolded me, an' then she laughed, an' I laughed—an' so, when I see a stick or two o' beech to-day, I kind o' picked it out a-purpose."

John's horse stamped impatiently from the gate, and John, too, knew it was time to go. His errand was not done, and he balked at it.

"Lucy Ann," said he, with the bluntness of resolve, "what you goin' to do?"

Lucy Ann looked sweetly at him through the dark. She had expected that. She smoothed her mother's dress with one hand, and it gave her courage.

"Do?" said she; "why, I ain't goin' to do nothin'. I've got enough to pull through on."

"Yes, but where you goin' to live?"

"Here."

"Alone?"

"I don't feel so very much alone," said she, smiling to herself. At that moment she did not. All sorts of sweet possibilities had made themselves real. They comforted her, like the presence of love.

John felt himself a messenger. He was speaking for others that with which his soul did not accord.

"The fact is," said he, "they're all terrible set ag'inst it. They say you're gittin' along in years. So you be. So are we all. But they will have it, it ain't right for you to live on here alone. Mary says she should be scairt to death. She wants you should come an' make it your home with us."

"Yes, I dunno but Mary would be scairt," said Lucy Ann placidly. "But I ain't. She's real good to ask me; but I can't do it, no more'n she could leave you an' the children an' come over here to stay with me. Why, John, this is my home!"

Her voice sank upon a note of passion. It trembled with memories of dewy mornings and golden eves. She had not grown here, through all her youth and middle life, like moss upon a rock, without fitting into the hollows and softening the angles of her poor habitation. She had drunk the sunlight and the rains of one small spot, and she knew how both would fall. The place, its sky and clouds and breezes, belonged to her: but she belonged to it as well.

John stood between two wills, his own and that of those who had sent him. Left to himself, he would not have harassed her. To him, also, wedded to a hearth where he found warmth and peace, it would have been sweet to live there always, though alone, and die by the light of its dying fire. But Mary thought otherwise, and in matters of worldly judgment he could only yield.

"I don't want you should make a mistake," said he. "Mebbe you an' I don't look for'ard enough. They say you'll repent it if you stay, an' there'll be a hurrah-boys all round. What say to makin' us a visit? That'll kind o' stave it off, an' then we can see what's best to be done."

Lucy Ann put her hands to her delicate throat, where her mother's gold beads lay lightly, with a significant touch. She, like John, had an innate gentleness of disposition. She distrusted her own power to judge.

"Maybe I might," said she faintly. "Oh, John, do you think I've got to?"

"It needn't be for long," answered John briefly, though he felt his eyes moist with pity of her. "Mebbe you could stay a month?"

"Oh, I couldn't do that!" cried Lucy Ann, in wild denial. "I never could in the world. If you'll make it a fortnight, an' harness up yourself, an' bring me home, mebbe I might."

John gave his word, but when he took his leave of her, she leaned forward into the dark, where the impatient horse was fretting, and made her last condition.

"You'll let me turn the key on things here jest as they be? You won't ask me to break up nuthin'?"

"Break up!" repeated John, with the intensity of an oath. "I guess you needn't. If anybody puts that on you, you send 'em to me."

So Lucy Ann packed her mother's dresses into a little hair trunk that had stood in the attic unused for many years, and went away to make her visit. When she drove up to the house, sitting erect and slender in her mother's cashmere shawl and black bonnet, Mary, watching from the window, gave a little cry, as at the risen dead. John had told her about Lucy Ann's transformation, but she put it all aside as a crazy notion, not likely to last: now it seemed less a pathetic masquerade than a strange by-path taken by nature itself.

The children regarded it with awe, and half the time called Lucy Ann "grandma." That delighted her. Whenever they did it, she looked up to say, with her happiest smile,—

"There! that's complete. You'll remember grandma, won't you? We mustn't ever forget her."

Here, in this warm-hearted household, anxious to do her service in a way that was not her own, she had some happiness, of a tremulous kind; but it was all built up of her trust in a speedy escape. She knit mittens, and sewed long seams; and every day her desire to fill the time was irradiated by the certainty that twelve hours more were gone. A few more patient intervals, and she should be at home. Sometimes, as the end of her visit drew nearer, she woke early in the morning with a sensation of irresponsible joy, and wondered, for an instant, what had happened to her. Then it always came back, with an inward flooding she had scarcely felt even in her placid youth. At home there would be so many things to do, and, above all, such munificent leisure! For there she would feel no need of feverish action to pass the time. The hours would take care of themselves; they would fleet by, while she sat, her hands folded, communing with old memories.

The day came, and the end of her probation. She trembled a good deal, packing her trunk in secret, to escape Mary's remonstrances; but John stood by her, and she was allowed to go.

"You'll get sick of it," called Mary after them. "I guess you'll be glad enough to see the children again, an' they will you. Mind, you've got to come back an' spend the winter."

Lucy Ann nodded happily. She could agree to anything sufficiently remote; and the winter was not yet here.

The first day in the old house seemed to her like new birth in Paradise. She wandered about, touching chairs and tables and curtains, the manifest symbols of an undying past. There were loving duties to be done, but she could not do them yet. She had to look her pleasure in the face, and learn its lineaments.

Next morning came brother Ezra, and Lucy Ann hurried to meet him with an exaggerated welcome. Life was never very friendly to Ezra, and those who belonged to him had to be doubly kind. They could not change his luck, but they might sweeten it. They said the world had not gone well with him; though sometimes it was hinted that Ezra, being out of gear, could not go with the world. All the rivers ran away from him, and went to turn some other mill. He was ungrudging of John's prosperity, but still he looked at it in some disparagement, and shook his head. His cheeks were channeled long before youth was over; his feet were weary with honest serving, and his hands grown hard with toil. Yet he had not arrived, and John was at the goal before him.

"We heard you'd been stayin' with John's folks," said he to Lucy Ann. "Leastways, Abby did, an' she thinks mebbe you've got a little time for us now, though we ain't nothin' to offer compared to what you're used to over there."

"I'll come," said Lucy Ann promptly. "Yes, I'll come, an' be glad to."

It was part of her allegiance to the one who had gone.

"Ezra needs bracin'," she heard her mother say, in many a sick-room gossip. "He's got to be flattered up, an' have some grit put into him."

It was many weeks before Lucy Ann came home again. Cousin Rebecca, in Saltash, sent her a cordial letter of invitation for just as long as she felt like staying; and the moneyed cousin at the Ridge wrote in like manner, following her note by a telegram, intimating that she would not take no for an answer. Lucy Ann frowned in alarm when the first letter came, and studied it by daylight and in her musings at night, as if some comfort might lurk between the lines. She was tempted to throw it in the fire, not answered at all. Still, there was a reason for going. This cousin had a broken hip, she needed company, and the flavor of old times. The other had married a "drinkin' man," and might feel hurt at being refused. So, fortifying herself with some inner resolution she never confessed, Lucy Ann set her teeth and started out on a visiting campaign. John was amazed. He drove over to see her while she was spending a few days with an aunt in Sudleigh.

"When you been home last, Lucy Ann?" asked he.

A little flush came into her face, and she winked bravely.

"I ain't been home at all," said she, in a low tone. "Not sence August."

John groped vainly in mental depths for other experiences likely to illuminate this. He concluded that he had not quite understood Lucy Ann and her feeling about home; but that was neither here nor there.

"Well," he remarked, rising to go, "you're gittin' to be quite a visitor."

"I'm tryin' to learn how," said Lucy Ann, almost gayly. "I've been a-cousinin' so long, I sha'n't know how to do anything else."

But now the middle of November had come, and she was again in her own house. Cousin Titcomb had brought her there and driven away, concerned that he must leave her in a cold kitchen, and only deterred by a looming horse-trade from staying to build a fire. Lucy Ann bade him good-by, with a gratitude which was not for her visit, but all for getting home; and when he uttered that terrifying valedictory known as "coming again," she could meet it cheerfully. She even stood in the door, watching him away; and not until the rattle of his wheels had ceased on the frozen road, did she return to her kitchen and stretch her shawled arms pathetically upward.

"I thank my heavenly Father!" said Lucy Ann, with the fervency of a great experience.

She built her fire, and then unpacked her little trunk, and hung up the things in the bedroom where her mother's presence seemed still to cling.

"I'll sleep here now," she said to herself. "I won't go out of this no more."

Then all the little homely duties of the hour cried out upon her, like children long neglected; and, with the luxurious leisure of those who may prolong a pleasant task, she set her house in order. She laid out a programme to occupy her days. The attic should be cleaned to-morrow. In one day? Nay, why not three, to hold Time still, and make him wait her pleasure? Then there were the chambers, and the living-rooms below. She felt all the excited joy of youth; she was tasting anticipation at its best.

"It'll take me a week," said she. "That will be grand." She could hardly wait even for the morrow's sun; and that night she slept like those of whom much is to be required, and who must wake in season. Morning came, and mid-forenoon, and while she stepped about under the roof where dust had gathered and bitter herbs told tales of summers past, John drove into the yard. Lucy Ann threw up the attic window and leaned out.

"You put your horse up, an' I'll be through here in a second," she called. "The barn's open."

John was in a hurry.

"I've got to go over to Sudleigh, to meet the twelve o'clock," said he. "Harold's comin'. I only wanted to say I'll be over after you the night before Thanksgivin'. Mary wants you should be sure to be there to breakfast. You all right? Cephas said you seemed to have a proper good time with them."

John turned skillfully on the little green and drove away. Lucy Ann stayed at the window watching him, the breeze lifting her gray curls, and the sun smiling at her. She withdrew slowly into the attic, and sank down upon the floor, close by the window. She sat there and thought, and the wind still struck upon her unheeded. Was she always to be subject to the tyranny of those who had set up their hearth-stones in a more enduring form? Was her home not a home merely because there were no men and children in it? She drew her breath sharply, and confronted certain problems of the greater world, not knowing what they were. To Lucy Ann they did not seem problems at all. They were simply touches on the individual nerve, and she felt the pain. Her own inner self throbbed in revolt, but she never guessed that any other part of nature was throbbing with it. Then she went about her work, with the patience of habit. It was well that the attic should be cleaned, though the savor of the task was gone.

Next day, she walked to Sudleigh, with a basket on her arm. Often she sent her little errands by the neighbors; but to-day she was uneasy, and it seemed as if the walk might do her good. She wanted some soda and some needles and thread. She tried to think they were very important, though some sense of humor told her grimly that household goods are of slight use to one who goes a-cousining. Her day at John's would be prolonged to seven; nay, why not a month, when the winter itself was not too great a tax for them to lay upon her? In her deserted house, soda would lose its strength, and even cloves decay. Lucy Ann felt her will growing very weak within her; indeed, at that time, she was hardly conscious of having any will at all.

It was Saturday, and John and Ezra were almost sure to be in town. She thought of that, and how pleasant it would be to hear from the folks: so much pleasanter than to be always facing them on their own ground, and never on hers. At the grocery she came upon Ezra, mounted on a wagon-load of meal-bags, and just gathering up the reins.

"Hullo!" he called. "You didn't walk?"

"Oh, I jest clipped it over," returned Lucy Ann carelessly. "I'm goin' to git a ride home. I see Marden's wagon when I come by the post-office."

"Well, I hadn't any expectation o' your bein' here," said Ezra. "I meant to ride round to-morrer. We want you to spend Thanksgivin' Day with us. I'll come over arter you."

"Oh, Ezra!" said Lucy Ann, quite sincerely, with her concession to his lower fortunes, "why didn't you say so! John's asked me."

"The dogs!" said Ezra. It was his deepest oath. Then he drew a sigh. "Well," he concluded, "that's our luck. We al'ays come out the leetle end o' the horn. Abby'll be real put out. She 'lotted on it. Well, John's inside there. He's buyin' up 'bout everything there is. You'll git more'n you would with us."

He drove gloomily away, and Lucy Ann stepped into the store, musing. She was rather sorry not to go to Ezra's, if he cared. It almost seemed as if she might ask John to let her take the plainer way. John would understand. She saw him at once where he stood, prosperous and hale, in his great-coat, reading items from a long memorandum, while Jonathan Stevens weighed and measured. The store smelled of spice, and the clerk that minute spilled some cinnamon. Its fragrance struck upon Lucy Ann like a call from some far-off garden, to be entered if she willed. She laid a hand on her brother's arm, and her lips opened to words she had not chosen:—

"John, you shouldn't ha' drove away so quick, t'other day. You jest flung out your invitation an' run. You never give me no time to answer. Ezra's asked me to go there."

"Well, if that ain't smart!" returned John. "Put in ahead, did he? Well, I guess it's the fust time he ever got round. I'm terrible sorry, Lucy. The children won't think it's any kind of a Thanksgivin' without you. Somehow they've got it into their heads it's grandma comin'. They can't seem to understand the difference."

"Well, you tell 'em I guess grandma's kind o' pleased for me to plan it as I have," said Lucy Ann, almost gayly. Her face wore a strange, excited look. She breathed a little faster. She saw a pleasant way before her, and her feet seemed to be tending toward it without her own volition. "You give my love to 'em. I guess they'll have a proper nice time."

She lingered about the store until John had gone, and then went forward to the counter. The storekeeper looked at her respectfully. Everybody had a great liking for Lucy Ann. She had been a faithful daughter, and now that she seemed, in so mysterious a way, to be growing like her mother, even men of her own age regarded her with deference.

"Mr. Stevens," said she, "I didn't bring so much money with me as I might if I'd had my wits about me. Should you jest as soon trust me for some Thanksgivin' things?"

"Certain," replied Jonathan. "Clean out the store, if you want. Your credit's good." He, too, felt the beguilement of the time.

"I want some things," repeated Lucy Ann, with determination. "Some cinnamon an' some mace—there! I'll tell you, while you weigh."

It seemed to her that she was buying the spice islands of the world; and though the money lay at home in her drawer, honestly ready to pay, the recklessness of credit gave her an added joy. The store had its market, also, at Thanksgiving time, and she bargained for a turkey. It could be sent her, the day before, by some of the neighbors. When she left the counter, her arms and her little basket were filled with bundles. Joshua Marden was glad to take them.

"No, I won't ride," said Lucy Ann. "Much obliged to *you*. Jest leave the things inside the fence. I'd ruther walk. I don't git out any too often."

She took her way home along the brown road, stepping lightly and swiftly, and full of busy thoughts. Flocks of birds went whirring by over the yellowed fields. Lucy Ann could have called out to them, in joyous understanding, they looked so free. She, too, seemed to be flying on the wings of a fortunate wind.

All that week she scrubbed and regulated, and took a thousand capable steps as briskly as those who work for the home-coming of those they love. The neighbors dropped in, one after another, to ask where she was going to spend Thanksgiving. Some of them said, "Won't you pass the day with us?" but Lucy Ann replied blithely:—

"Oh, John's invited me there!"

All that week, too, she answered letters, in her cramped and careful hand; for cousins had bidden her to the feast. Over the letters she had many a troubled pause, for one cousin lived near Ezra, and had to be told that John had invited her; and to three others, dangerously within hail of each, she made her excuse a turncoat, to fit the time. Duplicity in black and white did hurt her a good deal, and she sometimes stopped, in the midst of her slow transcription, to look up piteously and say aloud:—

"I hope I shall be forgiven!" But by the time the stamp was on, and the pencil ruling erased, her heart was light again. If she had sinned, she was finding the path intoxicatingly pleasant.

Through all the days before the festival, no house exhaled a sweeter savor than this little one on the green. Lucy Ann did her miniature cooking with great seriousness and care. She seemed to be dwelling in a sacred isolation, yet not altogether alone, but with her mother and all their bygone years. Standing at her table, mixing and tasting, she recalled stories her mother had told her, until, at moments, it seemed as if she not only lived her own life, but some previous one, through that being whose blood ran with hers. She was realizing that ineffable sense of possession born out of knowledge that the enduring part of a personality is ours forever, and that love is an unquenched fire, fed by memory as well as hope.

On Thanksgiving morning, Lucy Ann lay in bed a little later, because that had been the family custom. Then she rose to her exquisite house, and got breakfast ready, according to the unswerving programme of the day. Fried chicken and mince pie: she had had them as a child, and now they were scrupulously prepared. After breakfast, she sat down in the sunshine, and watched the people go by to service in Tiverton Church. Lucy Ann would have liked going, too; but there would be inconvenient questioning, as there always must be when we meet our kind. She would stay undisturbed in her seclusion, keeping her festival alone. The morning was still young when she put her turkey in the oven, and made the vegetables ready. Lucy Ann

was not very fond of vegetables, but there had to be just so
many—onions, turnips, and squash baked with molasses—for
her mother was a Cape woman, preserving the traditions of
dear Cape dishes. All that forenoon, the little house throbbed
with a curious sense of expectancy. Lucy Ann was preparing so
many things that it seemed as if somebody must surely keep her
company; but when dinner-time struck, and she was still alone,
there came no lull in her anticipation. Peace abode with her,
and wrought its own fair work. She ate her dinner slowly, with
meditation and a thankful heart. She did not need to hear the
minister's careful catalogue of mercies received. She was at
home; that was enough.

After dinner, when she had done up the work, and left the
kitchen without spot or stain, she went upstairs, and took out
her mother's beautiful silk poplin, the one saved for great
occasions, and only left behind because she had chosen to be
buried in her wedding gown. Lucy Ann put it on with careful
hands, and then laid about her neck the wrought collar she had
selected the day before. She looked at herself in the glass, and
arranged a gray curl with anxious scrutiny. No girl adorning for
her bridal could have examined every fold and line with a more
tender care. She stood there a long, long moment, and approved
herself.

"It's a wonder," she said reverently. "It's the greatest mercy
anybody ever had."

The afternoon waned, though not swiftly; for Time does not
always gallop when happiness pursues. Lucy Ann could almost
hear the gliding of his rhythmic feet. She did the things set aside
for festivals, or the days when we have company. She looked
over the photograph album, and turned the pages of the "Ladies'
Wreath." When she opened the case containing that old daguerreotype, she scanned it with a little distasteful smile, and
then glanced up at her own image in the glass, nodding her
head in thankful peace. She was the enduring portrait. In
herself, she might even see her mother grow very old. So the
hours slipped on into dusk, and she sat there with her dream,
knowing, though it was only a dream, how sane it was, and
good. When wheels came rattling into the yard, she awoke with
a start, and John's voice, calling to her in an inexplicable alarm,

did not disturb her. She had had her day. Not all the family
fates could take it from her now. John kept calling, even while
his wife and children were climbing down, unaided, from the
great carryall. His voice proclaimed its own story, and Lucy Ann
heard it with surprise.

"Lucy! Lucy Ann!" he cried. "You here? You show yourself,
if you're all right."

Before they reached the front door, Lucy Ann had opened it
and stood there, gently welcoming.

"Yes, here I be," said she. "Come right in, all of ye. Why, if
that ain't Ezra, too, an' his folks, turnin' into the lane. When'd
you plan it?"

"Plan it! we didn't plan it!" said Mary testily. She put her hand
on Lucy Ann's shoulder, to give her a little shake; but, feeling
mother's poplin, she forbore.

Lucy Ann retreated before them into the house, and they all
trooped in after her. Ezra's family, too, were crowding in at the
doorway; and the brothers, who had paused only to hitch the
horses, filled up the way behind. Mary, by a just self-election,
was always the one to speak.

"I declare, Lucy!" cried she, "if ever I could be tried with you,
I should be now. Here we thought you was at Ezra's, an' Ezra's
folks thought you was with us; an' if we hadn't harnessed up,
an' drove over there in the afternoon, for a kind of surprise
party, we should ha' gone to bed thinkin' you was somewhere,
safe an' sound. An' here you've been, all day long, in this
lonesome house!"

"You let me git a light," said Lucy Ann calmly. "You be takin'
off your things, an' se' down." She began lighting the tall astral
lamp on the table, and its prisms danced and swung. Lucy Ann's
delicate hand did not tremble; and when the flame burned up
through the shining chimney, more than one started, at seeing
how exactly she resembled grandma, in the days when old Mrs.
Cummings had ruled her own house. Perhaps it was the royalty
of the poplin that enwrapped her; but Lucy Ann looked very
capable of holding her own. She was facing them all, one hand
resting on the table, and a little smile flickering over her face.

"I s'pose I was a poor miserable creatur' to git out of it that
way," said she. "If I'd felt as I do now, I needn't ha' done it. I

could ha' spoke up. But then it seemed as if there wa'n't no other way. I jest wanted my Thanksgivin' in my own home, an' so I throwed you off the track the best way I could. I dunno's I lied. I dunno whether I did or not; but I guess, anyway, I shall be forgiven for it."

Ezra spoke first: "Well, if you didn't want to come"—

"Want to come!" broke in John. "Of course she don't want to come! She wants to stay in her own home, an' call her soul her own—don't you, Lucy?"

Lucy Ann glanced at him with her quick, grateful smile.

"I'm goin' to, now," she said gently, and they knew she meant it.

But, looking about among them, Lucy Ann was conscious of a little hurt unhealed; she had thrown their kindness back.

"I guess I can't tell exactly how it is," she began hesitatingly; "but you see my home's my own, jest as yours is. You couldn't any of you go around cousinin', without feelin' you was tore up by the roots. You've all been real good to me, wantin' me to come, an' I s'pose I should make an awful towse if I never was asked; but now I've got all my visitin' done up, cousins an' all, an' I'm goin' to be to home a spell. An' I do admire to have company," added Lucy Ann, a bright smile breaking over her face. "Mother did, you know, an' I guess I take arter her. Now you lay off your things, an' I'll put the kettle on. I've got more pies 'n you could shake a stick at, an' there's a whole loaf o' fruit-cake, a year old."

Mary, taking off her shawl, wiped her eyes surreptitiously on a corner of it, and Abby whispered to her husband, "Dear creatur'!" John and Ezra turned, by one consent, to put the horses in the barn; and the children, conscious that some mysterious affair had been settled, threw themselves into the occasion with an irresponsible delight. The room became at once vocal and with talk and laughter, and Lucy Ann felt, with a swelling heart, what a happy universe it is where so many bridges lie between this world and that unknown state we call the next. But no moment of that evening was half so sweet to her as the one when little John, the youngest child of all, crept up to her and pulled at her poplin skirt, until she bent down to hear.

"Grandma," said he, "when 'd you get well?"

Mary E. Wilkins Freeman

Old Woman Magoun
1905

Mary E. Wilkins Freeman (1852–1930), after an adolescence unsettled by increasing financial hardship, moved with her family from their familiar Randolph, Massachusetts home to Brattleboro, Vermont. There, attempts to achieve security and stability ended with the successive deaths of her only sibling, her younger sister Nan, in 1876, her mother in 1880, and her father in 1883. She was left alone, needing to support herself in a time when the only careers open to a young woman of her class were teaching and literature. She returned to Randolph and moved in with the family of her life-long friend Mary Wales, where she stayed through the years of her literary apprenticeship, and the years of her greatest success, until her ill-fated marriage to Charles Freeman, a New Jersey physician, in 1902. Their marriage was soon disrupted by Dr. Freeman's increasing alcoholism and its associated illnesses.

Freeman lived most of her life in a world of women and, when she became restless, her literary success gave her the financial independence to travel. She was part of the network of literary women whose hub was Annie Fields, the wife of Henry Fields, publisher and editor of the Atlantic Monthly. *Among these women were Sarah Orne Jewett, who had been the young Mary Wilkins's literary inspiration and model, and Alice Brown.*

Her first literary success came with the acceptance in 1883 by Harper's Bazaar *of the story "Two Old Lovers." By 1887 enough stories had been published in that periodical and in* Harper's New Monthly Magazine *to compile her first collection:* A Humble Romance and Other Stories. *A second collection,* A New England Nun and Other Stories, *appeared in 1891.*

Although Freeman left little in the way of personal reminiscence about her mother, at some point in her career she changed her given middle name of Ella to Eleanor, which had been her mother's name. The characteristic pair in many of her stories is either a mother and daughter, two sisters (one almost old enough to be the other's mother), or two women who stand, as in "Old Woman Magoun," in the stead of mother and daughter to each other. Intense and supportive relationships between such pairs are often central to her stories.

Freeman's genius lay in her ability to penetrate and illuminate the conjunction between necessity and desire in a woman's life. She tells her truths in ways that pierce the reader's heart as if with a boning knife. Her stories often focus on that moment in a woman's life when she must act in the face of conflict between her personal values and the demands of the "real world," whether social or natural. Her heroines often must make choices in no-win situations.

"Old Woman Magoun," first published in Harper's in October 1905, and later included in her 1909 collection, The Winning Lady and Others, reflects elements of the Demeter and Persephone myth explored in depth in recent years by feminist scholars. Freeman was an erudite woman, and the powerful myths of the early Hebrew, Greek, and Roman cultures as they were encoded in the Hebrew Bible and in classical Greek and Roman drama left strong imprints on her fiction.

"Old Woman Magoun" is a transformation of a classical Greek tragedy: Euripedes' Medea. The story of the mother who murders her children to protect them from their corrupt father and to punish him for his betrayal and desertion of their mother is brought forward in time more than two millennia. The major force energizing this retelling is wrought by the shift in focus from the vision of a male storyteller to a female storyteller.

Additionally, the custom of Freeman's times called for the polite masking of barbarism, and so motivated certain changes in the figures through whom the story is told. The killing of the child becomes the passive act of a mother-surrogate rather than the act of a mother stabbing her children with a knife. The betrayed and deserted Medea, wife and mother, is divided into two characters—Old Woman Magoun and her long-dead daughter. And the figure of the father is split into two men: one who exercises his patriarchal right to demand sexual access to his daughter, and the other who will actually carry out the rape.

The story can be read as a study of the incest theme, couched in Victorian gentility. The threat of incest and the sexual exploitation of female children by men with the privilege, the opportunity, and the habit of self-indulgence is the most important threat to the mother-daughter couple. This story is a model for stories in the category of mother and daughter vis-à-vis the patriarchy.

Mary E. Wilkins Freeman received the Howells Medal of the American Academy of Arts and Letters and was elected to the National Institute of Arts and Letters in 1926. Although her writing has often been narrowly categorized and stereotypically misinterpreted, it has never been completely unavailable and she has always retained an audience.

Freeman's first two volumes of stories have remained in print almost continually since their publication. Ten more volumes of her short stories have been reprinted in recent years: Pot of Gold and Other Stories *(1892);* Young Lucretia and Other Stories *(1892);* People of Our Neighborhood *(1898);* Silence and Other Stories *(1898);* Love of Parson Lord and Other Stories *(1900);* Understudies *(1901);* Six Trees *(1903);* The Wind in the Rose Bush and Other Stories of the Supernatural *(1903);* The Givers *(1904); and* Copy-Cat and Other Stories *(1914). Several others are unavailable. Five of her novels are back in print.*

The hamlet of Barry's Ford is situated in a sort of high valley among the mountains. Below it the hills lie in moveless curves like a petrified ocean; above it they rise in green-cresting waves which never break. It is *Barry's* Ford because one time the Barry family was the most important in the place; and *Ford* because just at the beginning of the hamlet the little turbulent Barry River is fordable. There is, however, now a rude bridge across the river.

Old Woman Magoun was largely instrumental in bringing the bridge to pass. She haunted the miserable little grocery, wherein whisky and hands of tobacco were the most salient features of the stock in trade, and she talked much. She would elbow herself into the midst of a knot of idlers and talk.

"That bridge ought to be built this very summer," said Old Woman Magoun. She spread her strong arms like wings, and sent the loafers, half laughing, half angry, flying in every direction. "If I were a *man*," said she, "I'd go out this very minute and lay the fust log. If I were a passel of lazy men layin' round, I'd start up for once in my life, I would." The men cowered visibly—all except Nelson Barry; he swore under his breath and strode over to the counter.

Old Woman Magoun looked after him majestically. "You can cuss all you want to, Nelson Barry," said she; "I ain't afraid of you. I don't expect you to lay ary log of the bridge, but I'm goin' to have it built this very summer." She did. The weakness of the masculine element in Barry's Ford was laid low before such strenuous feminine assertion.

Old Woman Magoun and some other women planned a treat—

two sucking pigs, and pies, and sweet cake—for a reward after the bridge should be finished. They even viewed leniently the increased consumption of ardent spirits.

"It seems queer to me," Old Woman Magoun said to Sally Jinks, "that men can't do nothin' without havin' to drink and chew to keep their sperits up. Lord! I've worked all my life and never done nuther."

"Men is different," said Sally Jinks.

"Yes, they be," assented Old Woman Magoun, with open contempt.

The two women sat on a bench in front of Old Woman Magoun's house, and little Lily Barry, her granddaughter, sat holding her doll on a small mossy stone near by. From where they sat they could see the men at work on the new bridge. It was the last day of the work.

Lily clasped her doll—a poor old rag thing—close to her childish bosom, like a little mother, and her face, round which curled her long yellow hair, was fixed upon the men at work. Little Lily had never been allowed to run with the other children at Barry's Ford. Her grandmother had taught her everything she knew—which was not much, but tending at least to a certain measure of spiritual growth—for she, as it were, poured the goodness of her own soul into this little receptive vase of another. Lily was firmly grounded in her knowledge that it was wrong to lie or steal or disobey her grandmother. She had also learned that one should be very industrious. It was seldom that Lily sat idly holding her doll baby, but this was a holiday because of the bridge. She looked only a child, although she was nearly fourteen; her mother had been married at sixteen. That is, Old Woman Magoun said that her daughter, Lily's mother, had married at sixteen; there had been rumors, but no one had dared openly gainsay the old woman. She said that her daughter had married Nelson Barry and he had deserted her. She had lived in her mother's house, and Lily had been born there, and she had died when the baby was only a week old.

Lily's father, Nelson Barry, was the fairly dangerous degenerate of a good old family. Nelson's father before him had been bad. He was now the last of the family, with the exception of a sister of feeble intellect, with whom he lived in the old Barry house. He was a middle-aged man, still handsome. The shiftless population of Barry's Ford looked up to him as to an evil deity. They wondered how Old Woman Magoun dared brave him as she did. But Old Woman Magoun had within her a mighty sense of reliance upon herself as being on the right track in the midst of a maze of evil, which gave her courage. Nelson Barry had manifested no interest whatever in his daughter. Lily seldom saw her father. She did not often go to the store which was his favorite haunt. Her grandmother took care that she should not do so.

However, that afternoon she departed from her usual custom and sent Lily to the store.

She came in from the kitchen, whither she had been to baste the roasting pig. "There's no use talkin'," said she, "I've got to have some more salt. I've jest used the very last I had to dredge over that pig. I've got to go to the store."

Sally Jinks looked at Lily. "Why don't you send her?" she asked.

Old Woman Magoun gazed irresolutely at the girl. She was herself very tired. It did not seem to her that she could drag herself up the dusty hill to the store. She glanced with covert resentment at Sally Jinks. She thought that she might offer to go. But Sally Jinks said again, "Why don't you let her go?" and looked with a languid eye at Lily holding her doll on the stone.

Lily was watching the men at work on the bridge, with her childish delight in a spectacle of any kind, when her grandmother addressed her.

"Guess I'll let you go down to the store an' git some salt, Lily," said she.

The girl turned uncomprehending eyes upon her grandmother at the sound of her voice. She had been filled with one of the innocent reveries of childhood. Lily had in her the making of an artist or a poet. Her prolonged childhood went to prove it, and also her retrospective eyes, as clear and blue as blue light itself, which seemed to see past all that she looked upon. She had not come of the old Barry family for nothing. The best of the strain was in her, along with the splendid stanchness in humble lines which she had acquired from her grandmother.

"Put on your hat," said Old Woman Magoun; "the sun is hot

and you might git a headache." She called the girl to her, and put back the shower of fair curls under the rubber band which confined the hat. She gave Lily some money, and watched her knot it into a corner of her little cotton handkerchief. "Be careful you don't lose it," said she, "and don't stop to talk to anybody, for I am in a hurry for that salt. Of course, if anybody speaks to you answer them polite, and then come right along."

Lily started, her pocket handkerchief weighted with the small silver dangling from one hand, and her rag doll carried over her shoulder like a baby. The absurd travesty of a face peeped forth from Lily's yellow curls. Sally Jinks looked after her with a sniff.

"She ain't goin' to carry that rag doll to the store?" said she.

"She likes to," replied Old Woman Magoun, in a half-shamed yet defiantly extenuating voice.

"Some girls at her age is thinkin' about beaux instead of rag dolls," said Sally Jinks.

The grandmother bristled, "Lily ain't big nor old for her age," said she. "I ain't in any hurry to have her git married. She ain't none too strong."

"She's got a good color," said Sally Jinks. She was crocheting white cotton lace, making her thick fingers fly. She really knew how to do scarcely anything except to crochet that coarse lace; somehow her heavy brain or her fingers had mastered that.

"I know she's got a beautiful color," replied Old Woman Magoun, with an odd mixture of pride and anxiety, "but it comes an' goes."

"I've heard that was a bad sign," remarked Sally Jinks, loosening some thread from her spool.

"Yes, it is," said the grandmother. "She's nothin' but a baby, though she's quicker than most to learn."

Lily Barry went on her way to the store. She was clad in a scanty short frock of blue cotton; her hat was tipped back, forming an oval frame for her innocent face. She was very small, and walked like a child, with the clap-clap of little feet of babyhood. She might have been considered, from her looks, under ten.

Presently she heard footsteps behind her; she turned around a little timidly to see who was coming. When she saw a handsome well-dressed man, she felt reassured. The man came alongside and glanced down carelessly at first; then his look deepened. He smiled, and Lily saw he was very handsome indeed, and that his smile was not only reassuring but wonderfully sweet and compelling.

"Well, little one," said the man, "where are you bound, you and your dolly?"

"I am going to the store to buy some salt for grandma," replied Lily, in her sweet treble. She looked up in the man's face, and he fairly started at the revelation of its innocent beauty. He regulated his pace by hers, and the two went on together. The man did not speak again at once. Lily kept glancing timidly up at him, and every time that she did so the man smiled and her confidence increased. Presently when the man's hand grasped her little childish one hanging by her side, she felt a complete trust in him. Then she smiled up at him. She felt glad that this nice man had come along, for just here the road was lonely.

After a while the man spoke. "What is your name, little one?" he asked, caressingly.

"Lily Barry."

The man started. "What is your father's name?"

"Nelson Barry," replied Lily.

The man whistled. "Is your mother dead?"

"Yes, sir."

"How old are you, my dear?"

"Fourteen," replied Lily.

The man looked at her with surprise. "As old as that?"

Lily suddenly shrank from the man. She could not have told why. She pulled her little hand from his, and he let it go with no remonstrance. She clasped both her arms around her rag doll, in order that her hand should not be free for him to grasp again.

She walked a little farther away from the man, and he looked amused.

"You still play with your doll?" he said, in a soft voice.

"Yes, sir," replied Lily. She quickened her pace and reached the store.

When Lily entered the store, Hiram Gates, the owner, was behind the counter. The only man besides in the store was

Nelson Barry. He sat tipping his chair back against the wall; he
was half asleep, and his handsome face was bristling with a
beard of several days' growth and darkly flushed. He opened
his eyes when Lily entered, the strange man following. He
brought his chair down on all fours, and he looked at the man—
not noticing Lily at all—with a look compounded of defiance
and uneasiness.

"Hullo, Jim!" he said.

"Hullo, old man!" returned the stranger.

Lily went over to the counter and asked for the salt, in her
pretty little voice. When she had paid for it and was crossing
the store, Nelson Barry was on his feet.

"Well, how are you, Lily? It is Lily, isn't it?" he said.

"Yes, sir," replied Lily, faintly.

Her father bent down and, for the first time in her life, kissed
her, and the whisky odor of his breath came into her face.

Lily involuntarily started, and shrank away from him. Then
she rubbed her mouth violently with her little cotton handkerchief, which she held gathered up with the rag doll.

"Damn it all! I believe she is afraid of me," said Nelson Barry,
in a thick voice.

"Looks a little like it," said the other man, laughing.

"It's that damned old woman," said Nelson Barry. Then he
smiled again at Lily. "I didn't know what a pretty little daughter
I was blessed with," said he, and he softly stroked Lily's pink
cheek under her hat.

Now Lily did not shrink from him. Heredity instincts and
nature itself were asserting themselves in the child's innocent,
receptive breast.

Nelson Barry looked curiously at Lily. "How old are you,
anyway, child?" he asked.

"I'll be fourteen in September," replied Lily.

"But you still play with your doll?" said Barry, laughing kindly
down at her.

Lily hugged her doll more tightly, in spite of her father's kind
voice. "Yes, sir," she replied.

Nelson glanced across at some glass jars filled with sticks of
candy. "See here, little Lily, do you like candy?" said he.

"Yes, sir."

"Wait a minute."

Lily waited while her father went over to the counter. Soon he returned with a package of the candy.

"I don't see how you are going to carry so much," he said, smiling. "Suppose you throw away your doll?"

Lily gazed at her father and hugged the doll tightly, and there was all at once in the child's expression something mature. It became the reproach of a woman. Nelson's face sobered.

"Oh, it's all right, Lily," he said; "keep your doll. Here, I guess you can carry this candy under your arm."

Lily could not resist the candy. She obeyed Nelson's instructions for carrying it, and left the store laden. The two men also left, and walked in the opposite direction, talking busily.

When Lily reached home, her grandmother, who was watching for her, spied at once the package of candy.

"What's that?" she asked, sharply.

"My father gave it to me," answered Lily, in a faltering voice. Sally regarded her with something like alertness.

"Your father?"

"Yes, ma'am."

"Where did you see him?"

"In the store."

"He gave you this candy?"

"Yes, ma'am."

"What did he say?"

"He asked me how old I was, and—"

"And what?"

"I don't know," replied Lily; and it really seemed to her that she did not know, she was so frightened and bewildered by it all, and, more than anything else, by her grandmother's face as she questioned her.

Old Woman Magoun's face was that of one upon whom a long-anticipated blow had fallen. Sally Jinks gazed at her with a sort of stupid alarm.

Old Woman Magoun continued to gaze at her grandchild with that look of terrible solicitude, as if she saw the girl in the clutch of a tiger. "You can't remember what else he said?" she asked, fiercely, and the child began to whimper softly.

"No, ma'am," she sobbed. "I—don't know, and—"

"And what? Answer me."

"There was another man there. A real handsome man."

"Did he speak to you?" asked Old Woman Magoun.

"Yes, ma'am; he walked along with me a piece," confessed Lily, with a sob of terror and bewilderment.

"What did *he* say to you?" asked Old Woman Magoun, with a sort of despair.

Lily told, in her little, faltering, frightened voice, all of the conversation which she could recall. It sounded harmless enough, but the look of the realization of a long-expected blow never left her grandmother's face.

The sun was getting low and the bridge was nearing completion. Soon the workmen would be crowding into the cabin for their promised supper. There became visible in the distance, far up the road, the heavily plodding figure of another woman who had agreed to come and help. Old Woman Magoun turned again to Lily.

"You go right upstairs to your own chamber now," said she.

"Good land! ain't you goin' to let that poor child stay up and see the fun?" said Sally Jinks.

"You jest mind your own business," said Old Woman Magoun, forcibly, and Sally Jinks shrank. "You go right up there now, Lily," said the grandmother, in a softer tone, "and grandma will bring you up a nice plate of supper."

"When be you goin' to let that girl grow up?" asked Sally Jinks when Lily had disappeared.

"She'll grow up in the Lord's good time," replied Old Woman Magoun, and there was in her voice something both sad and threatening. Sally Jinks again shrank a little.

Soon the workmen came flocking noisily into the house. Old Woman Magoun and her two helpers served the bountiful supper. Most of the men had drunk as much as, and more than, was good for them, and Old Woman Magoun had stipulated that there was to be no drinking of anything except coffee during supper.

"I'll git you as good a meal as I know how," she said, "but if I see ary one of you drinkin' a drop, I'll run you all out. If you want anything to drink, you can go up to the store afterward. That's the place for you to go to, if you've got to make hogs of yourselves. I ain't goin' to have no hogs in my house."

Old Woman Magoun was implicitly obeyed. She had a curious authority over most people when she chose to exercise it. When the supper was in full swing, she quietly stole upstairs and carried some food to Lily. She found the girl, with the rag doll in her arms, crouching by the window in her little rocking-chair—a relic of her infancy, which she still used.

"What a noise they are makin', grandma!" she said, in a terrified whisper, as her grandmother placed the plate before her on a chair.

"They've 'most all of 'em been drinkin'. They air a passel of hogs," replied the old woman.

"Is the man that was with—with my father down there?" asked Lily, in a timid fashion. Then she fairly cowered before the look in her grandmother's eyes.

"No, he ain't, and what's more, he never will be down there if I can help it," said Old Woman Magoun, in a fierce whisper. "I know who he is. They can't cheat me. He's one of them Willises—that family the Barrys married into. They're worse than the Barrys, ef they *have* got money. Eat your supper, and put him out of your mind, child."

It was after Lily was asleep, when Old Woman Magoun was alone, clearing away her supper dishes, that Lily's father came. The door was closed, and he knocked, and the old woman knew at once who was there. The sound of that knock meant as much to her as the whir of a bomb to the defender of a fortress. She opened the door, and Nelson Barry stood there.

"Good evening, Mrs. Magoun," he said.

Old Woman Magoun stood before him, filling up the doorway with her firm bulk.

"Good evening, Mrs. Magoun," said Nelson Barry again.

"I ain't got no time to waste," replied the old woman, harshly. "I've got my supper dishes to clean up after them men."

She stood there and looked at him as she might have looked at a rebellious animal which she was trying to tame. The man laughed.

"It's no use," said he. "You know me of old. No human being can turn me from my way when I am once started in it. You may as well let me come in."

Old Woman Magoun entered the house, and Barry followed her.

Barry began without any preface. "Where is the child?" asked he.

"Upstairs. She has gone to bed."

"She goes to bed early."

"Children ought to," returned the old woman, polishing a plate.

Barry laughed. "You are keeping her a child a long while," he remarked, in a soft voice which had a sting in it.

"She *is* a child," returned the old woman, defiantly.

"Her mother was only three years older when Lily was born."

The old woman made a sudden motion toward the man which seemed fairly menacing. Then she turned again to her dish washing.

"I want her," said Barry.

"You can't have her," replied the old woman, in a still stern voice.

"I don't see how you can help yourself. You have always acknowledged that she was my child."

The old woman continued her task, but her strong back heaved. Barry regarded her with an entirely pitiless expression.

"I am going to have the girl, that is the long and short of it," he said, "and it is for her best good, too. You are a fool, or you would see it."

"Her best good?" muttered the old woman.

"Yes, her best good. What are you going to do with her, anyway? The girl is a beauty, and almost a woman grown, although you try to make out that she is a baby. You can't live forever."

"The Lord will take care of her," replied the old woman, and again she turned and faced him, and her expression was that of a prophetess.

"Very well, let Him," said Barry, easily. "All the same I'm going to have her, and I tell you it is for her best good. Jim Willis saw her this afternoon, and—"

Old Woman Magoun looked at him. "Jim Willis!" she fairly shrieked.

"Well, what of it?"

"One of them Willises!" repeated the old woman, and this time her voice was thick. It seemed almost as if she were stricken with paralysis. She did not enunciate clearly.

The man shrank a little. "Now what is the need of your making such a fuss?" he said. "I will take her, and Isabel will look out for her."

"Your half-witted sister?" said Old Woman Magoun.

"Yes, my half-witted sister. She knows more than you think."

"More wickedness."

"Perhaps. Well, a knowledge of evil is a useful thing. How are you going to avoid evil if you don't know what it is like? My sister and I will take care of my daughter."

The old woman continued to look at the man, but his eyes never fell. Suddenly her gaze grew inconceivably keen. It was as if she saw through all externals.

"I know what it is!" she cried. "You have been playing cards and you lost, and this is the way you will pay him."

Then the man's face reddened, and he swore under his breath.

"Oh, my God!" said the old woman; and she really spoke with her eyes aloft as if addressing something outside of them both. Then she turned again to her dish washing.

The man cast a dogged look at her back. "Well, there is no use talking. I have made up my mind," said he, "and you know me and what that means. I am going to have the girl."

"When?" said the old woman, without turning around.

"Well, I am willing to give you a week. Put her clothes in good order before she comes."

The old woman made no reply. She continued washing dishes. She even handled them so carefully they did not rattle.

"You understand," said Barry. "Have her ready a week from today."

"Yes," said Old Woman Magoun, "I understand."

Nelson Barry, going up the mountain road, reflected that Old Woman Magoun had a strong character, that she understood much better than her sex in general the futility of withstanding the inevitable.

"Well," he said to Jim Willis when he reached home, "the old woman did not make such a fuss as I expected."

"Are you going to have the girl?"

"Yes; a week from today. Look here, Jim; you've got to stick to your promise."

"All right," said Willis. "Go you one better."

The two were playing at cards in the old parlor, once magnificent, now squalid, of the Barry house. Isabel, the half-witted sister, entered, bringing some glasses on a tray. She had learned with her feeble intellect some tricks, like a dog. One of them was the mixing of sundry drinks. She set the tray on a little stand near the two men, and watched them with her silly simper.

"Clear out now and go to bed," her brother said to her, and she obeyed.

Early the next morning Old Woman Magoun went up to Lily's little sleeping chamber, and watched her a second as she lay asleep, with her yellow locks spread over the pillow. Then she spoke. "Lily," said she—"Lily, wake up. I am going to Greenham across the new bridge, and you can go with me."

Lily immediately sat up in bed and smiled at her grandmother. Her eyes were still misty, but the light of awakening was in them.

"Get right up," said the old woman. "You can wear your new dress if you want to."

Lily gurgled with pleasure like a baby. "And my new hat?" said she.

"I don't care."

Old Woman Magoun and Lily started for Greenham before Barry's Ford, which kept late hours, was fairly awake. It was three miles to Greenham. The old woman said that, since the horse was a little lame, they would walk. It was a beautiful morning, with a diamond radiance of dew over everything. Her grandmother had curled Lily's hair more punctiliously than usual. The little face peeped like a rose out of two rows of golden spirals. Lily wore her new muslin dress with a pink sash, and her best hat of a fine white straw trimmed with a wreath of rosebuds; also the neatest black openwork stockings and pretty shoes. She even had white cotton gloves. When they set out, the old, heavily stepping woman, in her black gown and cape and bonnet, looked down at the little pink fluttering figure. Her face was full of the tenderest love and admiration, and yet there was something terrible about it. They crossed the new bridge—a primitive structure built of logs in a slovenly fashion. Old Woman Magoun pointed to a gap.

"Jest see that," said she. "That's the way men work."

"Men ain't very nice, be they?" said Lily, in her sweet little voice.

"No, they ain't, take them all together," replied her grandmother.

"That man that walked to the store with me was nicer than some, I guess," Lily said, in a wishful fashion. Her grandmother reached down and took the child's hand in its small cotton glove. "You hurt me, holding my hand so tight," Lily said presently, in a deprecatory little voice.

The old woman loosened her grasp. "Grandma didn't know how tight she was holding your hand," said she. "She wouldn't hurt you for nothin', except it was to save your life, or somethin' like that." She spoke with an undertone of tremendous meaning which the girl was too childish to grasp. They walked along the country road. Just before they reached Greenham they passed a stone wall overgrown with blackberry vines, and, an unusual thing in that vicinity, a lusty spread of deadly nightshade full of berries.

"Those berries look good to eat, grandma," Lily said.

At that instant the old woman's face became something terrible to see. "You can't have any now," she said, and hurried Lily along.

"They look real nice," said Lily.

When they reached Greenham, Old Woman Magoun took her way straight to the most pretentious house there, the residence of the lawyer, whose name was Mason. Old Woman Magoun bade Lily wait in the yard for a few moments, and Lily ventured to seat herself on a bench beneath an oak tree; then she watched with some wonder her grandmother enter the lawyer's office door at the right of the house. Presently the lawyer's wife came out and spoke to Lily under the tree. She had in her hand a little tray containing a plate of cake, a glass of milk, and an early apple. She spoke very kindly to Lily; she even kissed her, and offered her the tray of refreshments, which Lily accepted gratefully. She sat eating, with Mrs. Mason watching her, when Old Woman Magoun came out of the lawyer's office with a ghastly face.

"What are you eatin'?" she asked Lily, sharply. "Is that a sour apple?"

"I thought she might be hungry," said the lawyer's wife, with loving, melancholy eyes upon the girl.

Lily had almost finished the apple. "It's real sour, but I like it; it's real nice, grandma," she said.

"You ain't been drinkin' milk with a sour apple?"

"It was real nice milk, grandma."

"You ought never to have drunk milk and eat a sour apple," said her grandmother. "Your stomach was all out of order this mornin', an' sour apples and milk is always apt to hurt anybody."

"I don't know but they are," Mrs. Mason said, apologetically, as she stood on the green lawn with her lavender muslin sweeping around her. "I am real sorry, Mrs. Magoun. I ought to have thought. Let me get some soda for her."

"Soda never agrees with her," replied the old woman, in a harsh voice. "Come," she said to Lily, "it's time we were goin' home."

After Lily and her grandmother had disappeared down the road, Lawyer Mason came out of his office and joined his wife, who had seated herself on the bench beneath the tree. She was idle, and her face wore the expression of those who review joys forever past. She had lost a little girl, her only child, years ago, and her husband always knew when she was thinking about her. Lawyer Mason looked older than his wife; he had a dry, shrewd, slightly one-sided face.

"What do you think, Maria?" he said. "That old woman came to me with the most pressing entreaty to adopt that little girl."

"She is a beautiful little girl," said Mrs. Mason, in a slightly husky voice.

"Yes, she is a pretty child," assented the lawyer, looking pityingly at his wife; "but it is out of the question, my dear. Adopting a child is a serious measure, and in this case a child who comes from Barry's Ford!"

"But the grandmother seems a very good woman," said Mrs. Mason.

"I rather think she is. I never heard a word against her. But the father! No, Maria, we cannot take a child with Barry blood in her veins. The stock has run out; it is vitiated physically and morally. It won't do, my dear."

"Her grandmother had her dressed up as pretty as a little girl could be," said Mrs. Mason, and this time the tears welled into her faithful, wistful eyes.

"Well, we can't help that," said the lawyer, as he went back to his office.

Old Woman Magoun and Lily returned, going slowly along the road to Barry's Ford. When they came to the stone wall where the blackberry vines and the deadly nightshade grew, Lily said she was tired, and asked if she could not sit down for a few minutes. The strange look on her grandmother's face had deepened. Now and then Lily glanced at her and had a feeling as if she were looking at a stranger.

"Yes, you can set down if you want to," said Old Woman Magoun, deeply and harshly.

Lily started and looked at her, as if to make sure that it was her grandmother who spoke. Then she sat down on a stone which was comparatively free of the vines.

"Ain't you goin' to set down, grandma?" Lily asked, timidly.

"No; I don't want to get into that mess," replied her grandmother. "I ain't tired. I'll stand here."

Lily sat still; her delicate little face was flushed with heat. She extended her tiny feet in her best shoes and gazed at them. "My shoes are all over dust," said she.

"It will brush off," said her grandmother, still in that strange voice.

Lily looked around. An elm tree in the field behind her cast a spray of branches over her head; a little cool puff of wind came on her face. She gazed at the low mountains on the horizon, in the midst of which she lived, and she sighed, for no reason that she knew. She began idly picking at the blackberry vines; there were no berries on them; then she put her little fingers on the berries of the deadly nightshade. "These look like nice berries," she said.

Old Woman Magoun, standing stiff and straight in the road, said nothing.

"They look good to eat," said Lily.

Old Woman Magoun still said nothing, but she looked up into the ineffable blue of the sky, over which spread at intervals great white clouds shaped like wings.

Lily picked some of the deadly nightshade berries and ate them. "Why, they are real sweet," said she. "They are nice." She picked some more and ate them.

Presently her grandmother spoke. "Come," she said, "it is time we were going. I guess you have set long enough."

Lily was still eating the berries when she slipped down from the wall and followed her grandmother obediently up the road.

Before they reached home, Lily complained of being very thirsty. She stopped and made a little cup of a leaf and drank long at a mountain brook. "I am dreadful dry, but it hurts me to swallow," she said to her grandmother when she stopped drinking and joined the old woman waiting for her in the road. Her grandmother's face seemed strangely dim to her. She took hold of Lily's hand as they went on. "My stomach burns," said Lily, presently. "I want some more water."

"There is another brook a little farther on," said Old Woman Magoun, in a dull voice.

When they reached that brook, Lily stopped and drank again, but she whimpered a little over her difficulty in swallowing. "My stomach burns, too," she said, walking on, "and my throat is so dry, grandma." Old Woman Magoun held Lily's hand more tightly. "You hurt me, holding my hand so tight, grandma," said Lily, looking up at her grandmother, whose face she seemed to see through a mist, and the old woman loosened her grasp.

When at last they reached home, Lily was very ill. Old Woman Magoun put her on her own bed in the little bedroom out of the kitchen. Lily lay there and moaned, and Sally Jinks came in.

"Why, what ails her?" she asked. "She looks feverish."

Lily unexpectedly answered for herself. "I ate some sour apples and drank some milk," she moaned.

"Sour apples and milk are dreadful apt to hurt anybody," said Sally Jinks. She told several people on her way home that Old Woman Magoun was dreadful careless to let Lily eat such things.

Meanwhile Lily grew worse. She suffered cruelly from the burning in her stomach, the vertigo, and the deadly nausea. "I am so sick, I am so sick, grandma," she kept moaning. She could no longer see her grandmother as she bent over her, but she could hear her talk.

Old Woman Magoun talked as Lily had never heard her talk before, as nobody had ever heard her talk before. She spoke from the depths of her soul; her voice was as tender as the coo of a dove, and it was grand and exalted. "You'll feel better very soon, little Lily," said she.

"I am so sick, grandma."

"You will feel better very soon, and then—"

"I am sick."

"You shall go to a beautiful place."

Lily moaned.

"You shall go to a beautiful place," the old woman went on.

"Where?" asked Lily, groping feebly with her cold little hands. Then she moaned again.

"A beautiful place, where the flowers grow tall."

"What color? Oh, grandma, I am so sick."

"A blue color," replied the old woman. Blue was Lily's favorite color. "A beautiful blue color, and as tall as your knees, and the flowers always stay there, and they never fade."

"Not if you pick them, Grandma? Oh!"

"No, not if you pick them; they never fade, and they are so sweet you can smell them a mile off; and there are birds that sing, and all the roads have gold stones in them, and the stone walls are made of gold."

"Like the ring grandpa gave you? I am so sick, grandma."

"Yes, gold like that. And all the houses are built of silver and gold, and the people all have wings, so when they get tired walking they can fly, and—"

"I am so sick, grandma."

"And all the dolls are alive," said Old Woman Magoun. "Dolls like yours can run, and talk, and love you back again."

Lily had her poor old rag doll in bed with her, clasped close to her agonized little heart. She tried very hard with her eyes, whose pupils were so dilated that they looked black, to see her grandmother's face when she said that, but she could not. "It is dark," she moaned, feebly.

"There where you are going it is always light," said the grandmother, "and the commonest things shine like that breast-pin Mrs. Lawyer Mason had on today."

Lily moaned pitifully, and said something incoherent. Delirium was commencing. Presently she sat straight up in bed and raved; but even then her grandmother's wonderful compelling voice had an influence over her.

"You will come to a gate with all the colors of the rainbow," said her grandmother; "and it will open, and you will go right in and walk up the gold street, and cross the field where the blue flowers come up to your knees, until you find your mother, and she will take you home where you are going to live. She has a little white room all ready for you, white curtains at the windows, and a little white looking-glass, and when you look in it you will see—"

"What will I see? I am so sick, grandma."

"You will see a face like yours, only it's an angel's; and there will be a little white bed, and you can lay down an' rest."

"Won't I be sick, grandma?" asked Lily. Then she moaned and babbled wildly, although she seemed to understand through it all what her grandmother said.

"No, you will never be sick any more. Talkin' about sickness won't mean anything to you."

It continued. Lily talked on wildly, and her grandmother's great voice of soothing never ceased, until the child fell into a deep sleep, or what resembled sleep; but she lay stiffly in that sleep, and a candle flashed before her eyes made no impression on them.

Then it was that Nelson Barry came. Jim Willis waited outside the door. When Nelson entered he found Old Woman Magoun on her knees beside the bed, weeping with dry eyes and a might of agony which fairly shook Nelson Barry, the degenerate of a fine old race.

"Is she sick?" he asked, in a hushed voice.

Old Woman Magoun gave another terrible sob, which sounded like the gasp of one dying.

"Sally Jinks said that Lily was sick from eating milk and sour apples," said Barry, in a tremulous voice. "I remember that her mother was very sick once from eating them."

Lily lay still, and her grandmother on her knees shook with her terrible sobs.

Suddenly Nelson Barry started. "I guess I had better go to Greenham for a doctor if she's as bad as that," he said. He went close to the bed and looked at the sick child. He gave a great start. Then he felt of her hands and reached down under the bedclothes for her little feet. "Her hands and feet are like ice," he cried out. "Good God! why didn't you send for some one— for me—before? Why, she's dying; she's almost gone!"

Barry rushed out and spoke to Jim Willis, who turned pale and came in and stood by the bedside.

"She's almost gone," he said, in a hushed whisper.

"There's no use going for the doctor; she'd be dead before he got here," said Nelson, and he stood regarding the passing child with a strange, sad face—unutterably sad, because of his incapability of the truest sadness.

"Poor little thing, she's past suffering, anyhow," said the other man, and his own face also was sad with a puzzled, mystified sadness.

Lily died that night. There was quite a commotion in Barry's Ford until after the funeral, it was all so sudden, and then everything went on as usual. Old Woman Magoun continued to live as she had done before. She supported herself by the produce of her tiny farm; she was very industrious, but people said that she was a trifle touched, since every time she went over the log bridge with her eggs or her garden vegetables to sell in Greenham, she carried with her, as one might have carried an infant, Lily's old rag doll.

Fannie Hurst

Oats for the Woman
1917

Fannie Hurst (1889–1968) took as her subject matter what she called the "common people." In her 1958 autobiography, Anatomy of Me, *dedicated "To My Friend The Anonymous Public," she remembers looking out of the window in the Hotel Astor*

"... on the anonymous masses ... the people who were to make up my social register. The unhyphenated Smiths and Joneses. The people who, if killed in a plane crash, were designated as 'and others.' . . . Those people down there . . . were composed of persons. People were persons!"

When she left her parents and her St. Louis home to live in New York City, she immersed herself in the city's crowds—on the subways, in the lunchrooms, along the avenues. She was a writer researching her subject.

In this choice of subject matter, she recognized her predecessors and colleagues as the great European realists and naturalists: Tolstoy, Dostoyevsky, Gorki, Dumas, Balzac, de Maupassant, Ibsen, Strindberg, Wedekind, Lagerloff, Undset, Bennett; and the Americans: O. Henry, Edwin Markham, and Edgar Lee Masters. At the same time that Hurst identified these writers with whom she felt kinship, she also insisted on her literary independence: "I do not recall that I ever consciously became the disciple of any one author. . . . "

While on the one hand, she saw herself as a sui generis primitive, as a sort of "sport" or mutant, arising from a nurturant and loving but uncomprehending environment as artiste complete, on the other hand, she was widely read, well educated, and a diligent student of the history of her craft. Besides the typically demanding and intense curriculum of the urban American high school at the turn of the century, Hurst also had had a fine classical literary education at Washington University in St. Louis as an undergraduate and later as a graduate student. She completed two additional years of graduate work at Columbia University. She always read and studied with the eye of an apprentice. From her earliest years, she wrote ceaselessly.

The apparently contradictory images of Fannie Hurst as naive self-created artist and as sophisticated inheritor and practitioner of an old literary tradition result from contradictions in her own life. As an American educated in the tradition of the "the best" in Western cultural history, her access to this past was undisputed. However, as a second generation, American-born, German-Jewish descendant of peasants, she knew of no literary tradition that was really hers. The duality of her hyphenated identity explains the duality of her self-image. Because she was a woman, she was set apart from literary achievement by both the Jewish tradition and the Western Christian tradition that had, by her time, come to be identified as the American tradition. This accounts for her perception of herself as an artist without precedent. She did not know of a feminist, or even a female, immigrant Jewish literary tradition.

Critics have often dismissed Fannie Hurst's characters as sentimental stereotypes. The critics who labeled her "sob sister" (borrowing the title of one of her own early stories) tended to think of the working class and of immigrants and their American-born children as "milling crowds" and "huddling masses," as collections of types, rather than as the persons she insisted in her life and her work that they were. The critics never really impugned the accuracy of her portrayals; rather, they denigrated her subject matter. They have thus far been successful in ridiculing her into ill-deserved obscurity.

But the millions of readers who made her the most beloved and one of the wealthiest writers in history, who belonged to the groups of persons about which she wrote—the waitresses, the models, the department store clerks, the laborers, the small business owners, the struggling immigrant mothers and fathers—found her characters and their stories every bit as real, as compelling, as individualized, as their relatives, their friends, and their own selves. They often wrote to ask her if she had been eavesdropping on their lives. A social activist and feminist, Hurst was a colleague of Eleanor Roosevelt from an early shared struggle for better wages and working conditions for domestic workers. She fought against racism, anti-Semitism, sexism, and homophobia, striving to alleviate the suffering she witnessed and wrote about. She has been accused of including too many happy endings, of falsifying the lives of her characters and betraying the inevitability of their stories. But she also wrote about those who didn't triumph. The stories of personal defeat are almost always women's stories, in which a woman comes into conflict with the patriarchy, not stories in which an immigrant comes into conflict with America.

Fannie Hurst published a total of nine volumes of short stories, seventeen novels, three plays, many articles on a variety of subjects, and she collaborated on several of the many films made from her stories and novels. Her work has been translated into eleven languages. "Oats for the Woman" was first published in Cosmopolitan *in June 1917, and was included in* Humoresque *(1919), her fourth volume of short stories.*

The story is both a surrogate mother story and one of a mother and daughter being confronted by the patriarchy in such a way that the happiness and safety of one can only be preserved by the sacrifice of the other. As is often the case in surrogate mother stories, where the absence of biological connection between the mother and the daughter makes the subject more abstract and less evocative of prurience, the real subject of the story is the threat of incest and the mother's anguish in the face of it. As in "Old Woman Magoun" and "Recuerdo," where the implicit threat is the same, the adolescent daughter's childlike innocence and trust are emphasized along with the maternal figure's helplessness and the complicity of all male figures, who might be expected to intervene and protect the women.

That women who toil not neither do they spin might know the feel of fabrics so cunningly devised that they lay to the flesh like the inner petals of buds, three hundred and fifty men, women, and children contrived, between strikes, to make the show-rooms of the Kessler Costume Company, Incorporated, a sort of mauve and mirrored Delphi where buyers from twenty states came to invoke forecast of the mood of skirts, the caprice of sleeves, and the rumored flip to the train. Before these flips and moods, a gigantic industry held semi-annual pause, destinies of lace-factories trembling before a threatened season of strictly tailor-mades, velvet-looms slowing at the shush of taffeta. When woman would be sleazy, petticoat manufacturers went overnight into an oblivion from which there might or might not be returning. The willow plume waved its day, making and unmaking merchants.

Destiny loves thus to spring from acorn beginnings. Helen smiled, and Troy fell. Roast pork, and I doubt not then and there the apple sauce, became a national institution because a small boy burnt his fingers.

That is why, out from the frail love of women for the flesh and its humors, and because for the webby cling of chiffon too often no price is too high, the Kessler Costume Company employed, on the factory side of the door, the three hundred and fifty sewers and cutters, not one of whose monthly wage could half buy the real-lace fichu or the painted-chiffon frock of his own handiwork.

On the show-room side of the door, painted mauve within and not without, *mannequins,* so pink finger-tipped, so tilted of instep, and so bred in the thrust to the silhouette, trailed these sleazy products of thick fingers across mauve-colored carpet and before the appraising eyes of twenty states.

Often as not, smoke rose in that room from the black cigar of the Omaha Store, Omaha, or Ladies' Wear, Cleveland. In season, and particularly during the frenzied dog-days of August, when the fate of the new waist-line or his daring treatment of cloth of silver hung yet in the balance, and the spirit of Detroit must be browbeaten by the dictum of the sleeveless thing in evening frocks, Leon Kessler himself smoked a day-long chain of cigarettes, lighting one off the other.

In the model-room, a long, narrow slit, roaringly ventilated by a whirling machine, lined in frocks suspended from hangers, and just wide enough for two very perfect thirty-sixes to stand abreast, August fell heavily. So heavily that occasionally a cloak-model, her lot to show next December's conceit in theater wraps, fainted on the show-dais; or a cloth-of-gold evening gown, donned for the twentieth time that sweltering day, would suddenly, with its model, crumple, a glittering huddle, to the floor.

Upon Miss Hattie Becker, who within the narrow slit had endured eight of these Augusts with only two casual faints and a swoon or two nipped in the bud, this ninth August came in so furiously that, sliding out of her sixth showing of a cloth-of-silver and blue-fox opera wrap, a shivering that amounted practically to chill took hold of her.

"Br-r-r!" she said, full of all men's awe at the carbon-dioxide paradox. "I'm so hot I'm cold!"

Miss Clarice Delehanty slid out of a shower of tulle-of-gold dancing-frock and into an Avenue gown of rough serge. The tail of a very arched eyebrow threatened, and then ran down in a black rill.

> "If Niagara Falls was claret lemonade,
> You'd see me beat it to a watery grave.

"That'll be enough canary-talk out of you, Clare. Hand me my shirt-waist there off the hook."

"Didn't Kess say we had to show Keokuk the line before lunch?"

"If the King of England was buying ermine sport coats this morning, I wouldn't show 'em before I had a cold cut and a long drink in me. Hurry! Hand me my waist, Clare, before the girls come in from showing the bridesmaid line."

Miss Delehanty flung the garment down the narrow length of the room.

"Minneapolis don't know it, but after this showing he's going to blow me to the frappiest little lunch on the Waldorf roof."

Miss Becker buttoned her flimsy blouse with three pearl beads down its front, wiping constantly at a constantly dampening brow.

"You'd shove over the Goddess of Liberty if you thought she had her foot on a meal ticket."

"Yes; and if I busted her, you could build a new one on the lunch money you've saved in your time."

"Waldorf! You've got a fine chance with Minneapolis. You mean the Automat, and two spoons for the ice-cream."

Miss Delehanty adjusted a highly eccentric hat, a small green velvet, outrageously tilted off the rear of its *bandeau*, and a wide black streamer flowing down over one shoulder. It was the match to the explosive effect of the *trotteur* gown. She was Fashion's humoresque, except that Fashion has no sense of humor. Very presently Minneapolis would appraise her at two hundred and seventy-five as is. Miss Delehanty herself came cheaper.

"Say, Hattie, don't let being an old man's darling go to your head. The grandchildren may issue an injunction."

A flare of crimson rushed immediately over Miss Becker's face, spreading down into her neck.

"You let him alone! He's a darn sight better than anything I've seen you girls picking for yourselves. You never met a man in your life whose name wasn't Johnnie. You couldn't land a John in a million years."

Miss Delehanty raised her face from over a shoe-buckle. A stare began to set in, as obviously innocent as a small boy's between spitballs.

"Well, who said anything about old St. Louis, I'd like to know?"

"You did, and you leave him alone! What do you know about a real man? You'd pass up a Ford ride to sit still in a pasteboard limousine every time!"

"Well, of all things! Did I say anything?"

"Yes, you did!"

"Why, for my part, he can show you a good time eight nights in the week and Sundays, too."

"He 'ain't got grandchildren—if you want to know it."

"Did I say he had?"

"Yes, you did!"

"Why, I don't blame any girl for showing grandpa a good time."

"You could consider yourself darn lucky, Clarice Delehanty, if one half as good ever—"

"Ask the girls if I don't always say old St. Louis is all to the good. Three or four years ago, right after his wife died, I said to Ada, I said—"

A head showed suddenly through the lining side of the mauve portières, blue-eyed, blue-shaved, and with a triple ripple of black hair trained backward.

"Hurry along there with fifty-seven, Delehanty! Heyman's got to see the line and catch that six-two Chicago flier."

Miss Delehanty fell into pose, her profile turned back over one shoulder.

"Tell him to chew a clove; it's good for breathless haste," she said, disappearing through portières into the show-room.

Miss Becker thrust herself from a hastily-found-out aperture, patting, with final touch, her belt into place.

"Have I been asking you for five years, Kess, to knock before you poke your head in on us girls?"

Mr. Leon Kessler appeared then fully between the curtains, letting them drape heavily behind him. Gotham garbs her poets and her brokers, her employers and employees, in the national pin-stripes and sack coat. Except for a few pins stuck upright in his coat lapel, Mr. Kessler might have been his banker or his salesman. Typical New-Yorker is the pseudo, half enviously bestowed upon his kind by *hinter* America. It signifies a bi-weekly manicure femininely administered; a hotel lobbyist who can outstare a seatless guest; the sang-froid to add up a dinner check; spats. When Mr. Kessler tipped, it did not clink; it rustled. In theater, at each interval between acts, he piled out over ladies' knees and returned chewing a mint. He journeyed twice a year to a famous Southern spa, and there won or lost his expenses. He regarded Miss Becker, peering at her around the fluff of a suspended frock of pink tulle.

"What's the idea, Becker? Keokuk wants to see you in the wrap line."

Miss Becker swallowed hard, jamming down and pinning into a small taffy-colored turban, her hair, the exact shade of it, escaping in scallops. Carefully powdered-out lines of her face seemed to emerge suddenly through the conserved creaminess of her skin. Thirty-four, in its unguarded moments, will out. Miss Becker had almost detained twenty's waistline and twenty-two's ardent thrust of face. It was only the indentures of time that had begun to tell slightly—indentures that powder could not putty out. There was a slight bagginess of throat where the years love to eat in first, and out from the eyes a spray of fine lines. It was these lines that came out now indubitably.

"If you want me to lay down on you, Kess, for sure, just ask me to show the line again before lunch. I'm about ready to keel. And you can't put me off again. I'm ready, and you got to come now."

He dug so deeply into his pockets that his sleeves crawled up.

"Say, look here. I've got my business to attend to, and, when my trade's in town, my trade comes first. See? Take off and show Keokuk a few numbers. I want him to see that chinchilla drape."

She reached out, closing her hand over his arm.

"I'll show him the whole line, Kess, when we're back from lunch. I got to talk to you, I tell you. You put me off yesterday and the day before, and this—this is the last."

"The last what?"

"Please, Kess, if you only run over to Rinehardt's with me. I got to tell you something. Something about me and—and—"

He regarded her in some perplexity. "Tell it to me here. Now!"

"I can't. The girls'll be swarming in any minute. I can't get you anywheres but lunch. It's the first thirty minutes of your time I've asked in five years, Kess—is that little enough? Let Cissie show Keokuk the blouses till we get back. It's something, Kess, I can't put off. Kess, please!"

Her face was so close to him and so eager that he turned to back out.

"Wait for me at the Thirty-first Street entrance," he said, "and I'll shoot you across to Rinehardt's."

She caught up her small silk hand-bag and ran out toward the elevators. Down in Thirty-first Street a wave of heat met, almost overpowering her. New York, enervated from sleepless nights on fire-escapes and in bedrooms opening on areaways, moved through it at half-speed, hugging the narrow shade of buildings. Infant mortality climbed with the thermometer. In Fifth Avenue, cool, high bedrooms were boarded and empty. In First Avenue, babies lay naked on the floor, snuffing out for want of oxygen.

Across that man-made Grand Cañon men leap sometimes, but seldom. Mothers whose babies lie naked on the floor look out across it, damning.

Out into this flaying heat Miss Becker stepped gingerly, almost immediately rejoined by Mr. Leon Kessler, crowningly touched with the correct thing in straw sailors.

"Get a move on," he said, guiding her across the soft asphalt.

In Rinehardt's, one of a thousand such *Rathskeller* retreats designed for a city that loves to dine in fifteen languages, the noonday cortège of summer widowers had not yet arrived. Waiters moved through the dim, pink-lit gloom, dressing their tables temptingly cool and white, dipping ice out from silver buckets into thin tumblers.

They seated themselves beneath a ceiling fan, Miss Becker's taffy-colored scallops stirring in the scurry of air.

"Lordy!" she said, closing her eyes and pressing her finger-tips against them, "I wish I could lease this spot for the summer!"

He pushed a menu-card toward her. "What'll you have? There's plenty under the 'ready to serve.' "

She peeled out of her white-silk gloves.

"Some cold cuts and a long ice-tea."

He ordered after her and more at length, then lighted a cigarette.

"Well?" he said, waving out a match.

She leaned forward, already designing with her fork on the table-cloth.

"Kess, can you guess?"

"Come on with it!"

"Have you—noticed anything?"

"Say, I'd have a sweet time keeping up with you girls!"

She looked at him now evenly between the eyes.

"You kept up with me pretty close for three years, didn't you?"

"Say, you knew what you were doing!"

"I—I'm not so sure of that by a long shot. I—I was fed up with the most devilish kind of promises there are. The kind you was too smart to put in words or—or in writing. You—you only looked 'em."

"I suppose you was kidnapped one dark and stormy night while the villain pursued you, eh? Is that it?"

"Oh, what's the use—rehashing! After that time at Atlantic City and—and then the—flat, it—it just seemed the way I felt about you then—that nothing you wanted could be wrong. I guess I knew what I was doing all right, or, if I didn't, I ought to have. I was rotten—or I couldn't have done it, I guess. Only, deep inside of me I was waiting and banking on you like—like poor little Cissie is now. And you knew it; you knew it all them three years."

"Say, did you get me over here to—"

"I only hope to God when you're done with Cissie you'll—"

"You let me take care of my own affairs. If it comes right down to it, there's a few things I could tell you, girl, that ain't so easy to listen to. Let's get off the subject while the going's good."

"Oh, anybody that plays as safe as you—"

He raised his voice, shoving back his chair. "Well, if you want me to clear out of this place quicker than you can bat your eye, you just—"

"No, no, Kess! 'Sh-h-h-h!"

"If there ever was a girl in my place had a square deal, that girl's been you."

" 'Square deal!' Because after I held on and—ate out my heart for three years, you didn't—take away my job, too? Somebody ought to pin a Carnegie medal on you!"

"You've held down a twenty-dollar-a-week job season in and season out, when there've been times it didn't even pay for the ink it took to write you on the pay-roll."

"There's nothing I ever got out of you I didn't earn three times over."

"A younger figure than yours is getting to be wouldn't hurt the line any, you know. It's because I make it a rule not to throw off the old girls when their waist-lines begin to spread that makes you so grateful, is it? There's not a firm in town keeps on a girl after she begins to heavy up. If you got to know why I took you off the dress line and put you in the wraps, it's because I seen you widening into a thirty-eight, and a darn poor one at that. I can sell two wraps off Cissie to one off you. You're getting hippy, girl, and, since you started the subject, you can be darn glad you know where your next week's salary's coming from."

She was reddening so furiously that even her earlobes, their tips escaping beneath the turban, were tinged.

"Maybe I—I'm getting hippy, Kess; but it'll take more than anything you can ever do for me to make up for—"

"Gad!" he said, flipping an ash in some disgust, "I wish I had a ten-cent piece for every one since!"

"Oh," she cried, her throat jerking, "you eat what you just said! You eat it, because you know it ain't so!"

"Now look here," he said, straightening up suddenly, "I don't know what your game is, but if you're here to stir up the old dust that's been laid for five years—"

"No, no, Kess! It's only that—what I got to tell you—I—it makes a difference, I—"

"What?"

"There's nothing in these years since, I swear to God, or in the years before, that I got to be ashamed of!"

"All right! All right!"

"If ever a girl came all of a sudden to her senses, it was me. If ever a girl has lived a quiet life, picking herself up and brushing the dust off, it's been me. Oh, I don't say I 'ain't been entertained by the trade—I didn't dodge my job—but it's been a straight kind of a time—straight!"

"I'm not asking for an alibi, Becker. What's the idea?"

"Kess," she said, leaning forward, with tears popping out in her eyes, "I. W. Goldstone has asked me to marry him."

He laid down his roll in the act of buttering it, gazing across at her with his knife upright in his hand.

"Huh?"

"Night before last, Kess, in the poppy-room at Shalif's."

"Are you crazy?"

"It's the God's truth, Kess. He's begging me for an answer by to-night, before he goes back home."

"I. W. Goldstone, of Goldstone & Auer, ladies' wear?"

She nodded, her hand to her throat.

"Well, I'll be strung up!"

"He—he says, Kess, it's been on his mind for a year and a half, ever since his spring trip a year ago. He wants to take me back with him, Kess, home."

"Whew!" said Mr. Kessler, wiping his brow and the back of his collar.

"You're no more surprised than me, Kess. I—I nearly fell off the Christmas tree."

"Good Lord! Why, his wife—he had her in the store it seems yesterday!"

"She's been dead four years and seven months, Kess."

"Old I. W. and you!"

"He's only fifty-two, Kess; I'm thirty-four."

"I. W. Goldstone!"

"I know it. I can't realize it, neither."

"Why, he's worth two hundred thousand, if he's worth a cent!"

"I know it, Kess."

"The old man's stringing you, girl. His kind stop, look, and listen."

"He's not stringing me! I tell you he's begging me to marry him and go back home with him. He's even told his—daughter about me."

"Good Lord—little Effie! I was out there once when she was a kid. Stopped off on my way to Hot Springs. They live in a kind of park—Forest Park Street or something or other. Why, I've done business with Goldstone & Auer for fifteen years, and my father before me! Good Lord!"

"What'll I do, Kess?"

"So that's the size of the fish you went out and landed!"

"I didn't! I didn't! He's been asking me out the last three trips, and post-cards in between, but I never thought nothing of it."

"Why, he can't get away with this!"

"Why?"

"They won't stand for it out in that Middle West town. He's the head of a big business. He's got a grown daughter."

"He's got her fixed, Kess—settled on her."

"Hattie Becker, Mrs. I. W. Goldstone! Gad! can you beat it? Can't you just see me, when I come out to St. Louis pretty soon, having dinner out at Mrs. I. W. Goldstone's house? Say, am I seeing things?"

"What'll I do, Kess? What'll I do?"

"I tell you that you can't get away with it, girl. The old man's getting childish; they'll have to have him restrained. Why, the woman he was married to for twenty years, Lenie Goldstone, never even seen a skirt-dance. I remember once he brought her to New York and then wouldn't let her see a cabaret show. He won't even buy sleeveless models for his French room."

"I tell you, Kess, he'll take me to Jersey to-morrow and marry me, if I give the word."

"Not a chance!"

"I tell you yes. That's why I got to see you. I got to tell him to-night, Kess. He—goes back to-morrow."

He regarded her slowly, watching her throat where it throbbed.

"Well, what are you going to do?"

"I—I don't know."

"Where do you stand with him? Sweet sixteen and never been kissed?"

"He—he don't ask questions, Kess. I—I'm his ideal, he says, of the—kind of—woman can take up for him where his wife left off. He says we're alike in everything but looks, and that a man who was happy in marriage like him can't be happy outside of it. He—he's sized up pretty well the way I live, and—and—he knows I don't expect too much out of life no more. Just a quiet kind of team-work, he puts it—pulling together fifty-fifty, and somebody's hand to hold on to when old fellow Time hits you a whack in the knees from behind. But he ain't old when he talks that way, Kess; he—he's beautiful to me."

"Does he wear a mask when he makes love?"

"He's got a fine face."

"So that's the way you're playing it, is it? Love-stuff?"

"Oh, I've had all the love-stuff knocked out of me. Three years of eating out my heart is about all the love-stuff I can handle for a while. He don't want that in a woman. I don't want it in him. He's just a plain, good man I never in my life could dream of having. A good home in a good town where life ain't like a red-eyed devil ready to hit in deep between the shoulder-blades. I know why he says he can see his wife in me. He knows I'm the kind was cut out for that kind of life—home and kitchen and my own parsley in my own back yard. He knows, if he marries me, carpet slippers seven nights in the week is my speed. I never want to see a 'roof,' or a music-show, or a cabaret again to the day I die. He knows I'll fit in home like a goldfish in its bowl. Life made a mistake with me, and it's going to square itself. It's fate, Kess; that's what it is—fate!"

She clapped her hands to her face, sobbing down into them.

He glanced about him in quick and nervous concern.

"Pull yourself together there, Becker; we're in a public place."

"If only I could go to him and tell him."

"Well, you can't."

"It's not you that keeps me. Only, I know that with his kind of man and at his age, a woman is—is one thing or another and that ends it. With a grown daughter, he wouldn't—couldn't—he's too set in his ways to know how it was with me—and—what'll I do, Kess?"

"Say, I'm not going to stand in your light, if that's what's eating you. If you can get away with it, I don't wish you nothing but well. Looks to me like all right, if you want to make the try. I'll even come and break bread with you when I go out to see my Middle West trade pretty soon. That's the kind of a hairpin I am."

"It's like I keep saying to myself, Kess. If—if he'd ask me anything, it—it would be different. He—he says he never felt so satisfied that a woman had the right stuff in her. And I have! There's nothing in the world can take that away from me. I can give him what he wants. I know I can. Why, the way I'll make up to that little girl out there and love her to death! I ask so little, Kess—just a decent life and rest—peace. I'm tired. I want to let myself get fat. I'm built that way, to get fat. It was nothing but diet gave me the anæmia last summer. He says he wants me to plump out. Perfect thirty-six don't mean nothing in his life except for the trade. No more rooming-houses with the kitchenette in the bath-room. A kitchen, he says, Kess, half the size of the show-room, with a butler's pantry. He likes to play pinochle at night, he says, next to the sitting-room fire. He tried to learn me the rules of the game the other night in the poppy-room. It's easy. His first wife was death on flowers. She used to train roses over their back fence. He loved to see her there. He wants me to like to grow them. He wants to take me back to a home of my own and peace, where life can't look to a girl like a devil with horns. He wants to take me home. What'll I do, Kess? Please, please, what'll I do?"

He was rather inarticulate, but reached out to pat her arm. "Go—to it—girl, and—God bless you!"

Forest Park Boulevard comes in sootily, smoke-stacks, gas-tanks, and large areas of scarred vacant lots boding ill enough for its destiny. But after a while, where Taylor Avenue bisects, it begins to retrieve itself. Here it is parked down its center, a narrow strip set out in shrubs, and on either side, traffic, thus divided, flows evenly up and down a macadamized roadway. In summer the shrubs thicken, half concealing one side of Forest Park Boulevard from its other. Houses suddenly take on detached and architectural importance, often as not a gravel driveway dividing lawns, and out farther still, where the street eventually flows into Forest Park, the Italian Renaissance invades, somebody's rococo money's worth.

I. W. Goldstone's home, so near the park that, in spring, the smell of lilacs and gasolene hovers over it, pretends not to period or dynasty. Well detached, and so far back from the sidewalk that interlocking trees conceal its second-story windows, an alcove was frankly a bulge on its red-brick exterior. Where the third-floor bath-room, an afterthought, led off the hallway, it jutted out, a shingled protuberance on the left end of the house. A tower swelled out of its front end, and all year round geraniums and boxed climbing vines bloomed in its three stories.

Across a generous ledge of veranda, more vines grew quite

furiously, reaching their height and then growing down upon themselves. Behind those vines, and so cunningly concealed by them that not even the white wrapper could flash through to the passerby, Mrs. I. W. Goldstone, in a chair that would rock rhythmically with her, loved to sit in the first dusk of evening, pleasantly idle. A hose twirling on the lawn spun up the smell of green, abetted by similar whirlings down the wide vista of adjoining lawns. Occasionally, a prideful and shirt-sleeved landed proprietor wielded his own hose, flushing the parched sidewalk or shooting spray against hot bricks that drank in thirstily.

As Mrs. Goldstone rocked she smiled, tilting herself backward off the balls of her feet. The years had cropped out in her suddenly, surprisingly, and with a great deal of geniality. The taffy cast to her hair had backslid to ashes of roses. Uncorseted and in the white wrapper, she was quite frankly widespread, her hips fitting in tight between the chair-arms, and her knees wide.

A screen door snapped sharply shut on its spring, Mr. I. W. Goldstone emerging. There was a great rotundity to his silhouette, the generous outward curve to his waist-line giving to his figure a swayback erectness, the legs receding rather short and thin from the bay of waistcoat.

"Hattie?"

"Here I am, I. W."

"I looped up the sweet-peas."

"Good!"

He sat down beside her, wide-kneed, too, the smooth top of his head and his shirt sleeves spots in the darkness.

"Get dressed a little, Hattie, and I'll get out the car and ride you out to Forest Park Highlands."

She slowed, but did not cease to rock.

"It's so grand at home this evening, I.W. I'm too comfortable to even dress myself."

He felt for her hand in the gloom; she put it out to him.

"You huck home too much, Hattie."

"I guess I do, honey; but it's like I can never get enough of it. The first year I was a home body, and the second and third year I'm two of 'em."

"That's something you'll never hear me complain of in a

woman. There's a world of good in the woman who loves her home."

"It's not that, I. W. It's because I—I never dreamed that there was anything like this coming to me. To live around in rooms, year in and year out, in the lonesomest town in the world, and then, all of a sudden, a home of your own and a hubby of your own and a daughter of your own, why—I dunno—sometimes when I think of them days it's like life was a big red devil with horns and a tail that I'd got away from. Why, if it was to get me again, I—I dunno, honey, I dunno—I—just—dunno."

"You're a good woman, Hattie, and you deserve all that's coming to you. I wish it was more."

"And you're a good man—they don't come no better."

"I'm satisfied with my bargain."

"And me with mine, honey, if—if you don't mind the talk."

"S-ay, this town would talk if you cut its tongue out."

"You're my nice old hubby!"

"If I ever was a little uneasy it was in the beginning, Hattie— the girl—those things don't always turn out."

"It's her as much as me, I. W. She's the sweetest little thing."

"Never seen the like the way you took hold, though. I'll bet there's not one woman in a hundred could have worked it out easier."

"That's right—kid me to death."

" 'Kid,' she says, the minute I tell her the truth."

"Put on your cap, I. W.; it's getting damp."

He felt under the chair-cushions, drawing out and adjusting a black skull-cap.

"Want to go to the picture-show awhile, Hattie?"

"No. When Lizzie's done the dishes, I want to set some dough."

"Let's walk, then, a little. I ate too much supper."

"Just in the side yard, I. W. It's a shame the way I don't dress evenings."

"S-ay, in your own home, shouldn't you have your own comfort? You can take it from me, Hattie, no matter what Effie tells you, you're twice the looking woman with some skin on your bones. I want my wife when she sits down to table she should not look blue-faced when the gravy is passed. Maybe it's

not the style, but if it suits your old man, we should worry who
else it suits."

"It's not right, I. W., but I love it—this feeling at home for—
for good." She rose out of the low mound she had made in the
chair, tucking up the white wrapper at both sides. "Come; let's
walk in the side yard."

A narrow strip of asphalt ran across the house-frontage,
turning in a generous elbow and then back the depth of the lot.
They paced it quietly in the gloom, arm in arm, and their voices
under darkness.

"Next month is my New York trip. All of a sudden Effie begs
I should take her. We'll all go. What you say, Hattie? It'll do us
good."

"You take the kid, I. W. Lizzie needs watching. Yesterday I
had to make her do the whole butler's pantry over. She just
naturally ain't clean."

"You got such luck with your roses, Hattie; it's wonderful!"

They were beneath a climbing bush of them that ran along,
glorifying a wooden fence.

She pulled a fan of them to her face. "M-m-m-m!"

"I must spray for worms to-morrow," he said.

They resumed their soft walking in the gloom. "Where's
Effie?"

"Telephoning."

"I ask you, is it a shame a child should hang on to the telephone
an hour at a time? Fifty minutes since she was interrupted from
supper she's been there."

"What's the harm in a young girl telephoning, I. W.? All
young folks like to gad over the wire."

"What can a girl have to say over the telephone for fifty
minutes? Altogether in my life I never talked that long into the
telephone."

"Let the child alone, I. W."

"Who can she get to listen to her for fifty minutes?"

"Birdie Harberger usually calls up at this time."

"Always at supper-time! Never in my life has that child sat
down at the table it don't ring in our faces. The next time what

it happens you can take sides with her all you want, not one step does she move till she's finished with her supper."

"As easy with her as you are, I. W., just as unreasonable you can get."

"On the stairs-landing for an hour a child should giggle into the telephone! I'm ashamed for the operators. You take sides with her yet."

"I don't, I. W.; only—"

"You do!"

A patch of light from an upper window sprang then across their path.

"She's in her room now, I. W.!" cried Mrs. Goldstone. "She hasn't been telephoning all this time at all. Now, crosspatch!"

"You know much! Can't you see she just lit up? Effie!"

A voice came down to them, clear and with a quality to it like the ring of thin glass.

"Coming, pop!"

The light flashed out again, and in a length of time that could only have meant three steps at a bound she was around the elbow of the asphalt walk, a coat dangling off one arm, her summery skirts flying backward and her head ardently forward.

"You'll never guess!"

She flung herself between the two of them, linking into each of their elbows.

"By my watch, Effie, fifty minutes! If it happens again that you get rung up supper-time, I—"

"It was Leon Kessler, pop; he didn't leave on the six-two. Can you beat it? Down at the station he got to thinking of me and turned back. Oh, my golly! how the boys love me!"

She was jumping now on the tips of her toes, her black curls bouncing.

"You don't tell me!" said Mr. Goldstone. "To-day in the store he says he must be back in New York by Monday morning."

She thrust her face outward, its pink-and-white vividness very close to his.

"Is my daddy's daughter going out in a seventy horse-power to Delmar Garden? She is!"

"Them New York boys spend too much money on the girls when they come. They spoil them for the home young men."

"Can I help it if he couldn't tear himself away?"

"S-ay, don't fool yourself! I said to him to-day he should stay over Sunday. After the bill of goods I bought from him this morning, and the way he only comes out to see his trade once in five or six years, he should stay and mix with them a little longer. That fellow knows good business."

She turned her face with a fling of curls to the right of her, linking closer into the soft arm there.

"Listen to him, Mamma Hat! Let's shove a brick house over on him."

When Mrs. Goldstone finally spoke there was a depth to her voice that seemed to create sudden quiet.

"Effie, Effie, why didn't you let him go?"

"Let him? Did I tie any strings to him? I said good-by to him in the store this afternoon. Can I help it that the boys love me? Why didn't I let him go, she says!"

Her father pinched her slyly at that. "*Echta* fresh kid," he said.

To her right, the hand at her arm clung closer.

"Effie, you—you're so young, honey. Leon Kessler's an old-timer—"

"I hate kids. Give me a *man* every time. I like them when they've got enough sense to—"

"Why didn't you let him go, Effie? Ain't I right, I. W.? Ain't I right?"

"S-ay, what's the difference if he likes to show her a good time? If I was a young man, I wouldn't pass her up myself."

"But, I. W., she's—so young!"

"Who's young? I'm nineteen, going on—"

"You've been running with him all the three days he's been here, honey. What's the use getting yourself talked about?"

"Well, any girl in town would be glad to get herself talked about if Leon Kessler was rushing her."

"Effie, I won't let you—I won't—"

Miss Goldstone unhinged her arm, jerking it free in anger.

"Well, I like that!"

"Effie, I—"

"You ain't my boss!"

"Effie!"

"But, papa, she—"

There was a booming in Mr. Goldstone's voice and a suddenly projected vibrancy.

"You apologize to your mother—this minute! You talk to your mother the way you know she's to be talked to!"

"I. W., she didn't—"

"You hear me!"

"I. W.! Don't holler at her; she—"

"She ain't your boss? Well, she just is your boss! You take back them words and say you're sorry! You apologize to your mother!" Immediate sobs were rumbling up through Miss Goldstone.

"Well, she— I—I didn't do anything. She's down on him. She—"

"Oh, Effie, would I say anything if it wasn't for your own good?"

"You—you were down on him from the start!"

"Effie darling, you must be mad! Would I say anything if it wasn't for our girl's good to—"

"I—oh, Mamma Hat, I'm sorry, darling! I never meant a word. I didn't! I didn't, darling!"

They embraced there in the shrouding darkness, the tears flowing.

"Oh, Effie—Effie!"

"I didn't mean one word I said, darling! I just get nasty like that before I know it. I didn't mean it!"

"My own Effie!"

"My darling Mamma Hat!"

In the shadow of a flowering shrub Mr. Goldstone stood by, mopping. Mrs. Goldstone took the small face between her hands, peering down into it.

"Effie, Effie, don't let—"

Just beyond the enclosing hedge, a motor-car drew up, honking, at the curb, two far-flung paths of light whitening the street and a disused iron negro-boy hitching-post. Miss Goldstone reared back.

"That's him!"

"Effie!"

"Let me go, dearie; let me go!"

"But, Effie—"

"Say, Hattie, I don't want to butt in, but it don't hurt the child should go riding a little while out by Delmar Garden—a man that can handle a car like Leon Kessler. Anyways, it don't pay to hurt the firm's feelings."

There was a constant honking now at the curb, and violent throbbing of engine.

"But, I. W.—"

"Popsie darling, I'll be back early. Mamma Hat, please!"

"Your mother says yes, baby. Tell Kess he should come for Sunday dinner to-morrow."

She was a white streak across the grass, her nervous feet flying. Almost instantly the honk of a horn came streaming back, faint, fainter.

Left standing there, Goldstone was instantly solicitous of his wife, feeling along her arm up under the loose sleeve.

"It don't pay, Hattie, to hurt Kessler's feelings, and, anyhow, what's the difference just so we know who she's running with? It's like this house was a honey-pot and the boys flies."

She turned to him now with her voice full of husk, and even in the dark her face bleached and shrunken from its plumpness.

"You oughtn't to let her! You—hadn't the right! She's too young and too—sweet for a man like him. You oughtn't to let her!"

He stepped out in front of her, taking her by the elbows and holding them close down against her sides.

"Why, Hattie, that child's own mother that loved her like an angel couldn't worry no more foolishly about her than you do. Gad! I think you wimmin love it! It was the same kind of worrying shortened her mother's life. Always about nothing, too. 'Lenie,' I used to say to her, just to quiet her, 'it was worry killed a Maltese cat; don't let it kill you.' That child is all right, Hattie. What if he does like her pretty well? Worse could happen."

"No, it couldn't! No!"

"Why not? He 'ain't seen her since a child, and all of a sudden he comes West and finds in front of him an eye-opener."

"He's twice her age—more!"

"The way girls demand things nowadays, a man has got to be twice her age before he can provide for her. Leon Kessler is big rich."

"He—he's fast."

"Show me the one that 'ain't sowed his wild oats. Them's the kind that settle down quickest into good husbands."

"He—"

"S-ay, it 'ain't happened yet. I'm the last one to wish my girl off my hands. I only say not a boy in this town could give it to her so good. Fifteen years I've done business with that firm, and with his father before him. A-1 house! S-ay, I should worry that he ain't a Sunday-school boy. Show me the one that is. Your old man in his young days wasn't such a low flier, neither, if anybody should ask you." He made a whirring noise in his throat at that, pinching her cold cheek. She was walking rapidly now toward the house. "Well, since our daughter goes out riding in a six-thousand-dollar car, to show that we're sports, lets her father and mother take themselves out for a ride in their six-hundred-dollar car. I drive you out as far as Yiddle's farm for some sweet butter, eh?"

"No, no; I'm cold. It's getting damp."

"S-ay, you can't hurt my feelings. On a cool night like this, a brand-new sleeping-porch ain't the worst spot in the world."

They were on the veranda, the hall light falling dimly out and over them.

"She's so young—"

"Now, now, Hattie; worry killed a Maltese cat. Come to bed."

"You go. I want to wait up."

"Hattie, you want to make of yourself the laughingstock of the neighborhood. A grown-up girl goes out riding with a man like Leon Kessler, and you wants to wait up and catch your death of cold. If we had more daughters, I wouldn't have no more wife; I'd have a shadow from worry. Come!"

"I'll be up in a minute, I. W."

He regarded her in some concern.

"Why, Hattie, if there's anything in the world to worry about, wouldn't I be the first? Ain't you well?"

"Yes."

"Then come. I'll get a pitcher of ice-water to take up-stairs."

"I'll be up in a minute."

"I don't want, Hattie, you should wait up for that child and take your death of cold. Because I sleep like a log when I once hit the bed, don't you play no tricks on me."

"I'll be up in a minute, I. W."

He moved into the house and, after a while, to the clinking of ice against glass, up the stairs.

"Come, Hattie; and be sure and leave the screen door un-hooked for her."

"Yes, I. W."

An hour she sat in the shrouded darkness of the elbow of the veranda. Street noises died. The smell of damp came out. Occasionally a motor-car sped by, or a passer-by, each step clear on the asphalt. The song of crickets grated against the darkness. An infant in the right-side house raised a fretful voice once or twice, and then broke into a sustained and coughy fit of crying. Lights flashed up in the windows, silhouettes moving across drawn shades. Then silence again. The university clock, a mile out, chimed twelve, and finally a sonorous one. Mrs. Goldstone lay huddled in her chair, vibrant for sound. At two o'clock the long, high-power car drew up at the curb again, this time without honking. She sat forward, trembling.

There followed a half-hour of voices at the curb, a low voice of undeniable tensity, high laughter that shot up in joyous geysers. It was a fifteen-minute process from the curb to the first of the porch steps, and then Mrs. Goldstone leaned forward, her voice straining to keep its pitch.

"Effie!"

The young figure sprang around the porch pillar.

"Mamma Hat! Honey, you didn't wait up for me?"

Mr. Kessler came forward, goggles pushed up above his cap-visor.

"Well, I'm hanged! What did you think—that I was kidnapping the kid?"

"How—how dared you! It's after two, and—"

Miss Goldstone began then to jump again upon her toes, linking her arm in his.

"Tell her, Leon! Tell her! Oh, Mamma Hat! Mamma Hat!"

She was suddenly in Mrs. Goldstone's arms, her ardent face burning through the white wrapper.

Mr. Kessler removed his cap, flinging it upward again and catching it.

"Tell her, Leon!"

"Well, what would you say, Becker, what would you say if I was to come out here and swipe that little darling there?"

"Oh, Leon—kidder!"

"If—what?"

"I said it!"

"Tell her, Kess; tell it out! Oh, mommie, mommie!"

He leaned forward with his hand on the back of the turbulent head of curls.

"You little darling, I'm going to put you on my back and carry you off to New York."

"Oh, mommie," cried Miss Goldstone, flinging back her head so that her face shone up, "he asked me in Delmar Garden! We're going to live in New York, darling, and Rockaway in summer. He don't care a rap about the New York girls compared to me. We're going to Cuba on our honeymoon. I'm engaged, darling! I got engaged to-night!"

"That's the idea, Twinkle-pinkle. I'd carry you off to-night if I could!"

"Mommie Hat, ain't you glad?"

"Effie—Effie—"

"Mommie, what is it? What's the matter, darling? What?"

"I—it's just that I got cold, honey, sitting here waiting—the surprise and all. Run, honey, and get me a drink. Crack some ice, dearie, and then run up-stairs in the third floor back and see if there's some brandy up there. Be sure to look for—the brandy. I—I'll be all right."

"My poor, darling, cold mommie!"

She was off on the slim, quick feet, the screen door slamming and vibrating.

Then Mrs. Goldstone sprang up.

"You wouldn't dare! Such a baby—you wouldn't dare!"

"Dare what?"

"You can't have the child! You can't!"

"What do you mean?"

"What do I mean?"

He advanced a step, his voice and expression lifted in incredulity.

"Say, look here, Becker, are you stark, raving crazy? Is it

possible you don't know that, in your place, nobody but a crazy woman would open her mouth?"

"Maybe; but I don't care. Just leave her alone, Kess, please! That little baby can stand nothing but happiness."

"Why, woman, you're crazy with the heat. If you want to know it, I'm nuts over that little kid. Gad! never ran across anything so full of zip in my life! I'm going to make life one joy ride after another for that joy baby. That kid's the showpiece of the world. She's got me so hipped I'm crazy, and the worst of it is I like it. You don't need to worry. As the boys say, when I settle down, I'm going to settle hard."

"You ain't fit to have her!"

"Say, the kind of life I've lived I ain't ashamed to tell her own father. He's a man, and I'm a man, and life's life."

"You—"

"Now look here, Becker. That'll be about all. If you're in your right senses, you're going to ring the joy bells louder than any one around here. What you got on your chest you can just as well cut your throat as tell; so we'll both live happy every after. There's not one thing in my life that any jury wouldn't pass, and—"

"I've seen you drunk."

"Well, what of it? It took three of us to yank old I. W. out from under the table at my sister's wedding."

"You— What about you and Cissie and—"

The light run of feet, and almost instantly Miss Goldstone was pirouetting in between them.

"Here, dearie! There wasn't anything like brandy up in the third floor. I found some cordial in the pantry. Drink it down, dearie; it 'll warm you."

They hovered together, Miss Goldstone trembling between solicitude and her state of intensity.

"Kessie darling, you've got to go now. I want to get mommie up-stairs to bed. You got to go, darling, until to-morrow. Oh, why isn't it to-morrow? I want everybody to know. Don't let on, Mamma Hat. I'll pop it on popsie at breakfast while I'm opening his eggs for him. You come for breakfast, Leon. You're in the family now." He lifted her bodily from her feet, pressing a necklace of kisses round her throat.

"Good night, Twinkle-pinkle, till to-morrow."

"Good night, darling. I won't sleep a wink, waiting for you."

"Me, neither."

"One more, darling—a French one."

"Two for good measure."

"Sleep tight, beautiful! Good night!"

"Good night, beautifulest!"

She stood poised forward on the topmost step, watching him between backward waves of the hand crank, throw his clutch, and steer off. Then she turned inward, a sigh trembling between her lips.

"Oh, Mamma Hat, I—"

But Mrs. Goldstone's chair was empty. Into it with a second and more tremulous sigh sank Miss Goldstone, her lips lifted in the smile that had been kissed.

When Mr. Goldstone slept, every alternate breath started with a rumble somewhere down in the depths of him and, drawn up like a chain from a well, petered out into a thin whistle before the next descent. Beside him, now, on her knees, Mrs. Goldstone shook at his shoulder.

"I. W.! I. W.! Quick! Wake up!"

He let out a shuddering, abysmal breath.

"I. W.! Please!"

He moaned, turning his face from her.

She tugged him around again, now raising his face between her hands from the pillow.

"I. W.! Try to wake up! For God's sake, I. W.!" He sprang up in a terrified daze, sitting upright in bed.

"My God! Who? What's wrong? Effie! Hattie."

"No, no; don't get excited, I. W. It's me—Hattie!"

"What?"

"Nothing, I. W. Nothing to get excited about. Only I got to tell you something."

"Where's Effie?"

"She's home."

"What time is it?"

"Three."

"Come back to bed, then; you got the nightmare."

"No, no!"

"You ain't well, Hattie? Let me light up."

"No, no; only, I got to tell you something! I 'ain't been to bed; I been waiting up, and—"

"And what?"

"She just came home—engaged!"

"My God! Effie?"

He blinked in the darkness, drawing up his knees to a hump under the sheet.

"Engaged—how?"

"I. W., don't you remember? Wake up, honey. To Kess, to Leon Kessler that she went automobiling with."

"Our Effie engaged—to Leon Kessler?"

"Yes, I. W.—our little Effie!"

A smile spread over his face slowly, and he clasped his hands in an embrace about his knees.

"You don't tell me!"

"Oh, I. W., please—"

"Our little girl. S-ay, how poor Lenie would have loved this happiness! Our little girl engaged to get married!"

"I. W., she—"

"We do the right thing by them—eh, Hattie? Furnish them up as many rooms as they want. But, s-ay, they don't need help from us. He's a lucky boy who gets her, I don't care who he is. Her papa's little Effie, a baby—old enough to get engaged!"

"I. W., she's too—young. Don't give him our little Effie; she's too young!"

"I married her mother, Hattie, when she wasn't yet eighteen."

"I know, I. W., but not to Leon Kessler. She's such a baby, I. W. He—didn't I work for him nine years, I. W.—don't I know what he is!"

"I'm surprised, Hattie, you should hold so against a man his wild oats."

"Then why ain't oats for the man oats for the woman? It's the men that sow the wild oats and the women—us women that's got to reap them!"

"S-ay, life is life. Do you want to put your head up against a brick wall?"

"A wall that men built!"

"It's always hard, Hattie, for good women like you and like poor Lenie was to understand. It's better you don't. You shouldn't even think about it."

"But, I. W.—"

"If I didn't know Leon Kessler was no worse than ninety-nine good husbands in a hundred, you think I would let him lay a finger on the apple of my eye? I don't understand, Hattie; all of a sudden this evening, you're so worked up. Instead of happiness, you come like with a funeral. Is that why you wake me up out of a sleep? To cry about it? Don't think, Hattie, that just as much as you I haven't got the good of my child at heart. Out of a sound sleep she wakes me to cry because a happiness has come to us. Leon Kessler can have any girl in this town he wants. Maybe he wasn't a Sunday-school boy in his day—but say, show me one that was."

She drew herself up, grasping him at the shoulders.

"I. W., don't let him have our little Effie!"

"Nonsense!" he said, in some distaste for her voice choked with tears. "Cut out this woman foolishness now and come to bed. Is this something new you're springing on me? I got no patience with women who indulge themselves with nervous breakdowns. I never thought, Hattie, you had nothing like that in you."

Her voice was rising now in hysteria, slipping up frequently beyond her control.

"If you do, I can't stand it! I can't stand it, I. W.!"

He peered at her in the starlight that came down through the screened-in top of the sleeping-porch.

"Why?" he said, suddenly awake, and shortly.

"I worked for him nine years, I. W. I—I know him."

"How?"

"I know him, I. W. She's too good for him."

"How do you know him?"

"I—the girls, I. W. One little girl now, Cissie—I—I hear it all from my friend Delehanty—sometimes she—she writes to me. I—the models and—the girls and—and the lady buyers—they—they used to gossip in the factory and—I—I used to hear about it. I. W., don't! Let go! You hurt!" His teeth and his hands were very tight, and he hung now over the side of the bed and toward her.

"He—I. W.—he—"

"He what? He what?"

"He—ain't good enough."

"I say he is!"

"But he—I. W.—she—she's such a baby and he—he— You hurt!"

"Then tell me, he what?"

"I. W., you're hurting me!"

"He what—do you hear?—he what?"

"Don't make me say it! Don't! It—it just happened—with him meaning one thing all the time and—me another. I was thrown with that kind of a crowd, I. W., all my life. All the girls, they— It don't make me worse than it makes him. With me it was once; with him it's—it's— I didn't know, I. W. My mother she died that year before, and—I needed the job, and I swear to God, I. W., I—kept hoping even if he never put it in words he'd fix it. Kill me, if you want to, I. W., but don't throw our Effie to him! Don't! Don't! Don't!"

She was pounding the floor with her bare palms, her face so distorted that the mouth drawn tight over the teeth was as wide and empty as a mask's, and sobs caught and hiccoughed in her throat.

"I didn't know, I. W.! Don't kill me for what I didn't know!"

She crouched back from his knotted face, and he sprang then out of bed, nightshirt flapping about his knees, and his fists and his bulging eyes raised to the quiet stars.

"God," he cried, "help me to keep hold of myself! Help me! You—you—"

His voice was so high and so tight in his throat that it stuck, leaving him in inarticulate invocation.

"I. W.!"

"My child engaged to—to her mother's—you—you—"

"I. W.! Do you see now? You wouldn't let him have her! You wouldn't, I. W.! Tell me you wouldn't!"

"I want him if he touches her to be struck dead! I want him to be struck dead!"

"Thank God!" said Mrs. Goldstone, weeping now tears that eased her breathing.

Suddenly he leaned toward her, his voice rather quieter, but his forefinger waggling out toward the open door.

"You go!" he said, and then in a gathering hurricane of fury, "go!"

"I. W., don't yell! Don't! Don't!"

"Go—while I'm quiet. Go—you hear?"

She edged around him where he stood, in fear of his white, crouched attitude.

"I. W.!"

He made a step toward her, and, at the sound in his throat, she ran out into the hallway and down the stairs to the porch. In the deep shade of the veranda's elbow a small figure lay deep in sleep in the wicker rocker, one bare arm up over her head and lips parted.

In a straight chair beside her Mrs. Goldstone sat down. She was shuddering with chill and repeating to herself, quite aloud and over and over again:

"What have I done? What have I done? What have I done?"

She was suddenly silent then, staring out ahead, her hands clutching the chair-arms.

To her inflamed fancy, it was as if, beyond the hedge, the old disused hitching-post had become incarnate and, in the form of her naive and horned conception, was coming toward her with the whites of his eyes bloodshot.

Helen Rose Hull

The Fire
1917

Helen Rose Hull (1888–1971) grew up in Albion, Michigan, the daughter of teachers and the granddaughter of a printer. Her grandfather printed one of her stories when she was eight years old, and, thereafter, she thought of herself as a writer. She attended Michigan State University and completed a degree in philosophy at the University of Chicago, where she later did graduate work. She taught English at Wellesley College for three years. After collecting enough rejection slips to paper a wall in her house, she published her first story in 1915; eventually, her work appeared in such periodicals as Harper's *Magazine,* Century, Colliers, Cosmopolitan, The Ladies' Home Journal, *and* The Saturday Evening Post. *In 1916 she moved to New York City to begin her long dual career, teaching at Columbia University for nine months of the year and writing during the summer at her home in Maine.*

*A lesbian, Hull shared a long and productive life with Mabel Louise Robinson, a member of the creative writing faculty at Columbia. Three of Hull's first four novels—*Quest *(1922);* Labyrinth *(1923); and* Islanders *(1927)—reflect her commitment to the feminist issues of her time. Two of them depict lesbian couples in secondary roles, providing a sane and stable backdrop against which all the other characters and relationships are contrasted. Dorothea Brande, in a review of* Labyrinth *in* The New Republic *(November 7, 1923), complained that the "most satisfactory human relationship . . . is one between two women characters. Marriage shows up beside it as something dingy and unalluring, a whining and exacting state."*

The house with detached writing studio where Hull and Robinson spent their summers had been carefully renovated and they cherished it until Mabel's death at eighty-eight, when Helen was in her early seventies. The two of them had collaborated on a book about writing, Creative Writing, the Story Form, *in 1932. Along with Roger Sherman Loomis they also co-edited* The Art of Writing Prose, *a collection of essays by various well-known writers on their craft, in 1936.*

Helen Hull also published two collections of her short stories: Uncommon People *(1936), and* Octave, A Book of Stories *(1947); a collection of novellas,* The Flying Yorkshireman *(1938); and a collection of four short novels (or long short stories),* Experiment *(1940). There were more than a dozen other novels as well. Her literary output was prolific.*

In her story "Second Fiddle," a character exclaims, "We feel too much respect for forms—marriage and families. Have to take the lid off and look inside." That probing of family dynamics was the consuming focus of all her fiction. She looked at the effect on the sensitive child of growing up with a "weak" father and a "strong" mother, and then reversed the construct, examining the impact on a similarly lonely, sensitive, and idealistic child of an overpowering father and a shrinking mother. She frequently explored the pain of conflicting loyalties, sometimes portraying a child torn between parents at war with each other, and sometimes portraying young adulthood, when children separate from their parents to enter into new alliances.

Such a story is told in "The Fire," originally published in Century, *November 1917, and reprinted in the lesbian periodical* The Ladder *and later in* Lesbians Home Journal: Stories from the Ladder *in 1976. Barbara Grier, co-editor of* The Ladder *and publisher of The Naiad Press, an American lesbian publishing house, wrote in her note on this story, "It is a tribute to the universality of [Hull's] talent that this story still has relevance today in defining the puberty patterns of the Lesbian."*

"The Fire" is discussed further by Lillian Faderman in Surpassing the Love of Men *(New York: William Morrow, 1981). Faderman writes,*

> There does in fact seem to be an erotic element in [Miss Egert's and Cynthia's] relationship which is inextricably mixed with their roles as the mentor of beauty and courage and the devoted pupil. . . . Although Cynthia bows to her mother's pressure and gives up Miss Egert, it is made clear that she will not give up Miss Egert's influence, which is portrayed as entirely positive and constructive in contrast with the pathetically narrow ideals that Cynthia's parents try to impose on their daughter.

Cynthia blotted the entry in the old ledger and scowled across the empty office at the door. Mrs. Moriety had left it ajar when

she departed with her receipt for the weekly fifty cents on her
"lot." If you supplied the missing gilt letters, you could read the
sign on the glass of the upper half: "H. P. Bates. Real Estate.
Notary Public." Through the door at Cynthia's elbow came the
rumbling voice of old Fleming, the lawyer down the hall; he
had come in for his Saturday night game of chess with her
father.

Cynthia pushed the ledger away from her, and with her elbows
on the spotted, green felt of the desk, her fingers burrowing
into her cheeks, waited for two minutes by the nickel clock;
then, with a quick, awkward movement, she pushed back her
chair and plunged to the doorway, her young face twisted in a
sort of fluttering resolution.

"Father—"

Her father jerked his head toward her, his fingers poised over
a pawn. Old Fleming did not look up.

"Father, I don't think anybody else will be in."

"Well, go on home, then." Her father bent again over the
squares, the light shining strongly on the thin places about his
temples.

"Father, please,"— Cynthia spoke hurriedly,—"you aren't going
for a while? I want to go down to Miss Egert's for a minute."

"Eh? What's that?" He leaned back in his chair now, and Mr.
Fleming lifted his severe, black beard to look at this intruder.
"What for? You can't take any more painting lessons. Your
mother doesn't want you going there any more."

"I just want to get some things I left there. I can get back to
go home with you."

"But your mother said she didn't like your hanging around
down there in an empty house with an old maid. What did she
tell you about it?"

"Couldn't I just get my sketches, Father, and tell Miss Egert
I'm not coming any more? She would think it was awfully funny
if I didn't. I won't stay. But she—she's been good to me—"

"What set your mother against her, then? What you been
doing down there?"

Cynthia twisted her hands together, her eyes running from
Fleming's amused stare to her father's indecision. Only an

accumulated determination could have carried her on into speech.

"I've just gone down once a week for a lesson. I want to get my things. If I'm not going, I ought to tell her."

"Why didn't you tell her that last week?"

"I kept hoping I could go on."

"Um." Her father's glance wavered toward his game. "Isn't it too late?"

"Just eight, Father." She stepped near her father, color flooding her cheeks. "If you'll give me ten cents, I can take the car—"

"Well—" He dug into his pocket, nodding at Fleming's grunt, "The women always want cash, eh, Bates?"

Then Cynthia, the dime pressed into her palm, tiptoed across to the nail where her hat and sweater hung, seized them, and still on tiptoe, lest she disturb the game again, ran out to the head of the stairs.

She was trembling as she pulled on her sweater; as she ran down the dark steps to the street the tremble changed to a quiver of excitement. Suppose her father had known just what her mother *had* said! That she could not see Miss Egert again; could never go hurrying down to the cluttered room they called the studio for more of those strange hours of eagerness and pain when she bent over the drawing-board, struggling with the mysteries of color. That last sketch—the little, purpling mint-leaves from the garden—Miss Egert had liked that. And they thought she could leave those sketches there! Leave Miss Egert, too, wondering why she never came again! She hurried to the corner, past the bright store-windows. In thought she could see Miss Egert setting out the jar of brushes, the dishes of water, pushing back the litter of magazines and books to make room for the drawing-board, waiting for her to come. Oh, she had to go once more, black as her disobedience was!

The half-past-eight car was just swinging round the curve. She settled herself behind two German housewives, shawls over their heads, market-baskets beside them. They lived out at the end of the street; one of them sometimes came to the office with payments on her son's lot. Cynthia pressed against the dirty window, fearful lest she miss the corner. There it was, the new street light shining on the sedate old house! She ran to the platform, pushing against the arm the conductor extended.

"Wait a minute, there!" He released her as the car stopped, and she fled across the street.

In front of the house she could not see a light, up-stairs or down, except staring reflections in the windows from the white arc light. She walked past the dark line of box which led to the front door. At the side of the old square dwelling jutted a new, low wing; and there in two windows were soft slits of light along the curtain-edges. Cynthia walked along a little dirt path to a door at the side of the wing. Standing on the door-step, she felt in the shadow for the knocker. As she let it fall, from the garden behind her came a voice:

"I'm out here. Who is it?" There was a noise of feet hurrying through dead leaves, and as Cynthia turned to answer, out of the shadow moved a blur of face and white blouse.

"Cynthia! How nice!" The woman touched Cynthia's shoulder as she pushed open the door. "There, come in."

The candles on the table bent their flames in the draft; Cynthia followed Miss Egert into the room.

"You're busy?" Miss Egert had stood up by the door an old wooden-toothed rake. "I don't want to bother you." Cynthia's solemn, young eyes implored the woman and turned hastily away. The intensity of defiance which had brought her at such an hour left her confused.

"Bother? I was afraid I had to have my grand bonfire alone. Now we can have it a party. You'd like to?"

Miss Egert darted across to straighten one of the candles. The light caught in the folds of her crumpled blouse, in the soft, drab hair blown out around her face.

"I can't stay very long." Cynthia stared about the room, struggling to hide her turmoil under ordinary casualness. "You had the carpenter fix the bookshelves, didn't you?"

"Isn't it nice now! All white and gray and restful—just a spark of life in that mad rug. A good place to sit in and grow old."

Cynthia looked at the rug, a bit of scarlet Indian weaving. She wouldn't see it again! The thought poked a derisive finger into her heart.

"Shall we sit down just a minute and then go have the fire?"

Cynthia dropped into the wicker chair, wrenching her fingers through one another.

"My brother came in to-night, his last attempt to make me see reason," said Miss Egert.

Cynthia lifted her eyes. Miss Egert wasn't wondering why she had come; she could stay without trying to explain.

Miss Egert wound her arms about her knees as she went on talking. Her slight body was wrenched a little out of symmetry, as though from straining always for something uncaptured; there was the same lack of symmetry in her face, in her eyebrows, in the line of her mobile lips. But her eyes had nothing fugitive, nothing pursuing in their soft, gray depth. Their warm, steady eagerness shone out in her voice, too, in its swift inflections.

"I tried to show him it wasn't a bit disgraceful for me to live here in a wing of my own instead of being a sort of nurse-maid adjunct in his house." She laughed, a soft, throaty sound. "It's my house. It's all I have left to keep me a person, you see. I won't get out and be respectable in his eyes."

"He didn't mind your staying here and taking care of—them!" cried Cynthia.

"It's respectable, dear, for an old maid to care for her father and mother; but when they die she ought to be useful to some one else instead of renting her house and living on an edge of it."

"Oh,"—Cynthia leaned forward,—"I should think you'd hate him! I think families are—terrible!"

"Hate him?" Miss Egert smiled. "He's nice. He just doesn't agree with me. As long as he lets the children come over—I told him I meant to have a beautiful time with them, with my real friends—with you."

Cynthia shrank into her chair, her eyes tragic again.

"Come, let's have our bonfire!" Miss Egert, with a quick movement, stood in front of Cynthia, one hand extended.

Cynthia crouched away from the hand.

"Miss Egert,"—her voice came out in a desperate little gasp,— "I can't come down any more. I can't take any more painting lessons." She stopped. Miss Egert waited, her head tipped to one side. "Mother doesn't think I better. I came down—after my things."

"They're all in the workroom." Miss Egert spoke quietly. "Do you want them now?"

"Yes." Cynthia pressed her knuckles against her lips. Over her hand her eyes cried out. "Yes, I better get them," she said heavily.

Miss Egert, turning slowly, lifted a candle from the table.

"We'll have to take this. The wiring isn't done." She crossed the room, her thin fingers, not quite steady, bending around the flame.

Cynthia followed through a narrow passage. Miss Egert pushed open a door, and the musty odor of the store-room floated out into a queer chord with the fresh plaster of the hall.

"Be careful of that box!" Miss Egert set the candle on a pile of trunks. "I've had to move all the truck from the attic and studio in here. Your sketches are in the portfolio, and that's—somewhere!"

Cynthia stood in the doorway, watching Miss Egert bend over a pile of canvases, throwing up a grotesque, rounded shadow on the wall. Round the girl's throat closed a ring of iron.

"Here they are, piled up—"

Cynthia edged between the boxes. Miss Egert was dragging the black portfolio from beneath a pile of books.

"And here's the book I wanted you to see." The pile slipped crashing to the floor as Miss Egert pulled out a magazine. "Never mind those. See here." She dropped into the chair from which she had knocked the books, the portfolio under one arm, the free hand running through the pages of an old art magazine. The chair swung slightly; Cynthia, peering down between the boxes, gave a startled "Oh!"

"What is it?" Miss Egert followed Cynthia's finger. "The chair?" She was silent a moment. "Do you think I keep my mother prisoner here in a wheel-chair now that she is free?" She ran her hand along the worn arm. "I tried to give it to an old ladies' home, but it was too used up. They wanted more style."

"But doesn't it remind you—" Cynthia hesitated.

"It isn't fair to remember the years she had to sit here waiting to die. You didn't know her. I've been going back to the real years—" Miss Egert smiled at Cynthia's bewildered eyes. "Here, let's look at these." She turned another page. "See, Cynthia. Aren't they swift and glad? That's what I was trying to tell you the other day. See that arm, and the drapery there! Just a line—"

The girl bent over the page, frowning at the details the quick finger pointed out. "Don't they catch you along with them?" She held the book out at arm's-length, squinting at the figures. "Take it along. There are several more." She tucked the book into the portfolio and rose. "Come on; we'll have our fire."

"But, Miss Egert,"—Cynthia's voice hardened as she was swept back into her own misery,—"I can't take it. I can't come any more."

"To return a book?" Miss Egert lowered her eyelids as if she were again sizing up a composition. "You needn't come just for lessons."

Cynthia shook her head.

"Mother thinks—" She fell into silence. She couldn't say what her mother thought—dreadful things. If she could only swallow the hot pressure in her throat!

"Oh. I hadn't understood." Miss Egert's fingers paused for a swift touch on Cynthia's arm, and then reached for the candle. "You can go on working by yourself."

"It isn't that—" Cynthia struggled an instant, and dropped into silence again. She couldn't say out loud any of the things she was feeling. There were too many walls between feeling and speech: loyalty to her mother, embarrassment that feelings should come so near words, a fear of hurting Miss Egert.

"Don't mind so much, Cynthia." Miss Egert led the way back to the living-room. "You can stay for the bonfire? That will be better than sitting here. Run into the kitchen and bring the matches and marshmallows—in a dish in the cupboard."

Cynthia, in the doorway, stared at Miss Egert. Didn't she care at all! Then the dumb ache in her throat stopped throbbing as Miss Egert's gray eyes held her steadily a moment. She did care! She did! She was just helping her. Cynthia took the candle and went back through the passageway to the kitchen, down at the very end.

She made a place on the table in the litter of dishes and milk-bottles for the candle. The matches had been spilled on the shelf of the stove and into the sink. Cynthia gathered a handful of the driest. Shiftlessness was one of her mother's counts against Miss Egert. Cynthia flushed as she recalled her stumbling defense: Miss Egert had more important things to do; dishes were kept in their proper place; and her mother's: "Important! Mooning about!"

"Find them, Cynthia?" The clear, low voice came down the hall, and Cynthia hurried back.

Out in the garden it was quite black. As they came to the far end, the old stone wall made a dark bank against the sky, with a sharp star over its edge. Miss Egert knelt; almost with the scratch of the match the garden leaped into yellow, with fantastic moving shadows from the trees and in the corner of the wall. She raked leaves over the blaze, pulled the great mound into firmer shape, and then drew Cynthia back under the wall to watch. The light ran over her face; the delighted gestures of her hands were like quick shadows.

"See the old apple-tree dance! He's too old to move fast."

Cynthia crouched by the wall, brushing away from her face the scratchy leaves of the dead hollyhocks. Excitement tingled through her; she felt the red and yellow flames seizing her, burning out the heavy rebellion, the choking weight. Miss Egert leaned back against the wall, her hands spread so that her thin fingers were fire-edged.

"See the smoke curl up through those branches! Isn't it lovely, Cynthia?" She darted around the pile to push more leaves into the flames.

Cynthia strained forward, hugging her arms to her body. Never had there been such a fire! It burned through her awkwardness, her self-consciousness. It ate into the thick, murky veils which hung always between her and the things she struggled to find out. She took a long breath, and the crisp scent of smoke from the dead leaves tingled down through her body.

Miss Egert was at her side again. Cynthia looked up; the slight, asymmetrical figure was like the apple-tree, still, yet dancing!

"Why don't you paint it?" demanded Cynthia, abruptly, and then was frightened as Miss Egert's body stiffened, lost its suggestion of motion.

"I can't." The woman dropped to the ground beside Cynthia, crumpling a handful of leaves. "It's too late." She looked straight at the fire. "I must be content to see it." She blew the pieces of leaves from the palm of her hand and smiled at Cynthia. "Perhaps some day you'll paint it—or write it."

"I can't paint." Cynthia's voice quivered. "I want to do something. I can't even see things except what you point out. And now—"

Miss Egert laid one hand over Cynthia's clenched fingers. The girl trembled at the cold touch.

"You must go on looking." The glow, as the flames died lower, flushed her face. "Cynthia, you're just beginning. You mustn't stop just because you aren't to come here any more. I don't know whether you can say things with your brush; but you must find them out. You mustn't shut your eyes again."

"It's hard alone."

"That doesn't matter."

Cynthia's fingers unclasped, and one hand closed desperately around Miss Egert's. Her heart fluttered in her temples, her throat, her breast. She clung to the fingers, pulling herself slowly up from an inarticulate abyss.

"Miss Egert,"—she stumbled into words,—"I can't bear it, not coming here! Nobody else cares except about sensible things. You do, beautiful, wonderful things."

"You'd have to find them for yourself, Cynthia." Miss Egert's fingers moved under the girl's grasp. Then she bent toward Cynthia, and kissed her with soft, pale lips that trembled against the girl's mouth. "Cynthia, don't let any one stop you! Keep searching!" She drew back, poised for a moment in the shadow before she rose. Through Cynthia ran the swift feet of white ecstasy. She was pledging herself to some tremendous mystery, which trembled all about her.

"Come, Cynthia, we're wasting our coals."

Miss Egert held out her hands. Cynthia, laying hers in them, was drawn to her feet. As she stood there, inarticulate, full of a strange, excited, shouting hope, behind them the path crunched. Miss Egert turned, and Cynthia shrank back.

Her mother stood in the path, making no response to Miss Egert's "Good evening, Mrs. Bates."

The fire had burned too low to lift the shadow from the mother's face. Cynthia could see the hem of her skirt swaying where it dipped up in front. Above that two rigid hands in gray cotton gloves; above that the suggestion of a white, strained face.

Cynthia took a little step toward her.

"I came to get my sketches," she implored her. Her throat was dry. What if her mother began to say cruel things—the things she had already said at home.

"I hope I haven't kept Cynthia too late," Miss Egert said. "We were going to toast marshmallows. Won't you have one, Mrs. Bates?" She pushed the glowing leaf-ashes together. The little spurt of flame showed Cynthia her mother's eyes, hard, angry, resting an instant on Miss Egert and then assailing her.

"Cynthia knows she should not be here. She is not permitted to run about the streets alone at night."

"Oh, I'm sorry." Miss Egert made a deprecating little gesture. "But no harm has come to her."

"She has disobeyed me."

At the tone of her mother's voice Cynthia felt something within her breast curl up like a leaf caught in flame.

"I'll get the things I came for." She started toward the house, running past her mother. She must hurry, before her mother said anything to hurt Miss Egert.

She stumbled on the door-step, and flung herself against the door. The portfolio was across the room, on the little, old piano. The candle beside it had guttered down over the cover. Cynthia pressed out the wobbly flame, and, hugging the portfolio, ran back across the room. On the threshold she turned for a last glimpse. The row of Botticelli details over the bookcases were blurred into gray in the light of the one remaining candle; the Indian rug had a wavering glow. Then she heard Miss Egert just outside.

"I'm sorry Cynthia isn't to come any more," she was saying.

Cynthia stepped forward. The two women stood in the dim light, her mother's thickened, settled body stiff and hostile, Miss Egert's slight figure swaying toward her gently.

"Cynthia has a good deal to do," her mother answered. "We can't afford to give her painting lessons, especially—" Cynthia moved down between the women—"especially," her mother continued, "as she doesn't seem to get much of anywhere. You'd think she'd have some pictures to show after so many lessons."

"Perhaps I'm not a good teacher. Of course she's just beginning."

"She'd better put her time on her studies."

"I'll miss her. We've had some pleasant times together."

Cynthia held out her hand toward Miss Egert, with a fearful little glance at her mother.

"Good-by, Miss Egert."

Miss Egert's cold fingers pressed it an instant.

"Good night, Cynthia," she said slowly.

Then Cynthia followed her mother's silent figure along the path; she turned her head as they reached the sidewalk. Back in the garden winked the red eye of the fire.

They waited under the arc light for the car, Cynthia stealing fleeting glances at her mother's averted face. On the car she drooped against the window-edge, away from her mother's heavy silence. She was frightened now, a panicky child caught in disobedience. Once, as the car turned at the corner below her father's office, she spoke:

"Father will expect me—"

"He knows I went after you," was her mother's grim answer.

Cynthia followed her mother into the house. Her small brother was in the sitting-room, reading. He looked up from his book with wide, knowing eyes. Rebellious humiliation washed over Cynthia; setting her lips against their quivering, she pulled off her sweater.

"Go on to bed, Robert," called her mother from the entry, where she was hanging her coat. "You've sat up too late as it is."

He yawned, and dragged his feet with provoking slowness past Cynthia.

"Was she down there, Mama?" He stopped on the bottom step to grin at his sister.

"Go on, Robert. Start your bath. Mother'll be up in a minute."

"Aw, it's too late for a bath." He leaned over the rail.

"It's Saturday. I couldn't get back sooner."

Cynthia swung away from the round, grinning face. Her mother went past her into the dining-room. Robert shuffled upstairs; she heard the water splashing into the tub.

Her mother was very angry with her. Presently she would come back, would begin to speak. Cynthia shivered. The familiar room seemed full of hostile, accusing silence, like that of her mother. If only she had come straight home from the office, she would be sitting by the table in the old Morris chair, reading, with her mother across from her sewing, or glancing through the evening paper. She gazed about the room at the neat scrolls of the brown wall-paper, at a picture above the couch, cows by a stream. The dull, ordinary comfort of life there hung about her, a reproaching shadow, within which she felt the heavy, silent discomfort her transgression dragged after it. It would be much easier to go on just as she was expected to do. Easier. The girl straightened her drooping body. That things were hard didn't matter. Miss Egert had insisted upon that. She was forgetting the pledge she had given. The humiliation slipped away, and a cold exaltation trembled through her, a remote echo of the hope that had shouted within her back there in the garden. Here it was difficult to know what she had promised, to what she had pledged herself—something that the familiar, comfortable room had no part in.

She glanced toward the dining-room, and her breath quickened. Between the faded green portières stood her mother, watching her with hard, bright eyes. Cynthia's glance faltered; she looked desperately about the room as if hurrying her thoughts to some shelter. Beside her on the couch lay the portfolio. She took a little step toward it, stopping at her mother's voice.

"Well, Cynthia, have you anything to say?"

Cynthia lifted her eyes.

"Don't you think I have trouble enough with your brothers? You, a grown girl, defying me! I can't understand it."

"I went down for this." Cynthia touched the black case.

"Put that down! I don't want to see it!" The mother's voice rose, breaking down the terrifying silences. "You disobeyed me. I told you you weren't to go there again. And then I telephoned your father to ask you to do an errand for me, and find you there—with that woman!"

"I'm not going again." Cynthia twisted her hands together. "I had to go a last time. She was a friend. I could not tell her I wasn't coming—"

"A friend! A sentimental old maid, older than your mother! Is that a friend for a young girl? What were you doing when I found you? Holding hands! Is that the right thing for you? She's turned your head. You aren't the same Cynthia, running off to her, complaining of your mother."

"Oh, no!" Cynthia flung out her hand. "We were just talking." Her misery confused her.

"Talking? About what?"

"About—" The recollection rushed through Cynthia—"about beauty." She winced, a flush sweeping up to the edge of her fair hair, at her mother's laugh.

"Beauty! You disobey your mother, hurt her, to talk about beauty at night with an old maid!"

There was a hot beating in Cynthia's throat; she drew back against the couch.

"Pretending to be an artist," her mother drove on, "to get young girls who are foolish enough to listen to her sentimentalizing."

"She was an artist," pleaded Cynthia. "She gave it up to take care of her father and mother. I told you all about that—"

"Talking about beauty doesn't make artists."

Cynthia stared at her mother. She had stepped near the table, and the light through the green shade of the reading-lamp made queer pools of color about her eyes, in the waves of her dark hair. She didn't look real. Cynthia threw one hand up against her lips. She was sucked down and down in an eddy of despair. Her mother's voice dragged her again to the surface.

"We let you go there because you wanted to paint, and you maunder and say things you'd be ashamed to have your mother hear. I've spent my life working for you, planning for you, and you go running off—" Her voice broke into a new note, a trembling, grieved tone. "I've always trusted you, depended on you: now I can't even trust you."

"I won't go there again. I had to explain."

"I can't believe you. You don't care how you make me feel."

Cynthia was whirled again down the sides of the eddy.

"I can't believe you care anything for me, your own mother."

Cynthia plucked at the braid on her cuff.

"I didn't do it to make you sorry," she whispered. "I—it was—" The eddy closed about her, and with a little gasp she dropped down on the couch, burying her head in the sharp angle of her elbows.

The mother took another step toward the girl; her hand hovered above the bent head and then dropped.

"You know mother wants just what is best for you, don't you? I can't let you drift away from us, your head full of silly notions."

Cynthia's shoulders jerked. From the head of the stairs came Robert's shout:

"Mama, tub's full!"

"Yes; I'm coming."

Cynthia looked up. She was not crying. About her eyes and nostrils strained the white intensity of hunger.

"You don't think—" She stopped, struggling with her habit of inarticulateness. "There might be things—not silly—you might not see what—"

"Cynthia!" The softness snapped out of the mother's voice.

Cynthia stumbled up to her feet; she was as tall as her mother. For an instant they faced each other, and then the mother turned away, her eyes tear-brightened. Cynthia put out an awkward hand.

"Mother," she said piteously, "I'd like to tell you—I'm sorry—"

"You'll have to show me you are by what you do." The woman started wearily up the stairs. "Go to bed. It's late."

Cynthia waited until the bath-room door closed upon Robert's splashings. She climbed the stairs slowly, and shut herself into her room. She laid the portfolio in the bottom drawer of her white bureau; then she stood by her window. Outside, the big elm-tree, in fine, leafless dignity, showed dimly against the sky, a few stars caught in the arch of its branches.

A swift, tearing current of rebellion swept away her unhappiness, her confused misery; they were bits of refuse in this new flood. She saw, with a fierce, young finality that she was pledged to a conflict as well as to a search. As she knelt by the window and pressed her cheek on the cool glass, she felt the house about her, with its pressure of useful, homely things, as a very prison. No more journeyings down to Miss Egert's for glimpses of escape. She must find her own ways. Keep searching! At the phrase, excitement again glowed within her; she saw the last red wink of the fire in the garden.

Helen Reimensnyder Martin

Mrs. Gladfelter's Revolt
1923

There is scant biographical information available about Helen Reimensnyder Martin (1868–1939). She was born in Lancaster, Pennsylvania, to Henrietta Thurman and the Reverend Cornelius Reimensnyder, an immigrant German Lutheran pastor. Educated as a special student in English at Swarthmore and Radcliffe, she taught at a fashionable private school in New York City where she came in contact with the wealthy. After her marriage to Frederic C. Martin, a music teacher, in 1899, they settled in Harrisburg, Pennsylvania, where Helen Martin began to write. She published a novel every year, eventually producing thirty-six novels and two volumes of short stories. The couple had one daughter and one son. She wrote for middle-class literate audiences, publishing stories in McClure's, Century, Cosmopolitan, and other periodicals. Her husband died in 1936 and she died three years later, at the age of seventy, in her daughter's home.

She had one subject—the oppression of women—which she explored in two settings: sophisticated white high society and rural Pennsylvania Dutch society. Her high-society novels were not well received until after she had achieved recognition and success with her ethnic material.

Her work was successfully translated to the stage and screen. Her most famous and frequently reprinted novel, Tillie: A Mennonite Maid (1904), was filmed in 1922 and produced on stage in 1924. Her 1914 Mennonite novel, Barnabetta, was turned into a play at the request of Minnie Maddern Fiske (1865–1932), one of the greatest theatrical artists in United States history.

After a two-year absence from the stage during which Fiske acted in the earliest cinematic versions of Thomas Hardy's Tess of the D'Urbervilles *(1913) and William Thackeray's* Vanity Fair *(1915), Fiske, who had introduced Henrik Ibsen to American audiences, returned to the stage in the starring role in "Erstwhile Susan" (1916), the theatrical version of* Barnabetta. *It was later made into a film. Finally, two of Martin's society novels became films:* The Parasite *(1913) in 1925, starring Owen Moore and Madge Bellamy, and* The Snob *(1924) in 1924, starring John Gilbert and Norma Shearer.*

Martin has been variously praised for the authenticity of her portrayals of the Pennsylvania German ethnic community and for the comic exaggerations of characteristics presumed to be typical of its members. She has also been castigated for those same exaggerations, which have been labeled extreme, unfair, and cruel caricatures. In a 1916 interview published in the New York Evening Post, *to defend herself from these attacks, she said,*

> . . . the Pennsylvania Dutchman is parsimonious with
> everything but the labor of his women. He'll buy modern
> plows, an automobile to take his products to market,
> modern harness to save his horse. Up-to-dateness in the
> barn means more money in his pocket. But he won't
> spend a cent to save his wife or daughter a bit of work.
> That is what they are for—to work for men folk in the
> kitchen or near it.

She campaigned actively for women's suffrage and for socialism. Seeing significant connections between capitalism and the organized church, she opposed both of them. Beverly Seaton, a modern critic, has written about Martin that her central message was "The absolute necessity for a person to be independent of others, educated, able to earn a living, free to choose a vocation," adding that, for a woman, "money of her own is the key to control of her own life."

"Mrs. Gladfelter's Revolt" was first published in The Nation *on October 10, 1923, and later collected in Martin's second volume of short stories,* Yoked With a Lamb and Other Stories, *1930, which, along with her 1907 collection,* The Betrothal of Elypholate and Other Tales of the Pennsylvania Dutch, *has recently been reprinted. Of her novels, only* Tillie *is now in print.*

Unlike Mary E. Wilkins Freeman's better-known story, "The Revolt of Mother," (in A New England Nun, *1891) with which many readers have compared this story, "Mrs. Gladfelter's Revolt" not only involves a confrontation with the husband/father who embodies patriarchal authority, but does so for the purpose of expanding opportunities for the daughter and initiating real changes in the lives of mother, daughter, and father. In addition, the undercurrent of sexual feeling between the parents makes the story more complex than most stories portraying the struggle of a mother with her husband for the sake of their daughter.*

Written only three years after passage of the Nineteenth Amendment and published less than one month before the 1923 general election, this story might also be read as encouragement to newly enfranchised women to exercise their right to vote and as discouragement to men from interfering with women's impetus to do so.

I

Although Jacob Gladfelter's four robust sons had come out from under the rule of his heavy hand as strong, self-reliant young men, his wife and his only daughter had become, year after year, more and more submissive and cowed. To be sure, Jacob had always been a little more tolerant of self-assertion on the part of the males of the household, seeing that they would, in the end, have to be their own masters; but as a woman must always, according to the Pennsylvania Dutch standard of what was "womanly," acquiesce in the dominance of a man, either her father or her "mister," there was not the same reason for relaxing one's sway over them as in the case of the boys.

It had never occurred to Meely, Jacob's wife, to question her man's right to rule his own household. She would have thought him less than a man and would not have respected him if he had not governed her and their children with a firm hand. From that night when, meeting her for the first time at a barn dance, he had boldly snatched her from her partner, carried her bodily to his own sleigh and driven away with her under the very eyes of her dumfounded and indignant escort, she had been his abject slave.

Her sons loved and petted their little mother and their comely young sister Weezy—and walked over them rough-shod. In this they only followed the example of their father. Although Jacob Gladfelter, prosperous proprietor of the only general store in Virginsville, had always been, according to his lights, a kind, indulgent husband and father, he was first and foremost a man of strict conscientious scruples and he would have considered himself just as sadly lacking in his duty if he had ever let his women folks get out of hand as if he had failed to be a "good-purvider" or had neglected to engage the best procurable midwife for his wife's many confinements, keeping her on the job for as much as two weeks—which in Virginsville was almost going to the ragged edge of sentimentality. Jacob's contempt for the few men of his acquaintance who were so weak as to "leave the women boss" was unutterable. Besides this, in spite of his reputedly amiable disposition, there was a streak of obstinacy in his character that, once he had taken a stand, would not let him yield.

So jealously did Jacob guard his prerogative to decide all household matters that for his wife and daughter to make a suggestion was only to invite a sure denial of what they wanted. If he indulged them it must be in his own way, at his own convenience, and in what *he* considered pleasant for them. Was a new carpet to be bought, Mr. Gladfelter selected it. He would see no point in consulting his wife's taste in the matter because if she did not share his decided preferences as to carpets her preference would, of course, have to be sacrificed; and if she did share them, no use to consult her. Did the kitchen range wear out, it was Jacob who said whether it should be replaced by a gas-cooking stove. And on such questions as the higher schooling of the children Jacob simply announced to her what he intended to do.

When suffrage was given to women the four Gladfelter boys were hilarious at the idea of "Mom's wotin'." Jacob, considering the Amendment unscriptural and subversive of a stable social order, laid down the law for his family: "I won't give you the dare to wote, Mom! As fur Weezy, till she's at the wotin' age, I guess she'll be married and it'll be fur her mister to say dare she wote or not."

"It wonders me how a man ever knows who *to* wote fur," said Mrs. Gladfelter. "The candidates all seems all right till they're *in* oncet—and then—"

"Yes, *and then!* You said it!" blustered her son Elmer. "And then it's hell! Ain't?"

"Yes, ain't!" responded all the men.

When Weezy reached the age for "sittin' up Sa'rdays and

keepin' comp'ny with a Steady-Regular," her father magnani-
mously told her one evening at supper that he would now get
a new suite of furniture for the parlor. He had expected this
news to be received with gratitude and pleasure by Weezy and
her mother, and he was surprised at the awkward silence that
answered him. The truth was Meely and Weezy had come to
dread Jacob's taste in household furnishings.

"Please, Pop," Weezy ventured, "don't get yellow!"

Mrs. Gladfelter looked anxiously across the supper table to
note the effect upon her husband of such boldness. Jacob, eating
sausage and fried potatoes, did not reply.

"Yellow kreistles me!" Weezy shuddered.

No reply from Jacob.

"I like red better or such dark blue."

Jacob noisily sipped his coffee.

"Sooner'n have yellow, I'd *let* the parlor."

"So would I!" Mrs. Gladfelter, unexpectedly though timidly,
spoke in. "It's going on twenty years that I lived with our parlor
furniture and I'm used to it a little. I'd sooner let it be than get
new."

"You always were so much for yellow, Pop!" pleaded Weezy.
"I wouldn't like to keep comp'ny with a fellow with yellow
furniture!"

"And it's Weezy would use the room, not us," Mrs. Gladfelter
reasoned, taking refuge in addressing her son Albert rather than
her husband. "If Weezy don't favor yellow, I think it's a pity to
get yel—"

"Be peaceable, Mom!" Jacob quietly ordered her, with that
look of deadly obstinacy on his face which she and Weezy knew
to be the stone wall to any further advancement of *their* side of
a question. But something in her daughter's wistful, worried
eyes made her, this evening, strangely persistent.

"Us we might as well get what Weezy would like and yellow
ain't just to say so tasty in parlor furniture—it's not so bad in
wallpaper or carpet, though I'd sooner purfer red or blue, like
Weezy says, but yellow furniture, yet—"

"Be peaceable, Mom!"

"But Weezy's gettin' full-growed now, and if she don't take to yellow, it's her has to set in the parlor, *we* never do, and it's her—"

"Mom! Be peaceable!"

And Mrs. Gladfelter, with a long sigh, subsided.

Mr. Gladfelter felt it to be his clear duty, in view of this incipient insubordination of his wife and daughter, to establish his rightful authority by getting a parlor suite of the yellowest yellow plush he could find.

It was when her father announced, upon Weezy's having finished the village school course, that she was now "done school," and must henceforth stay at home and help with the housework and the general store, that Mrs. Gladfelter, for the first time in her married life, was jolted into a real protest.

"Weezy not go to Millersville Normal!" she almost gasped, "like all our boys have went! But Pop! Me I always conceited you'd leave Weezy have schoolage, too, like our boys!"

Jacob did not think it necessary to offer any explanation of his decision.

"But Weezy she was always smarter'n any of our boys, Pop—her teachers all sayed she was smart! And she's always *counted* on goin' to Millersville Normal. She's planned all her life to be a school teacher!"

Jacob paid less attention to her plaints than he would have paid to a fly's buzzing.

"I always missed it so myself, not having no schoolage, Pop, I did think now my dotter was to have it! Why, look, Pop, how much better she could marry, too, if she got good educated!"

Weezy, during this monologue of her mother's, was silently weeping over her untasted supper.

Jacob, rising from the table, took a clothes-brush from a shelf, brushed first his clothes, then his hair with the same brush, and then, still without replying, turned away and walked into his store in the front of the house.

Mrs. Gladfelter regarded her weeping daughter in an agony of sympathy. That Weezy, so very much "smarter at the books" than her big brothers, should be denied an education for no other reason than that she was not a boy—for the first time in her life the bald unreasonableness and injustice of such a philosophy cut deep into her soul. She loved this daughter, her only girl, with a passionate devotion such as her rowdy, unmanageable boys had not called forth from her. Weezy, always so tender and thoughtful for her, was the poetry and romance of her life. It seemed to her that she could not calmly submit to this ruthless destruction of her child's dearest hopes. She suddenly rose, went to Weezy and put her arms about her. "Never you mind, Weezy, I've always counted on your gettin' a good education and you're *a-goin'* to get it! Don't cry! *You're not stoppin' your schoolage!*"

Weezy dried her eyes and looked at her mother incredulously. "But, Mom, what can we do if Pop says no? The more we coax, the more stubborn-headed he'll get!"

"I know that. We won't coax. But you're a-goin' to get your nice education all the same!"

"But how, Mom? How will you get round Pop?"

"You know I got my interest money?"

"But Pop never gives it to you."

"I've never ast it off of him. But it comes in sich little pieces of paper called cupons. Pop keeps 'em in the safe. They give six hundred dollars a year. They're mine. My Pop inherited 'em to me. That'll be enough to keep you at school."

"But, Mom, what would Pop *say* if you took them cupons?"

"I don't mind what he says compared to how I mind your not goin' to school. I got to just choose between them two things— Pop bein' cross at me or you losin' your schoolin'."

"I never saw Pop really cross at you, Mom!"

"I have never gave him no reason to be. He can't rightly have cross at me fur takin' what's my own. Your Pop's a awful honest man, Weezy. Why, here this morning, Sally Bergstresser come in our store to buy a spool of thread off Pop, and Pop he reminded her she owed him a cent on the last spool she got— her not having knew thread had went up a cent and having only five cents along that time. Pop tol' her, 'It ain't that I want that cent, Sally, but there's my income tax, you see. I got to be wery honest about that, you understand.' Sally she laughed till I thought she'd bust! She sayed, 'Now, Jake Gladfelter, if that ain't like you! Takin' the trouble to get your income tax right to the penny!—where *some* wouldn't bother none if they was off a dollar or more!' Yes, Weezy, your Pop is that pertikkler that folks laughs at him yet! So I can't see that he could get cross at me fur takin' my own."

"Does he think it *is* yours, Mom, when you're married to him?"

"Well, the law calls it mine."

"The law gives you dare to wote, too, and Pop won't leave you."

"It makes me nothing, Weezy, if Pop is cross, so long as I can get you a good education."

Weezy shook her head hopelessly. "I'm under age. Pop could fetch me home from Normal."

Her mother's eyes gleamed with an adventurous daring that made her look to Weezy like a stranger. "Could he? Then I'll put you to a school that he won't know where you're at!"

"Why, Mom, you don't sound like yourself!" Weezy softly exclaimed. almost alarmed.

"Where could I find out about another school, Weezy?"

"Uriah Bergstresser mebby could tell you, Mom."

"Yi Bergstresser! Him!" Her mother was skeptical. "Why, him he was that dumb at Millersville Normal that they shed him at the end of the term!"

"I know, but he's traveled 'round a good bit."

"Yes, that's so, too. I mind that time he was to New York over, with his Pop. You mind how he tol' us New York's so big they couldn't find the end of it!"

"You mind, Mom, how he told us about the nice things they're got in that Metropolitan *Mu*-zeem in New York? Sich mummies and all. Och, me, I'd like now to see that *Mu*-zeem! Ain't, Mom? You mind Yi said that as far as *he* could see, they didn't seem to use that great big handsome building for a thing 'ceptin' to store all them things!"

"If you think, Weezy, Yi *could* tell us the name of another school than Millersville Normal, I'll ast him right aways."

"All right, Mom."

II

One Sunday morning early in September, when Weezy and her mother started out as usual for church, the girl surprised her father by kissing him good-by. Demonstrations of family affection being rare among the Pennsylvania Dutch, kissing being scarcely ever indulged in even when parting for a long time, Jake was puzzled—and pleased. He was very fond of little Weezy.

"Ain't you some early startin'?" he asked.

"It gives such a nice day, we thought we'd walk a piece-ways," answered his wife.

When the mother and daughter reached the church, they did not go in, but walked on to the Square where you took the trolley to the near-by city of Lancaster. From Lancaster, Mrs. Gladfelter sent a telegram to her husband: "Taking Weezy to Normal School. Be home Wednesday."

They stopped in Lancaster with Mrs. Gladfelter's brother Sam, who had recently moved there from Columbia unknown to Jacob. On Monday Sam helped his sister procure money on her bond and Mrs. Sam went with her and Weezy to outfit the girl for school. For the first time in her life Weezy was permitted to choose her own clothes, never having presumed to object to wear whatever her father had seen fit to buy for her.

Not even to her brother and his wife would Mrs. Gladfelter trust her secret—the name of the Normal School to which she was taking her daughter. "Millersville Normal," the only one they had ever heard of, being just four miles from Lancaster, she knew that they (and her husband too) would assume that that was where Weezy was going.

"It wonders me, Meely, that Jake leaves *you* to tend to all this business for Weezy—the money and buyin' and all! It ain't like him! Is he sick or whatever, and how's your Monday washin' gettin' done?" asked her sister-in-law.

"Fur oncet I'm just lettin' the washin', Mame! I'm lettin' everything! Fur oncet I don't care! I feel that light-headed and indiff'runt, I don't har'ly know what's over me!"

"Mebby you better see a doctor—not? What does Jake say at your bein' so light-headed and indiff'runt?"

"It makes me nothing what he says!" laughed Meely.

"My souls, Meely, you *better* see a doctor—it must be some serious!"

But Meely only laughed.

She doubted not that Jacob, immediately upon receiving her

telegram on Sunday, had gone to "Millersville Normal" to force her and Weezy to come home. She marveled at her own unruffled calmness in contemplating his amazement at not finding them there.

"Do you think, Mom, you *can* keep it from Pop where I'm at?" Weezy wondered.

"Weezy, your Pop will *never get it out of me!*"

When the time came to part with her daughter and return home, Mrs. Gladfelter's high spirits suddenly dropped.

"Och, Mom, I hate for you to go back home and face Pop!" Weezy mourned.

"It ain't facin' your Pop, I mind. It's—the thought of what home will be without you, Weezy."

Weezy clasped her close. "Mom! I love you so!"

But on her homeward trip, Mrs. Gladfelter's sadness at leaving her daughter lifted somewhat and the unconquerable buoyancy that had possessed her ever since her flight was again in the ascendancy. This first and only adventure of her whole life, this first taste of freedom, had seemed to re-create her into a new being—she was almost a stranger to herself.

When at four o'clock on Wednesday afternoon she walked blithely through the general store where her husband and two of her sons were at the moment waiting on customers, she greeted them gayly as she passed on out to the sitting-room back of the store. "Well, Jake! Well, boys!"

The boys stared at her, too bewildered to reply. But her husband did not look up. Not until she called them all to supper did Jake deign to come near her, and even then he did not speak to her or even look at her as he sat down and at once began to help himself to fried "ponhaus" and "smear case." Meely suddenly realized that however strong she might be to meet reproaches, his holding himself silently and icily aloof from her would be more than she could live with! If *this* was to be the weapon with which he would try to wrest her secret from her and regain his dominance—

"I was talkin' to such a lady educator here the other day," she smilingly told them as she poured their coffee, "and she explained me the arguments how it's my dooty now to use the wote. So at the next election, Pop, I'm wotin'," she cheerfully stated.

Her husband made no sign. But the boys who, affected by their father's grim mood, had been discreetly silent, sent up a shout of laughter at the huge joke of their timid little mother's going to the polls to vote.

"Here's the new woman!"

"Have a cig-arette, Mom?"

"It wonders me you didn't have your hair so bobbed while you was to Lancaster over!"

After supper Jake at once went back into the store, still without speaking to her. She had expected him to demand, the moment she appeared at home, what she had done with Weezy; and she had been fully prepared to resist his insisting upon knowing. But when that night he went to sleep at her side without having spoken to her, she saw that until she voluntarily offered him the explanations and apologies he considered due him, he meant to hold himself thus aloof. She knew how stubbornly he could hold out in a course like this. She could not live with him in such alienation. It would kill her in a month! They had never quarreled before in all the twenty years of their married life.

The next morning she stopped him as he was about to go into the store. "Please, Pop, leave Al tend store till I speak somethin' to you."

Jake, directing Albert with a backward motion of his thumb to go into the store, stood still and waited for his wife to speak.

"I've made up my mind, Jake, fur our Weezy to have a nice education like you gev our boys—and, Jake, you better know right aways that if I have to die fur it, I'm a-goin' to see that she gets it!"

"Where's she at?"

"I'll tell you when you pass me your promise you won't go and fetch her home."

"Where's she at?" he repeated, bringing his knuckles down upon the table with a shock that rattled the dishes.

Meely's answer was to meet his cold eyes with such unflinching determination in her own that in his utter astonishment at its unfamiliarity, he relaxed, his jaw dropped, and he stared at her in confusion.

"Jake, I want fur my dotter to be somepin' more'n I always

was—a cabbage-head. Our Weezy's a-goin' to have her chanct to get more out of livin' than I ever had a'ready."

Jake stared at her stupidly, incredulously. "I don't favor females bein' book-learnt! It's agin Nature!"

"An awful lot of females is goin' agin Nature then, fur there's a thousand girls at that there Normal School Weezy's at. If I'd been a little book learnt myself, I guess I wouldn't o' waited *this* long till I took my own mind fur somepin' oncet!"

"Where is that Normal School where Weezy's at?"

"Do you pass your promise like I sayed?"

"Answer to me, Meely!"

"When you pass your promise!"

"Meely!" he exclaimed, utterly exasperated, "if I'd o' knowed you'd ever turn out like this here, I sure never woulda married you!"

"Why, Jake!" protested Meely, shocked, "when us we're got three growed children, it's har'ly maur'l to say such a thing as that!—that you wouldn't o' married me!"

"But I don't har'ly *know* you like this, Meely!—you seem like a stranger to me!"

"Well, but, Pop, that must seem a pleasant change to you. Me, I'd *like* it to have a little change. I'm awful used to you, Pop," she sighed. "A little change would do me good—"

"Meely! What fur talk is this?"

"Yes, well, I mean it, Jake. Sometimes I think I'm a little tired of you—that I do."

Again their eyes met and Jake, with a strange pang of fear in his heart, saw, in the straight, fearless gaze of the little woman whom, up to this hour, he had always regarded with a queer mingling of affection and contempt, that for once in his life he had encountered his match in obstinacy. Deep down in his soul he knew that he was beaten.

Tess Slesinger

Mother to Dinner
1935

Tess Slesinger's mother never forgave her for writing "Mother to Dinner," according to Janet Sharistanian, Slesinger's biographer.

Augusta Slesinger, daughter of a Russian-Jewish immigrant, had been the dominant presence in her daughter's childhood—and she was an extremely unconventional mother. She successfully directed a child guidance clinic, ran the Jewish Big Sister organization, and helped establish the New School for Social Research. Late in life, she became a dedicated psychoanalyst—while her husband, a Hungarian-Jewish immigrant who had studied to be a lawyer, plodded away in his father-in-law's business at a garment industry job he despised. On the day after their fiftieth wedding anniversary, Slesinger's parents separated and never saw one another again.

Tess Slesinger (1905–1945) observed her mother's competence, energy, and power—and absorbed her parents' liberal ideas about sexuality and self-expression. A neighbor reported her astonishment at the sight of Tess's brothers singing and dancing around a table in celebration of her first menstrual period.

As a child, Tess had declared that she would be a writer and nothing else. "I was born with the curse of intelligent parents, a happy childhood, and nothing valid to rebel against," she once said, "So I rebelled against telling the truth. I told whoppers at three, tall stories at four, a home-run at five: from six to sixteen I wrote them into a diary."

At Ethical Culture Society schools, Slesinger absorbed socialist ideals; at Swarthmore College she studied creative writing and Freud, and later claimed she had been dropped for flunking algebra and being caught smoking on campus. In 1927 she was graduated from the Columbia School of Journalism, where she studied fiction, and in 1928 she married Herbert Solow, the scholarly, intense assistant editor of the Menorah Journal, *a Jewish/Marxist magazine. The* Menorah Journal *crowd argued Marxism, pursued their ambitions as writers, and saw themselves as stars in the intellectual drama of the 1930s. In 1934 they picketed a publisher who, they felt, treated his staff unfairly—and Slesinger was one of eighteen writers arrested and jailed.*

Many of Slesinger's colleagues argued abstractly about "the workers" or "alienated labor" or "class politics," but Slesinger, a skeptic, took a down-to-earth personal view. In her short stories, many of her male characters declaim and act on high principles, but they miss the everyday details and emotional currents that women see. It was the friction between these emotional realities and the high principles that provided the conflict in many of the short stories she published in the Menorah Journal, The New Yorker, Scribner's, Vanity Fair, *and other prestigious magazines. In a late unfinished novel, Slesinger described a political organizer as "a brilliant imitation of a complex human being," but in her short stories she used pointed and poignant details to describe women, such as the daughter "sliding the bread into the shining modern breadbox" and feeling "a strong nostalgia for the worn-out tin that had stood for years on her mother's shelf."*

New York intellectual circles grew too narrow for Slesinger. Her marriage lasted only four years. She published The Unpossessed *(1934, reprinted 1984, The Feminist Press) and* Time: the Present *(her short story collection, 1935)— and headed west. She replaced an unfulfilling marriage with one combining love and work. With her second husband, Frank Davis, she wrote screenplays, gave birth to two children, and joined the bitter struggle to form the Screen Writers Guild.*

Slesinger's screen credits include "The Good Earth," based on Pearl Buck's novel about Chinese women's struggles for survival as wives and mothers and daughters. She also adapted A Tree Grows in Brooklyn, *Betty Smith's bittersweet novel about a girl's coming of age and learning to side with her mother in the battles between men and women.*

Slesinger rarely wrote short stories after she went to Hollywood and never finished her own second novel. She died of cancer in 1945 at the age of thirty-nine. Augusta Slesinger, who lived to be seventy-nine, outlived her daughter by seven years.

"Mother to Dinner" is about how daughters love, honor, fear, hide from, and long for their mothers—and how that mother-daughter knot is invisible to men. When Augusta Slesinger read "Mother to Dinner" as an insult from her daughter, she saw only the pain in it, and denied the longing.

Katherine Benjamin, who had been Katherine Jastrow for something less than a year, said Goodafternoon to the groceryman and, stooping to the counter, gathered two large and unwieldy packages close to her body, balancing one elbow on her hip so that the hand, crawling to the top, could hold sternly separate the bottle of milk from the package of Best Eggs. The thin, one-eyed errand boy who sprawled on an empty packing-box near the door leaped to his feet and opened it with a flourish and a "hot, isn't it?" And sliding past him, curving her body to make a nest for the projecting bundle, she heard the screen door swing lightly closed behind her, flutter against the wood frame in a series of gently diminishing taps.

Why did one say Goodafternoon instead of Goodbye to tradesmen and teachers, she wondered, following her packages as they bobbed evenly down the street before her, recalling (as she adjusted her gait to her burden) countless times when she had waited, in middies and broad sailor hats, for her mother's comforting "Good*morning*, Mr Schmidt," and Mr Schmidt's answering "*Good*morning, Mrs Benjamin, *good*morning I'm sure." And now Katherine, no longer in middies or accompanied by her mother but modestly wearing a ring on her left hand, heard herself kindly bidding Mr Papenmeyer Goodafternoon, and feeling, as she said it, very close to her mother, feeling almost, as she nodded firmly to him, that she was her mother. (Gerald predicted with scorn that it would not be long before Katherine would speak of Mr Papenmeyer as "my Mr Papenmeyer" and he suspected that she would even add, in time, "he never disappoints"; but she was not to suppose, he said, that he would glance benignly over his *Saturday Evening Post* as her father did, and listen.)

Katherine hugged her packages like babies; in them lay, wrapped in glossy wax paper, in brown paper bags, in patent boxes, the dinner to which Katherine's mother and father were coming as guests ... The dinner over which Katherine would frown at Gerald politely insulting Mrs Benjamin; over which Mr Benjamin would cough and insist on the worst cuts of everything ... She hoped nervously that Gerald would not be insolent and argumentative, that her mother would not be stupid. ... She must protect them both ... And she began to dread the strangeness which always oppressed her on beholding her mother in a house which was her home and not her mother's. ...

Ridiculous, she said brightly, I'm not going to let *that* happen again . . .

The spire of the church on the corner raised itself in the form of a huge salt-shaker against the mild, colorless sky. The sun, a blurred yellow lamp, glimmered palely behind veils of soiled cloud; it might rain, for the air was sodden, the leaves on the tree before the church hovered on the air with a peculiar waiting indifference, like dead fish turned over on their backs and floating in still water.

And for years to come she, "Mrs Gerald Jastrow," would walk, heavily laden with her thoughts and her packages, in Fall, in Winter, and in Spring, from Mr Papenmeyer's meat-and-grocery store through these same streets, past the church with its salt-shaker spire, past the row of low brick houses, past the tall india-rubber apartment with the liveried doorman shuffling his feet under the awning, stretched like a hollow wrinkled caterpillar to the curb, to her own home, which she shared with Gerald, of whom she had never heard two years before . . .

Katherine's fingers, tapping the sagging bundles, reviewed their contents. Meat—Mr Papenmeyer's recommended cut for four—bread, milk, corn, tomatoes—without her asking, the clerk had passionately assured her they were firm—two large packages it amounted to, one small slippery one under her elbow, and her purse. By a minute flexing of her left hand she could feel the key tucked neatly in her glove to save her trouble when she reached her door. An absurd ritual, that, said Gerald; one which in the sum total could not save her much trouble. You've picked up all these damn habits, he said, from your mother: they're a waste of time, they take more time to remember than simply to leave out; be careful, Katherine, before you know it you will be keeping a platinum-framed market-list. But these little rituals made doing the things fun, Katherine argued; when she re-membered, at the grocer's before picking up her packages, to tuck the key in her glove, a horde of vague recollections, almost recollections of recollections, unravelled pleasantly in her mind. They gave meaning to what would otherwise be just marketing; they formed a link not only with yesterday and tomorrow, but with other women squinting at scales and selecting dinners for strange men to whom they found themselves married; with, if you like, her mother, who had been doing these things every day for thirty years. You may say pooh Gerald, she said, but there are many things which you, who are after all a man, cannot be expected to know; why two years ago you didn't even know *me* . . .

Were the flat faces she had left haggling over green peas and punching cantaloupes aware of the waiting uncertainties, the uprooting, the transplanting, the bleeding, involved in their calmly leaving their homes to go to live with strangers? Strangers—husbands—Gerald A. Jastrow—I met a boy named Gerald A. Jastrow at a party, he asked to take me home—I am sorry, I am seeing a boy named Gerald Jastrow, he has a cowlick which trembles when he argues—but mother I am seeing Gerald tonight—Gerald says, Gerald thinks—I am going to be married—his name? (*whose* name?—oh, the Stranger's)—his name is Jastrow, Gerald Jastrow—I've been married for eleven months—my husband's name is Gerald Jastrow, no I don't know him, he's a Stranger to me, but I put away his male-smelling underwear. . . . Katherine reached the sidewalk just in time to avoid a cab which sped down the street in front of her house.

She smiled brightly at the elevator man, an expert, busy, kindly smile; she felt again like her mother. "Wouldn't be surprised if a storm blew up," Albert said to her shrewdly, resting his hand in a friendly way on the lever. (A storm, she didn't want a storm, Katherine thought, suddenly frightened; Gerald might say what he liked about the risk of motoring being greater than that of flying, and the chance of being murdered in sleep greater than that of being struck by lightning: she *wouldn't* fly, and she cowered before thunder and lightning.) "Oh do you think so?" said Mrs. Gerald Jastrow, and she looked in awe at the elevator man, as if it was all in his hands whether a storm came or not. "Oh I hope not," she pleaded. The elevator stopped on a level with her floor, her door was before her, familiar, with its arty streaks, its brass knob and keyhole, the number 21 in black painted letters. Albert, slamming the door of his cage, determined to go the whole hog. "Well I wouldn't be surprised," he said, and dropped suddenly out of sight.

Katherine could not bear to drop a single one of her burdens, now that she had come so far; she made a series of supreme efforts, balancing, juggling, squirming, forcing her key out of her glove with fractional, inch-worm motions, still carefully separating the bottle of milk from the package of Best Eggs, evoking a new muscle to keep the small package from slipping.

And then she was in, in her own house, with the door shut behind her, and the yellow curtains dancing on the window panes, the stove standing, homely and patient, in the small kitchen, the chairs sitting in friendly fashion, as if themselves guests at a tea-party, just as she had left them . . .

Suddenly she was overcome by a swift engulfing depression. She stood at the door of the yellow room and was unable to put down the packages in her arms. The air in the room stood hot and heavy, waiting, like Albert, with melancholy assurance, for storm; the curtains flapped treacherously.

What nonsense, she said crisply, amazingly comforted by a slant of faint sunlight which quivered through the gloom. Look, she said, it is my own house . . . Reassured, she dropped her packages on the kitchen table. But someone should be there to greet her, she felt, to rise from one of those friendly chairs and say to her: What did you buy? How was Mr Papenmeyer the butcher? Was the one-eyed errand boy there today? Come in, take off your hat and gloves, I am glad you are home . . . A year ago she would have stood at the door and shouted *Moth-er*, where *are* you? And if Mrs Benjamin had not come in haste at her call, a white-aproned German maid (Mrs Benjamin chaperoned their love-affairs so successfully that they generally stayed with her for years, like obedient nuns) would have come and said, Oh Miss Katy, your mother said to tell you she went over to your Aunt Sarah, your uncle's not feeling just right.

But she would call *up* her mother, she thought gleefully, running to the telephone: Hel*lo*, mother, what do you think I bought for supper? The butcher said . . . Do you think there will be a storm, mother? . . . As she lifted the receiver from its hook she thought she heard faint steps behind her; Gerald, she thought in a flash, and slid the receiver back to its place. Of course it wasn't Gerald, at four o'clock in the afternoon, of course it wasn't anybody; but suppose he had come upon her telephoning her mother: she could hear him say, as he had said last Sunday, catching her at the telephone (and of course one thought of one's mother on a long Sunday), Oh for God's sake, Katherine, like a two-year-old baby you are always running home to mother ... Cut off from her mother. Yet Gerald was right, she mustn't, she mustn't.

Loneliness surrounded Katherine like a high black fence. Then why not call up Gerald, why not rush to the telephone and call Gerald at his office (where she could never visualize him); if only she could call him up and say to him: I have just come home to our house. It is pleasant and cool, the curtains are still yellow. I shall take off my dress and read. Then I shall cook dinner, for you, for me, for my father and mother—you haven't forgotten they are coming? you'll come early?—*Gerald, what are you doing?* But she knew his firm "Jastrow speaking," and she could guess, if she dared to go beyond it, at his business-like: "What do you *want*, dear?" Well, what *did* she want, she wondered impatiently, and strained to discover whether that was thunder or furniture moving.

Probably Gerald was right, she thought wearily—for he was so often "right" in a logical, meaningless way—that thinking about every small thing, attaching significances to every moment, wishing to communicate every small thought, was, besides being sentimental, "an imbecilic waste of time." Gerald railed against sentimentality, and, charmingly, disarmingly, gave way to it at moments. When the moment passed Gerald shed it like a wet bathing suit, and emerged cool and casual, forgetful and untouched. But with her mother, these moments grew into comfortable hours, never forgotten, linking one with another, remaining always, a steady undercurrent, ready to rise and fill them at the lightest touch.

And sliding the bread into the shining modern breadbox she felt a strong nostalgia for the worn-out tin that had stood for years on her mother's shelf. This cold affair of shelves and sliding doors, glittering knobs and antiseptic lettering suggested too much newness, too little use and familiarity; her mother's loomed in contrast, a symbol of security, almost a refuge from storm. And yet Mrs Benjamin, with the vision of that old, battered, loyal thing in the back of her mind, had come with

Katherine graciously, gayly even, to buy this tawdry substitute. (My little girl, she had said to the clerk, smiling ironically at him and drawing him into her sympathy, would like that Modern Breadbox. It was as if she had said, My little girl has tired of her old mother, she wants the latest thing in young men, one that can scientifically explain away the fear of lightning.) Feeling warmly bound to her mother, she caught herself opening and slamming the little door a second, unnecessary time, an old nervous habit of her mother's. For a moment she felt purified, intensely loyal, as if by this gesture she had renounced the new for the old. She walked from the kitchen with her mother's tired, elastic step, the step of a stout woman who has shopped all day, whose weary body will neither submit to rest nor ignore the stern orders of fashion. It was a step singularly unsuited to Katherine's slimness, but it was comfortable now, familiar; she slid gratefully into it, like one falling into a cushioned rocker which is too large for the body but provides, nevertheless, a warm and comfortable harbor. And so she bent her body back from the waist and became her mother, balancing her stout body, carrying the heaviest part bravely before her. (Your mother navigates like a boat, Gerald had said to her once. Katherine, ruefully succumbing to the justice of the description, had come starkly awake on the edge of falling asleep that night, and cried bitterly, not because Gerald, whom she hated for sleeping soundly beside her, had said it, but because she had laughed.)

Oh of course Gerald was "right," she told herself. And yet, this coming home eagerly, her arms aching with pleasant weights, delighting in facing those yellow curtains again, with no one to greet her, and unable to telephone because what she had to say to her husband was irrelevant—her mother wouldn't like it, she felt. But between two people who lived together, why should anything be irrelevant? nothing she could ever say, she knew, would be irrelevant to her mother: how eagerly Mrs Benjamin had awaited reports of adventures no more important than a shopping expedition, a subway jam, a lunch engagement. (Oh but that had been stupid, stupid—inadequate. You told your mother insignificant things because you knew she wouldn't understand the important ones. Gerald's words: but true, true.) But Gerald himself had so *little* concern for the small things she did all day that she refrained from telling him anecdotes which she passionately feared might bore him, but which, nevertheless, she collected like bouquets of precious flowers to lay before him if she dared. Looking about the empty room, Gerald's desk standing solidly in one corner reproved her; she became irritated that her mind flew so often to thoughts of her mother. . . .

Like a human shuttle she wove her way between these two, between Gerald and her mother, the two opposites who supported her web. (Why couldn't they both leave her alone?) When she was with her mother she could not rest, for she thought continually of the beacon of Gerald's intelligence, which must be protected from her mother's sullying incomprehension. And when she was with Gerald her heart ached for her deserted mother, she longed for her large enveloping sympathy in which to hide away from Gerald's too-clear gaze. From sheer hopelessness and irritation, tears filled her eyes. . . .

She was glad to escape from the kitchen, for she had begun to hate Mr Papenmeyer's excellent foods, which would merge artfully and serve as the camouflage of a family battle. As long as the dinner lasted, she knew the conversation could be kept meager and on a safely mediocre level. But Katherine, sitting between her mother and father, and eyeing her husband with apprehension, would know that around her own table, consuming food she herself had prepared, a victim would be fattened for slaughter, a victor strengthened for battle. And whoever won, Katherine lost . . . Oh come, she told herself, exasperated, this isn't the Last Supper . . .

But that wasn't furniture moving, she told herself grimly, crouching on the window-sill and regarding the street which was lying quietly in its place before her house—not twice, she said, that's Albert's thunder. It rumbled from a great distance, as though it were in hiding.

Certainly, she thought, her mind returning, like a dog worrying a bone, she lived with Gerald on a higher plane—if her misery was sometimes more acute, her pleasure, in proportion, was more poignant. While they had felt nothing deeply, Katherine and her mother, as they had built up, over tea-tables, simple patterns of thought, simplified ways of looking at things. What if Katherine had had to stoop her mind so that they might stay together? at least they could talk, at least they kept each other company. (Gerald said their talk was no more than gossip; he said that Katherine and her mother had shut themselves up in a hot-house, talking and comforting each other for griefs that could never come to them while they remained in their lethargic half-life.) But in a world like this, thought Katherine, where thunder-storms can creep on one ruthlessly, why shouldn't two people who love each other hide away and give one another comfort?

Thunder rumbled more constantly now. Katherine, suspicious of it, in spite of its distance, detected in its muffled rolling a growing concentration, as if it were slowly gathering its strength, as if it were winding itself up for a tremendous spring. Should she telephone Gerald?—*no*.

The thought of Gerald frightened her. He led such a curious existence apart from her every day from nine till six. Katherine and her mother had always known exactly what the other was doing, at almost every hour in the day. It was a comfort to stop suddenly, look at one's watch, and think "Mother's at the dentist's now" or "I should think mother would be on the way home now." But there were times when Gerald was in the room with her, sitting beside her, lying beside her in bed, when she didn't know exactly where he was. . . .

Gerald said—and with some justice, she admitted to herself— that she and her mother had lived like two spoiled wives in a harem kept by a simple old gentleman who demanded nothing of them beyond their presence and the privilege of supporting them. But because of his docility one could not take seriously a possible injustice to him. Beside his work downtown, Mr Benjamin mailed their letters, called for their purchases, or did any of the little errands which they had spent the day in pleasantly avoiding. If he entered the room where Katherine and her mother were talking, it had seemed quite natural for Mrs Benjamin to say, "Dear, we are talking"; it seemed natural because of the peaceful expression with which Mr Benjamin picked up his *Saturday Evening Post* on the way out of the room. All Katherine's uncles were disposed of in the same way by her aunts.

Gerald referred to the Benjamin men as "poor devils," as "emasculated boobs". You resent me, he said to Katherine, because you have a preconceived idea of the rôle to which all husbands are relegated by their wives; you'd like to laugh me out of any important existence. (Indeed, it was only at moments when he was away and when she was performing, in his absence, some intimate service for him, that she could look upon Gerald as her mother looked upon her father; with ease, with possession, with a maternal tolerance touched by affectionate irony. Here were things of which she could be certain: that he rolled his underwear into a ball and dropped it on the floor, that he left his shoes to lie where they fell, that he draped yesterday's tie around the back of a chair. But she could never achieve this intimacy in his presence: when Gerald was with her, when she *thought* about Gerald, it faded; there was more strangeness.) Gerald again! She was aware of a wish to sink Gerald into the bottom of her mind: she was too much aware of him; when she read, when she visited, when she noticed things, it was always with the desire to report back to Gerald: nothing was complete until Gerald had been told.

She and her mother had discussed and reported everything. But she could no longer be alone with her mother, for it seemed as though Gerald sat in taunting effigy between them, forcing Katherine for her mother's sake to deprecate him, for his sake to protect him, from obscurity, from misrepresentation, from neglect . . .

His presence, even now, while she was alone, sat heavily, reproachfully, in the empty rooms, forbidding her to call him up, forbidding her to recall comfortably past days she had spent with her mother. This was not living, Gerald said, to spend one's hours in introspective analysis, to brood over the past. Katherine's flights he called "a worthless luxury, like the visits of the rich to Palm Beach or Paris." But it was living, Katherine knew unhappily; she was living most acutely.

The room darkened suddenly. Something of the tension which would be upon her later, as it always was when her mother and Gerald were in the same room, came upon her now, as she sat straining for the sound of thunder, watching shades of gloom silently lay themselves in the hot room. Katherine held her breath waiting for thunder, for rain, anything. Voices of children floated reassuringly up from the street, and in a moment the sunlight reappeared, tentative, tempting one to believe in it for all its faintness. The thunder sounded like the chopping of wood in a far-off field. Katherine longed for her mother. She wished she were not so near the heart of the storm.

She hated herself for thinking of her mother. But not to think of her demanded a complete uprooting, demanded a final shoving off from a safe dock into unknown waters. Besides, she felt guilty toward her mother, she brooded over her as one does over a victim, pitying him, resenting him and utterly unable to forget him.

For against her mother Katherine felt that she had committed a crime. She had abandoned that elderly lady for a young man who, from her mother's point of view, had been merely one of several who had taken her to dances, to dinner, who had kissed her in the parlor, with whom finally, inexplicably, she had come to have more dates than with any other. She had abandoned her mother, left her sitting at home with no more evening gowns to "take in", no one to sit up for, no young men to laugh about in the bathroom at four o'clock in the morning when Katherine came home. She had left her to sit opposite an old man at dinner every evening, she had imposed upon her the tragedy of being a guest in her own daughter's house; she had reduced her to a stranger.

But a little bit her mother had the advantage. She had seen Gerald, after all, in the absurd rig of tuxedo and stiff shirt, calling upon her daughter with flowers, with books, leaping to his feet when she (Mrs Benjamin) entered the room. She had watched Gerald for a year politely talking parlor politics with Katherine's father, posturing ridiculously when he held Katherine's coat, becoming perforce friendly with the elevator boys in the Benjamin apartment, slinking shamefacedly before a doorman who had seen him too often. Nothing, Katherine reflected, could be more unreal, more unconvincing, than a young man in the act of courting. She could never forgive Gerald for having let her mother observe him in that rôle. (Equally she could never forgive her mother, blameless as she was, for having seen him.) Her mother could never take seriously, surely, a marriage which had grown from love-making in taxi-cabs which had been reported to her with amusement by Katherine, brushing her teeth in the bathroom. She had not shared with her mother the tortuous transition which had left her no longer an amused observer, but a helpless, suffering participant. All the indication Mrs Benjamin had had of Katherine's growing need of Gerald was a burst of hysteria and a state of nervous irritability which had succeeded the usual calm of Katherine's disposition—before suddenly one evening, preparing her charity report in a black lace dress, she was confronted by two embarrassed young people who declared their ridiculous intention to marry.

This, Katherine felt, she should have spared her mother. She should not have caused her, so heartbreakingly, to drop her charity report on the marble table and to look suddenly at her daughter with reproachful eyes, saying, half-humorously, What, daughter, tired of your old mother already?

She had left her parents for no reason, they had given her no cause to leave them, she had left them for no better reason than that when Gerald said to her that he would never again ask her to marry him, she had been seized with panic lest he meant it.

Gerald, who two years before had not existed. Whereas her father and mother had fed her porridge, given her blackboards, measured her growth against a door, for a long period of twenty years during which Gerald had never heard of her. She was unsafe, she cried internally. She was living with a stranger in a strange land where storms evolved closely about one. She was living with a stranger who had no knowledge of the first twenty years of her life, the major portion of her life. She was living in a strange land where her childhood had no existence. It was unreal, it was unsafe, it was terrifying. Gerald liked to hear her tell stories of her childhood; but it was as if, when she told him little things she remembered, she and he were together contemplating the childhood of a stranger. She held tightly to the arms of her chair, but the slippery wood was repelling. Suddenly everything was reduced to an absurdity. It was, to Gerald, as though she had not begun to exist until he had noticed her two years before, at a party, and asked to take her home; but suppose

she had not come to the party—she had come only out of
boredom; or suppose, to make it more ridiculous, she had not
worn the particular blue dress which had caught Gerald's eye?
and he hadn't asked to take her home? Their life together
seemed no more than the result of a series of insignificant
accidents. Could it be real? Could she share the rest of her life
with a stranger whose eye had casually fallen on a blue dress?
With someone who had known her for only two years out of
her twenty-two?

Katherine felt herself to be struggling somewhere in the
middle, between two harbors, unable to decide whether to swim
backward or forward, tempted almost to close her eyes and
quietly drown where she was. Shuttle, shuttle, she murmured
to herself, miserably, exasperated at her weakness, her helplessness.

Smoking in the yellow room, she waited with unhappy certainty
for Albert's storm which would surely come now. The air was
oppressive, sullenly pregnant. It was as if an evil thing crouched
in the room, waiting for birth. Dark was gathering in shades,
permitting still a faint yellowish gloom. Wind was dead. Katherine, fearing and hating the coming storm, nevertheless feared
and hated the moments of waiting even more. A clock on the
mantel slowly ticked off the moments she would have to wait; it
was in league with the coming storm. Her body was chill in the
midst of heat.

She was weary already with the nervous effort she would make
to bring Gerald and her mother close to each other, with her
own struggle to remain equally close to both of them, simulta-
neous with her desperate attempt to conceal from each the
affection she felt for the other. Gerald and her mother sitting
and eating in this room, which now was the home of the storm,
would be a cat and mouse, quietly stalking each other under
cover. (Was this true? or did their struggle for supremacy take
place merely in her own mind? Because she must know, she
must know.) Katherine would twist herself this way and that to
keep the evening characterless and blessedly dull, rather than
immerse them all in the horror of an argument, in which their
superficial sides would represent symbolically their eternal,

fundamental resentment. Katherine must take no sides, Katherine must flit nervously from one side to the other, breaching gaps with hysterical giggles, throwing herself into outbursts of hysterical affection, making a clown of herself in order to distract these two who fought silently for her. She was loathsome to herself.

Her mind struggled with a remote memory. Something—perhaps the slumbering quality of the air which sheltered the coming storm so that its pent-up evil would suddenly roll forth and smother the world—reminded her of a thing which seemed to have happened when she was a child. Frowning, she gazed into herself to recall. And it came back to her. She had cried one day for her mother and they had told her that Mrs Benjamin had gone to Atlantic City for two days and that this young lady would take care of Katherine while her mother was away. Katherine kicked and screamed, but Miss Anna proved so entertaining—she showed her how to make a whole family of paper dolls live through a day's work and play—that she forgot her mother and was surprised to hear the next day that she would be home in an hour. Suddenly she hated Miss Anna, and when Mrs Benjamin came home she found her daughter crying angrily, Miss Anna bewildered, murmuring, But she seemed so happy, she seemed perfectly happy . . . I was not happy for a minute, Katherine screamed, I was waiting the whole time for my mother to come back.

Enraged with herself, she wondered whether she retained somewhere the idea that because her life had begun with her mother, it would end with her, whether some childish part of her could not accept their parting as final and looked upon her life with Gerald as no more than an interlude. Oh Gerald, Gerald, she sobbed, I am worse than unfaithful to you . . . I hate my mother, she is a venomous old woman who tries to keep me from you. . . . The injustice to her mother overwhelmed her. She hated herself. She felt like the child of divorced parents, driven from one to the other and unable with either to make a home.

I have been married during every month except June, she thought, lifting her head and quietly looking, as if to remember, about the room. She was comforted by Gerald's desk, which had been with her during eleven months. Thunder, blasting the earth in a distant place, filled the room. She had been married for eleven months and had never told her mother anything but housekeeping troubles. Why? A second roll of thunder sounded.

She was surrounded, she could not escape. She was suspended, she could take refuge with neither Gerald nor her mother, she was caught fairly by the thunder . . .

Deception had begun with her engagement. One had to keep one's eyes constantly glowing, however terrifiedly they looked at the approaching cliff, one's words constantly gay and effervescent, lest one's mother look searchingly at the prospective bride and say, But are you sure, Darling, absolutely *sure*? Of course one was not sure. One was suspended, even as now, with thunders rolling in from all sides. (I ought to start the dinner, I ought to start the dinner: I *can't*, I can't.)

During a wedding trip one was awakened to innumerable things, most of them delightful, all of them terrifying. A longing had filled Katherine intermittently to be back from this trip of surprises: she pictured herself talking to her mother all day for many days, sharing with her, not details, but the contemplation, of intimacies. It seemed to her the most delicious part of the trip, that she would return and talk about it to her mother. Gerald's jealous allusions to her mother she had accepted with a tolerant smile; his analyses—for it was then that he had violently expounded his harem theory—meant nothing to her, they seemed to have no connection with reality. "Dearest mother," she had written, "all the things I have to tell you! I can hardly wait to see you . . . So many things have happened. And of course, Gerald being a man . . ." (Was that lightning, or was it the mere lifting of the curtain by the wind? The dinner, the dinner was waiting to be cooked: I won't *touch* it.)

The awful farce at the station, where Mr and Mrs Benjamin had come to meet them, came to her vividly now. Mr Benjamin, having screwed his courage to the point of making Katherine remember his presence long enough to kiss him, retiring to help Gerald, competently wasting time with the luggage in the background, mother and daughter swaying in a series of embraces—Katherine was suddenly lost, locked, imprisoned, in the body of a stout, fashionable stranger. Why doesn't she look at me? she thought, all she wants is to hold me, to squeeze me, to choke me to death, it never occurs to her to look in my face. Sweeping her daughter to one side, Mrs Benjamin sprang forth to smother Gerald. She had no right to, cried Katherine wildly to herself, as she turned from her father's vague embrace, and all the things which Gerald had said of her mother came back to her and they seemed true. And at the same time she felt passionately that Mrs Benjamin must not expose herself to Gerald's unsympathetic eye; horrible embarrassment arose in her, when, thank God, she saw that Mrs Benjamin in her eagerness had missed her aim; her kiss floated on past Gerald's clean indifferent cheek—he at least was unsullied, and at the same time her mother was protected from nakedness. Mrs Benjamin, discarding Gerald, threw her arms around Katherine once more, with force and meaning, and kissed her in great wet gulps. "Katherine, Katherine," she sobbed, rocking her great body from side to side, "I've got you again, darling. Let's leave all these men and go off together, darling." Katherine felt fastidious, she drew her body back delicately from the impact of her mother's.

Mrs Benjamin shook off the two men, she carried Katherine off to a tea-room—their old favorite tea-room—for lunch, a confidential lunch it was supposed to be, but Katherine had grown to hate tea-rooms, a month with Gerald had taught her to hate shrimp salad . . . Mrs Benjamin, suddenly squeezing her hand under the candle-lit table, looked into her eyes, her own eyes fatuous, confident, worried and questioning, "Katherine, darling Katherine, now tell me the 'many things' you wrote about." Katherine, looking into her mother's avid eyes, knew that she could never tell her anything again.

How horribly she must have hurt her, thought Katherine, gravely hurt herself at the recollection. In bed beside Gerald that night she had lain, trying to make the night go faster, so that she might see her mother and change what she had done. She thought of her mother lying sleepless, even as she was, beside a sleeping husband, thinking, bitterly thinking, of the thing that had happened between them. But Katherine could never undo the thing that was between them, for it was Gerald who stood between her mother and herself, just as her mother stood between herself and Gerald.

Well, *was* Albert's storm coming or wasn't it, she thought impatiently, and beat out her cigarette on the window-sill, dropped the dead stub and watched it hurtle past awnings and window-boxes and land haphazardly in the gutter. (And what about the dinner?)

A clap of thunder brought her trembling to her feet. It had traveled with treacherous silence from a great distance to burst like a shell in her ear. And now lightning quivered across the pewter sky in a blinding streak. Katherine, trembling, holding to the mantel, felt all the elements of storm gathering closely about her. The intense heat and stillness in the room vibrated with suppressed force. She had a sense of something evil, something unhealthy, waiting beneath the table to be born. The room was alive, awake, crouching before the storm, waiting in every sense for its approach.

She laughed aloud, nervously, when the thunder sounded next, meek and far-off; it rumbled for a few seconds, then it rolled toward her with increasing force until something cut it off sharply in the height of its passion. The storm was playing with her; it was here, but it played at hiding, it retreated and advanced so that she could never be sure of it.

What was she to do, what was she to do? Should she, could she telephone?—*no*.

Thunder shook the house. Malicious streaks of lightning drew themselves across the sky, lighting up the gloom until the day shone for a second like steel. Suddenly night came. Winds came alive and tore drunkenly down the street. Another long reverberating crash of thunder, incredibly near and ear-splitting. There was a moment of suspension, while only the wind moved. And then the sky retched and large cold drops of rain like stones pelted the windowpanes . . .

Panic seized Katherine. She rushed to the window to escape. She was afraid of the room. It rocked with unhappy speculation. She stood at the window facing in, and saw how the storm was fed from within her room. The lightning lit it like quick fire, the thunder sounded in it long after it had died outside.

The thunder bounced about the room, striking at corners, rolling over furniture, shaking the walls, groveling derisively at her feet.

It seemed to her that before the next clap of thunder she must have reached a decision or she would die. But what decision, she cried, striking her fist against the window? What decision? about what? The problem was obscure. (She imagined her mother struck by lightning, her stout body collapsing with dignity under a tree, she heard herself telling Gerald with triumph as an overtone to her grief, My mother is dead, I have only you now.) And if the problem was obscure, how much more obscure the solution. (She imagined Gerald struck by lightning, a look of hurt surprise in his eyes as he fell beneath a tree, murmuring something about scientific chance, she heard herself telling her mother, strange relief mingling with her sorrow, Gerald is gone, mother, I shall have to come back to you.) And the next thunder rolled down a hill, louder and louder, faster and nearer, and fell to the bottom, bursting into cannon balls, exploding with insane crashes, and in a thousand voices splitting the earth in its center. Katherine burst into passionate tears.

Now everything was the storm. The storm, which had circled about the room, wished for closer nucleus, and entered her body. The lightning pierced her stomach, the thunder shook her limbs, and retreated, growling, to its home in her bowels. There was no escape for her; she was no longer imprisoned in the storm: the storm was imprisoned in her.

She stood in a shaking lethargy, she had no will, no feeling. She was frozen; she was a shell in which storm raged without her will. All the world had entered the room . . .

It came to her slowly that there was a new sound in the air, a sharp metallic ring that repeated itself at intervals. She had no idea how long she might have been hearing it in the back of her head before she took notice of it. Now it rang again, sharply, there seemed to be fright in it, or anger, she could not tell which. On stiff legs she ran down the hall toward the door, by reflex knowing that it was the doorbell which had sounded. But with her hand on the knob something held her back. She could not force herself to turn the knob, to move her hand, even to call out, Wait, wait . . .

Was it her mother, or was it Gerald? Which, in the midst of storm, did she want it to be? It seemed to her that she could not open the door until she knew. A great ball of thunder followed her out of the room she had left, hurtled down the hall and broke beside her, and in the midst of it the terrified bell rang repeatedly, in small staccato notes, shrilling through the depth of the thunder, prodding . . .

She did not know. She knew only, as she closed her eyes and slowly turned the handle of the door, and drew it in toward herself, that she wished that one of them, Gerald or her mother, were dead.

Hisaye Yamamoto

Seventeen Syllables
1949

The second of eight stories by Hisaye Yamamoto published between 1948 and 1961, "Seventeen Syllables" first appeared in Partisan Review *in November 1949. A 1951 story, "Yoneko's Earthquake," which also has a mother-daughter theme, was included in Martha Foley's* Best American Short Stories *of 1952. Since 1969, five of Yamamoto's stories have been reprinted at least twenty times in one or more of twelve anthologies specializing either in Asian-American, United States minority, regional, or women writers. For more than twenty-five years, Yamamoto has contributed poetry, book reviews, essays, and reminiscences to a variety of Japanese-American publications. Herself a Nisei (second generation Japanese American), she has written with tenderness and humor about the relationships between Japanese immigrants and their American-born children and grandchildren. She has also written about the experience of Japanese Americans incarcerated in U.S. prison camps during World War II.*

Hisaye Yamamoto was born in Redondo Beach, California in 1921 and grew up in various small southern California towns. Her parents had emigrated from Kumamoto, Japan. She studied at Excelsior Union High School and Compton Junior College, majoring in foreign languages. She received encouragement from an English teacher, Lela May Garver, and became friendly with several other young Asian-American women interested in writing. Then came World War II and she, along with 110,000 other Japanese Americans, was subjected to relocation and imprisonment mandated by the Japanese Relocation Act of 1942.

During the war, she moved to Massachusetts for a summer, but returned to camp, and then to California in 1945, where she was employed by the Los Angeles Tribune, *a black weekly newspaper. Her brother Jemo helped support her for a few months when she left the* Tribune *to try writing full time. An insurance bequest from her brother Johnny, killed at the age of nineteen fighting with the American army in Italy, added more time to that struggle. In 1950 she was awarded a John Hay Whitney Foundation Opportunity Fellowship. She was already raising an adopted son and, although the support included funds for nearby babysitting, she remembers in "Writing," an autobiographical essay, that " . . . he used to pound on the door, demanding to be let in, or he would wedge himself between the typewriter and me and, spreading out his arms, say, 'Don't type!' " In her thirties, she married Anthony De Soto and became the mother of four more children. She is now also a grandmother.*

Frank Chin and Shawn Wong, co-editors of Yardbird Reader, No. 3, *a 1974 collection of Asian-American writing, have called her "Asian America's most accomplished living fiction writer." However, in "Writing," she states, "But, alas, when I have occasion to fill out a questionnaire, I must in all honesty list my occupation as housewife."*

"Seventeen Syllables" weaves together several of the mother-daughter categories, for it is an occasional story commemorating two life-cycle events: a daughter's menarche and a mother's death. It is a "disgraceful mother" story, and a story about multiple confrontations with the patriarchy, a story speaking to the experiences of multiple oppressions—racism and classism as well as sexism. Commenting on the story in a letter (March 12, 1984), Yamamoto writes,

> . . . it is so painful, when I think of how [my mother] could have used a more understanding daughter at the time—but, of course, I was wrapped up in myself at that age. Even though none of the details are true, "Seventeen Syllables" is [my mother's] story. It is the most reprinted of all the stories. Maybe she, wherever she is, guided the writing of it, and, even now, the propagation of it—in textbooks yet, from junior high to community college level—so her story would be known. Or is this too far-fetched to contemplate?

"Seventeen Syllables," like so many of the stories in this collection, is a testimony of a daughter's powerful love and respect for her mother. The existence of such stories is strong evidence of the history of love and alliance between mothers and daughters.

The first Rosie knew that her mother had taken to writing poems was one evening when she finished one and read it aloud for her daughter's approval. It was about cats, and Rosie pretended to understand it thoroughly and appreciate it no end, partly because she hesitated to disillusion her mother about the quantity and quality of Japanese she had learned in all the years now that she had been going to Japanese school every Saturday (and Wednesday, too, in the Summer). Even so, her mother must have been skeptical about the depth of Rosie's understanding, because she explained afterwards about the kind of poem she was trying to write.

See, Rosie, she said, it was a *haiku*, a poem in which she must pack all her meaning into seventeen syllables only, which were divided into three lines of five, seven, and five syllables. In the one she had just read, she had tried to capture the charm of a kitten, as well as comment on the superstition that owning a cat of three colors meant good luck.

"Yes, yes, I understand. How utterly lovely," Rosie said, and her mother, either satisfied or seeing through the deception and resigned, went back to composing.

The truth was that Rosie was lazy; English lay ready on the tongue but Japanese had to be searched for and examined, and even then put forth tentatively (probably to meet with laughter). It was so much easier to say yes, yes, even when one meant no, no. Besides, this was what was in her mind to say: I was looking through one of your magazines from Japan last night, Mother, and towards the back I found some *haiku* in English that delighted me. There was one that made me giggle off and on until I fell asleep—

> It is morning, and lo!
> I lie awake, comme il faut,
> sighing for some dough.

Now, how to reach her mother, how to communicate the melancholy song? Rosie knew formal Japanese by fits and starts, her mother had even less English, no French. It was much more possible to say yes, yes.

It developed that her mother was writing the *haiku* for a daily newspaper, the *Mainichi Shinbun*, that was published in San Francisco. Los Angeles, to be sure, was closer to the farming community in which the Hayashi family lived and several

Japanese vernaculars were printed there, but Rosie's parents said they preferred the tone of the northern paper. Once a week, the *Mainichi* would have a section devoted to *haiku,* and her mother became an extravagant contributor, taking for herself the blossoming pen name, Ume Hanazono.

So Rosie and her father lived for awhile with two women, her mother and Ume Hanazono. Her mother (Tome Hayashi by name) kept house, cooked, washed, and, along with her husband and the Carrascos, the Mexican family hired for the harvest, did her ample share of picking tomatoes out in the sweltering fields and boxing them in tidy strata in the cool packing shed. Ume Hanazono, who came to life after the dinner dishes were done, was an earnest, muttering stranger who often neglected speaking when spoken to and stayed busy at the parlor table as late as midnight scribbling with pencil on scratch paper or carefully copying characters on good paper with her fat, pale green Parker.

The new interest had some repercussions on the household routine. Before, Rosie had been accustomed to her parents and herself taking their hot baths early and going to bed almost immediately afterwards, unless her parents challenged each other to a game of flower cards or unless company dropped in. Now, if her father wanted to play cards, he had to resort to solitaire (at which he always cheated fearlessly), and if a group of friends came over, it was bound to contain someone who was also writing *haiku,* and the small assemblage would be split in two, her father entertaining the nonliterary members and her mother comparing ecstatic notes with the visiting poet.

If they went out, it was more of the same thing. But Ume Hanazono's life span, even for a poet's, was very brief—perhaps three months at most.

One night they went over to see the Hayano family in the neighboring town to the west, an adventure both painful and attractive to Rosie. It was attractive because there were four Hayano girls, all lovely and each one named after a season of the year (Haru, Natsu, Aki, Fuyu), painful because something had been wrong with Mrs. Hayano ever since the birth of her first child. Rosie would sometimes watch Mrs. Hayano, reputed to have been the belle of her native village, making her way about a room, stooped, slowly shuffling, violently trembling (*always* tembling), and she would be reminded that this woman, in this same condition, had carried and given issue to three babies. She would look wonderingly at Mr. Hayano, handsome, tall, and strong, and she would look at her four pretty friends. But it was not a matter she could come to any decision about.

On this visit, however, Mrs. Hayano sat all evening in the rocker, as motionless and unobtrusive as it was possible for her to be, and Rosie found the greater part of the evening practically anaesthetic. Too, Rosie spent most of it in the girls' room, because Haru, the garrulous one, said almost as soon as the bows and other greetings were over, "Oh, you must see my new coat!"

It was a pale plaid of grey, sand, and blue, with an enormous collar, and Rosie, seeing nothing special in it, said, "Gee, how nice."

"Nice?" said Haru, indignantly. "Is that all you can say about it? It's gorgeous! And so cheap, too. Only seventeen-ninety-eight, because it was a sale. The saleslady said it was twenty-five dollars regular."

"Gee," said Rosie. Natsu, who never said much and when she said anything said it shyly, fingered the coat covetously and Haru pulled it away.

"Mine," she said, putting it on. She minced in the aisle between two large beds and smiled happily. "Let's see how your mother likes it."

She broke into the front room and the adult conversation, and went to stand in front of Rosie's mother, while the rest watched from the door. Rosie's mother was properly envious. "May I inherit it when you're through with it?"

Haru, pleased, giggled and said yes, she could, but Natsu reminded gravely from the door, "You promised me, Haru."

Everyone laughed but Natsu, who shamefacedly retreated into the bedroom. Haru came in laughing, taking off the coat. "We were only kidding, Natsu," she said. "Here, you try it on now."

After Natsu buttoned herself into the coat, inspected herself solemnly in the bureau mirror, and reluctantly shed it, Rosie, Aki, and Fuyu got their turns, and Fuyu, who was eight, drowned in it while her sisters and Rosie doubled up in amusement. They all went into the front room later, because Haru's mother quaveringly called to her to fix the tea and rice cakes and open a can of sliced peaches for everybody. Rosie noticed that her mother and Mr. Hayano were talking together at the little table— they were discussing a *haiku* that Mr. Hayano was planning to send to the *Mainichi*, while her father was sitting at one end of the sofa looking through a copy of *Life*, the new picture magazine. Occasionally, her father would comment on a photograph, holding it toward Mrs. Hayano and speaking to her as he always did—loudly, as though he thought someone such as she must surely be at least a trifle deaf also.

The five girls had their refreshments at the kitchen table, and it was while Rosie was showing the sisters her trick of swallowing peach slices without chewing (she chased each slippery crescent down with a swig of tea) that her father brought his empty teacup and untouched saucer to the sink and said, "Come on, Rosie, we're going home now."

"Already?" asked Rosie.

"Work tomorrow," he said.

He sounded irritated, and Rosie, puzzled, gulped one last yellow slice and stood up to go, while the sisters began protesting, as was their wont.

"We have to get up at five-thirty," he told them, going into the front room quickly, so that they did not have their usual chance to hang onto his hands and plead for an extension of time.

Rosie, following, saw that her mother and Mr. Hayano were sipping tea and still talking together, while Mrs. Hayano concentrated, quivering, on raising the handleless Japanese cup to her lips with both her hands and lowering it back to her lap. Her father, saying nothing, went out the door, onto the bright porch, and down the steps. Her mother looked up and asked, "Where is he going?"

"Where is he going?" Rosie said. "He said we were going home now."

"Going home?" Her mother looked with embarrassment at

Mr. Hayano and his absorbed wife and then forced a smile. "He must be tired," she said.

Haru was not giving up yet. "May Rosie stay overnight?" she asked, and Natsu, Aki, and Fuyu came to reinforce their sister's plea by helping her make a circle around Rosie's mother. Rosie, for once, having no desire to stay, was relieved when her mother, apologizing to the perturbed Mr. and Mrs. Hayano for her father's abruptness at the same time, managed to shake her head no at the quartet, kindly but adamant, so that they broke their circle to let her go.

Rosie's father looked ahead into the windshield as the two joined him. "I'm sorry," her mother said. "You must be tired." Her father, stepping on the starter, said nothing. "You know how I get when it's *haiku*," she continued, "I forget what time it is." He only grunted.

As they rode homeward, silently, Rosie sitting between, felt a rush of hate for both, for her mother for begging, for her father for denying her mother. I wish this old Ford would crash, right now, she thought, then immediately, no, no, I wish my father would laugh, but it was too late: already the vision had passed through her mind of the green pick-up crumpled in the dark against one of the mighty eucalyptus trees they were just riding past, of the three contorted, bleeding bodies, one of them hers.

Rosie ran between two patches of tomatoes, her heart working more rambunctiously than she had ever known it to. How lucky it was that Aunt Taka and Uncle Gimpachi had come tonight, though, how very lucky. Otherwise, she might not have really kept her half-promise to meet Jesus Carrasco. Jesus, who was going to be a senior in September at the same school she went to, and his parents were the ones helping with the tomatoes this year. She and Jesus, who hardly remembered seeing each other at Cleveland High, where there were so many other people and two whole grades between them, had become great friends this Summer—he always had a joke for her when he periodically drove the loaded pick-up up from the fields to the shed where she was usually sorting while her mother and father did the packing, and they laughed a great deal together over infinitesimal repartee during the afternoon break for chilled watermelon or ice cream in the shade of the shed.

What she enjoyed most was racing him to see which could finish picking a double row first. He, who could work faster, would tease her by slowing down until she thought she would surely pass him this time, then speeding up furiously to leave her several sprawling vines behind. Once he had made her screech hideously by crossing over, while her back was turned, to place atop the tomatoes in her green-stained bucket a truly monstrous, pale green worm (it had looked more like an infant snake). And it was when they had finished a contest this morning, after she had pantingly pointed a green finger at the immature tomatoes evident in the lugs at the end of his row and he had returned the accusation (with justice), that he had startlingly brought up the matter of their possible meeting outside the range of both their parents' dubious eyes.

"What for?" she had asked.

"I've got a secret I want to tell you," he said.

"Tell me now," she demanded.

"It won't be ready till tonight," he said.

She laughed. "Tell me tomorrow then."

"It'll be gone tomorrow," he threatened.

"Well, for seven hakes, what is it?" she had asked, more than twice, and when he had suggested that the packing shed would be an appropriate place to find out, she had cautiously answered maybe. She had not been certain she was going to keep the appointment until the arrival of her mother's sister and her husband. Their coming seemed a sort of signal of permission, of grace, and she had definitely made up her mind to lie and leave as she was bowing them welcome.

So, as soon as everyone appeared settled back for the evening, she announced loudly that she was going to the privy outside. "I'm going to the *benjo!*" and slipped out the door. And now that she was actually on her way, her heart pumped in such an undisciplined way that she could hear it with her ears. It's because I'm running, she told herself, slowing to a walk. The shed was up ahead, one more patch away, in the middle of the fields. Its bulk, looming in the dimness, took on a sinisterness that was funny when Rosie reminded herself that it was only a wooden frame with a canvas roof and three canvas walls that made a slapping noise on breezy days.

Jesus was sitting on the narrow plank that was the sorting platform and she went around to the other side and jumped backwards to seat herself on the rim of a packing stand. "Well, tell me," she said, without greeting, thinking her voice sounded reassuringly familiar.

"I saw you coming out the door," Jesus said. "I heard you running part of the way, too."

"Uh-huh," Rosie said, "Now tell me the secret."

"I was afraid you wouldn't come," he said.

Rosie delved around on the chicken-wire bottom of the stall for number two tomatoes, ripe, which she was sitting beside, and came up with a left-over that felt edible. She bit into it and began sucking out the pulp and seeds. "I'm here," she pointed out.

"Rosie, are you sorry you came?"

"Sorry? What for?" she said. "You said you were going to tell me something."

"I will, I will," Jesus said, but his voice contained disappointment, and Rosie, fleetingly, felt the older of the two, realizing a brand-new power which vanished without category under her recognition.

"I have to go back in a minute," she said. "My aunt and uncle are here from Wintersburg. I told them I was going to the privy."

Jesus laughed. "You funny thing," he said. "You slay me!"

"Just because you have a bathroom *inside*," Rosie said. "Come on, tell me."

Chuckling, Jesus came around to lean on the stand facing her. They still could not see each other very clearly, but Rosie noticed that Jesus became very sober again as he took the hollow tomato from her hand and dropped it back into the stall. When he took hold of her empty hand, she could find no words to protest; her vocabulary had become distressingly constricted and she thought desperately that all that remained intact now was yes and no and oh, and even these few sounds would not easily out.

Thus, kissed by Jesus, Rosie fell, for the first time, entirely victim to a helplessness delectable beyond speech. But the terrible, beautiful sensation lasted no more than a second, and the reality of Jesus' lips and tongue and teeth and hands made her pull away with such strength that she nearly tumbled.

Rosie stopped running as she approached the lights from the windows of home. How long since she had left? She could not guess, but gasping yet, she went to the privy in back and locked herself in. Her own breathing deafened her in the dark, close space, and she sat and waited until she could hear at last the nightly calling of the frogs and crickets. Even then, all she could think to say was oh, my, and the pressure of Jesus' face against her face would not leave.

No one had missed her in the parlor, however, and Rosie walked in and through quickly, announcing that she was next going to take a bath. "Your father's in the bathhouse," her mother said, and Rosie, in her room, recalled that she had not seen him when she entered. There had been only Aunt Taka and Uncle Gimpachi with her mother at the table, drinking tea. She got her robe and straw sandals and crossed the parlor again to go outside. Her mother was telling them about the *haiku* competition in the *Mainichi* and the poem she had entered.

Rosie met her father coming out of the bathhouse. "Are you through, Father?" she asked. "I was going to ask you to scrub my back."

"Scrub your own back," he said shortly, going toward the main house.

"What have I done now?" she yelled after him. She suddenly felt like doing a lot of yelling. But he did not answer, and she went into the bathhouse. Turning on the dangling light, she removed her denims and T-shirt and threw them in the big carton for dirty clothes standing next to the washing machine. Her other things she took with her into the bath compartment to wash after her bath. After she had scooped a basin of hot water from the square wooden tub, she sat on the grey cement of the floor and soaped herself at exaggerated leisure, singing "Red Sails in the Sunset" at the top of her voice and using da-da-da where she suspected her words. Then, standing, still singing, for she was possessed by the notion that any attempt now to analyze would result in spoilage and she believed that the larger her volume the less she would be able to hear herself think, she obtained more hot water and poured it on until she was free of lather. Only then did she allow herself to step into the steaming vat, one leg first, then the remainder of her body inch by inch until the water no longer stung and she could move around at will.

She took a long time soaking, afterwards remembering to go around outside to stoke the embers of the tin-lined fireplace beneath the tub and to throw on a few more sticks so that the water might keep its heat for her mother, and when she finally returned to the parlor, she found her mother still talking *haiku* with her aunt and uncle, the three of them on another round of tea. Her father was nowhere in sight.

At Japanese school the next day (Wednesday, it was), Rosie was grave and giddy by turns. Preoccupied at her desk in the row for students on Book Eight, she made up for it at recess by performing wild mimicry for the benefit of her friend Chizuko. She held her nose and whined a witticism or two in what she considered was the manner of Fred Allen; she assumed intoxication and a British accent to go over the climax of the Rudy Vallee recording of the pub conversation about William Ewart Gladstone; she was the child Shirley Temple piping "On the Good Ship Lollipop"; she was the gentleman soprano of the Four Inkspots trilling "If I Didn't Care." And she felt reasonably satisfied when Chizuko wept and gasped, "Oh, Rosie, you ought to be in the movies!"

Her father came after her at noon, bringing her sandwiches of minced ham and two nectarines to eat while she rode, so that she could pitch right into the sorting when they got home. The lugs were piling up, he said, and the ripe tomatoes in them would probably have to be taken to the cannery tomorrow if they were not ready for the produce haulers tonight. "This heat's not doing them any good. And we've got no time for a break today."

It *was* hot, probably the hottest day of the year, and Rosie's blouse stuck damply to her back even under the protection of the canvas. But she worked as efficiently as a flawless machine and kept the stalls heaped, with one part of her mind listening in to the parental murmuring about the heat and the tomatoes and with another part planning the exact words she would say to Jesus when he drove up with the first load of the afternoon. But when at last she saw that the pick-up was coming, her hands went berserk and the tomatoes started falling in the wrong stalls, and her father said, "Hey, hey! Rosie, watch what you're doing!"

"Well, I have to go to the *benjo*," she said, hiding panic.

"Go in the weeds over there," he said, only half-joking.

"Oh, Father!" she protested.

"Oh, go on home," her mother said. "We'll make out for awhile."

In the privy, Rosie peered through a knothole toward the fields, watching as much as she could of Jesus. Happily she thought she saw him look in the direction of the house from time to time before he finished unloading and went back toward the patch where his mother and father worked. As she was heading for the shed, a very presentable black car purred up the dirt driveway to the house and its driver motioned to her. Was this the Hayashi home, he wanted to know. She nodded. Was she a Hayashi? Yes, she said, thinking that he was a good-looking man. He got out of the car with a huge, flat package and she saw that he warmly wore a business suit. "I have something here for your mother then," he said, in a more elegant Japanese than she was used to.

She told him where her mother was and he came along with her, patting his face with an immaculate white handkerchief and saying something about the coolness of San Francisco. To her surprised mother and father, he bowed and introduced himself as, among other things, the *haiku* editor of the *Mainichi Shinbun*, saying that since he had been coming as far as Los Angeles anyway, he had decided to bring her the first prize she had won in the recent contest.

"First prize?" her mother echoed, believing and not believing, pleased and overwhelmed. Handed the package with a bow, she bobbed her head up and down numerous times to express her utter gratitude.

"It is nothing much," he added, "but I hope it will serve as a token of our great appreciation for your contributions and our great admiration of your considerable talent."

"I am not worthy," she said, falling easily into his style. "It is I who should make some sign of my humble thanks for being permitted to contribute."

"No, no, to the contrary," he said, bowing again.

But Rosie's mother insisted, and then saying that she knew she was being unorthodox, she asked if she might open the package because her curiosity was so great. Certainly she might. In fact, he would like her reaction to it, for personally, it was one of his favorite *Hiroshiges*.*

Rosie thought it was a pleasant picture, which looked to have been sketched with delicate quickness. There were pink clouds, containing some graceful calligraphy, and a sea that was a pale blue except at the edges, containing four sampans with indications of people in them. Pines edged the water and on the far-off beach there was a cluster of thatched huts towered over by pine-dotted mountains of grey and blue. The frame was scalloped and gilt.

After Rosie's mother pronounced it without peer and somewhat prodded her father into nodding agreement, she said Mr. Kuroda must at least have a cup of tea, after coming all this way, and although Mr. Kuroda did not want to impose, he soon agreed that a cup of tea would be refreshing and went along with her to the house, carrying the picture for her.

"Ha, your mother's crazy!" Rosie's father said, and Rosie laughed uneasily as she resumed judgment on the tomatoes. She had emptied six lugs when he broke into an imaginary conversation with Jesus to tell her to go and remind her mother of the tomatoes, and she went slowly.

Mr. Kuroda was in his shirtsleeves expounding some *haiku* theory as he munched a rice cake, and her mother was rapt. Abashed in the great man's presence, Rosie stood next to her mother's chair until her mother looked up inquiringly, and then she started to whisper the message, but her mother pushed her gently away and reproached, "You are not being very polite to our guest."

---

* Japanese artist (1797–1858).

"Father says the tomatoes . . ." Rosie said aloud, smiling fool-ishly.

"Tell him I shall only be a minute," her mother said, speaking the language of Mr. Kuroda.

When Rosie carried the reply to her father, he did not seem to hear and she said again, "Mother says she'll be back in a minute."

"All right, all right," he nodded, and they worked again in silence. But suddenly, her father uttered an incredible noise, exactly like the cork of a bottle popping, and the next Rosie knew, he was stalking angrily toward the house, almost running, in fact, and she chased after him crying, "Father! Father! What are you going to do?"

He stopped long enough to order her back to the shed. "Never mind!" he shouted. "Get on with the sorting!"

And from the place in the fields where she stood, frightened and vacillating, Rosie saw her father enter the house. Soon Mr. Kuroda came out alone, putting on his coat. Mr. Kuroda got into his car and backed out down the driveway, onto the highway. Next her father emerged, also alone, something in his arms (it was the picture, she realized), and going over to the bathhouse woodpile, he threw the picture on the ground and picked up the axe. Smashing the picture, glass and all (she heard the explosion faintly), he reached over the kerosene that was used to encourage the bath fire and poured it over the wreckage. I am dreaming, Rosie said to herself, I am dreaming, but her father, having made sure that his act of cremation was irrevocable, was even then returning to the fields.

Rosie ran past him and toward the house. What had become of her mother? She burst into the parlor and found her mother at the back window, watching the dying fire. They watched together until there remained only a feeble smoke under the blazing sun. Her mother was very calm.

"Do you know why I married your father?" she said, without turning.

"No," said Rosie. It was the most frightening question she had ever been called upon to answer. Don't tell me now, she wanted to say, tell me tomorrow, tell me next week, don't tell me today. But she knew she would be told now, that the telling would combine with the other violence of the hot afternoon to level her life, her world (so various, so beautiful, so new?) to the very ground.

It was like a story out of the magazines, illustrated in sepia, which she had consumed so greedily for a period until the information had somehow reached her that those wretchedly unhappy autobiographies, offered to her as the testimonials of living men and women, were largely inventions: Her mother, at nineteen, had come to America and married her father as an alternative to suicide.

At eighteen, she had been in love with the first son of one of the well-to-do families in her village. The two had met whenever and wherever they could, secretly, because it would not have done for his family to see him favor her—her father had no money; he was a drunkard and a gambler besides. She had learned she was with child; an excellent match had already been arranged for her lover. Despised by her family, she had given premature birth to a stillborn son, who would be seventeen now. Her family did not turn her out, but she could no longer project herself in any direction without refreshing in them the memory of her indiscretion. She wrote to Aunt Taka, her favorite sister, in America, threatening to kill herself if Aunt Taka would not send for her. Aunt Taka hastily arranged a marriage with a young man, but lately arrived from Japan, of whom she knew, a young man of simple mind, it was said, but of kindly heart. The young man was never told why his unseen betrothed was so eager to hasten the day of meeting.

The story was told perfectly, with neither groping for words nor untoward passion. It was as though her mother had memorized it by heart, reciting it to herself so many times over that its nagging vileness had long since gone.

"I had a brother then?" Rosie asked, for this was what seemed to matter now; she would think about the other later, she assured herself, pushing back the illumination which threatened all that darkness that had hitherto been merely mysterious or even glamorous. "A half-brother?"

"Yes."

"I would have liked a brother," she said.

Suddenly, her mother knelt on the floor and took her by the

wrists. "Rosie," she said urgently, "promise me you will never marry!" Shocked more by the request than the revelation, Rosie stared at her mother's face. Jesus, Jesus, she called silently, not certain whether she was invoking the help of the son of the Carrascos or of God, until there returned sweetly the memory of Jesus' hand, how it had touched her and where. Still her mother waited for an answer, holding her wrists so tightly that her hands were going numb. She tried to pull free. "Promise," her mother whispered fiercely, "promise." "Yes, yes, I promise," Rosie said. But for an instant she turned away, and her mother, hearing the familiar glib agreement, released her, Oh, you, you, you, her eyes and twisted mouth said, you fool. Rosie, covering her face, began at last to cry, and the embrace and consoling hand came much later than she expected.

Tillie Olsen

I Stand Here Ironing
1956

Tillie Olsen was born in Nebraska in 1913 (or perhaps 1912), and has lived in San Francisco most of her life. Coming of age during the Depression, she points out that she fared better than most of her generation: She got almost all the way through high school. Public libraries were her college. Her origin, most of her life, and identification are primarily working class. She became early on a member of the world of "everyday" jobs. She wrote and published while young, but the necessity of rearing and supporting four children silenced her for twenty years. She was in her mid-forties when she began to write again.

Tell Me a Riddle, a collection of four short stories including "I Stand Here Ironing," was first published in 1962. The title story won the O. Henry Memorial Prize Award as the best story of 1961. In 1974, forty years after its opening chapter appeared in an early Partisan Review, her "lost" novel, Yonnondio: From the Thirties, was published. Silences, a collection of essays on the relationship between circumstances and human creativity, was published in 1978.

In recent years, Olsen has spoken on various topics on many university campuses. She has taught at Amherst, the Massachusetts Institute of Technology, Stanford, and the University of Massachusetts. She is the recipient of Ford Foundation and National Endowment for the Arts grants, a Guggenheim Fellowship, various other literary honors, and three honorary degrees, including Doctor of Arts and Letters from the University of Nebraska, her home state. In 1980, the Unitarian Women's Federation conferred on her their annual "Ministry to Women Award." Also in 1980, in conjunction with their issuance of stamps commemorating Emily Bronte, Charlotte Bronte, George Eliot, and Elizabeth Gaskell, the British Post Office (and Business and Professional Women) *selected Olsen for a special award. May 18, 1981 was proclaimed "Tillie Olsen Day" in San Francisco by the Mayor and Board of Supervisors of that city.*

"I Stand Here Ironing" originally appeared in 1956 in Pacific Spectator, *a publication of the Pacific Coast Committee for the Humanities of the American Council of Learned Societies. Along with the three other stories in* Tell Me a Riddle, *it has been anthologized in dozens of places, performed on numerous college campuses and in stage productions, and adapted into films and an opera. It is one of the very few stories, and perhaps the first, written about the mother-daughter relationship from the perspective of a mother.*

The late Elizabeth Fisher, feminist, novelist, anthropologist, essayist, and founder and editor of Aphra: The Feminist Literary Magazine, *wrote in a 1972 review in* The Nation:

> "I Stand Here Ironing" is the story told by a mother of how, wanting to do the best for her daughter, she was so often forced to do the worst, and it is one that every parent can recognize. In tight, economical prose she tears us with the parental experience, how we listen, wrongly, to other people, or are just imprisoned by events we could not foresee—desertion, poverty, expanding families; it is also a hopeful story of how children survive, sometimes even making strength, or talent, out of the deprivations they've endured. Tillie Olsen's is an unsparing but tender vision in which love is a need that is rarely answered, a vision of communication on strange, imperfect, levels, and, above all, of resilience, a belief that human beings are not passive, that there is more in them "than this dress on the ironing board, helpless before the iron."

As we see in this story, mothers are given responsibilities for the rearing and well-being of their children that are too heavy to bear successfully under the best of circumstances—and rarely do the best of circumstances exist. Mothers must learn to look at the lives of children, to see and understand how they have been damaged, how their potential to love and work, to trust and create, has been diminished because as mothers we have been unable to accomplish on their behalf all that mothers are charged to accomplish. We must learn to see and understand their losses while simultaneously we learn to refuse the blame. Maternal guilt muddies our ability to analyze the causes and understand the sources of children's and women's pain and deprivations. Mothers and daughters must absolve each other of guilt and learn to share a vision of a world in which the responsibilities are shared and the potentials can be fulfilled.

Toward the end of "A Dream-Vision," a reminiscence of her mother as she lay dying, Olsen writes about such a shared mother-daughter vision:

I had seen my mother but three times in my adult life, separated as we were by the continent between, by lack of means, by jobs I had to keep and by the needs of my four children. She could scarcely write English—her only education in this country, a few months of night school.

When at last I flew to her, it was in the last days she had language at all. Too late to talk with her of what was in our hearts; or of harms and crucifyings and strengths as she had known and experienced them; or of whys and knowledge, of wisdom. She died a few weeks later.

She, who had no worldly goods to leave, yet left to me an inexhaustible legacy. Inherent in it, this heritage of summoning resources to make out of song, food, warmth, expressions of human love—courage, hope, resistance, belief; this vision of universality and illimitability born with each human infant, before the lessenings, harms, divisions of the world are visited upon it.

As she sheltered and carried us and others, she sheltered and carried that belief, that wisdom throughout a lifetime lived in a world whose season was, as still it is, a time of winter.

I stand here ironing, and what you asked me moves tormented back and forth with the iron.

"I wish you would manage the time to come in and talk with me about your daughter. I'm sure you can help me understand her. She's a youngster who needs help and whom I'm deeply interested in helping."

"Who needs help. . . ." Even if I came, what good would it do? You think because I am her mother I have a key, or that in some way you could use me as a key? She has lived for nineteen years. There is all that life that has happened outside of me, beyond me.

And when is there time to remember, to sift, to weigh, to estimate, to total? I will start and there will be an interruption and I will have to gather it all together again. Or I will become engulfed with all I did or did not do, with what should have been and what cannot be helped.

She was a beautiful baby. The first and only one of our five that was beautiful at birth. You do not guess how new and uneasy her tenancy in her now-loveliness. You did not know her all those years she was thought homely, or see her poring over her baby pictures, making me tell her over and over how beautiful she had been—and would be, I would tell her—and was now, to the seeing eye. But the seeing eyes were few or non-existent. Including mine.

I nursed her. They feel that's important nowadays. I nursed all the children, but with her, with all the fierce rigidity of first motherhood, I did like the books then said. Though her cries battered me to trembling and my breasts ached with swollenness, I waited till the clock decreed.

Why do I put that first? I do not even know if it matters, or if it explains anything.

She was a beautiful baby. She blew shining bubbles of sound. She loved motion, loved light, loved color and music and textures. She would lie on the floor in her blue overalls patting the surface so hard in ecstasy her hands and feet would blur. She was a miracle to me, but when she was eight months old I had to leave her daytimes with the woman downstairs to whom she was no miracle at all, for I worked or looked for work and for Emily's father, who "could no longer endure" (he wrote in his good-bye note) "sharing want with us."

I was nineteen. It was the pre-relief, pre-WPA world of the depression. I would start running as soon as I got off the streetcar, running up the stairs, the place smelling sour, and awake or asleep to startle awake, when she saw me she would break into a clogged weeping that could not be comforted, a weeping I can hear yet.

After a while I found a job hashing at night so I could be with her days, and it was better. But it came to where I had to bring her to his family and leave her.

It took a long time to raise the money for her fare back. Then she got chicken pox and I had to wait longer. When she finally came, I hardly knew her, walking quick and nervous like her father, looking like her father, thin, and dressed in a shoddy red that yellowed her skin and glared at the pockmarks. All the baby loveliness gone.

She was two. Old enough for nursery school they said, and I

did not know then what I know now—the fatigue of the long day, and the lacerations of group life in the kinds of nurseries that are only parking places for children.

Except that it would have made no difference if I had known. It was the only place there was. It was the only way we could be together, the only way I could hold a job.

And even without knowing, I knew. I knew the teacher that was evil because all these years it has curdled into my memory, the little boy hunched in the corner, her rasp, "why aren't you outside, because Alvin hits you? that's no reason, go out, scaredy." I knew Emily hated it even if she did not clutch and implore "don't go Mommy" like the other children, mornings.

She always had a reason why we should stay home. Momma, you look sick. Momma, I feel sick. Momma, the teachers aren't there today, they're sick. Momma, we can't go, there was a fire there last night. Momma, it's a holiday today, no school, they told me.

But never a direct protest, never rebellion. I think of our others in their three-, four-year-oldness—the explosions, the tempers, the denunciations, the demands—and I feel suddenly ill. I put the iron down. What in me demanded that goodness in her? And what was the cost, the cost to her of such goodness?

The old man living in the back once said in his gentle way: "You should smile at Emily more when you look at her." What *was* in my face when I looked at her? I loved her. There were all the acts of love.

It was only with the others I remembered what he said, and it was the face of joy, and not of care or tightness or worry I turned to them—too late for Emily. She does not smile easily, let alone almost always as her brothers and sisters do. Her face is closed and sombre, but when she wants, how fluid. You must have seen it in her pantomimes, you spoke of her rare gift for comedy on the stage that rouses a laughter out of the audience so dear they applaud and applaud and do not want to let her go.

Where does it come from, that comedy? There was none of it in her when she came back to me that second time, after I had had to send her away again. She had a new daddy now to learn to love, and I think perhaps it was a better time.

Except when we left her alone nights, telling ourselves she was old enough.

"Can't you go some other time, Mommy, like tomorrow?" she would ask. "Will it be just a little while you'll be gone? Do you promise?"

The time we came back, the front door open, the clock on the floor in the hall. She rigid awake. "It wasn't just a little while. I didn't cry. Three times I called you, just three times, and then I ran downstairs to open the door so you could come faster. The clock talked loud. I threw it away, it scared me what it talked."

She said the clock talked loud again that night I went to the hospital to have Susan. She was delirious with the fever that comes before red measles, but she was fully conscious all the week I was gone and the week after we were home when she could not come near the new baby or me.

She did not get well. She stayed skeleton thin, not wanting to eat, and night after night she had nightmares. She would call for me, and I would rouse from exhaustion to sleepily call back: "You're all right, darling, go to sleep, it's just a dream," and if she still called, in a sterner voice, "now go to sleep, Emily, there's nothing to hurt you." Twice, only twice, when I had to get up for Susan anyhow, I went in to sit with her.

Now when it is too late (as if she would let me hold and comfort her like I do the others) I get up and go to her at once at her moan or restless stirring. "Are you awake, Emily? Can I get you something?" And the answer is always the same: "No, I'm all right, go back to sleep, Mother."

They persuaded me at the clinic to send her away to a convalescent home in the country where "she can have the kind of food and care you can't manage for her, and you'll be free to concentrate on the new baby." They still send children to that place. I see pictures on the society page of sleek young women planning affairs to raise money for it, or dancing at the affairs, or decorating Easter eggs or filling Christmas stockings for the children.

They never have a picture of the children so I do not know if the girls still wear those gigantic red bows and the ravaged looks on the every other Sunday when parents can come to visit "unless otherwise notified"—as we were notified the first six weeks.

Oh it is a handsome place, green lawns and tall trees and fluted flower beds. High up on the balconies of each cottage the children stand, the girls in their red bows and white dresses, the boys in white suits and giant red ties. The parents stand below shrieking up to be heard and the children shriek down to be heard, and between them the invisible wall "Not To Be Contaminated by Parental Germs or Physical Affection."

There was a tiny girl who always stood hand in hand with Emily. Her parents never came. One visit she was gone. "They moved her to Rose Cottage" Emily shouted in explanation. "They don't like you to love anybody here."

She wrote once a week, the labored writing of a seven-year-old. "I am fine. How is the baby. If I write my leter nicly I will have a star. Love." There never was a star. We wrote every other day, letters she could never hold or keep but only hear read—once. "We simply do not have room for children to keep any personal possessions," they patiently explained when we pieced one Sunday's shrieking together to plead how much it would mean to Emily, who loved so to keep things, to be allowed to keep her letters and cards.

Each visit she looked frailer. "She isn't eating," they told us.

(They had runny eggs for breakfast or mush with lumps, Emily said later, I'd hold it in my mouth and not swallow. Nothing ever tasted good, just when they had chicken.)

It took us eight months to get her released home, and only the fact that she gained back so little of her seven lost pounds convinced the social worker.

I used to try to hold and love her after she came back, but her body would stay stiff, and after a while she'd push away. She ate little. Food sickened her, and I think much of life too. Oh she had physical lightness and brightness, twinkling by on skates, bouncing like a ball up and down up and down over the jump rope, skimming over the hill; but these were momentary.

She fretted about her appearance, thin and dark and foreign-looking at a time when every little girl was supposed to look or thought she should look a chubby blonde replica of Shirley Temple. The doorbell sometimes rang for her, but no one seemed to come and play in the house or be a best friend. Maybe because we moved so much.

There was a boy she loved painfully through two school semesters. Months later she told me how she had taken pennies from my purse to buy him candy. "Licorice was his favorite and I brought him some every day, but he still liked Jennifer better'n me. Why, Mommy?" The kind of question for which there is no answer.

School was a worry to her. She was not glib or quick in a world where glibness and quickness were easily confused with ability to learn. To her overworked and exasperated teachers she was an overconscientious "slow learner" who kept trying to catch up and was absent entirely too often.

I let her be absent, though sometimes the illness was imaginary. (How different from my now-strictness about attendance with the others.) I wasn't working. We had a new baby, I was home anyhow. Sometimes, after Susan grew old enough, I would keep her home from school, too, to have them all together.

Mostly Emily had asthma, and her breathing, harsh and labored, would fill the house with a curiously tranquil sound. I would bring the two old dresser mirrors and her boxes of collections to her bed. She would select beads and single earrings, bottle tops and shells, dried flowers and pebbles, old postcards and scraps, all sorts of oddments; then she and Susan would play Kingdom, setting up landscapes and furniture, peopling them with action.

Those were the only times of peaceful companionship between her and Susan. I have edged away from it, that poisonous feeling between them, that terrible balancing of hurts and needs I had to do between the two, and did so badly, those earlier years.

Oh there are conflicts between the others too, each one human, needing, demanding, hurting, taking—but only between Emily and Susan, no Emily toward Susan that corroding resentment. It seems so obvious on the surface, yet it is not obvious. Susan, the second child, Susan, golden- and curly-haired and chubby, quick and articulate and assured, everything in appearance and manner Emily was not; Susan, not able to resist Emily's precious things, losing or sometimes clumsily breaking them; Susan telling jokes and riddles to company for applause while Emily sat silent (to say to me later: that was *my* riddle, Mother, I told it to Susan); Susan, who for all the five years' difference in age was just a year behind Emily in developing physically.

I am glad for that slow physical development that widened the difference between her and her contemporaries, though she suffered over it. She was too vulnerable for that terrible world of youthful competition, of preening and parading, of constant measuring of yourself against every other, of envy, "If I had that copper hair," "If I had that skin. . . ." She tormented herself enough about not looking like the others, there was enough of the unsureness, the having to be conscious of words before you speak, the constant caring—what are they thinking of me? without having it all magnified by the merciless physical drives.

Ronnie is calling. He is wet and I change him. It is rare there is such a cry now. That time of motherhood is almost behind me when the ear is not one's own but must always be racked and listening for the child cry, the child call. We sit for a while and I hold him, looking out over the city spread in charcoal with its soft aisles of light. "*Shoogily*," he breathes and curls closer. I carry him back to bed, asleep. *Shoogily*. A funny word, a family word, inherited from Emily, invented by her to say: *comfort*.

In this and other ways she leaves her seal, I say aloud. And startle at my saying it. What do I mean? What did I start to gather together, to try and make coherent? I was at the terrible, growing years. War years. I do not remember them well. I was working, there were four smaller ones now, there was not time for her. She had to help be a mother, and housekeeper, and shopper. She had to set her seal. Mornings of crisis and near hysteria trying to get lunches packed, hair combed, coats and shoes found, everyone to school or Child Care on time, the baby ready for transportation. And always the paper scribbled on by a smaller one, the book looked at by Susan then mislaid, the homework not done. Running out to that huge school where she was one, she was lost, she was a drop; suffering over her unpreparedness, stammering and unsure in her classes.

There was so little time left at night after the kids were bedded down. She would struggle over books, always eating (it was in those years she developed her enormous appetite that is legendary in our family) and I would be ironing, or preparing food for the next day, or writing V-mail to Bill, or tending the baby. Sometimes, to make me laugh, or out of her despair, she would imitate happenings or types at school.

I think I said once: "Why don't you do something like this in the school amateur show?" One morning she phoned me at work, hardly understandable through the weeping: "Mother, I did it. I won, I won; they gave me first prize; they clapped and clapped and wouldn't let me go."

Now suddenly she was Somebody, and as imprisoned in her difference as she had been in her anonymity.

She began to be asked to perform at other high schools, even in colleges, then at city and state-wide affairs. The first one we went to, I only recognized her that first moment when thin, shy, she almost drowned herself into the curtains. Then: Was this Emily? The control, the command, the convulsing and deadly clowning, the spell, then the roaring, stamping audience, unwilling to let this rare and precious laughter out of their lives.

Afterwards: You ought to do something about her with a gift like that—but without money or knowing how, what does one do? We have left it all to her, and the gift has as often eddied inside, clogged and clotted, as been used and growing.

She is coming. She runs up the stairs two at a time with her light graceful step, and I know she is happy tonight. Whatever it was that occasioned your call did not happen today.

"Aren't you ever going to finish the ironing, Mother? Whistler painted his mother in a rocker. I'd have to paint mine standing over an ironing board." This is one of her communicative nights and she tells me everything and nothing as she fixes herself a plate of food out of the icebox.

She is so lovely. Why did you want me to come in at all? Why were you concerned? She will find her way.

She starts up the stairs to bed. "Don't get *me* up with the rest in the morning." "But I thought you were having midterms." "Oh, those," she comes back in, kisses me, and says quite lightly, "in a couple of years when we'll all be atom-dead they won't matter a bit."

She has said it before. She *believes* it. But because I have been dredging the past, and all that compounds a human being is so heavy and meaningful in me, I cannot endure it tonight.

I will never total it all. I will never come in to say: She was a child seldom smiled at. Her father left me before she was a year old. I had to work her first six years when there was work, or I sent her home and to his relatives. There were years she had care she hated. She was dark and thin and foreign-looking in a world where the prestige went to blondeness and curly hair and dimples, she was slow where glibness was prized. She was a child of anxious, not proud, love. We were poor and could not afford for her the soil of easy growth. I was a young mother, I was a distracted mother. There were the other children pushing up, demanding. Her younger sister seemed all that she was not. There were years she did not let me touch her. She kept too much in herself, her life was such she had to keep too much in herself. My wisdom came too late. She has much to her and probably little will come of it. She is a child of her age, of depression, of war, of fear.

Let her be. So all that is in her will not bloom—but in how many does it? There is still enough left to live by. Only help her to know—help make it so there is cause for her to know—that she is more than this dress on the ironing board, helpless before the iron.

Guadalupe Valdes

Recuerdo
1963

In her commentary on the origins of this story, its place in her life, and the course of her life since the writing of the story, Guadalupe Valdes attributes to her mother the intellectual encouragement and creative support that made it possible for her to write. But, at the same time, like so many women, the disappointments Valdes experienced as a young married mother of two small children seemed to her to be her mother's fault.

My story "Recuerdo" might well be entitled "Mother's Advice." It is a bitter story, written at a time in which I was angry about my own life and about having followed my own mother's counsel. I was trying to make sense of the world, trying to understand why one could follow all the rules and yet end up unhappy. I felt betrayed, trapped, and all alone.

Until recently, it had not occurred to me that my mother has also been betrayed and trapped. . . . like so many women, she had also tried to follow rules; to make sense of so many things that seemed unfair; and to hope that somehow, for her daughters, things would be different.

Clearly, my anger was misdirected. My mother gave me what she could. She said, "Marry a man who doesn't drink." Amazing that, like the mother in "Recuerdo," her formula for happiness was so simple. She focused on the one thing that had made her life unhappy, and she wanted more for *me*. It seems sad now, that I blamed her for so many years, blamed her because I believed her,

blamed her because the formula was not complete and
did not bring happiness.

*Like many women writers, among them in this collection Elizabeth Stuart
Phelps, Hisaye Yamamoto, Alice Walker, and Joanna Russ, Valdes testifies to
her mother's strong influence on her own ability to imagine herself as a writer.
The artist's mother as artist manqué is a figure revealed more and more frequently
as scholars have begun to look at the maternal influence on writers. Valdes
writes:*

My mother had a lot to do with my writing. I can
remember bringing her the first poems I ever wrote. She
found them brilliant, of course, and praised me warmly.
Recently in looking through old papers, I found them.
She had kept them all these years.

I began to write in the fourth grade. I wrote in English,
the language that I learned at school, the language of the
country that I spent eight hours in every day, before
recrossing the border back to my Mexican world. I wrote
in English, and took the poems home and showed them
to my mother. It didn't seem strange to me.

She always read them carefully. For she liked poetry
too; and had thick scrapbooks of poems she'd typed out,
or copied, or cut out from books and magazines. And it's
only now that I'm aware that those poems were all in
English too.

"Recuerdo" (meaning "Remembrance") was first published in De Colores
Journal *in 1976, thirteen years after its original composition. "At the time I
sent the story everywhere, and of course, it was rejected," comments Valdes.
"Minority themes only recently became popular." She continues:*

. . . one day, looking in an old file, I found "Recuerdo."
Having become an expert at sending things out, I sent it
off to a new "minority" little magazine; and it was published. I was pleased and yet saddened. I remembered the
young woman (myself at 20) who had written it; and
wondered how different her life would have been if only
it had been published then.

*In this story, as in "A Marriage of Persuasion," the mother is portrayed as a
woman who fails her daughter—who, indeed, cannot do other than fail her
daughter. But because the stories are written by artists who transcend their
personal feelings about and understandings of their own mothers, these fictional
mothers are portrayed as vulnerable and victimized women without power. The
reader can see, however, that the mother is not to blame for anything.*

It was noon. It was dusty. And the sun, blinding in its brightness, shone unmercifully on the narrow dirty street.

It was empty. And to Rosa, walking slowly past the bars and the shops and the curios stands, it seemed as if they all were peering out at her, curiously watching what she did.

She walked on . . . toward the river, toward the narrow, muddy strip of land that was the dry Rio Grande; and she wished suddenly that it were night and that the tourists had come across, making the street noisy and gay and full of life.

But it was noon. And there were no happy or laughing Americanos; no eager girls painted and perfumed and waiting for customers; no blaring horns or booming bongos . . . only here and there a hungry dog, a crippled beggar, or a drunk thirsty and broke from the night before.

She was almost there. She could see the narrow door and the splintered wooden steps. And instinctively she stopped. Afraid suddenly, feeling the hollow emptiness again, and the tightness when she swallowed.

And yet, it was not as if she did not know why he had wanted her to come, why he had sent for her. It was not as though she were a child. Her reflection in a smudged and dirty window told her that she was no longer even a girl.

And still, it was not as if she were old, she told herself, it was only that her body was rounded and full, and her eyes in the dark smooth face were hard and knowing, mirroring the pain and the disappointment and the tears of thirty-five years . . .

She walked to the narrow door slowly, and up the stairs . . . thumping softly on the creaking swollen wood. At the top, across a dingy hallway, she knocked softly at a door. It was ajar, and Rosa could see the worn chairs and the torn linoleum and the paper-littered desk. But she did not go in. Not until the man came to the door and looked out at her impatiently.

He saw her feet first and the tattered sandals. Then her dress clean but faded, a best dress obviously, because it was not patched. Finally, after what seemed to Rosa an eternity, he looked at her face, at her dark black hair knotted neatly on top of her head; and at last, into her eyes.

"Come in, Rosa," he said slowly, "I am glad that you could come."

"Buenas tardes Don Lorenzo," Rosa said meekly, looking up uneasily at the bulky smelly man. "I am sorry I am late."

"Yes," he said mockingly; and turning, he walked back into the small and dirty room.

Rosa followed him, studying him, while he could not see her, seeing the wrinkled trousers, the sweat stained shirt, and the overgrown greasy hair on the back of his pudgy neck.

He turned suddenly, his beady eyes surveying his domain smugly; then deliberately, he walked to the window and straightened the sign that said:

DIVORCES
LORENZO PEREZ SAUZA
ATTORNEY AT LAW

It was not as important as the neon blinking sign, of course, but sometimes people came from the side street, and it was good to be prepared.

"Well, Rosa," he said, looking at her again, "and where is Maruca?"

"She is sick, señor."

"Sick?"

"Yes, she has had headaches and she is not well . . . she . . ."

"Has she seen a doctor, Rosa?" The question was mocking again.

"No . . . she . . . it will pass, señor . . . It's only that now . . . I do not think that she should come to work."

"Oh?" He was looking out of the window distractedly, ignoring her.

"I am sorry, I should have come before," she continued meekly . . .

"Maruca is very pretty, Rosa," Don Lorenzo said suddenly.

"Thank you, señor, you are very kind." She was calmer now . . .

"She will make a man very happy, someday," he continued.

"Yes."

"Do you think she will marry soon then?" he asked her, watching her closely.

"No," she hesitated, "that is, I don't know, she . . . there isn't anyone yet."

"Ah!" It was said quietly but somehow triumphantly . . .
And Rosa waited, wondering what he wanted, sensing something
and suddenly suspicious.

"Do you think she likes me, Rosa," he asked her deliberately,
baiting her.

And she remembered Maruca's face, tear-stained, embarrassed
telling her: "I can't go back, mama. He does not want me to
help in his work. He touches me, mother . . . and smiles. And
today, he put his large sweaty hand on my breast, and held it,
smiling, like a cow. Ugly!"

"Why, yes, Don Lorenzo," she lied quickly. "She thinks you
are very nice." Her heart was racing now, hoping and yet not
daring to—

"I am much of a man, Rosa," he went on slowly, "and the girl
is pretty . . . I would take care of her . . . if she let me."

"Take care of her?" Rosa was praying now, her fingers crossed
behind her back.

"Yes, take care of her," he repeated. "I would be good to her,
you would have money. And then, perhaps, if there is a child
. . . she would need a house . . ."

"A house." Rosa repeated dully. A house for Maruca. That it
might be. That it might be, really, was unbelievable. To think
of the security, of the happy future frightened her suddenly,
and she could only stare at the fat man, her eyes round and
very black.

"Think about it, Rosita," he said smiling benevolently . . . "You
know me . . ." And Rosa looked at him angrily, remembering,
and suddenly feeling very much like being sick.

The walk home was long; and in the heat Rosa grew tired.
She wished that she might come to a tree, so that she could sit
in the shade and think. But the hills were bare and dry, and
there were no trees. There were only shacks surrounded by
hungry crying children.

And Rosa thought about her own, about the little ones. The
ones that still depended on her even for something to eat. And
she felt it again, the strange despair of wanting to cry out:
"Don't, don't depend on me! I can hardly depend on myself."

But they had no one else; and until they could beg or steal a
piece of bread and a bowl of beans, they would turn to her, only
to her, not ever to Pablo.

And it wasn't because he was drunk and lazy, or even because only the last two children belonged to him. He was kind enough to all of them. It was, though, as if they sensed that he was only temporary.

And still it was not that Pablo was bad. He was better actually than the others. He did not beat her when he drank, or steal food from the children. He was not even too demanding. And it gave them a man, after all, a man to protect them . . . It was enough, really.

True, he had begun to look at Maruca, and it had bothered Rosa. But perhaps it *was* really time for Maruca to leave. For the little ones, particularly. Because men are men, she said to herself, and if there is a temptation. . . .

But she was not fooling anyone, and when at last she saw the tin and cardboard shack against the side of the hill, with its cluttered front and screaming children, she wanted to turn back.

Maruca saw her first.

"There's mama," she told the others triumphantly, and at once they took up the shout: "mama! mama! mama!"

The other girl, standing with Maruca, turned to leave as Rosa came closer.

"Buenas tardes," she said uncomfortably, sensing the dislike and wanting to hurry away.

"What did Petra want?" Rosa asked Maruca angrily, even before Petra was out of earshot.

"Mama, *por favor*, she'll hear you."

"I told you I did not want her in this house."

"We were only talking, mama. She was telling me about her friends."

"Her friends!" Rosa cut in sharply, "as if we did not know that she goes with the first American that looks at her. Always by the river that one, with one soldier and another, her friends indeed!"

"But she says she has fun, mama, and they take her to dance and buy her pretty things."

"Yes, yes, and tomorrow, they will give her a baby . . . And where is the fun then . . . eh? She is in the streets . . . no?" Rosa was shaking with anger. "Is that what you want? Do you?"

"No, mama," Maruca said meekly, "I was just listening to her talk."

"Well, remember it," Rosa snapped furiously, but then seeing Maruca's face, she stopped suddenly. "There, there, it's alright," she said softly. "We will talk about it later."

And Rosa watched her, then, herding the children into the house gently, gracefully; slim and small, angular still, with something perhaps a little doltish in the way she held herself, impatient, and yet distrusting, not quite daring to go forward.

And she thought of Don Lorenzo, and for a moment, she wished that he were not so fat, or so ugly, and especially, so sweaty.

But it was an irrecoverable chance! Old men with money did not often come into their world, and never to stay.

To Rosa, they had been merely far away gods at whose houses she had worked as a maid or as a cook; faultless beings who were to be obeyed without question; powerful creatures who had commanded her to come when they needed variety or adventure . . .

But only that.

She had never been clever enough, or even pretty enough to make it be more.

But Maruca! Maruca could have the world.

No need for her to marry a poor young bum who could not even get a job. No need for her to have ten children all hungry and crying. No need for her to dread, even, that the bum might leave her. No need at all.

"Maruca," Rosa said decidedly, turning to where she sat playing with the baby, "I went to see Don Lorenzo."

"Oh?" There was fear in the bright brown eyes.

"And he wants to take care of you," Rosa continued softly. "He thinks you're pretty, and he likes you."

"Take care of me?" It was more of a statement than a question.

"He wants to make an arrangement with you, Maruca." Rosa too was afraid now. "He would come to see you . . . and . . . well . . . if there is a baby, there might very well be a house."

"A baby?" The face was pale now, the eyes surprised and angry. "You want me to go to bed with Don Lorenzo? You want me to let him put his greasy hands all over me, and make love to me? You want that? Is that how much better I can do than Petra?"

"Don't you see, I want you to be happy, to be safe. I want you to have pretty things and not to be afraid. I want you to love your babies when you have them, to hear them laugh with full fat stomachs . . . I want you to love life, to be glad that you were born."

"To be happy?" Maruca repeated slowly, as if it had never occurred to her that she was not.

"Yes, to be happy."

"And sleeping with Don Lorenzo," Maruca asked uncertainly, "will that make me glad that I was born?"

And Rosa looked at her, saw her waiting for an answer, depending on it . . .

And she wanted to scream out. "No, no! You will hate it probably, and you will dread his touch on you and his breath smelling of garlic. But it isn't *he,* that will make you happy. It's the rest of it. Don't you see, can't you understand how important *he* is?"

But the brown eyes stared at her pleadingly, filling with tears, like a child's, and Rosa said quietly: "Yes, Maruca, it will make you happy."

But then suddenly, unexpectedly, she felt alone and very, very tired.

"Go on to church now," she said slowly, "it's time for benediction and you have the novena to complete." And Rosa watched her go, prayer book clutched tightly in one hand, hopeful still, trusting still, and so very, very young still. And she wondered if she would change much, really, after Don Lorenzo, and the baby and the house. She wondered if she would still be gay and proud and impatient.

But then suddenly Maruca was out of sight, and Rosa turned to the others, kissing one, patting another's head, and hurrying to have the beans hot and the house tidy for the time that Pablo would come home.

James Tiptree, Jr.

The Women Men Don't See
1973

The Science Fiction Writers of America annually vote to determine who among them shall be honored by their colleagues with the Nebula Award for the best work in a variety of genres. James Tiptree, Jr. (b. 1915) was awarded the Nebula for best short story in 1973, for "Love is the Plan, the Plan is Death"; for best novella in 1976, for "Houston, Houston, Do You Read?"; and for the best novelette in 1977, for "The Screwfly Solution," published under the pseudonym Racoona Sheldon. Science fiction fans, who also vote on annual literary prizes, awarded the 1974 Hugo for the best novella to "The Girl Who Was Plugged In" (included in The Other Woman, *ed. Susan Koppelman,* The Feminist Press, 1984*).*

Tiptree has published four volumes of short stories: Ten Thousand Light-Years From Home, *(1973),* Warm Worlds and Otherwise *(1975),* Star-Songs of an Old Primate *(1978), and* Out of the Everywhere and Other Extraordinary Visions *(1981), and one novel,* Up the Walls of the World *(1978).*

Tiptree's biography includes an exotic childhood (as the only one of ten siblings to survive beyond birth) spent largely in Africa and India on exploratory expeditions with extraordinarily talented, accomplished, adventuresome, and achievement-oriented parents; an early career as a graphic artist and painter; a stint in the United States air force during World War II as a photo-intelligence officer; involvement in the creation of the Central Intelligence Agency; a midlife career change leading to the successful pursuit of a Ph.D. in experimental psychology; and a brief teaching career. Tiptree has written that the early exposure to "dozens of cultures and sub-cultures whose values, taboos, imperatives, religions, languages, and mores conflicted with each other" resulted in "profound alienation from any nominal peers, and an enduring cultural relativism."

Among Tiptree's experiences as a youngster was that of being given "one of the most expensive debutante parties ever seen, in the middle of the Depression." Like the nineteenth-century writers George Eliot, George Sand, and Ellis, Acton, and Currer Bell (Emily, Anne, and Charlotte Bronte), James Tiptree, Jr. is a woman. (Tiptree is not the only writer in this collection to use a male pseudonym. Alice Brown's story, "The Way of Peace," was published under the name of Martin Redfield.) Tiptree, whose real name is Alice Sheldon, explains her choice of a male nom de plume on the grounds that "it seemed like a good camouflage. I had the feeling that a man would slip by less observed. . . . Men have so pre-empted the area of human experience that when you write about universal motives, you are assumed to be writing like a man." That male name gives the writer the privilege of assuming that her perspective is normative. That which makes the work distinctive is not gender, but other, chosen and personal matters.

One of the aspects of Tiptree's distinctiveness is the authorial assumption that her reader is leisured, well-educated, and well-travelled. Her stories are filled with geographical and cultural details reflecting her own wide experience. When a woman writer is presumptuous about her audience in this way, she is often criticized as an elitist, while a man making similar use of his life experience is honored as erudite and sophisticated. The reader has to work hard when reading Tiptree's stories, but as her colleagues and fans have indicated by the awards they have voted her work, the effort is well worth it.

"The Women Men Don't See" was first published in The Magazine of Fantasy and Science Fiction in December 1973 and collected in Warm Worlds and Otherwise two years later. In his introduction to the book, Robert Silverberg, who didn't know the secret of Tiptree's identity (Joanna Russ has called Alice Sheldon's masquerade the most successful and the most sustained in literary history), pays special attention to this story, labelling it a "masterpiece of short-story writing," and observing:

> The thematic solution is an ancient s-f cliche . . . re-
> deemed and wholly transformed by its sudden shattering
> vision of women, stolid and enduring, calmly trading one
> set of alien masters for another that may be more tolera-
> ble. It is a profoundly feminist story told in entirely mas-
> culine manner, and deserves close attention by those in
> the front lines of the wars of sexual liberation, male and
> female.

I see her first while the Mexicana 727 is barreling down to Cozumel Island. I come out of the can and lurch into her seat, saying "Sorry," at a double female blur. The near blur nods quietly. The younger one in the window seat goes on looking out. I continue down the aisle, registering nothing. Zero. I never would have looked at them or thought of them again.

Cozumel airport is the usual mix of panicky Yanks dressed for the sand pile and calm Mexicans dressed for lunch at the Presidente. I am a used-up Yank dressed for serious fishing; I extract my rods and duffel from the riot and hike across the field to find my charter pilot. One Captain Estéban has contracted to deliver me to the bonefish flats of Belize three hundred kilometers down the coast.

Captain Estéban turns out to be four feet nine of mahogany Mayan *puro*. He is also in a somber Maya snit. He tells me my Cessna is grounded somewhere and his Bonanza is booked to take a party to Chetumal.

Well, Chetumal is south; can he take me along and go on to Belize after he drops them? Gloomily he concedes the possibility—*if* the other party permits, and *if* there are not too many *equipajes*.

The Chetumal party approaches. It's the woman and her young companion—daughter?—neatly picking their way across the gravel and yucca apron. Their Ventura two-suiters, like themselves, are small, plain and neutral-colored. No problem. When the captain asks if I may ride along, the mother says mildly "Of course," without looking at me.

I think that's when my inner tilt-detector sends up its first faint click. How come this woman has already looked me over carefully enough to accept on her plane? I disregard it. Paranoia hasn't been useful in my business for years, but the habit is hard to break.

As we clamber into the Bonanza, I see the girl has what could be an attractive body if there was any spark at all. There isn't. Captain Estéban folds a serape to sit on so he can see over the cowling and runs a meticulous check-down. And then we're up and trundling over the turquoise Jello of the Caribbean into a stiff south wind.

The coast on our right is the territory of Quintana Roo. If you haven't seen Yucatán, imagine the world's biggest absolutely flat green-gray rug. An empty-looking land. We pass the white ruin of Tulum and the gash of the road to Chichén Itzá, a half-dozen coconut plantations, and then nothing but reef and low scrub jungle all the way to the horizon, just about the way the conquistadors saw it four centuries back.

Long strings of cumulus are racing at us, shadowing the coast. I have gathered that part of our pilot's gloom concerns the weather. A cold front is dying on the henequen fields of Mérida to the west, and the south wind has piled up a string of coastal storms: what they call *llovisnos*. Estéban detours methodically around a couple of small thunderheads. The Bonanza jinks, and I look back with a vague notion of reassuring the women. They are calmly intent on what can be seen of Yucatán. Well, they were offered the copilot's view, but they turned it down. Too shy?

Another *llovisno* puffs up ahead. Estéban takes the Bonanza upstairs, rising in his seat to sight his course. I relax for the first time in too long, savoring the latitudes between me and my desk, the week of fishing ahead. Our captain's classic Maya profile attracts my gaze: forehead sloping back from his predatory nose, lips and jaw stepping back below it. If his slant eyes had been any more crossed, he couldn't have made his license. That's a handsome combination, believe it or not. On the little Maya chicks in their minishifts with iridescent gloop on those cockeyes, it's also highly erotic. Nothing like the oriental doll thing; these people have stone bones. Captain Estéban's old grandmother could probably tow the Bonanza . . .

I'm snapped awake by the cabin hitting my ear. Estéban is barking into his headset over a drumming racket of hail; the windows are dark gray.

One important noise is missing—the motor. I realize Estéban is fighting a dead plane. Thirty-six hundred; we've lost two thousand feet!

He slaps tank switches as the storm throws us around; I catch something about *gasolina* in a snarl that shows his big teeth. The Bonanza reels down. As he reaches for an overhead toggle, I see the fuel gauges are high. Maybe a clogged gravity feed line; I've heard of dirty gas down here. He drops the set; it's a million to one nobody can read us through the storm at this range anyway. Twenty-five hundred—going down.

His electric feed pump seems to have cut in: the motor explodes—quits—explodes—and quits again for good. We are suddenly out of the bottom of the clouds. Below us is a long white line almost hidden by rain: the reef. But there isn't any beach behind it, only a big meandering bay with a few mangrove flats—and it's coming up at us fast.

This is going to be bad, I tell myself with great unoriginality. The women behind me haven't made a sound. I look back and see they've braced down with their coats by their heads. With a stalling speed around eighty, all this isn't much use, but I wedge myself in.

Estéban yells some more into his set, flying a falling plane. He is doing one jesus job, too—as the water rushes up at us he dives into a hair-raising turn and hangs us into the wind—with a long pale ridge of sandbar in front of our nose.

Where in hell he found it I never know. The Bonanza mushes down, and we belly-hit with a tremendous tearing crash—bounce—hit again—and everything slews wildly as we flat-spin into the mangroves at the end of the bar. Crash! Clang! The plane is wrapping itself into a mound of strangler fig with one wing up. The crashing quits with us all in one piece. And no fire. Fantastic.

Captain Estéban pries open his door, which is now in the roof. Behind me a woman is repeating quietly, "Mother. Mother." I climb up the floor and find the girl trying to free herself from her mother's embrace. The woman's eyes are closed. Then she opens them and suddenly lets go, sane as soap. Estéban starts hauling them out. I grab the Bonanza's aid kit and scramble out after them into brilliant sun and wind. The storm that hit us is already vanishing up the coast.

"Great landing, Captain."

"Oh, *yes!* It was beautiful." The women are shaky, but no hysteria. Estéban is surveying the scenery with the expression his ancestors used on the Spaniards.

If you've been in one of these things, you know the slow-motion inanity that goes on. Euphoria, first. We straggle down the fig tree and out onto the sandbar in the roaring hot wind, noting without alarm that there's nothing but miles of crystalline water on all sides. It's only a foot or so deep, and the bottom is the olive color of silt. The distant shore around us is all flat mangrove swamp, totally uninhabitable.

"Bahía Espiritu Santo." Estéban confirms my guess that we're down in that huge water wilderness. I always wanted to fish it.

"What's all that smoke?" The girl is pointing at the plumes blowing around the horizon.

"Alligator hunters," says Estéban. Maya poachers have left burn-offs in the swamps. It occurs to me that any signal fires we make aren't going to be too conspicuous. And I now note that our plane is well-buried in the mound of fig. Hard to see it from the air.

Just as the question of how the hell we get out of here surfaces in my mind, the older woman asks composedly, "If they didn't hear you, Captain, when will they start looking for us? Tomorrow?"

"Correct," Estéban agrees dourly. I recall that air-sea rescue is fairly informal here. Like, keep an eye open for Mario, his mother says he hasn't been home all week.

It dawns on me we may be here quite some while.

Furthermore, the diesel-truck noise on our left is the Caribbean piling back into the mouth of the bay. The wind is pushing it at us, and the bare bottoms on the mangroves show that our bar is covered at high tide. I recall seeing a full moon this morning in—believe it, St. Louis—which means maximal tides. Well, we can climb up in the plane. But what about drinking water?

There's a small splat! behind me. The older woman has sampled the bay. She shakes her head, smiling ruefully. It's the first real expression on either of them; I take it as the signal for introductions. When I say I'm Don Fenton from St. Louis, she tells me their name is Parsons, from Bethesda, Maryland. She says it so nicely I don't at first notice we aren't being given first names. We all compliment Captain Estéban again.

His left eye is swelled shut, an inconvenience beneath his attention as a Maya, but Mrs. Parsons spots the way he's bracing his elbow in his ribs.

"You're hurt, Captain."

"*Roto*—I think is broken." He's embarrassed at being in pain.

We get him to peel off his Jaime shirt, revealing a nasty bruise in his superb dark-bay torso.

"Is there tape in that kit, Mr. Fenton? I've had a little first-aid training."

She begins to deal competently and very impersonally with the tape. Miss Parsons and I wander to the end of the bar and have a conversation which I am later to recall acutely.

"Roseate spoonbills," I tell her as three pink birds flap away.

"They're beautiful," she says in her tiny voice. They both have tiny voices. "He's a Mayan Indian, isn't he? The pilot, I mean."

"Right. The real thing, straight out of the Bonampak murals. Have you seen Chichén and Uxmal?"

"Yes. We were in Mérida. We're going to Tikal in Guatemala . . . I mean, we were."

"You'll get there." It occurs to me the girl needs cheering up. "Have they told you that Maya mothers used to tie a board on the infant's forehead to get that slant? They also hung a ball of tallow over its nose to make the eyes cross. It was considered aristocratic."

She smiles and takes another peek at Estéban. "People seem different in Yucatán," she says thoughtfully. "Not like the Indians around Mexico City. More, I don't know, independent."

"Comes from never having been conquered. Mayas got massacred and chased a lot, but nobody ever really flattened them. I bet you didn't know that the last Mexican-Maya war ended with a negotiated truce in nineteen thirty-five?"

"No!" Then she says seriously, "I like that."

"So do I."

"The water is really rising very fast," says Mrs. Parsons gently from behind us.

It is, and so is another *llovisno*. We climb back into the Bonanza. I try to rig my parka for a rain catcher, which blows loose as the storm hits fast and furious. We sort a couple of malt bars and my bottle of Jack Daniels out of the jumble in the cabin and make ourselves reasonably comfortable. The Parsons take a sip of whiskey each, Estéban and I considerably more. The Bonanza begins to bump soggily. Estéban makes an ancient one-eyed Mayan face at the water seeping into his cabin and goes to sleep. We all nap.

When the water goes down, the euphoria has gone with it, and we're very, very thirsty. It's also damn near sunset. I get to work with a bait-casting rod and some treble hooks and manage to foul-hook four small mullets. Estéban and the women tie the Bonanza's midget life raft out in the mangroves to catch rain. The wind is parching hot. No planes go by.

Finally another shower comes over and yields us six ounces of water apiece. When the sunset envelops the world in golden smoke, we squat on the sandbar to eat wet raw mullet and Instant Breakfast crumbs. The women are now in shorts, neat but definitely not sexy.

"I never realized how refreshing raw fish is," Mrs. Parsons says pleasantly. Her daughter chuckles, also pleasantly. She's on Mamma's far side away from Estéban and me. I have Mrs. Parsons figured now; Mother Hen protecting only chick from male predators. That's all right with me. I came here to fish.

But something is irritating me. The damn women haven't complained once, you understand. Not a peep, not a quaver, no personal manifestations whatever. They're like something out of a manual.

"You really seem at home in the wilderness, Mrs. Parsons. You do much camping?"

"Oh goodness no." Diffident laugh. "Not since my girl scout days. Oh, look—are those man-of-war birds?"

Answer a question with a question. I wait while the frigate birds sail nobly into the sunset.

"Bethesda . . . Would I be wrong in guessing you work for Uncle Sam?"

"Why yes. You must be very familiar with Washington, Mr. Fenton. Does your work bring you there often?"

Anywhere but on our sandbar the little ploy would have worked. My hunter's gene twitches.

"Which agency are you with?"

She gives up gracefully. "Oh, just GSA records. I'm a librarian."

Of course. I know her now, all the Mrs. Parsonses in records divisions, accounting sections, research branches, personnel and administration offices. Tell Mrs. Parsons we need a recap on the external service contracts for fiscal '73. So Yucatán is on the tours now? Pity . . . I offer her the tired little joke. "You know where the bodies are buried."

She smiles deprecatingly and stands up. "It does get dark quickly, doesn't it?"

Time to get back into the plane.

A flock of ibis are circling us, evidently accustomed to roosting in our fig tree. Estéban produces a machete and a Mayan string hammock. He proceeds to sling it between tree and plane, refusing help. His machete stroke is noticeably tentative.

The Parsons are taking a pee behind the tail vane. I hear one of them slip and squeal faintly. When they come back over the hull, Mrs. Parsons asks, "Might we sleep in the hammock, Captain?"

Estéban splits an unbelieving grin. I protest about rain and mosquitoes.

"Oh, we have insect repellent and we do enjoy fresh air."

The air is rushing by about force five and colder by the minute.

"We have our raincoats," the girl adds cheerfully.

Well, okay, ladies. We dangerous males retire inside the damp cabin. Through the wind I hear the women laugh softly now and then, apparently cosy in their chilly ibis roost. A private insanity, I decide. I know myself for the least threatening of men; my non-charisma has been in fact an asset jobwise, over the years. Are they having fantasies about Estéban? Or maybe they really are fresh-air nuts . . . Sleep comes for me in invisible diesels roaring by on the reef outside.

We emerge dry-mouthed into a vast windy salmon sunrise. A diamond chip of sun breaks out of the sea and promptly submerges in cloud. I go to work with the rod and some mullet bait while two showers detour around us. Breakfast is a strip of wet barracuda apiece.

The Parsons continue stoic and helpful. Under Estéban's direction they set up a section of cowling for a gasoline flare in case we hear a plane, but nothing goes over except one unseen jet droning toward Panama. The wind howls, hot and dry and full of coral dust. So are we.

"They look first in the sea." Estéban remarks. His aristocratic frontal slope is beaded with sweat; Mrs. Parsons watches him concernedly. I watch the cloud blanket tearing by above, getting higher and dryer and thicker. While that lasts nobody is going to find us, and the water business is now unfunny.

Finally I borrow Estéban's machete and hack a long light pole. "There's a stream coming in back there, I saw it from the plane. Can't be more than two, three miles."

"I'm afraid the raft's torn." Mrs. Parsons shows me the cracks in the orange plastic; irritatingly, it's a Delaware label.

"All right," I hear myself announce. "The tide's going down. If we cut the good end of that air tube, I can haul water back in it. I've waded flats before."

Even to me it sounds crazy.

"Stay by plane," Estéban says. He's right, of course. He's also clearly running a fever. I look at the overcast and taste grit and old barracuda. The hell with the manual.

When I start cutting up the raft, Estéban tells me to take the serape. "You stay one night." He's right about that, too; I'll have to wait out the tide.

"I'll come with you," says Mrs. Parsons calmly.

I simply stare at her. What new madness has got into Mother Hen? Does she imagine Estéban is too battered to be functional? While I'm being astounded, my eyes take in the fact that Mrs. Parsons is now quite rosy around the knees, with her hair loose and a sunburn starting on her nose. A trim, in fact a very neat shading-forty.

"Look, that stuff is horrible going. Mud up to your ears and water over your head."

"I'm really quite fit and I swim a great deal. I'll try to keep up. Two would be much safer, Mr. Fenton, and we can bring more water."

She's serious. Well, I'm about as fit as a marshmallow at this time of winter, and I can't pretend I'm depressed by the idea of company. So be it.

"Let me show Miss Parsons how to work this rod."

Miss Parsons is even rosier and more windblown, and she's not clumsy with my tackle. A good girl, Miss Parsons, in her nothing way. We cut another staff and get some gear together. At the last minute Estéban shows how sick he feels: he offers me the machete. I thank him, but, no; I'm used to my Wirkkala knife. We tie some air into the plastic tube for a float and set out along the sandiest looking line.

Estéban raises one dark palm. "*Buen viaje.*" Miss Parsons has hugged her mother and gone to cast from the mangrove. She waves. We wave.

An hour later we're barely out of waving distance. The going is surely god-awful. The sand keeps dissolving into silt you can't walk on or swim through, and the bottom is spiked with dead mangrove spears. We flounder from one pothole to the next, scaring up rays and turtles and hoping to god we don't kick a moray eel. Where we're not soaked in slime, we're desiccated, and we smell like the Old Cretaceous.

Mrs. Parsons keeps up doggedly. I only have to pull her out once. When I do so, I notice the sandbar is now out of sight.

Finally we reach the gap in the mangrove line I thought was the creek. It turns out to open into another arm of the bay, with more mangroves ahead. And the tide is coming in.

"I've had the world's lousiest idea."

Mrs. Parsons only says mildly, "It's so different from the view from the plane."

I revise my opinion of the girl scouts, and we plow on past the mangroves toward the smoky haze that has to be shore. The sun is setting in our faces, making it hard to see. Ibis and herons fly up around us, and once a big permit spooks ahead, his fin cutting a rooster tail. We fall into more potholes. The flashlights get soaked. I am having fantasies of the mangrove as universal obstacle; it's hard to recall I ever walked down a street, for instance, without stumbling over or under or through mangrove roots. And the sun is dropping down, down.

Suddenly we hit a ledge and fall over it into a cold flow.

"The stream! It's fresh water!"

We guzzle and garble and douse our heads; it's the best drink I remember. "Oh my, oh my—!" Mrs. Parsons is laughing right out loud.

"That dark place over to the right looks like real land."

We flounder across the flow and follow a hard shelf, which turns into solid bank and rises over our heads. Shortly there's a break beside a clump of spiny bromels, and we scramble up and flop down at the top, dripping and stinking. Out of sheer reflex my arm goes around my companion's shoulder—but Mrs. Parsons isn't there; she's up on her knees peering at the burnt-over plain around us.

"It's so good to see land one can walk on!" The tone is too innocent. *Noli me tangere.*

"Don't try it." I'm exasperated; the muddy little woman, what does she think? "That ground out there is a crush of ashes over muck, and it's full of stubs. You can go in over your knees."

"It seems firm here."

"We're in an alligator nursery. That was the slide we came up. Don't worry, by now the old lady's doubtless on her way to be made into handbags."

"What a shame."

"I better set a line down in the stream while I can still see."

I slide back down and rig a string of hooks that may get us breakfast. When I get back Mrs. Parsons is wringing muck out of the serape.

"I'm glad you warned me, Mr. Fenton. It *is* treacherous."

"Yeah." I'm over my irritation; god knows I don't want to *tangere* Mrs. Parsons, even if I weren't beat down to mush. "In its quiet way, Yucatán is a tough place to get around in. You can see why the Mayas built roads. Speaking of which—look!"

The last of the sunset is silhouetting a small square shape a couple of kilometers inland; a Maya *ruina* with a fig tree growing out of it.

"Lot of those around. People think they were guard towers."

"What a deserted-feeling land."

"Let's hope it's deserted by mosquitoes."

We slump down in the 'gator nursery and share the last malt bar, watching the stars slide in and out of the blowing clouds. The bugs aren't too bad; maybe the burn did them in. And it isn't hot any more, either—in fact, it's not even warm, wet as we are. Mrs. Parsons continues tranquilly interested in Yucátan and unmistakably uninterested in togetherness.

Just as I'm beginning to get aggressive notions about how we're going to spend the night if she expects me to give her the serape, she stands up, scuffs at a couple of hummocks and says, "I expect this is as good a place as any, isn't it, Mr. Fenton?"

With which she spreads out the raft bag for a pillow and lies down on her side in the dirt with exactly half the serape over her and the other corner folded neatly open. Her small back is toward me.

The demonstration is so convincing that I'm halfway under my share of serape before the preposterousness of it stops me.

"By the way. My name is Don."

"Oh, of course." Her voice is graciousness itself, "I'm Ruth."

I get in not quite touching her, and we lie there like two fish on a plate, exposed to the stars and smelling the smoke in the wind and feeling things underneath us. It is absolutely the most intimately awkward moment I've had in years.

The woman doesn't mean one thing to me, but the obtrusive recessiveness of her, the defiance of her little rump eight inches from my fly—for two pesos I'd have those shorts down and introduce myself. If I were twenty years younger. If I wasn't so bushed . . . But the twenty years and the exhaustion are there, and it comes to me wryly that Mrs. Ruth Parsons has judged things to a nicety. If I *were* twenty years younger, she wouldn't be here. Like the butterfish that float around a sated barracuda, only to vanish away the instant his intent changes, Mrs. Parsons knows her little shorts are safe. Those firmly filled little shorts, so close . . .

A warm nerve stirs in my groin—and just as it does I become aware of a silent emptiness beside me. Mrs. Parsons is imperceptibly inching away. Did my breathing change? Whatever, I'm perfectly sure that if my hand reached, she'd be elsewhere—probably announcing her intention to take a dip. The twenty years bring a chuckle to my throat, and I relax.

"Good night, Ruth."

"Good night, Don."

And believe it or not, we sleep, while the armadas of the wind roar overhead.

Light wakes me—a cold white glare.

My first thought is 'gator hunters. Best to manifest ourselves as *turistas* as fast as possible. I scramble up, noting that Ruth has dived under the bromel clump.

"*Quién estás? A secorro!* Help, *señores!*"

No answer except the light goes out, leaving me blind.

I yell some more in a couple of languages. It stays dark. There's a vague scrabbling, whistling sound somewhere in the burn-off. Liking everything less by the minute, I try a speech about our plane having crashed and we need help.

A very narrow pencil of light flicks over us and snaps off.

"Eh-ep," says a blurry voice and something metallic twitters. They for sure aren't locals. I'm getting unpleasant ideas.

"Yes, help!"

Something goes *crackle-crackle whish-whish,* and all sounds fade away.

"What the holy hell!" I stumble toward where they were.

"Look." Ruth whispers behind me. "Over by the ruin."

I look and catch a multiple flicker which winks out fast.

"A camp?"

And I take two more blind strides. My leg goes down through the crust, and a spike spears me just where you stick the knife in to unjoint a drumstick. By the pain that goes through my bladder I recognize that my trick kneecap has caught it.

For instant basket-case you can't beat kneecaps. First you discover your knee doesn't bend any more, so you try putting some weight on it, and a bayonet goes up your spine and unhinges your jaw. Little grains of gristle have got into the sensitive bearing surface. The knee tries to buckle and can't, and mercifully you fall down.

Ruth helps me back to the serape.

"What a fool, what a god-forgotten imbecile—"

"Not at all, Don. It was perfectly natural." We strike matches; her fingers push mine aside, exploring. "I think it's in place, but it's swelling fast. I'll lay a wet handkerchief on it. We'll have to wait for morning to check the cut. Were they poachers, do you think?"

"Probably," I lie. What I think they were is smugglers.

She comes back with a soaked bandanna and drapes it on. "We must have frightened them. That light . . . it seemed so bright."

"Some hunting party. People do crazy things around here."

"Perhaps they'll come back in the morning."

"Could be."

Ruth pulls up the wet serape, and we say goodnight again. Neither of us are mentioning how we're going to get back to the plane without help.

I lie staring south where Alpha Centauri is blinking in and out of the overcast and cursing myself for the sweet mess I've made. My first idea is giving way to an even less pleasing one.

Smuggling, around here, is a couple of guys in an outboard

meeting a shrimp boat by the reef. They don't light up the sky
or have some kind of swamp buggy that goes whoosh. Plus a
big camp . . . paramilitary-type equipment?

I've seen a report of Guevarista infiltrators operating on the
British Honduran border, which is about a hundred kilometers—
sixty miles—south of here. Right under those clouds. If that's
what looked us over, I'll be more than happy if they don't come
back . . .

I wake up in pelting rain, alone. My first move confirms that
my leg is as expected—a giant misplaced erection bulging out
of my shorts. I raise up painfully to see Ruth standing by the
bromels, looking over the bay. Solid wet nimbus is pouring out
of the south.

"No planes today."

"Oh, good morning, Don. Should we look at that cut now?"

"It's minimal." In fact the skin is hardly broken, and no deep
puncture. Totally out of proportion to the havoc inside.

"Well, they have water to drink," Ruth says tranquilly. "Maybe
those hunters will come back. I'll go see if we have a fish—that
is, can I help you in any way, Don?"

Very tactful. I emit an ungracious negative, and she goes off
about her private concerns.

They certainly are private, too; when I recover from my own
sanitary efforts, she's still away. Finally I hear splashing.

"It's a big fish!" More splashing. Then she climbs up the bank
with a three-pound mangrove snapper—and something else.

It isn't until after the messy work of filleting the fish that I
begin to notice.

She's making a smudge of chaff and twigs to singe the fillets,
small hands very quick, tension in that female upper lip. The
rain has eased off for the moment; we're sluicing wet but warm
enough. Ruth brings me my fish on a mangrove skewer and sits
back on her heels with an odd breathy sigh.

"Aren't you joining me?"

"Oh, of course." She gets a strip and picks at it, saying quickly,
"We either have too much salt or too little, don't we? I should
fetch some brine." Her eyes are roving from nothing to noplace.

"Good thought." I hear another sigh and decide the girl scouts
need an assist. "Your daughter mentioned you've come from
Mérida. Have you seen much of Mexico?"

"Not really. Last year we went to Mazatlán and Cuerna-vaca . . . " She puts the fish down, frowning.

"And you're going to see Tikal. Going to Bonampak too?"

"No." Suddenly she jumps up brushing rain off her face. "I'll bring you some water, Don."

She ducks down the slide, and after a fair while comes back with a full bromel stalk.

"Thanks." She's standing above me, staring restlessly round the horizon.

"Ruth, I hate to say it, but those guys are not coming back and it's probably just as well. Whatever they were up to, we looked like trouble. The most they'll do is tell someone we're here. That'll take a day or two to get around, we'll be back at the plane by then."

"I'm sure you're right, Don." She wanders over to the smudge fire.

"And quit fretting about your daughter. She's a big girl."

"Oh, I'm sure Althea's all right . . . They have plenty of water now." Her fingers drum on her thigh. It's raining again.

"Come on, Ruth. Sit down. Tell me about Althea. Is she still in college?"

She gives that sighing little laugh and sits. "Althea got her degree last year. She's in computer programming."

"Good for her. And what about you, what do you do in GSA records?"

"I'm in Foreign Procurement Archives." She smiles mechanically, but her breathing is shallow. "It's very interesting."

"I know a Jack Wittig in Contracts, maybe you know him?"

It sounds pretty absurd, there in the 'gator slide.

"Oh, I've met Mr. Wittig. I'm sure he wouldn't remember me."

"Why not?"

"I'm not very memorable."

Her voice is factual. She's perfectly right, of course. Who was that woman, Mrs. Jannings, Janny, who coped with my per diem for years? Competent, agreeable, impersonal. She had a sick father or something. But dammit, Ruth is a lot younger and better-looking. Comparatively speaking.

"Maybe Mrs. Parsons doesn't want to be memorable."

She makes a vague sound, and I suddenly realize Ruth isn't listening to me at all. Her hands are clenched around her knees, she's staring inland at the ruin.

"Ruth. I tell you our friends with the light are in the next county by now. Forget it, we don't need them."

Her eyes come back to me as if she'd forgotten I was there, and she nods slowly. It seems to be too much effort to speak. Suddenly she cocks her head and jumps up again.

"I'll go look at the line, Don. I thought I heard something—" She's gone like a rabbit.

While she's away I try getting up onto my good leg and the staff. The pain is sickening; knees seem to have some kind of hot line to the stomach. I take a couple of hops to test whether the Demerol I have in my belt would get me walking. As I do so, Ruth comes up the bank with a fish flapping in her hands.

"Oh, no, Don! *No!*" She actually clasps the snapper to her breast.

"The water will take some of my weight. I'd like to give it a try."

"You mustn't!" Ruth says quite violently and instantly modulates down. "Look at the bay, Don. One can't see a thing."

I teeter there, tasting bile and looking at the mingled curtains of sun and rain driving across the water. She's right, thank god. Even with two good legs we could get into trouble out there.

"I guess one more night won't kill us."

I let her collapse me back onto the gritty plastic, and she positively bustles around, finding me a chunk to lean on, stretching the serape on both staffs to keep rain off me, bringing another drink, grubbing for dry tinder.

"I'll make us a real bonfire as soon as it lets up, Don. They'll see our smoke, they'll know we're all right. We just have to wait." Cheery smile. "Is there any way we can make you more comfortable?"

Holy Saint Sterculius: playing house in a mud puddle. For a fatuous moment I wonder if Mrs. Parsons has designs on me. And then she lets out another sigh and sinks back onto her heels with that listening look. Unconsciously her rump wiggles a little. My ear picks up the operative word: *wait.*

Ruth Parsons is waiting. In fact, she acts as if she's waiting so hard it's killing her. For what? For someone to get us out of here, what else? . . . But why was she so horrified when I got up to try to leave? Why all this tension?

My paranoia stirs. I grab it by the collar and start idly checking back. Up to when whoever it was showed up last night, Mrs. Parsons was, I guess, normal. Calm and sensible, anyway. Now she's humming like a high wire. And she seems to want to stay here and wait. Just as an intellectual pastime, why?

Could she have intended to come here? No way. Where she planned to be was Chetumal, which is on the border. Come to think, Chetumal is an odd way round to Tikal. Let's say the scenario was that she's meeting somebody in Chetumal. Somebody who's part of an organization. So now her contact in Chetumal knows she's overdue. And when those types appeared last night, something suggests to her that they're part of the same organization. And she hopes they'll put one and one together and come back for her?

"May I have the knife, Don? I'll clean the fish."

Rather slowly I pass the knife, kicking my subconscious. Such a decent ordinary little woman, a good girl scout. My trouble is that I've bumped into too many professional agilities under the careful stereotypes. *I'm not very memorable* . . .

What's in Foreign Procurement Archives? Wittig handles classified contracts. Lots of money stuff; foreign currency negotiations, commodity price schedules, some industrial technology. Or—just as a hypothesis—it could be as simple as a wad of bills back in that modest beige Ventura, to be exchanged for a packet from say, Costa Rica. If she were a courier, they'd want to get at the plane. And then what about me and maybe Estéban? Even hypothetically, not good.

I watch her hacking at the fish, forehead knotted with effort, teeth in her lip. Mrs. Ruth Parsons of Bethesda, this thrumming, private woman. How crazy can I get? *They'll see our smoke* . . .

"Here's your knife, Don. I washed it. Does the leg hurt very badly?"

I blink away the fantasies and see a scared little woman in a mangrove swamp.

"Sit down, rest. You've been going all out."

She sits obediently, like a kid in a dentist chair.

"You're stewing about Althea. And she's probably worried about you. We'll get back tomorrow under our own steam, Ruth."

"Honestly I'm not worried at all, Don." The smile fades; she nibbles her lip, frowning out at the bay.

"You know, Ruth, you surprised me when you offered to come along. Not that I don't appreciate it. But I rather thought you'd be concerned about leaving Althea alone with our good pilot. Or was it only me?"

This gets her attention at last.

"I believe Captain Estéban is a very fine type of man."

The words surprise me a little. Isn't the correct line more like "I trust Althea," or even, indignantly, "Althea is a good girl?"

"He's a man. Althea seemed to think he was interesting."

She goes on staring at the bay. And then I notice her tongue flick out and lick that prehensile upper lip. There's a flush that isn't sunburn around her ears and throat too, and one hand is gently rubbing her thigh. What's she seeing, out there in the flats?

Oho.

Captain Estéban's mahogany arms clasping Miss Althea Parsons' pearly body. Captain Estéban's archaic nostrils snuffling in Miss Parsons' tender neck. Captain Estéban's copper buttocks pumping into Althea's creamy upturned bottom . . . The hammock, very bouncy. Mayas know all about it.

Well, well. So Mother Hen has her little quirks.

I feel fairly silly and more than a little irritated. *Now* I find out . . . But even vicarious lust has much to recommend it, here in the mud and rain. I settle back, recalling that Miss Althea the computer programmer had waved good-bye very composedly. Was she sending her mother to flounder across the bay with me so she can get programmed in Maya? The memory of Honduran mahogany logs drifting in and out of the opalescent sand comes to me. Just as I am about to suggest that Mrs. Parsons might care to share my rain shelter, she remarks serenely, "The Mayas seem to be a very fine type of people. I believe you said so to Althea."

The implications fall on me with the rain. *Type.* As in breeding, bloodline, sire. Am I supposed to have certified Estéban not only as a stud but as a genetic donor?

"Ruth, are you telling me you're prepared to accept a half-Indian grandchild?"

"Why, Don, that's up to Althea, you know."

Looking at the mother, I guess it is. Oh, for mahogany gonads.

Ruth has gone back to listening to the wind, but I'm not about to let her off that easy. Not after all that *noli me tangere* jazz.

"What will Althea's father think?"

Her face snaps around at me, genuinely startled.

"Althea's father?" Complicated semismile. "He won't mind."

"He'll accept it too, eh?" I see her shake her head as if a fly were bothering her, and add with a cripple's malice: "Your husband must be a very fine type of a man."

Ruth looks at me, pushing her wet hair back abruptly. I have the impression that mousy Mrs. Parsons is roaring out of control, but her voice is quiet.

"There isn't any Mr. Parsons, Don. There never was. Althea's father was a Danish medical student . . . I believe he has gained considerable prominence."

"Oh." Something warns me not to say I'm sorry. "You mean he doesn't know about Althea?"

"No." She smiles, her eyes bright and cuckoo.

"Seems like rather a rough deal for her."

"I grew up quite happily under the same circumstances."

Bang, I'm dead. Well, well, well. A mad image blooms in my mind: generations of solitary Parsons women selecting sires, making impregnation trips. Well, I hear the world is moving their way.

"I better look at the fish line."

She leaves. The glow fades. *No.* Just no, no contact. Goodbye, Captain Estéban. My leg is very uncomfortable. The hell with Mrs. Parsons' long-distance orgasm.

We don't talk much after that, which seems to suit Ruth. The odd day drags by. Squall after squall blows over us. Ruth singes up some more fillets, but the rain drowns her smudge; it seems to pour hardest just as the sun's about to show.

Finally she comes to sit under my sagging serape, but there's no warmth there. I doze, aware of her getting up now and then to look around. My subconscious notes that she's still twitchy. I tell my subconscious to knock it off.

Presently I wake up to find her penciling on the water-soaked pages of a little notepad.

"What's that, a shopping list for alligators?"

Automatic polite laugh. "Oh, just an address. In case we—I'm being silly, Don."

"Hey," I sit up, wincing, "Ruth, quit fretting. I mean it. We'll all be out of this soon. You'll have a great story to tell."

She doesn't look up. "Yes . . . I guess we will."

"Come on, we're doing fine. There isn't any real danger here, you know. Unless you're allergic to fish?"

Another good-little-girl laugh, but there's a shiver in it.

"Sometimes I think I'd like to go . . . really far away."

To keep her talking I say the first thing in my head.

"Tell me, Ruth. I'm curious why you would settle for that kind of lonely life, there in Washington? I mean, a woman like you—"

"Should get married?" She gives a shaky sigh, pushing the notebook back in her wet pocket.

"Why not? It's the normal source of companionship. Don't tell me you're trying to be some kind of professional man-hater."

"Lesbian, you mean?" Her laugh sounds better. "With my security rating? No, I'm not."

"Well, then. Whatever trauma you went through, these things don't last forever. You can't hate all men."

The smile is back. "Oh, there wasn't any trauma, Don, and I *don't* hate men. That would be as silly as—as hating the weather." She glances wryly at the blowing rain.

"I think you have a grudge. You're even spooky of me."

Smooth as a mouse bite she says, "I'd love to hear about your family, Don?"

Touché. I give her the edited version of how I don't have one any more, and she says she's sorry, how sad. And we chat about what a good life a single person really has, and how she and her friends enjoy plays and concerts and travel, and one of them is head cashier for Ringling Brothers, how about that?

But it's coming out jerkier and jerkier like a bad tape, with her eyes going round the horizon in the pauses and her face listening for something that isn't my voice. What's wrong with her? Well, what's wrong with any furtively unconventional middle-aged woman with an empty bed. And a security clearance. An old habit of mind remarks unkindly that Mrs. Parsons represents what is known as the classic penetration target.

"—so much more opportunity now." Her voice trails off.

"Hurrah for women's lib, eh?"

"The lib?" Impatiently she leans forward and tugs the serape straight. "Oh, that's doomed."

The apocalyptic word jars my attention.

"What do you mean, doomed?"

She glances at me as if I weren't hanging straight either and says vaguely, "Oh . . . "

"Come on, why doomed? Didn't they get that equal rights bill?"

Long hesitation. When she speaks again her voice is different.

"Women have no rights, Don, except what men allow us. Men are more aggressive and powerful, and they run the world. When the next real crisis upsets them, our so-called rights will vanish like—like that smoke. We'll be back where we always were: property. And whatever has gone wrong will be blamed on our freedom, like the fall of Rome was. You'll see."

Now all this is delivered in a gray tone of total conviction. The last time I heard that tone, the speaker was explaining why he had to keep his file drawers full of dead pigeons.

"Oh, come on. You and your friends are the backbone of the system; if you quit, the country would come to a screeching halt before lunch."

No answering smile.

"That's fantasy." Her voice is still quiet. "Women don't work that way. We're a—a toothless world." She looks around as if she wanted to stop talking. "What women do is survive. We live by ones and twos in the chinks of your world-machine."

"Sounds like a guerrilla operation." I'm not really joking, here in the 'gator den. In fact, I'm wondering if I spent too much thought on mahogany logs.

"Guerrillas have something to hope for." Suddenly she switches on a jolly smile. "Think of us as opossums, Don. Did you know there are opossums living all over? Even in New York City."

I smile back with my neck prickling. I thought I was the paranoid one.

"Men and women aren't different species, Ruth. Women do everything men do."

"Do they?" Our eyes meet, but she seems to be seeing ghosts between us in the rain. She mutters something that could be "My Lai" and looks away. "All the endless wars . . . " Her voice is a whisper. "All the huge authoritarian organizations for doing unreal things. Men live to struggle against each other; we're just part of the battlefields. It'll never change unless you change the whole world. I dream sometimes of—of going away—" She checks and abruptly changes voice. "Forgive me, Don, it's so stupid saying all this."

"Men hate wars too, Ruth," I say as gently as I can.

"I know." She shrugs and climbs to her feet. "But that's your problem, isn't it?"

End of communication. Mrs. Ruth Parsons isn't even living in the same world with me.

I watch her move around restlessly, head turning toward the ruins. Alienation like that can add up to dead pigeons, which would be GSA's problem. It could also lead to believing some joker who's promising to change the whole world. Which could just probably be my problem if one of them was over in that camp last night, where she keeps looking. *Guerrillas have something to hope for . . . ?*

Nonsense. I try another position and see that the sky seems to be clearing as the sun sets. The wind is quieting down at last too. Insane to think this little woman is acting out some fantasy in this swamp. But that equipment last night was no fantasy; if those lads have some connection with her, I'll be in the way. You couldn't find a handier spot to dispose of the body . . . Maybe some Guevarista is a fine type of man?

Absurd. Sure . . . The only thing more absurd would be to come through the wars and get myself terminated by a mad librarian's boyfriend on a fishing trip.

A fish flops in the stream below us. Ruth spins around so fast she hits the serape. "I better start the fire," she says, her eyes still on the plain and her head cocked, listening.

All right, let's test.

"Expecting company?"

It rocks her. She freezes, and her eyes come swiveling around

at me like a film take captioned Fright. I can see her decide to
smile.

"Oh, one never can tell!" She laughs weirdly, the eyes not
changed. "I'll get the—the kindling." She fairly scuttles into the
brush.

Nobody, paranoid or not, could call *that* a normal reaction.

Ruth Parsons is either psycho or she's expecting something to
happen—and it has nothing to do with me; I scared her pissless.

Well, she could be nuts. And I could be wrong, but there are
some mistakes you only make once.

Reluctantly I unzip my body belt, telling myself that if I think
what I think, my only course is to take something for my leg
and get as far as possible from Mrs. Ruth Parsons before whoever
she's waiting for arrives.

In my belt also is a .32 caliber asset Ruth doesn't know about—
and it's going to stay there. My longevity program leaves the
shoot-outs to TV and stresses being somewhere else when the
roof falls in. I can spend a perfectly safe and also perfectly
horrible night out in one of those mangrove flats ... Am I
insane?

At this moment Ruth stands up and stares blatantly inland
with her hand shading her eyes. Then she tucks something into
her pocket, buttons up and tightens her belt.

That does it.

I dry-swallow two 100 mg tabs, which should get me ambulatory
and still leave me wits to hide. Give it a few minutes. I make
sure my compass and some hooks are in my own pocket and sit
waiting while Ruth fusses with her smudge fire, sneaking looks
away when she thinks I'm not watching.

The flat world around us is turning into an unearthly amber
and violet light show as the first numbness sweeps into my leg.
Ruth has crawled under the bromels for more dry stuff; I can
see her foot. Okay. I reach for my staff.

Suddenly the foot jerks, and Ruth yells—or rather, her throat
makes that *Uh-uh-hhh* that means pure horror. The foot disap-
pears in a rattle of bromel stalks.

I lunge upright on the crutch and look over the bank at a
frozen scene.

Ruth is crouching sideways on the ledge, clutching her stom-

ach. They are about a yard below, floating on the river in a skiff.
While I was making up my stupid mind, her friends have glided
right under my ass. There are three of them.

They are tall and white. I try to see them as men in some
kind of white jumpsuits. The one nearest the bank is stretching
out a long white arm toward Ruth. She jerks and scuttles further
away.

The arm stretches after her. It stretches and stretches. It
stretches two yards and stays hanging in the air. Small black
things are wiggling from its tip.

I look where their faces should be and see black hollow dishes
with vertical stripes. The stripes move slowly . . .

There is no more possibility of their being human—or anything
else I've ever seen. What has Ruth conjured up?

The scene is totally silent. I blink, blink—this cannot be real.
The two in the far end of the skiff are writhing those arms
around an apparatus on a tripod. A weapon? Suddenly I hear
the same blurry voice I heard in the night.

"Guh-give," it groans. "G-give . . ."

Dear god, it's real, whatever it is. I'm terrified. My mind is
trying not to form a word.

And Ruth—Jesus, of course—Ruth is terrified too; she's edging
along the bank away from them, gaping at the monsters in the
skiff, who are obviously nobody's friends. She's hugging something to her body. Why doesn't she get over the bank and circle
back behind me?

"G-g-give." That wheeze is coming from the tripod. "Pee-eeze
give." The skiff is moving upstream below Ruth, following her.
The arm undulates out at her again, its black digits looping.
Ruth scrambles to the top of the bank.

"Ruth!" My voice cracks. "Ruth, get over here behind me!"

She doesn't look at me, only keeps sidling farther away. My
terror detonates into anger.

"Come back here!" With my free hand I'm working the .32
out of my belt. The sun has gone down.

She doesn't turn but straightens up warily, still hugging the
thing. I see her mouth working. Is she actually trying to *talk* to
them?

"Please . . ." She swallows. "Please speak to me. I need your help."

"RUTH!!"

At this moment the nearest white monster whips into a great S-curve and sails right onto the bank at her, eight feet of snowy rippling horror.

And I shoot Ruth.

I don't know that for a minute—I've yanked the gun up so fast that my staff slips and dumps me as I fire. I stagger up, hearing Ruth scream "No! No! No!"

The creature is back down by his boat, and Ruth is still farther away, clutching herself. Blood is running down her elbow.

"Stop it, Don! They aren't attacking you!"

"For god's sake! Don't be a fool, I can't help you if you won't get away from them!"

No reply. Nobody moves. No sound except the drone of a jet passing far above. In the darkening stream below me the three white figures shift uneasily; I get the impression of radar dishes focusing. The word spells itself in my head: *Aliens.*

Extraterrestrials.

What do I do, call the President? Capture them single-handed with my peashooter? . . . I'm alone in the arse end of nowhere with one leg and my brain cuddled in meperidine hydrochloride.

"Prrr-eese," their machine blurs again. "Wa-wat hep . . ."

"Our plane fell down," Ruth says in a very distinct, eerie voice. She points up at the jet, out towards the bay. "My—my child is there. Please take us *there* in your boat."

Dear god. While she's gesturing, I get a look at the thing she's hugging in her wounded arm. It's metallic, like a big glimmering distributor head. What—?

Wait a minute. This morning: when she was gone so long, she could have found that thing. Something they left behind. Or dropped. And she hid it, not telling me. That's why she kept going under that bromel clump—she was peeking at it. Waiting. And the owners came back and caught her. They want it. She's trying to bargain, by god.

"—Water," Ruth is pointing again. "Take us. Me. And him."

The black faces turn toward me, blind and horrible. Later on I may be grateful for that "us." Not now.

"Throw your gun away, Don. They'll take us back." Her voice is weak.

"Like hell I will. You—who are you? What are you doing here?"

"Oh god, does it matter? He's frightened," she cries to them. "Can you understand?"

She's as alien as they, there in the twilight. The beings in the skiff are twittering among themselves. Their box starts to moan.

"Ss-stu-dens," I make out. "S-stu-ding . . . not—huh-arm-ing . . . w-we . . . buh . . . " It fades into garble and then says "G-give . . . we . . . g-go . . . "

Peace-loving cultural-exchange students—on the interstellar level now. Oh, no.

"Bring that thing here, Ruth—right now!"

But she's starting down the bank toward them saying, "Take me."

"Wait! You need a tourniquet on that arm."

"I know. Please put the gun down, Don."

She's actually at the skiff, right by them. They aren't moving.

"Jesus Christ." Slowly, reluctantly, I drop the .32. When I start down the slide, I find I'm floating; adrenaline and Demerol are a bad mix.

The skiff comes gliding toward me, Ruth in the bow clutching the thing and her arm. The aliens stay in the stern behind their tripod, away from me. I note the skiff is camouflaged tan and green. The world around us is deep shadowy blue.

"Don, bring the water bag!"

As I'm dragging down the plastic bag, it occurs to me that Ruth really is cracking up, the water isn't needed now. But my own brain seems to have gone into overload. All I can focus on is a long white rubbery arm with black worms clutching the far end of the orange tube, helping me fill it. This isn't happening.

"Can you get in, Don?" As I hoist my numb legs up, two long white pipes reach for me. *No you don't.* I kick and tumble in beside Ruth. She moves away.

A creaky hum starts up, it's coming from a wedge in the center of the skiff. And we're in motion, sliding toward dark mangrove files.

I stare mindlessly at the wedge. Alien technological secrets? I can't see any, the power source is under that triangular cover, about two feet long. The gadgets on the tripod are equally cryptic, except that one has a big lens. Their light?

As we hit the open bay, the hum rises and we start planing faster and faster still. Thirty knots? Hard to judge in the dark. Their hull seems to be a modified trihedral much like ours, with a remarkable absence of slap. Say twenty-two feet. Schemes of capturing it swirl in my mind. I'll need Estéban.

Suddenly a huge flood of white light fans out over us from the tripod, blotting out the aliens in the stern. I see Ruth pulling at a belt around her arm still hugging the gizmo.

"I'll tie that for you."

"It's all right."

The alien device is twinkling or phosphorescing slightly. I lean over to look, whispering, "Give that to me, I'll pass it to Estéban."

"No!" She scoots away, almost over the side. "It's theirs, they need it!"

"What? Are you crazy?" I'm so taken aback by this idiocy I literally stammer. "We have to, we—"

"They haven't hurt us. I'm sure they could." Her eyes are watching me with feral intensity; in the light her face has a lunatic look. Numb as I am, I realize that the wretched woman is poised to throw herself over the side if I move. With the alien thing.

"I think they're gentle," she mutters.

"For Christ's sake, Ruth, they're *aliens!*"

"I'm used to it," she says absently. "There's the island! Stop! Stop here!"

The skiff slows, turning. A mound of foliage is tiny in the light. Metal glints—the plane.

"Althea! Althea! Are you all right?"

Yells, movement on the plane. The water is high, we're floating over the bar. The aliens are keeping us in the lead with the light hiding them. I see one pale figure splashing toward us and a dark one behind, coming more slowly. Estéban must be puzzled by that light.

"Mr. Fenton is hurt, Althea. These people brought us back with the water. Are you all right?"

"A-okay." Althea flounders up, peering excitedly. "You all right? Whew, that light!" Automatically I start handing her the idiotic water bag.

"Leave that for the captain," Ruth says sharply. "Althea, can you climb in the boat? Quickly, it's important."

"Coming."

"No, no!" I protest, but the skiff tilts as Althea swarms in. The aliens twitter, and their voice box starts groaning. "Gu-give . . . now . . . give . . . "

"*Que llega?*" Estéban's face appears beside me, squinting fiercely into the light.

"Grab it, get it from her—that thing she has—" but Ruth's voice rides over mine. "Captain, lift Mr. Fenton out of the boat. He's hurt his leg. Hurry, please."

"Goddamn it, wait!" I shout, but an arm has grabbed my middle. When a Maya boosts you, you go. I hear Althea saying, "Mother, your arm!" and fall onto Estéban. We stagger around in water up to my waist; I can't feel my feet at all.

When I get steady, the boat is yards away. The two women are head-to-head, murmuring.

"Get them!" I tug loose from Estéban and flounder forward. Ruth stands up in the boat facing the invisible aliens.

"Take us with you. Please. We want to go with you, away from here."

"Ruth! Estéban, get that boat!" I lunge and lose my feet again. The aliens are chirruping madly behind their light.

"Please take us. We don't mind what your planet is like; we'll learn—we'll do anything! We won't cause any trouble. Please. Oh *please*." The skiff is drifting farther away.

"Ruth! Althea! Are you crazy? Wait—" But I can only shuffle nightmarelike in the ooze, hearing that damn voice box wheeze, "N-not come . . . more . . . not come . . . " Althea's face turns to it, open-mouthed grin.

"Yes, we understand," Ruth cries. "We don't want to come back. Please take us with you!"

I shout and Estéban splashes past me shouting too, something about radio.

"Yes-s-s" groans the voice.

Ruth sits down suddenly, clutching Althea. At that moment Estéban grabs the edge of the skiff beside her.

"Hold them, Estéban! Don't let her go."

He gives me one slit-eyed glance over his shoulder, and I recognize his total uninvolvement. He's had a good look at that camouflage paint and the absence of fishing gear. I make a desperate rush and slip again. When I come up Ruth is saying, "We're going with these people, Captain. Please take your money out of my purse, it's in the plane. And give this to Mr. Fenton."

She passes him something small; the notebook. He takes it slowly.

"Estéban! No!"

He has released the skiff.

"Thank you so much," Ruth says as they float apart. Her voice is shaky; she raises it. "There won't be any trouble, Don. Please send this cable. It's to a friend of mine, she'll take care of everything." Then she adds the craziest touch of the entire night. "She's a grand person; she's director of nursing training at N.I.H."

As the skiff drifts, I hear Althea add something that sounds like "Right on."

Sweet Jesus . . . Next minute the humming has started; the light is receding fast. The last I see of Mrs. Ruth Parsons and Miss Althea Parsons is two small shadows against that light, like two opossums. The light snaps off, the hum deepens—and they're going, going, gone away.

In the dark water beside me Estéban is instructing everybody in general to *chingarse* themselves.

"Friends, or something," I tell him lamely. "She seemed to want to go with them."

He is pointedly silent, hauling me back to the plane. He knows what could be around here better than I do, and Mayas have their own longevity program. His condition seems improved. As we get in I notice the hammock has been repositioned.

In the night—of which I remember little—the wind changes. And at seven thirty next morning a Cessna buzzes the sandbar under cloudless skies.

By noon we're back in Cozumel, Captain Estéban accepts his fees and departs laconically for his insurance wars. I leave the

Parsons' bags with the Caribe agent, who couldn't care less. The cable goes to a Mrs. Priscilla Hayes Smith, also of Bethesda. I take myself to a medico and by three PM I'm sitting on the Cabañas terrace with a fat leg and a double margharita, trying to believe the whole thing.

The cable said, *Althea and I taking extraordinary opportunity for travel. Gone several years. Please take charge our affairs. Love, Ruth.*

She'd written it that afternoon, you understand.

I order another double, wishing to hell I'd gotten a good look at that gizmo. Did it have a label. Made by Betelgeusians? No matter how weird it was, *how* could a person be crazy enough to imagine—?

Not only that but to hope, to plan? *If I could only go away . . .* That's what she was doing, all day. Waiting, hoping, figuring how to get Althea. To go sight unseen to an alien world . . .

With the third margharita I try a joke about alienated women, but my heart's not in it. And I'm certain there won't be any bother, any trouble at all. Two human women, one of them possibly pregnant, have departed for, I guess, the stars; and the fabric of society will never show a ripple. I brood: do all Mrs. Parsons' friends hold themselves in readiness for any eventuality, including leaving Earth? And will Mrs. Parsons somehow one day contrive to send for Mrs. Priscrlla Hayes Smith, that grand person?

I can only send for another cold one, musing on Althea. What suns will Captain Estéban's sloe-eyed offspring, if any, look upon? "Get in, Althea, we're taking off for Orion." "A-okay, Mother." Is that some system of upbringing? *We survive by ones and twos in the chinks of your world-machine . . . I'm used to aliens . . .* She'd meant every word. Insane. How could a woman choose to live among unknown monsters, to say good-bye to her home, her world?

As the margharitas take hold, the whole mad scenario melts down to the image of those two small shapes sitting side by side in the receding alien glare.

Two of our opossums are missing.

Alice Walker

Everyday Use
1973

Alice Walker (b. 1944), the youngest of eight children of sharecroppers in rural Georgia, has become one of the most critically acclaimed and widely loved writers in the United States. Walker was the baby of her family and cherished by her mother and other strong women in the community for her intelligence and her spirit—and also because she was "cute." She was favored, privileged, praised—until, at the age of eight, she was blinded in one eye in an accident. She lost her self-confidence and that special favor in her world until the appearance of the blinded eye was normalized again, in adolescence. Not until her late twenties did she overcome her estrangement from, and ambivalence about, her own appearance. That understanding and acceptance of shame and anger and inner vision and the appreciation of the impact of the perception of deformity, whether caused by sex or color or physical, emotional, or mental disability, illuminates all that she writes.

"Everyday Use," first published in Harper's Magazine *in April 1973, was included in Walker's first short story collection,* In Love and Trouble: Stories of Black Women *(1973). An extraordinarily versatile writer, Walker has published three volumes of poetry,* Once *(1968),* Revolutionary Petunias and Other Poems *(1973), and* Goodnight, Willie Lee, I'll See You in The Morning *(1979); and three novels,* The Third Life of Grange Copeland *(1970),* Meridian *(1976), and* The Color Purple *(1982), for which she received both the Pulitzer Prize and the American Book Award. In 1973 she published a biography for children,* Langston Hughes: American Poet. *She also edited* I Love Myself When I'm Laughing . . . And Then Again When I Am Looking Mean And Impressive: A Zora Neale*

Hurston Reader *(The Feminist Press, 1979) and most recently, a collection of her essays,* In Search of Our Mothers' Gardens *(1983).*

Alice Walker keeps a picture on her desk of herself at six—"dauntless eyes, springy hair, optimistic satin bow—and I look at it often; I realize I am always trying to keep faith with the child I was." Her sense of history and commitment to keeping faith with the past not only include herself and her own past, but also those whom she has identified as her people, black people, black women especially, and those individuals she has taken as mentors, in particular Zora Neale Hurston (1901–1960), the novelist and folklorist, in whose work she found inspiration and sustenance.

In her own work, Walker depicts the struggle of black women to survive the double oppressions of racism and sexism, poverty, a history of disempowerment, and physical, mental, and spiritual abuse. She portrays not only the triumphs in the struggle, but the costs and the defeats. She knows her subject matter from personal experience and the stories she grew up listening to, and also from her participation in the Civil Rights Movement. She has an international perspective and understands that "women's freedom is an idea whose time [has] come . . . an idea sweeping the world."

I will wait for her in the yard that Maggie and I made so clean and wavy yesterday afternoon. A yard like this is more comfortable than most people know. It is not just a yard. It is like an extended living room. When the hard clay is swept clean as a floor and the fine sand around the edges lined with tiny, irregular grooves, anyone can come and sit and look up into the elm tree and wait for the breezes that never come inside the house.

Maggie will be nervous until after her sister goes: she will stand hopelessly in corners, homely and ashamed of the burn scars down her arms and legs, eying her sister with a mixture of envy and awe. She thinks her sister has held life always in the palm of one hand, that "no" is a word the world never learned to say to her.

You've no doubt seen those TV shows where the child who has "made it" is confronted, as a surprise, by his own mother and father, tottering in weakly from backstage. (A pleasant surprise, of course: what would they do if parent and child came on the show only to curse out and insult each other?) On TV mother and child embrace and smile into each other's faces. Sometimes the mother and father weep, the child wraps them in his arms and leans across the table to tell how he would not have made it without their help. I have seen these programs.

Sometimes I dream a dream in which Dee and I are suddenly brought together on a TV program of this sort. Out of a dark and soft-seated limousine I am ushered into a bright room filled with many people. There I meet a smiling, gray, sporty man like Johnny Carson who shakes my hand and tells me what a fine girl I have. Then we are on the stage and Dee is embracing me with tears in her eyes. She pins on my dress a large orchid, even though she has told me once that she thinks orchids are tacky flowers.

In real life I am a large big-boned woman with rough, man-working hands. In the winter I wear flannel nightgowns to bed and overalls during the day. I can kill and clean a hog as mercilessly as a man. My fat keeps me hot in zero weather. I can work outside all day, breaking ice to get water for washing; I can eat pork liver cooked over the open fire minutes after it comes steaming from the hog. One winter I knocked a bull calf straight in the brain between the eyes with a sledgehammer and had the meat hung up to chill before nightfall. But of course all this does not show on television. I am the way my daughter would want me to be; a hundred pounds lighter, my skin like an uncooked barley pancake. My hair glistens in the hot bright lights. Johnny Carson has much to do to keep up with my quick and witty tongue.

But that is a mistake. I know even before I wake up. Who ever knew a Johnson with a quick tongue? Who can even imagine me looking a strange white man in the eye? It seems to me I have talked to them always with one foot raised in flight, with my head turned in whichever way is farthest from them. Dee, though. She would always look anyone in the eye. Hesitation was no part of her nature.

"How do I look, Mama?" Maggie says, showing just enough of her thin body enveloped in pink skirt and red blouse for me to know she's there almost hidden by the door.

"Come out into the yard," I say.

Have you ever seen a lame animal, perhaps a dog run over by some careless person rich enough to own a car, sidle up to someone who is ignorant enough to be kind to him? That is the way my Maggie walks. She has been like this, chin on chest, eyes on ground, feet in shuffle, ever since the fire that burned the other house to the ground.

Dee is lighter than Maggie, with nicer hair and a fuller figure. She's a woman now, though sometimes I forget. How long ago was it that the other house burned? Ten, twelve years? Sometimes I can still hear the flames and feel Maggie's arms sticking to me, her hair smoking and her dress falling off her in little black papery flakes. Her eyes seemed stretched open, blazed open by the flames reflected in them. And Dee. I see her standing off under the sweetgum tree she used to dig gum out of; a look of concentration on her face as she watched the last dingy gray board of the house fall in toward the red-hot brick chimney. Why don't you do a dance around the ashes? I'd wanted to ask her. She had hated the house that much.

I used to think she hated Maggie too. But that was before we raised the money, the church and me, to send her to Augusta to school. She used to read to us without pity; forcing words, lies, other folks' habits, whole lives upon us two, sitting trapped and ignorant underneath her voice. She washed us in a river of make-believe, burned us with a lot of knowledge we didn't necessarily need to know. Pressed us to her with the serious way she read, to shove us away, like dimwits, at just the moment we seemed about to understand.

Dee wanted nice things. A yellow organdy dress to wear to her graduation from high school; black pumps to match a green suit she'd made from an old suit somebody gave me. She was determined to stare down any disaster in her efforts. Her eyelids would not flicker for minutes at a time. Often I fought off the temptation to shake her. At sixteen she had a style of her own: and knew what style was.

I never had an education myself. After second grade the school was closed down. Don't ask me why: in 1927 colored asked fewer questions than they do now. Sometimes Maggie reads to me. She stumbles along good-naturedly but can't see well. She knows she is not bright. Like good looks and money, quickness passed her by. She will marry John Thomas (who has mossy teeth in an earnest face), and then I'll be free to sit here and I guess just sing church songs to myself. Although I never was a good singer. Never could carry a tune. I was always better at a man's job. I used to love to milk till I was hooked in the side in '49. Cows are soothing and slow and don't bother you, unless you try to milk them the wrong way.

I have deliberately turned my back on the house. It is three rooms, just like the one that burned, except the roof is tin; they don't make shingle roofs anymore. There are no real windows, just some holes cut in the sides, like the portholes in a ship, but not round and not square, with rawhide holding the shutters up on the outside. This house is in a pasture too, like the other one. No doubt when Dee sees it she will want to tear it down. She wrote me once that no matter where we "choose" to live, she will manage to come see us. But she will never bring her friends. Maggie and I thought about this and Maggie asked me, "Mama, when did Dee ever *have* any friends?"

She had a few. Furtive boys in pink shirts hanging about on washday after school. Nervous girls who never laughed. Impressed with her, they worshiped the well-turned phrase, the cute shape, the scalding humor that erupted like bubbles in lye. She read to them.

When she was courting Jimmy T she didn't have much time to pay to us, but turned all her fault-finding power on him. He *flew* to marry a cheap city girl from a family of ignorant, flashy people. She hardly had time to recompose herself.

When she comes I will meet . . . but there they are!

Maggie attempts to make a dash for the house, in her shuffling way, but I stay her with my hand. "Come back here," I say. And she stops and tries to dig a well in the sand with her toe.

It is hard to see them clearly through the strong sun. But even the first glimpse of leg out of the car tells me it is Dee. Her feet were always neat looking, as if God himself had shaped them with a certain style. From the other side of the car comes a short, stocky man. Hair is all over his head a foot long and hanging from his chin like a kinky mule tail. I hear Maggie suck in her breath. "Uhnnnh," is what it sounds like. Like when you see the wriggling end of a snake just in front of your foot on a road. "Uhnnnh."

Dee, next. A dress down to the ground, in this hot weather. A dress so loud it hurts my eyes. There are yellows and oranges enough to throw back the light of the sun. I feel my whole face warming from the heat waves it throws out. Earrings gold too, and hanging down to her shoulders. Bracelets dangling and making noises when she moves her arm up to shake the folds of the dress out of her armpits. The dress is loose and flows, and as she walks closer, I like it. I hear Maggie go "Uhnnnh" again. It is her sister's hair. It stands straight up like the wool on a sheep. It is black as night and around the edges are two long pigtails that rope about like small lizards disappearing behind her ears.

"Wa-su-zo-Tean-o!" she says, coming on in that gliding way the dress makes her move. The short stocky fellow with the hair to his navel is all grinning and he follows up with "Asalamalakim, my mother and sister!" He moves to hug Maggie but she falls back, right up against the back of my chair. I feel her trembling there, and when I look up I see the perspiration falling off her skin.

"Don't get up," says Dee. Since I am stout it takes something of a push. You can see me trying to move a second or two before I make it. She turns, showing white heels through her sandals, and goes back to the car. Out she peeks next with a Polaroid. She stoops down quickly and snaps off picture after picture of me sitting there in front of the house with Maggie cowering behind me. She never takes a shot without making sure the house is included. When a cow comes nibbling around the edge of the yard she snaps it and me and Maggie *and* the house. Then she puts the Polaroid on the back seat of the car, and comes up and kisses me on the forehead.

Meanwhile Asalamalakim is going through motions with Maggie's hand. Maggie's hand is as limp as a fish, and probably as cold, despite the sweat, and she keeps trying to pull it back. It looks like Asalamalakim wants to shake hands but wants to do it fancy. Or maybe he don't know how people shake hands. Anyhow, he soon gives up on Maggie.

"Well," I say, "Dee."

"No, Mama," she says. "Not 'Dee,' Wangero Leewanika Kemanjo!"

"What happened to 'Dee'?" I wanted to know.

"She's dead," Wangero said. "I couldn't bear it any longer, being named after the people who oppress me."

"You know well as me you was named after your aunt Dicie," I said. Dicie is my sister. She named Dee. We called her "Big Dee" after Dee was born.

"But who was *she* named after?" asked Wangero.

"I guess after Grandma Dee," I said.

"And who was she named after?" asked Wangero.

"Her mother," I said, and saw Wangero was getting tired. "That's about as far back as I can trace it," I said. Though, in fact, I probably could have carried it back beyond the Civil War through the branches.

"Well," said Asalamalakim, "there you are."

"Uhnnnh," I heard Maggie say.

"There I was not," I said, "before 'Dicie' cropped up in our family, so why should I try to trace it that far back?"

He just stood there grinning, looking down on me like somebody inspecting a Model A car. Every once in a while he and Wangero sent eye signals over my head.

"How do you pronounce this name?" I asked.

"You don't have to call me by it if you don't want to," said Wangero.

"Why shouldn't I?" I asked. "If that's what you want us to call you, we'll call you."

"I know it might sound awkward at first," said Wangero.

"I'll get used to it," I said. "Ream it out again."

Well, soon we got the name out of the way. Asalamalakim had a name twice as long and three times as hard. After I tripped over it two or three times he told me to just call him Hakim-a-barber. I wanted to ask him was he a barber, but I didn't really think he was, so I didn't ask.

"You must belong to those beef-cattle peoples down the road," I said. They said "Asalamalakim" when they met you too, but they didn't shake hands. Always too busy: feeding the cattle, fixing the fences, putting up salt-lick shelters, throwing down hay. When the white folks poisoned some of the herd, the men stayed up all night with rifles in their hands. I walked a mile and a half just to see the sight.

Hakim-a-barber said, "I accept some of their doctrines, but farming and raising cattle is not my style." They didn't tell me, and I didn't ask, whether Wangero (Dee) had really gone and married him.

We sat down to eat and right away he said he didn't eat collards and pork was unclean. Wangero, though, went on through the chitlins and corn bread, the greens and everything else. She talked a blue streak over the sweet potatoes. Everything delighted her. Even the fact that we still used the benches her daddy made for the table when we couldn't afford to buy chairs.

"Oh, Mama!" she cried. Then turned to Hakim-a-barber. "I never knew how lovely these benches are. You can feel the rump prints," she said, running her hands underneath her and along the bench. Then she gave a sigh and her hand closed over Grandma Dee's butter dish. "That's it!" she said. "I knew there was something I wanted to ask you if I could have." She jumped up from the table and went over in the corner where the churn stood, the milk in it clabber by now. She looked at the churn and looked at it.

"This churn top is what I need," she said. "Didn't Uncle Buddy whittle it out of a tree you all used to have?"

"Yes," I said.

"Uh huh," she said happily. "And I want the dasher too."

"Uncle Buddy whittle that too?" asked the barber.

Dee (Wangero) looked up at me.

"Aunt Dee's first husband whittled the dash," said Maggie so low you almost couldn't hear her. "His name was Henry, but they called him Stash."

"Maggie's brain is like an elephant's," Wangero said, laughing. "I can use the churn top as a centerpiece for the alcove table," she said, sliding a plate over the churn, "and I'll think of something artistic to do with the dasher."

When she finished wrapping the dasher the handle stuck out. I took it for a moment in my hands. You didn't even have to look close to see where hands pushing the dasher up and down to make butter had left a kind of sink in the wood. In fact, there were a lot of small sinks; you could see where thumbs and fingers had sunk into the wood. It was beautiful light yellow wood, from a tree that grew in the yard where Big Dee and Stash had lived.

After dinner Dee (Wangero) went to the trunk at the foot of my bed and started rifling through it. Maggie hung back in the kitchen over the dishpan. Out came Wangero with two quilts. They had been pieced by Grandma Dee, and then Big Dee and me had hung them on the quilt frames on the front porch and quilted them. One was in the Lone Star pattern. The other was Walk Around the Mountain. In both of them were scraps of dresses Grandma Dee had worn fifty and more years ago. Bits and pieces of Grandpa Jarrell's paisley shirts. And one teeny faded blue piece, about the size of a penny matchbox, that was from Great Grandpa Ezra's uniform that he wore in the Civil War.

"Mama," Wangero said sweet as a bird. "Can I have these old quilts?"

I heard something fall in the kitchen, and a minute later the kitchen door slammed.

"Why don't you take one or two of the others?" I asked. "These old things was just done by me and Big Dee from some tops your grandma pieced before she died."

"No," said Wangero. "I don't want those. They are stitched around the borders by machine."

"That'll make them last better," I said.

"That's not the point," said Wangero. "These are all pieces of dresses Grandma used to wear. She did all this stitching by hand. Imagine!" She held the quilts securely in her arms, stroking them.

"Some of the pieces, like those lavender ones, come from old clothes her mother handed down to her," I said, moving up to touch the quilts. Dee (Wangero) moved back just enough so that I couldn't reach the quilts. They already belonged to her.

"Imagine!" she breathed again, clutching them closely to her bosom.

"The truth is," I said, "I promised to give them quilts to Maggie, for when she marries John Thomas."

She gasped, like a bee had stung her.

"Maggie can't appreciate these quilts!" she said. "She'd probably be backward enough to put them to everyday use."

"I reckon she would," I said. "God knows I been saving 'em for long enough with nobody using 'em. I hope she will!" I didn't want to bring up how I had offered Dee (Wangero) a quilt when she went away to college. Then she had told me they were old-fashioned, out of style.

"But they're *priceless!*" she was saying now, furiously; for she has a temper. "Maggie would put them on the bed and in five years they'd be in rags. Less than that!"

"She can always make some more," I said. "Maggie knows how to quilt."

Dee (Wangero) looked at me with hatred. "You just will not understand. The point is these quilts, *these* quilts!"

"Well," I said, stumped, "what would *you* do with them?"

"Hang them," she said. As if that was the only thing you *could* do with quilts.

Maggie, by now, was standing in the door. I could almost hear the sound her feet made as they scraped over each other.

"She can have them, Mama," she said, like somebody used to never winning anything, of having anything reserved for her. "I can 'member Grandma Dee without the quilts."

I looked at her hard. She had filled her bottom lip with checkerberry snuff, and it gave her face a kind of dopey, hangdog look. It was Grandma Dee and Big Dee who taught her how to quilt herself. She stood there with her scarred hands hidden in the folds of her skirt. She looked at her sister with something like fear, but she wasn't mad at her. This was Maggie's portion. This was the way she knew God to work.

When I looked at her like that something hit me in the top of my head and ran down to the soles of my feet. Just like when I'm in church and the spirit of God touches me and I get happy and shout. I did something I never had done before: hugged Maggie to me, then dragged her on into the room, snatched the quilts out of Miss Wangero's hands and dumped them into Maggie's lap. Maggie just sat there on my bed with her mouth open.

"Take one or two of the others," I said to Dee.

But she turned without a word and went out to Hakim-a-barber.

"You just don't understand," she said, as Maggie and I came out to the car.

"What don't I understand?" I wanted to know.

"Your heritage," she said. And then she turned to Maggie, kissed her, and said, "You ought to try to make something of yourself too, Maggie. It's really a new day for us. But from the way you and Mama still live you'd never know it."

She put on some sunglasses that hid everything above the tip of her nose and her chin.

Maggie smiled; maybe at the sunglasses. But a real smile, not scared. After we watched the car dust settle I asked Maggie to bring me a dip of snuff. And then the two of us sat there just enjoying, until it was time to go in the house and go to bed.

┌─ Sherley Anne Williams ─┐

The Lawd Don't Like Ugly
1974

Writer, teacher, and critic Sherley Anne Williams (b. 1944) has published three books. Her first, Give Birth to Brightness *(1972), a volume of literary analysis, includes her definition of the black aesthetic and explores the notion of the hero in the work of Amiri Baraka, James Baldwin, and Ernest Gaines. Her two volumes of poetry are* The Peacock Poems *(1976), a National Book Award nominee, and* Someone Sweet Angel Chile *(1982). She has also published essays on black poetry and black music, including "The Blues Roots of Contemporary Afro-American Poetry" (*Massachusetts Review, *Autumn 1977), in which she defines her own literary goal as "the re-creation of a new tradition built on a synthesis of black oral traditions and Western literate forms." It is precisely that goal—the synthesis between oral and written traditions—that is one of the vitalizing stylistic characteristics of most of the best short stories written by women. In particular, this characteristic has distinguished the work of ethnic writers, such as Williams in the black tradition, and, earlier, Fannie Hurst in the Yiddish tradition.*

"The Lawd Don't Like Ugly" was first published in New Letters, *in December 1974. Two other stories by Williams have appeared: "Tell Martha Not to Moan," first published in* Massachusetts Review *in 1968 has been reprinted in* The Black Woman: An Anthology, *edited and with an introduction by Toni Cade (Bambara) (1970); and "Meditations on History" in* Midnight Birds: Stories of Contemporary Black Women Writers, *edited and with an introduction by Mary Helen Washington (1980). The story in* Midnight Birds *is preceded by a short but moving and informative autobiographical essay. A lengthy interview of Williams is included in Claudia Tate's 1983 volume,* Black Women Writers at Work *(New York: Crossroads Press).*

Williams was born in Bakersfield, California, into a family of agricultural workers who settled out of the migrant stream in Fresno. Only fifteen when her mother died, Williams came under the charge of her older, divorced sister, who struggled to care for her own child as well, while finishing high school and working as a maid and cook for a white family. Ill health finally forced the family onto welfare. Under the guidance and urging of her sister and other women in their community, Williams prepared for a career as a teacher, completing a B.A. at California State University at Fresno in 1966 and an M.A. in 1972 at Brown University. Realizing that she preferred creating literature to analyzing the literature of others, she left her Ph.D. program to teach and write. She is now a professor of literature and department head at the University of California, San Diego. She is the mother of one son.

Many of Williams's poems testify to her love and respect for the community of black women, struggling with racism, sexism, classism, poverty, and the welfare system, struggling to bring up their children to survive not just materially, but emotionally and spiritually. In "you were never miss brown to me" from Someone Sweet Angel Chile, *she offers tribute*

> to the women of that time,
> the mothers of friends, the friends
> of my mother, mamma
> herself . . .
> who taught what it is to be grown.

"The Lawd Don't Like Ugly," a surrogate-mother story, presents a version of the mother-daughter alliance in which the mother's lesson to her daughter about the conditions for survival of women in the patriarchy reveals the same pessimism that characterizes Tiptree's vision in "The Women Men Don't See." In both stories, we see the absolute necessity for women to achieve economic and emotional independence. The irony of Williams's story lies in the apparent brutality resulting from Miss Ead's tender regard for the girl becoming a woman. But perhaps by making clear to Queenie the essential connection between economics and sex, Queenie's own innocence and budding self-love are protected.

That *must* be Vista Park—and it actually looked good. Q.T. almost choked on her excitement as she leaned over the side of the old pick-up truck and watched the group of buildings that seemed to cover the city block grow larger, more distinct as the truck neared them. She had been waiting for this first glimpse ever since they turned off the highway back by the park. "There it is," she said and poked Sudy Mae. Sudy Mae lay in the bottom of the truck, her head resting against a bundle of clothes, a true confession magazine held close to her face; she didn't look up. Candy and Ryce were seated with their backs to the truck cab. Ryce looked over at Q.T. and smiled.

"Well," Ryce said, turning to Candy, "whatever it is, it couldn't be no worse than Salinas."

Candy laughed. "Salinas wa'n't that bad—once you got out them damn fields."

Ryce was laughing harder. "Girl—"

But Q.T. stopped listening. Bryant swung the truck past the front row of buildings and pulled up on the side street beside the third row of buildings. Bryant and Mo-Dear got out and stood a moment before going up the walk toward the door at the near end of the building.

Ryce stood up. "Let's go see what this mess looks like."

Candy didn't move. "Girl, ain't nothing in that house interest me. I want to see what's happenin back there on that road we come down."

"Well, it sho don't look like nothing ever go on here."

"That's wh—"

"Yo'all come on, start unloadin," Bryant called as he came down the walk.

From her perch on a bundle of bedding, Q.T. looked at the buildings, ignoring Bryant's impatient call to get a move on herself. This was Vista Park.

The night before, in Salinas, she had lain on the pallet she shared with Sudy Mae trying to picture the housing project in her mind. But she had never imagined anything like this, not the way the housing project sprawled over the city block in regulation ugliness. The buildings stood in lackluster formation, row after row of them all alike, like barracks or a fort. Each long building had four sets of steps leading up to four separate doors; two screened windows flanked each door and each window, each door looked across a small plot of grass, a sidewalk, to a repetition of the plot of grass and the windows and doors that faced them. Front to front and back to back, the long buildings seemed to march before her eyes.

There were trees, just as Bryant had told them, a sycamore

down toward the middle of this row of buildings and a couple
of smaller grey green olive trees and grass, some of it thick and
green. And even though Bryant hadn't said a thing about the
flaked and peeling green paint that trimmed the cream colored
houses—which were scarred and dirty—Q.T. lived there a long
time before she noticed that for herself. She had never seen so
many buildings alike. Front to front and back to back like the
game the kids played around the school grounds. Front to front,
they would hold hands and go around in pairs, chanting "front
to front and back to back" or "hey, hey, get out of my way; I
just got back and I'm here to stay," and she always wanted to
play, to have someone hold her hand—which was really like
saying they were friends—and skip around the grounds swinging
arms and turning bodies to show everyone that she could be
with someone, too. Back to back and front to front. That's what
the buildings reminded her of.

Look like, Q.T. thought, look like every row tellin the one
behind it, 'kiss my ass, kiss my natural ass.' But it wasn't so much
that Vista Park didn't look as good as it had in her mind ever
since Bryant had told them about the government housing
project—and Q.T. had hung on his every word. And it would
take a lot to be worse than the tents and one-room shacks of
the labor camps they had lived in—It was, well, if the houses
were telling each other to kiss ass, what would they tell her?

Where were the kids Bryant had told them about, the ones
who were supposed to be her friends? It took so much time to
make friends, so much time. And there had never been time
before, following the crops the way they had when Daddy was
alive or the time they had spent in Lanare after Daddy died. It
had been a new experience for her living in one place for longer
than it took to harvest a crop. And in some ways it had been
good, living on what Mo-dear called that ol wore out piece-a
ground (to which Mamma had always replied that it had been
good enough to feed her and ten other peoples in its time and
Mo-dear didn't seem to find it too 'wore out' to come back to
every time she needed something), feeding the chickens and
slopping the two hogs that they would slaughter come fall, and
helping Great-Uncle Jason with the other chores around the
small truck farm. And if Q.T. hated school, well, she managed

to miss the bus often enough and slip back into the fields to
help Uncle. He didn't ask questions and he didn't tell Mamma—
who would have taken a switch at her for playing truant—just
showed her what to do and explained that she had been helping
when Mamma asked why her clothes were so dirty. And Sudy
Mae never seemed to care one way or another about whether
Q.T. was with her on the bus.

Q.T. never told Uncle about the black kids who called her boy
and shorthair. She didn't know what to tell him about that. It
had never happened before—the black kids in the labor camps
always stuck together, especially in any school, sometimes banding together to fight the Mexicans or banding together with the
Mexicans to fight the white kids. But people really lived in
Lanare. They didn't just stay there until the work gave out, then
move on to another place where there was more work. She
thought it had to be that, that staying in one place that made
the kids in Lanare so different from the ones she'd known
before. But knowing there was a difference, even being able to
say to herself, this is the reason for the difference, didn't provide
her with the key that would make her one of them. She was the
girl with the funny name and short hair, the "boy." They had
made up things about her, saying she stank—and how could
that be true when Mamma took down the big zinc wash tub
every Saturday night, heated water on the new, yellow and green
gas stove and made her and Sudy Mae (and Ryce and Candy
too, if they were around) strip and bathe. She watched you as
you lathered up the large cake of yellow laundry soap muttering
about how Mo-dear wasn't teaching these kids a thing that would
ever be worth knowing. Then, for good measure, Mamma herself
would scrub your back and wash your ears, and, she made you
wash between your legs each morning. They made fun of her
because she wore levis with patches and Mamma made her stuff
her dress tails in the pants because she didn't think blouses
provided sufficient protection against the cold; they laughed at
her name, saying "what is a Q.T.?," "who ever heard of a Q.T.?"
"you must be a boy cause only boys ain't no first name." A
couple of times she started to ask Sudy Mae if the kids talked
about her, too, but she was too embarrassed; she wanted at least
to ask what she should do about it. Sudy Mae was already twelve

and twelve must make you know *some*thing, not as much as
Candy and Ryce (but they were always laughing and talking
between themselves, shutting everybody else out), but something.
She could never ask, though; she was always afraid that Sudy
Mae would laugh at her, too.

They stayed in Lanare until late March when Bryant had
come along with all his promises and seemingly endless money
and Mo-dear had packed up Q.T. and the other girls and
followed Bryant to Salinas. Q.T. had wanted to stay with
Mamma—Mamma worked you hard but she never got evil the
way Mo-dear could—but Mo-dear had said they needed her help
in the fields. And when she asked Mamma if she could stay on
in Lanare, Mamma had sighed, "I'm yo grandmother, true
enough, but Ryce Ann yo mother and you got to do what she
say do."

"Q.T." That was Mo-dear, and Q.T. moved, scrambling over
the heaped up bundles and boxes. Vista Park was home.

Shoulda knowed, she told herself as she carried a load of
bedding up the rickety wooden steps, I shoulda knowed Bryant
wa'n't doin nothing but lyin bout this town. He ain't done nothin
but lie since the first day Mo-dear brung him home. Tellin us
what a good time we have in Salinas. 'Pickin strawberries ain't
nothin like cutting grapes.' Well, he wa'n't lyin bout that, she
thought grimly. At least when you cut grapes, you were on your
knees, not all bent over and stooped down as you had to be to
pick strawberries. Fun, humph, and likin to eat strawberries ain't
got nothin to do with likin to pick em. And after he talk all his
talk, he want come tickle you and play with you, knowin all the
time he ain't gon be doin nothin. Just be layin up drinking his
wine while Mo-dear and us be workin.

The unloading was finished quickly—there really wasn't much
to unload, clothes, bedding, Ryce's and Candy's cots, the big
iron bedstead that supported Mo-dear's mattress and took up
most of the space in the small bedroom, the faded swayback
sofa couch that Bryant had picked up in Salinas for ten dollars
which Q.T. and Sudy Mae would let down at night and make
into a bed, and the dinette table that Mamma had given them.
A stove and refrigerator came with the apartment and Mo-dear
had promised to buy them chests of drawers as soon as grape-

cutting started in another month or so. Q.T. went into the older girls' bedroom; they had already left but Sudy Mae lay on one of the cots reading her magazine. Q.T. went to the closet, a recess in the wall with a rod across the front of it for hanging a curtain, and began to paw through the bundles on the floor.

"What you lookin for?" Sudy Mae asked.

"My clothes."

"Was they wrapped in that blue print?"

"Yeah."

"Over there beside that other cot. On the other side," she added when Q.T. hesitated. "And you betta put the community pile back in that closet fo Ryce see it and have a fit."

Q.T. began piling the clothes back in the closet. The pile contained some of everything, blouses, skirts, slips, even rags, all of it given to them by various people in various places, most of which they all wore at one time or another as night gowns or slop-around clothes but did not care to claim as their own; some of which none of them would ever wear but which they carted around with them on the chance that they might or that they might be able to pass an item on to someone else who could use it. Q.T. had her own personal bundle of clothing—all of them did—culled from the community pile but also a few items, like the pair of white panties with 'Sunday' embroidered across the front in red thread that Mamma had given her for Christmas, that had never belonged to anyone but her.

Q.T. opened the bundle and pulled out a yellow flowered dress with short puffed sleeves edged with small ruffles. The dress skirt was full and would flare out around her legs. Long thick sashes tied in the back and nipped the fitted bodice in at the waist line. The dress had been too large in the top, the waist dropping below her own waist line and the sleeve ruffles down to her elbows when Mamma gave it to her on her last birthday. One of the white women she sometimes worked for had given it to Mamma. Mamma had been reluctant to alter it because she was afraid that when it was let out again, the alterations would show in the fine cotton material. Q.T. had agreed that it was best to wait until she grew into it. It was the prettiest dress she had ever owned and she wanted nothing to mar it.

She took the dress and the panties into the bathroom and

closed the door. She had seen flush toilets in schools and big department stores but never in a house and she stared at it a moment. She had bragged to the other kids at the camp in Salinas about the house where Bryant was taking them. They had listened in envy and some disbelief to talk about the trees and swings and hot and cold running water. She'd only half believed the part about the inside flush toilet herself. She turned on both faucets on the sink and passed her hand under the streams of water, drawing it back quickly from the one on the left. It was hot. She looked at the open stall with a faucet hung overhead. The big zinc wash tub was set in the bottom of the stall. Well, least we ain't got to be totin water from the faucet to the tub, she thought. Then she grinned. This was the best they'd ever had it. She shimmied out of her baggy pedal pushers and over large tee shirt. No one could laugh at her, laugh at her name—not and they were doing this good. And she would just tell them her name, say it was Quotha. Quotha, after her daddy's second cousin. The name always seemed to stick in her throat when she tried to tell people that it was hers. But it wasn't exactly a lie. Daddy had had a second cousin named Quotha. Q.T. had seen a picture of her, a bright-skinned woman with long wavy hair, that was good, not straightened. And wasn't Candy, Candence after Daddy's Mamma, Ryce named after Mo-dear and Sudy Mae, Susan after Mamma. Maybe they had meant to name her Quotha and Mo-dear had been mad or something and decided not to do it out of spite. Mo-dear was always talking about Daddy's family, calling them shit-colored niggas who thought they were better than anybody else. And maybe they were; Q.T. had never seen any of them. But it was really hard not to wish that some of that long wavy hair and shit-color had rubbed off on her along with the name Quotha.

"Quotha," she whispered to herself. "Quotha. My name Quotha."

She brushed her hair with a little water and grease, trying to water-wave it, and stood on tip toe so that she could see herself in the small mirror that hung over the sink. She really did not know if her face were pretty, but she wanted it to be. The cute girls were the ones with the friends. She had almost given up hoping that her hair would grow, or that it would somehow turn out to be good and had settled for wanting to be cute. And it was not so much to look a certain way, cute could be anything, look at Alice Cunningham and Fay: one no lighter than she herself was, the other almost as black as the ace of spades and people called them cute, always wanted to play with them. And Alice sweated on her nose which meant she was mean. So, if people just *thought* she was cute, then she would be. They would treat her the same way they treated cute girls—like she was somebody, like she belonged to someone.

She pulled off the dirty underpants—almost bloomers, really; they were probably big enough for Mo-dear—and pulled on the white ones. They fitted nicely and she wagged her butt a little so that she could feel the cool rayon slide against her skin. She was Quotha Jean and Quotha Jean was pretty. She smiled at the mirror, a large grin showing her pinky brown gums and even white teeth. Quotha Jean was pretty.

She looked down at herself, smiling, posing, a favorite game she played when she could get by herself in front of the long mirror on Mamma's dresser. She could see the mound of her breasts, the dark brown rosette around the nipple seemed huge and she paused, remembering Miss Margarite in Salinas who'd told Mo-dear laughingly that she'd better get a bra for Q.T. because her titties were getting too big to flop around loose. Mamma had laughed, "This girl only ten years old, won't be eleven till way off in November—knowin I ain't never gon fo'git 19 and forty-four—but I put a bra on her and next thing you know I got mo little pissy tail boys hangin round her, jes like they be round Ryce and Candy. She betta be studyin at how Sudy Mae go on, steadda worryin bout some bra round her chest."

Miss Margarite had laughed too. "Okay but mind-out hers don't get to floppin down before they time."

It was a frightening conversation. When your breasts hung down, you had babies and she didn't even have a boyfriend to tease her or try to kiss her. The boys did pat her on the behind; she felt their touches were somehow connected with her growing breasts. They didn't do it around the teachers or other grown-ups and she knew the behind touching was on the way to doing something nasty, going in the bushes. But she knew that if having big breasts meant that she was included in a game the other kids played then she would take the touching, not go on in the bushes because if you did that people talked bad about you, but still brag about someone's wanting her to go.

She was reaching for the yellow dress when the door opened and Bryant came in. "Oh, 'cuse m—What you doin in here?" He came toward her slowly. "Getting to be a regular little lady, ain't you?" and he touched her breast lightly with one finger.

"I-I-I was just lookin at my tooth, it loose." She grabbed her dress and ran around him and out the door.

After dressing, she stood on the back stoop, tugging at the skirt of her dress; it was too short. The lines of her body were still lost in baby fat. This and her budding bust line made the bodice of her dress too tight. She ignored this fact for a moment as she surveyed the narrow space between the two rows of apartment units. A few patches of scorched grass dotted the ground. Farther down to the left, there were some swings and a slide. Several children were playing down there and Q.T. could plainly hear their shouts and laughter.

She fidgeted, trying to gather enough courage to join the children. She touched the dress, thinking how pretty it was. They would think it pretty. "Pretty dress," they'd say. Then, "What yo name?" "Quotha Jean? That's a pretty name." And it wouldn't be long before they'd say, "Let's play on the swings; I push you." The yellow dress would billow as she swung high in the air and her laughter would mingle with that of the other children. Yeah, it was all there; it was all true. She tugged once more at the dress and was rewarded with a dull plopping sound as two buttons came off. "Shoot, shoot, shoot. Ain't nothing goin right." But the vision of herself in the yellow dress beckoned to her and she plunged off the porch and ran down to where the other children were playing.

"Hi." There were three girls, all of them about her own age, and two boys who seemed a little older. The girls wore shorts and thin cotton tops. She felt suddenly uncomfortable in her torn dress that was already becoming stained with sweat.

"What yo name?" demanded the bigger of the three girls.

The bright-skinned girl with long thick hair giggled behind her hands. "I know what her name. Her name, 'Boy.' "

She could feel the prickly sweat in her armpits. It was always, always like this. Boy or—

"It ain't. It Q.T." And she had said it herself. Oh, shoot, shoot, shoot, *shoot*.

"Q.T.? That ain't no girl's name."

"That's cause she a boy."

They were talking so fast that she couldn't tell who was saying what, but she answered them all.

"I ain't. I ain't."

"Yes you is."

"Then what them letters stand for?"

"They stand for Queer Kinks."

"You can't even spell, Hattie Lee." But the girl was laughing. "How bout, Tiny Queers, cause she gots tiny hair."

Q.T. wanted to cry. "It's Quotha. Quotha Jean."

"Quotha," The little bright one was laughing so hard she could barely stand up. "Quotha Jean? You mean Quotha Boy."

Q.T. looked at them. They had formed a semi-circle around her, the boys standing a little to one side. They were grinning at her. They ain't gon never be my friends, she thought. "Go to hell, you ole black niggas," she screamed, "you ol shit-ass, you ol—"

"You bet'not be callin no black niggas," the bigger girl charged.

"Fight. Fight." Q.T. heard the boy's words dimly. She was lost in an effort first to keep her footing and then, after she had been knocked down, to keep the arms and legs out of her stomach. She had a hold on someone's hair while someone else pounded her on the back. The yellow dress was coming apart at the waistline.

"What goin on here? I declare, you chi'ren just gets worse and worse. Always fightin. Ain't yo mamma done told you the lawd don't like ugly?" Q.T. felt the weight being lifted from her and she rolled over, pulling her dress down.

"She started it, Miss Ead." The bright girl pointed a trembling finger at Q.T. and began to cry. "She called us niggas and we didn't even do nothin to her and then she started fightin all of us."

"You just be quiet, now, Hattie Lee. I knows what been goin on here. Now yo'all betta git on home fo I tells yo Mammas." The three girls scrambled up; the boys had already gone. As soon as she saw them disappear around the corner, Q.T. began to cry.

"Well, baby. Don't cry. Miss Ead knows all bout it." She hugged
Q.T. to a bosom that smelled of Lifebuoy and Cashmere Bouquet.
"You just moved in, huh? Yeah, I thought that truck I saw
stopped round here somewheres. Well, you sho got a fine
welcome to the neighborhood, didn't you?"

"They always makin fun of my hair, my name—"

"And what's that, baby?"

"Ain't nothin but Q.T., just only Q.T. and it don't stand for
nothin." It was almost like being with Mamma again, to have
this woman hold her, except that she would never have run
crying to Mamma. Mamma said you had to be strong and if all
it took to make you cry was some little old nothing words, and
spoken by kids at that, then she would spend many a day boo-
hooing. There would always be someone who would try to bring
you down or put you low, but they couldn't put you as low as
you put yourself by listening to them. Mamma just didn't seem
to believe that what people said could hurt you so bad, could
put you so low you couldn't get up by yourself. The only way
for it not to hurt, not to put you low was for them not to say it;
but Q.T. hadn't learned how to stop them.

"Well, now you know, 'Q' stand for Queen." The woman held
Q.T. away from her. "You a big girl," she said forcing Q.T. to
look at her, "big enough to know that. So it ain't nothin wrong
with having a 'Q' in yo name." She held her close once more.
"And 'T' is fo tall and fo true and fo a lotta good thangs. So I
wouldn't even let that worry me. And," she said, passing a hand
over Q.T.'s nubby head, "you come on over my house tomorrow
and I help you with this. I gots a growin hand; done growed
lottsa peoples hair—man and woman, child and grownup. I uses
a special brush and comb. You come on over tomorrow evenin,
bout seven." Q.T. settled herself against the big golden woman
as her voice crooned on and on and Miss Ead's hair brushed
softly against her tear-stained cheek.

Q.T. skipped along, her neatly braided head bobbing in time
to the tune she heard in her mind. "Goin down to Miss Ead's,
goin down to Miss Ead's. Gon get some hair on this head, when
I goes down to Miss Ead's." She laughed and skipped higher.

"Hey. Hey, Q.T."

Q.T. turned to see Melissa and Hattie Lee sitting in the shadows of Hattie Lee's front porch. "What you want?" she asked edging away from them. They were funny sometimes. Sometimes they'd let her play with them, but almost always they ended by making fun of her.

"You know how to ride a bike?" Melissa asked.

"Yeah."

Melissa smiled now. "Well, Hattie Lee just got a bike and she don't even know how to ride it." Q.T. laughed with her a little uncertainly. "We going to the playground and I gon hike Linda on mine. If you wanna go, you can hike Hattie Lee on her'n."

Q.T. hesitated.

"Teach you to do the Texas Hop, if you go." Hattie Lee said smiling.

"I can do that," Q.T. told her. She wanted to go, but it felt nice to have them asking her instead of having to tag along the way she usually did.

"Can you do the chicken?"

"Naw." Q.T. had seen some of the older kids doing that dance the last time they went to the playground, but she hadn't caught on enough to do it yet.

"Well, we teach you that if you want to go. Can you go?"

"Yeah."

Melissa and Hattie Lee stood up. "Come on."

"Oh, I can't go now. I gotta go down to Miss Ead's so she can do my hair."

There was a pause as Melissa considered. "How long you gon be?"

"Not long. It only take a few minutes," she said eagerly.

"Well, you don't be too long and we wait. We gotta wait for Linda, anyway," she said turning to Hattie Lee.

"I be right back." Q.T. ran on, the tune growing louder in her head. She knocked softly on Miss Ead's door and said a stilted "hello" when Miss Ead opened it. Even after two weeks she was still rather shy around her.

"Well, here's my little Queenie." Miss Ead called her that all the time now and Q.T. smiled self-consciously, each time. But she really liked the name. "You kinda late tonight. I done already started cleanin up." This cleaning up was part of their routine.

Q.T. would help Miss Ead tidy the house, then they would eat. After dinner and the washing up, Miss Ead would start on Q.T.'s hair.

"Miss Ead, I can't stay long tonight; I'm gon go to the playground with some friends." She could say that now. They had asked her; not the other way around and she wouldn't be just tagging along; she would be with them, with Hattie Lee, in fact, the cutest one. "They gon be leaving in a few minutes."

"Which kids is these?"

"Hattie Lee 'nem."

"Humph. They done finally asked you to play wid em, huh?"

"Yes."

"Well seem like, evil as they been to you, you wouldn't want to play wid em. It's otha kids round here."

Q.T. looked down. She would die before she'd tell Miss Ead that the other kids were just like Hattie Lee and Melissa, that she was the same with the other kids as she was with Hattie Lee and Melissa. It wasn't that they laughed at her or even about her. It was that she felt they were going to. Sometimes she could really *feel* that they were going to and she would tense up and get quiet and even after the moment passed and the taunt didn't come, she would be nervous. It was really easier to play with her stick doll or draw paper dolls or take one of Sudy Mae's love books and read, than it was to be with any of the kids. But they had asked her this time and it would be different.

"I want to go, Miss Ead," she said looking up.

"Well, come on," Miss Ead said turning away, "I be finished soon as I can."

It was always nice and cool in Miss Ead's house, and clean. Q.T. loved to feel the slick cleanness of the linoleum under her hot, dusty feet. This the way my house gon be, she thought as she wiggled her toes on the floor. Miss Ead pulled over a bar stool and settled her comfortable bottom on it. Q.T. sat in a kitchen chair.

"What yo'all gon do at the playground?"

"Play, I guess. And some nights they dance."

"Huh?" Miss Ead bent down. "Honey, you talk so low, sometimes I can't understand you." Q.T. repeated herself. "Well, I guess it good you gettin to be friends with these kids."

Miss Ead had been drinking; Q.T. smelled the liquor on her breath. Usually by the time she had finished with Q.T.'s hair, her trips to the bedroom—she never drank in front of Q.T.—would have made her high. "I happy drunk," she would say then; "I tipshe."

"Too bad you can't stay for supper. Miss Carr had two steaks left over from they supper. That white woman got so much, she ain't gon miss two steaks. I ever tell you bout Fred? That one man sho liked his steaks. He could pay for em too. Owned some 'partments. He tell everybody was movin in, 'Don't come runnin to me 'plainin bout nobody else and they won't come 'plaining bout you. If they gives a loud party one night, you just give one the next night. Then can't nobody say nothin. They be happy; you be happy; I be happy.' That what he tell em."

"Ain't nobody ever complain?"

Miss Ead laughed. "Nobody cept *his* neighbors. That nigga gave a party every night. He ain't never give his neighbors no chance to git back at him." They both laughed.

"You most finished, Miss Ead?" Q.T. asked a little impatiently.

"Yeah," Miss Ead said mimicking Q.T.'s tone. "I most finished."

She parted off another section of hair, then got up and went into the bedroom. When she came back the smell of liquor was stronger. She sat down again.

They listened to the drone of the swamp cooler. Q.T. could tell that Miss Ead was angry and she chewed her lip wondering if Miss Ead were angry with her. The silence was too much. "Me and Sudy Mae went to church Sunday." It was something to say.

"Well, that's nice." Miss Ead didn't sound too interested but at least she was talking.

"Sudy Mae had some of that grape juice and crackers, but that's not supposed to be fo kids, is it?"

"If you been baptised—least that's what the ol folks say."

"Well, Sudy Mae ain't been baptised."

"Oh, she still a sinner, huh?"

"I'on't know if she be *sinnin*," Q.T. said seriously, "but I know she ain't been baptised."

Miss Ead was laughing. "Baby, I'm only teasin. The ones what is, do as much dirt as the ones what ain't. There, that's the last one." Miss Ead got up and went over to the phonograph. "I sho

like the way this man sing," she said as she put on a record.
"*Mister* Ray Charles."

The record sounded almost like church music and Q.T. sat
listening, wanting to hear it all but conscious also of the time.
She moved uneasily and finally stood up. "Thank you."

"This the way they used to do it when I was young," Miss Ead
said swinging around. She was light on her feet and her heavy
body moved easily. "And I thought I would party jes till I had
a chile. So I balled with this un and that un—even got married
once. But I never did have me no baby. And it make me feel
bad, cause I ain't got no one, no one so's I can pass on to them
what I learned in my life. And I'm not sayin I know all there is
to know."

She stopped and Q.T. was frightened. Miss Ead's face was
shiny, the skin gathered in a knot between her eyes. The fullness
of her bottom lip was flattened against her teeth. She ran her
hands through the graying waves of her hair and shook her
head. "Go'n go, chile; go'n go. Can't no one stop you from yo
pain."

"Miss Ead—" Q.T. was breathing fast. She hadn't meant to
hurt Miss Ead, didn't know how or when she had hurt Miss Ead;
but she could see that Miss Ead was hurting.

Miss Ead smiled, "Hey, I'm drunk, you know." She reached
out and hugged Q.T. "But I am sober nough to tell you this:
you treat people like they treat you in this world—at least treat
em that way in yo heart if you can't treat em that way in yo
action."

Q.T. looked down. Miss Ead didn't want her to go to the
playground with Melissa and them. She was saying that they
wouldn't all of a sudden become her friends.

Miss Ead patted her shoulder and walked with her to the
door. "You have a good time at this playground, now. And be
careful. I be here." She smiled.

Q.T. looked up at her. Miss Ead knew she was going. And
Miss Ead would still go on, go on combing her hair in the
evening. "I be careful," she said, and shyly hugged the woman
around the waist.

They began cutting grapes in July, everybody except Candy

who had gotten into an argument with Mo-dear about working in the fields again. "I thought that was why you had Bryant. What the use of havin a nigga if he ain't brangin in nothin?" she asked, adding, "at least my daddy did work." Mo-dear had slapped her for talking back; as she had said then, fifteen which Candy was, wasn't grown. Candy had slammed out of the house, shouting back over her shoulder that she didn't have to work her fingers to the bones for a four dollar pair of shoes. Ryce had followed her but had come back late that same night. Candy didn't return for three days; when she did she had on a new, tight black skirt with a long split up the back, a thin nylon blouse with long puffed sleeves, red fox stockings, two inch spike heels and a new fushia lipstick. Her hair was curled in a poodle style and it was obvious that she had gotten it done at the beauty shop. Mo-dear called her a little whore ("Which," Q.T. heard Candy tell Ryce, "is a lie; I ain't gave *nothin* away."), but didn't say anything, not even when they got ready to go to the fields the next morning and Candy refused to get up. And Q.T. wondered about that; Candy, and Ryce, too, just seemed to not be the way they used to be when daddy was alive or even the way they had been in Lanare. Every time they said something to Mo-dear, they always seemed to be on the verge of talking back and quite a bit of the time actually doing it. And cutting raisin grapes was easier than picking strawberries; Mo-dear had even said that they could keep half of all the money they made— something they'd never been allowed before. Ryce and Sudy Mae were talking about buying purple quilted skirts and black sweaters and capizio shoes. All Q.T. wanted was a pair of penny loafers and Bonnie Donne socks and, since she was spreading trays for Sudy Mae, that was about all she would make enough to buy.

The days settled into a pattern, up early to be in the field by six o'clock where they worked until five or six in the afternoon. They would get home about seven and then everybody would wash up. Q. T. was last because she was the youngest. And when she was through, she would walk through the courts to Miss Eads. She liked that time of day best. It would be dusk then or just about and walking through the courts, Q.T. would think them almost beautiful. This not a bad place when you got some—

when you know people, she thought. It was late August, almost
September now and even though she got along with Melissa
and the other children, she never, even in her thoughts, called
them her friends any more. They still gon play wid me when
school start, when—she touched her hair. It hadn't grown much
in the two, almost three months she had been going to Miss
Ead's. She'd finally accepted the fact that Miss Ead could not
perform a miracle and make her hair long. But maybe, if I had
some clothes, they would be my friends. Mo-dear and her ol
boyfriend! But, she thought hopefully, Miss Ead know what to
do.

"Good evenin, Mamma Hattie."

"Hattie Lee not home, Q.T. She gon over her cousin's house
to spend the night." Hattie Lee's grandmother sat in a rocking
chair on the front stoop, her hands folded underneath her
droopy stomach.

"Oh." Q.T. pushed a pebble with her toe. Mamma Hattie
always managed to start talking about things and after saying
'hello' Q.T. never knew what else to say. She looked down,
knowing she must say something. Mamma Hattie continued to
rock placidly. "You know if Miss Ead home?"

"She just come in not five minutes ago. She really got yo hair
to growin. Pretty soon, yo hair be as long as Hattie Lee's. Ead
sho got a growing hand."

"Yes she do and she be waitin for me now." And throwing a
polite smile in the general direction of the porch, Q.T. went
down to Miss Ead's.

Tonight, the first part of the routine was quickly over. Miss
Ead stacked the dishes in the sink and pulled over the big bar
stool. "Yo mamma got a new boyfriend, I see." She settled on
the stool.

Q.T. sat in her usual chair, feeling a little surprised at how
much Miss Ead knew about what went on in the projects.
Sometimes in the evenings she would sit out on the lawn with
Melissa and Hattie Lee, Linda and some of the other kids and
listen to the grown-ups talk as they played whist or dominoes
under the big sycamore tree. Sometimes Miss Ead would join
them, catching up, as she called it, on the happenings. But even
though Miss Ead didn't go down to the tree that often, she could

give you an almost day by day account of what went on (and sometimes why) in the courts. Mo-dear had been down to the tree no more than once or twice. She called the women a bunch of biddies worried about keeping their lame-ass men (just like she'd want something like that) and trying to get into everybody's business. "Don't you say nothin bout what go on in this house, Q.T. I pays the rent here and ain't nobody got no business knowin what I do." Miss Ead was an exception, though; Q.T. knew she could tell Miss Ead anything and it wouldn't go any further.

"Yeah," she said now, "Mo-dear put Bryant out so we could get on the welfare. Mo-dear say he wa'n't doin enough fo us no way. Sides that, she think he got another woman."

"Well, I can see which one you think is most important, tween that woman and his takin care of yo all."

"But Miss Ead, you said if a man can't do nothin fo a woman than a woman don't need him."

"That right, chile. You learn that early, you won't have nothin to worry bout."

Q.T. grinned, then sobered. "Miss Ead, I think the new one, George come round and look in the window when Candy and Ryce be undressin."

"Tell yo mamma."

"I did."

"Have em pull the shades down."

There was pause and Q.T. squirmed in her chair, wanting to talk about the school clothes, but feeling reluctant to do so. She didn't want Miss Ead to think badly about Mo-dear but if she didn't tell Miss Ead about the clothes, if Miss Ead couldn't think up something, then she would have to go to school raggedty just like always.

"Yeah," Miss Ead said, "Yo mamma got that straight, at least. Don't care how many womens a nigga got, long as he puttin that money in the right pocket. Which is *mines*." She laughed. "Aw, yeah you can be a hypocrite bout it, talk bout how you don't want to be 'sharin yo stuff with nobody,' like I hear somma these ol foolish womens talkin. But only stuff that belongst to you is what's between you l—is you," she finished with a laugh. "Yeah, peoples sho will try to be hypocrites with they dirt. And if it one thing I can't stand it a hypocrite. I drinks my liquor but you don't see me sitting up in church on Sunday, makin like I ain't never touched a drop. But just cause I don't go to church, don't mean you shouldn't go. Yeah," she said tapping Q.T.'s shoulder with the comb, "I saw you out there last Sunday, playin wid them kids. It ugly when chi'ren don't go to church or Sunday School and the Lawd don't like ugly. But some people just be so hypocritical when they goes to church—"

It was one of Miss Ead's favorite subjects and Q.T. knew she'd never get a chance to say anything if Miss Ead really got wound up. "Miss Ead," she said swinging around to face her, "Mo-dear gived the money for our school clothes to George." Her lip quivered a moment as she struggled with her tears. "She say half that money gon be ours, for whatever we want to buy. That's all our grape cuttin money, what we worked for all summer and just cause George say he need just that little mo fo the down payment on that ol piece-a car, Mo-dear gived it to him. And now I ain't gon never get no penny loafers and Bonnie Donne socks." Q.T. buried her head in Miss Ead's lap.

Miss Ead rocked Q.T. for a moment. "Queenie. Queenie, I can probably squeeze out enough to get you that pair of shoes."

Q.T. felt better for a moment and then the words, 'probably squeeze out enough,' sank in. That's what Mamma always said when she really didn't have enough money to get what you'd asked for, but would scrimp on something else so you could have what you wanted, or else it was something she felt you really shouldn't have, didn't need and she might have second thoughts about getting it for you. She shook her head. She didn't want Miss Ead scrimping for her and if Miss Ead couldn't understand how badly she needed those loafers—everybody would have loafers, loafers or white saddle shoes.

"Chile sweet as you shouldn't have to rake and scrap fo nothin." Miss Ead held her tightly and rocked for a long time. Q.T. lay quiet and drowsy; the rhythm of Miss Ead's body keeping thought away. "Well, you come stay the night wid me tomorrow and I see what I can do. Okay?" Q.T. nodded. "Now you turn around so I can finish yo hair."

"Miss Ead, Mo-dear say fo me to come back quick, case the

L.B. Price man come collectin fo his bill, so I can answer the door." Q.T. grinned, feeling better now, knowing that somehow Miss Ead had made things right. "She say she ain't gon let no bill collector dun her to death."

"And they sho will try if you don't watch em close. But you ask if you can spend tomorrow night wid me. Be sho, now." She patted Q.T.'s shoulder and started on the last braid.

Q.T. could hear Miss Ead and Miss Ead's friend, Duncan, in the kitchen. They were drinking and every now and then Q.T. heard Duncan laugh or Miss Ead giggle. Miss Ead had sent Q.T. to bed when Duncan brought out the bottle. "Now you know, the lawd don't like ugly, Queenie; you go on to bed," she'd said when Q.T. seemed about to protest. Q.T. had gone with a falling sensation in her stomach, wondering how this could have anything to do with school clothes. Duncan her boyfriend, she thought now as she lay in the darkened bedroom; she must be gon talk him out the money. She strained to understand the low voices that came from the kitchen, then sighed in frustration and turned over. Her eyes caught the outline of a dress hanging on the closet door. It was her dress, a present from Duncan. "Ead done told me what a good girl you been so I brung you a present," he said as he kissed her forehead. Q.T. accepted the kiss, trying to conceal her impatience. When she was finally allowed to open the package, the dress wavered before her eyes and seemed for a moment to be one of her dreams come true. The dress, green with white stripes and a large, lace edged collar, felt good and looked good on her. "Now that's the way you should always look. Don't she look cute, Duncan?" Q.T. had bounced up and down in her excitement, and imagined herself in the dress on the first day of school. The picture danced before her eyes. First, everyone would gather around her to admire her dress. "You look good, girl." "That a pretty dress." Then they would ask her to play. "Queenie, that yo name?" And she would say, well, that's what some people call me. Maybe if she said it that way, the name would come out okay. She would be Queenie and not Q.T. Queenie was cute and then the kids would say, "Queenie, come on." "Queenie, the swings." "The—" The voices faded but their echo gave her 'thank you' an added fervency and her smile an added brilliance.

If Duncan wa'n't her friend, I bet Miss Ead'd call him a slick nigga, Q.T. thought. 'Black as tar, can't git to heaven on electric wire.' And he ain't even that big. She snapped her fingers. His ol boney knees look like they gon tear a hole through that suit every time he sit down. But that sho musta been a pretty suit when it was new. Wonder if it silk? I gon git me a silk suit one of these days, but I gon keep it good. It ain't never gon git ol and raggedty-looking like that one. Do women wear silk suits? I don't care. I is. She rolled over, squirming against the slickness of the new sheets. He sho keep his hair nice though. She felt funny about Duncan's hair. His beautifully processed hair was longer than hers and lay in smooth waves against his skinny head. Yeah, Q.T. nodded solemnly in the dark, he sho a slick nigga. But since he done come on in wid this dress, I tell the world he the best nigga ever was. She laughed at this last thought, thinking how much she sounded like Miss Ead.

She hadn't heard the door open and the squeaking of its hinges startled her. "Miss Ead?"

"No. It Duncan." He stood silhouetted in the door way, shoes in hand.

"What you want?"

"I comin to bed." He closed the door and moved toward the bed, unbuttoning his shirt.

"You supposed to sleep on the couch, ain't you?"

"No, I suppose to sleep right here."

By this time Duncan had pulled off his clothes and was slipping into the bed. As Q.T. felt his weight depressing the bed, she began to scream. "Miss Ead. Miss Ead, Duncan tryin' to get in bed wid me. Miss Ead. Miss—" Duncan put his hand over her mouth, whispering, "Shut up." Q.T. wiggled away from him and stood up in the bed, dragging the cover with her. She kicked out at him, screaming all the while. Duncan grabbed for the covers. Q.T. jumped back and jerked the covers out of his reach. "Stop it Duncan. You ain't even supposed to be here. Miss Ead." Duncan reached for her legs and fell flat when she moved out of his reach.

"Be still, girl. I ain't gon hurt you." He struggled to his knees and grabbed again for Q.T.'s legs. Q.T. dropped the covers on his head and leaped from the bed just in time. She picked up the bedside lamp and held it over her head, watching as Duncan struggled out of the tangled bed clothes. "You move Duncan and I throws it. Duncan. Dun—" Duncan moved. Q.T. threw the lamp and Miss Ead opened the door, turning on the light as the lamp caught Duncan in his chest and knocked him flat in the bed. He lay there panting.

Q.T. moved back against the wall. "Miss Ead," she stopped for breath. "Miss—"

"God damn it Ead," Duncan gasped. "Damn it, I thought you said she know what goin on. Damn it Ead, you too ol to be fumblin the way you do."

"Me? Fumblin?" Miss Ead's bosom heaved. "Me fumblin. Shit, you ol enough to know you ain't supposed to go round crawlin in peoples bed when it dark. Least you coulda done was turn on the lights. Fumblin! Shit. You git on outta here and let me talk to her."

Duncan picked up his clothes and started out. "Woman say, I got everythin un'er control. I know what goin down; I handle it. Ead, you can't handle shit."

"I ain't supposed to be handlin shit; I handlin this. Now go on Duncan, fo you mouth git yo ass in a world of hurt." Miss Ead waited until he closed the door, then came and sat down on the bed. She held out her arms, and, after a moment's hesitation, Q.T. scrambled across the bed to her and lay panting on her breast. Miss Ead rocked her silently. Then, she held her away and looked her in the eyes. "Queenie you member I always sayin if a nigga can't do nothing for you, then that a nigga you best be leavin alone? Well, Duncan do lots for you—that is, if you let him. But it a give and git world, and if he do for you, you gotta do for him too. You ain't really losin that much when you let him sleep in here, no way."

"That all he gon do is sleep?"

"Sometime, I think that all Duncan can do is sleep; he so silly," she said with a laugh. "But I wouldn't let him do nothin to hurt you."

There was a pause. Q.T. picked at the bedspread, her eyes

downcast. "The lady at church say it wrong for a boy and girl to do that," she said in low voice.

"That right, it is wrong for a boy and a girl. But," Miss Ead said, "Duncan a man. Now I gon tell him to come back, okay?" Q.T. said nothing. Her fingers still plucked at the bedspread. Finally Miss Ead rose to go. She stopped at the door. "Q.T." she spoke sharply and the use of her name made Q.T. look up. "Lawd don't like ugly. Now you be a pretty girl."

"Queenie?" Duncan's voice was hoarse. He stood in the doorway, his clothes clutched in front of him. His thin legs seemed to hang suspended from the too large legs of his boxer shorts. He grinned at her hesitantly showing the gap where a front tooth should have been.

Q.T. lowered her head and from the back of her mind, coming closer to the front, marched a vision of all the pretty dresses she could have. She could see herself on the first day of school, dressed in Duncan's present, hair pressed and curled. The admiring crowd, the voices joining together: "Come on, Queenie, let's play . . . Queenie let's swing . . . Come on . . ." You be a pretty girl.

She turned her back to him. "Turn out the light, Duncan."

─Joanna Russ─

Autobiography of My Mother
1975

Born in 1937 to second generation American Jewish school teacher parents, Joanna Russ, an only child, grew up in the Bronx. She was one of the top ten Westinghouse Science Talent Search winners in her senior year in high school. While an undergraduate at Cornell University, she studied with Vladimir Nabokov. Next, at the Yale Drama School, she completed an MFA in playwriting and dramatic literature. She had known from her pre-teen years that she wanted to write and in her last year at Yale she began writing science fiction while continuing to write plays. Her first published science fiction story, "Nor Custom Stale," appeared in The Magazine of Fantasy and Science Fiction *in 1959.*

While teaching full time (she is now a professor at the University of Washington in Seattle), she has managed to publish an impressive quantity of work, ranging from short stories to novels to literary criticism to a volume of literary theory and history. Russ's 1972 story, "When It Changed," literally changed—expanded—what readers and writers thought possible in the field of science fiction. It was chosen by the members of the Science Fiction Writers of America to receive the Nebula Award as the best short story of the year. Her feminist academic colleagues bestowed the Florence Howe Literary Criticism Award on her essay, "What Can a Heroine Do? Or, Why Women Can't Write," in 1974. [This essay opens the collection Images of Women in Fiction: Feminist Perspectives, *ed. Susan Koppelman Cornillon, 1972).] "Autobiography of My Mother," first published in* Epoch *at Cornell in 1975, was one of the 1977 O. Henry Memorial Prize Stories. In 1983, science fiction readers voted "Souls" the Hugo Award for best novella of the year.*

In his introduction to the 1976 Gregg Press reprinting of Alyx, *Russ's collection of four long stories and one short novel, Samuel Delany called* Picnic on Paradise, *her first novel, "an incredibly liberating work for the s-f genre,"* adding that *"it was a book which, after reading and rereading, has left me unable to think of writing quite so complacently as I had. And that is the highest compliment any writer can pay another."*

Her other books include the novels And Chaos Died *(1970)*, The Female Man *(1975)*, We Who are About To . . . *(1975)*, The Two Of Them *(1978), and* On Strike Against God *(1980); the childrens' book* Kittatinny: A Tale of Magic *(1978); the short story collection* The Zanzibar Cat *(1983); and* How to Suppress Women's Writing *(1983), an analysis of the ways in which women have been discouraged from writing.*

"Autobiography of My Mother" is a classical, yet unique, mother-daughter story. The daughter is portrayed encountering her mother at different periods in her mother's life, including a time before the daughter was born. These encounters enable the daughter to recognize her mother as a woman with needs, imperatives, and a history of her own. The daughter must also come to terms with what her birth and the responsibility for her care meant in her mother's life. The daughter is reconciled to her mother as a sister-woman and emerges as a woman who can look at her mother as a person in her own right and not solely as a mother. The daughter achieves a sense of continuity that will allow her to move into her own future as a woman with roots, strength, and love—roots in a woman's history, strength from understanding a woman's life, and love for and a sense of sisterhood with the woman who gave her life.

This story is classical in that it adheres to the pattern of a daughter questing for her origins and place in the history of women's lives. It is unique among quest stories, however, in that the mother in the story is not dead. In other stories of this type the quest is precipitated by, or becomes psychologically possible only after, the mother's death. "Autobiography of My Mother" represents a juncture among the genre of fantasy, women's history, and feminist utopianism (a theme that Russ developed further in The Female Man*). This type of imagining seems to have been unavailable until now. So while this story is firmly rooted in women's literary tradition, it is also a major breakthrough to something new.*

I'm an I.
Sometimes I'm a she.
Sometimes I'm even a he.
Sometimes I'm vervvery I.
Sometimes I'm my mother.

I WAS VISITING FRIENDS in Woodstock; you may find it surprising that I met my mother there for the first time. I certainly do.

She was two years old. My mother and I live on different ends of a balance; thus it's not surprising to find that when I'm thirty-five she's just a little tot. She sat on the living room rug and stared at me, with her legs bent under her in a position impossible to anyone but a baby. Babies might be lobsters or some other strange form of life, considering what positions they take up. A little light tug at the ornamental tassel of my shoe—not apologetic or tentative, she feels both modest and confident, but she has small hands. "What's that?" she says.

"That's a tassel." She decamped and settled her attention on the other shoe. "And what's *that*?"

"Another tassel." This baby has flossy black hair, a pinched little chin, and round pale-green eyes. Even at the age of two her upper lip is distinctive: long, obstinate, almost a chimp's. I think she thinks that every object has its own proper name and so—without intending to—I made her commit her first error. She said: "That's *a tassel*. That's *another tassel*." I nodded, bored. She's of the age at which they always take off their clothes; patiently, with her own understanding of what she likes and what's necessary to her, she took off all of hers: her little sailor dress, her patent leather shoes, her draggy black cotton stockings. It's only history that gave her these instead of a ruff and stomacher. She practiced talking in the corner of the living room for half an hour; then she came over to me, nude, without her underwear, and remarked:

"That's a tassel. That's another tassel."

"Uh-huh," I said. Pleased at having learned something, she pondered for a moment and then switched them around, declaring:

"That's *another tassel* and that's *a tassel*."

"No, no," I said. "They're both tassels. This is a tassel and that's a tassel."

She backed away from me. I don't think she likes me now. Later that night I saw her scream with excitement when her father came home; he held the tail of her nightshirt in one hand and her brother's in the other; they both played the great game of trying to scramble away from him on all fours. My mother shrieked and laughed. Even at the age of two she's addicted to pleasure.

It'll ruin her.

YOU GET STUCK IN TIME, not when you're born exactly, but when you "sit up and take notice," as they say, when you become aware that you have an individuality and there's something out there that either likes you or doesn't like you. This happens at about eighteen months. It isn't that you really prefer some other time, you don't know anything about that; you just back off (still crawling, perhaps), not shaking your head (for you don't know about that, either) just wary and knowing you don't like *that staircase* or *those visitors* or *this parent*. But what can be done about it? You're stuck. It would be the same if you could travel through time but not through space.

Like this story.

AT A CHINESE RESTAURANT: that is, a big room with a high ceiling and dun walls, like a converted gymnasium. Sepia-colored screens in front of the Men's and Ladies'. There is a fan of crimson coral over my mother's head and the chairs are high-backed and plain, the ultimate in chic for 1925. My mother is nineteen. When I was that age I discovered her diary and some poems she had written; they didn't mention the restaurant but here she is anyway, having dinner with her best friend. I've looked everywhere in them to find any evidence that she was abnormal, but there's none. Nobody hugs anybody or says anything they shouldn't, and if there's any morbidity, that's gone too. My mother's written remains are perfect. At that time I wasn't born yet. I'm not even a ghost in her thought because she's not going to get married or even have children; she's going to be a famous poet. It was known then that you had to have children. It was a fact, like the Empire State Building I saw every morning out of the corner of my eye at breakfast (through the kitchen window). When you looked at childlessness in those days you didn't even realize that you had made a judgment, an inference from one set of conditions to another, you just *knew*.

I sat down imprudently at my mother's table.

Now I'm not as pretty as she is (I don't look a bit like her with my big behind and my buck teeth) but I'm much better dressed, and having been able to arrange my entry to suit myself, I can turn on to the full that bullying, leering, ironical boldness I adopt so easily with women; I place my well-cut suede coat, my smart gloves, my modernique pearl earrings and Dior scarf directly in the track of my mother's green, beautiful, puzzled, nearsighted eyes. My mother didn't want me to sit next to her— she wanted her friend to come back. Strangers alarm her. When my mother is not with a good friend her spirits flag, she becomes vague, she loses control of herself and stares around the room, not because she wants to look at things but because she's diffused and anxious; it's a way of not meeting anyone's eye. She ducks her head and mutters (mannerisms that won't look so cute at fifty-nine). I want to protect her. Years later I'll hold her elbow when she crosses the street, suffer with her when she can't breathe in a crowd, but this is before she's perfected any such tricks, so I can only bare my teeth at her in a way that makes her uncomfortable. She essays a smile.

"Do you come here often?" I say and she draws on her gloves; that is, she wanted to draw on her gloves, began to move her hands as if she would do so, then didn't. She looked guilty. Mother has been taught to be nice to everybody but she doesn't want to be nice to me. Last week she wrote a romantic love story about a girl whose mouth was like a slow flame. When I'm eleven I will get felt up on my rear end in a crowd and will be too ashamed to run away. It may occur to you that the context between us is sexual. I think it is parental.

"Would you care to step outside?" I said politely. Mother demurred. Sitting there—I mean us sitting there—well, you might have taken us for cousins. I picked up the check and she suffered because she didn't know what to do. Her friend, who will never get here in time, forms in my mother's memory a little bright door. I dropped two anachronistic quarters on the tablecloth and then put my French purse back in my navy-blue suede bag, an easy forty-five dollars which she has never seen, no, not even in dreams.

"Do you mind if we chat?" I said; "Shall we have coffee?" and went on to explain: that I was a stranger in town, that I was new here, that I was going to catch a train in a few hours, I told her that I was her daughter, that she was going to marry eventually and after two spontaneous abortions bear me, that I didn't usually ask for favors but this was different.

"Consider what you gain by not marrying," I said. We walked

out onto Columbus Avenue. "All this can be yours." (Be the first one on your block; astonish your friends.) I told her that the most sacred female function was motherhood, that by her expression I knew that she knew it too, that nobody would dream of interfering with an already-accomplished pregnancy (and that she knew that) and that life was the greatest gift anybody could give, although only a woman could understand that or believe it. I said:

"And I want you to take it back."

WE WERE BOTH ELEVEN, on roller skates, skating towards Bronx Park with our braids flying behind us, but my mother was a little younger and a little slower, like my younger sister. I called her "Stupid."

IN THE FIRST PLACE I never borrowed it, in the second place it hasn't got a hole in it now, and in the third place it already had a hole in it when I borrowed it. I was going to show her all the kingdoms of the world. I wanted to protect my mother. Walking down Columbus Avenue in this expansive and generous mood—well, my mother didn't know what to make of me; like so many people she's puzzled by a woman who isn't beautiful, who doesn't make any pretense of being beautiful, and who yet flaunts herself. That's me. I asked my mother to tell me her daydreams, daydreams of meeting The Right Man, of being kept by an Older Woman, of inheriting money. Money means blood in dreams and blood means money. The autumn foliage in the park, for example, because the sun hadn't quite set. My mother was wearing a shapeless brown cloth coat that concealed her figure. It's very odd to think that this is 1921. Overheard: I thought it would be different.

I told my mother that when women first meet they dislike each other (because it's expected of them) but that's all right; that soon gives way to a feeling of mutual weakness and worthlessness and the feeling of being one species leads in turn to plotting, scheming, and shared conspiracies. I said that if we were going to be mother and daughter we ought to get to know each other. As we walked on the stone-flagged park paths my mother's soul flew out from under my fingers at every turn, to every man who passed, a terrible yearning, an awful lack, a down-on-your-knees appeal to anybody in the passing scene. She didn't like my company at all.

"Do you know what I want you to do?" I said. "Well, do you?"

"Well, do you?" my mother echoed earnestly, looking up at me with her nymph's green eyes.

"Look here—" I said.

("Look here—")

I suppose you expect me to say that I listened to her artlessly simple chatter, that I confided in her, or that next she will be a big girl and I the little one, but if you expect me to risk her being older than me, you're crazy. I remember what that was like from last time. I told her all of it—the blood, the sweat, the nastiness, the invasion of personality, the utter indecency (except in middle age, except with money) and she only looked up at me as if she knew things, that girl. She didn't like me. The palisade looking out over the river. The mild October air. We stood arm in arm, like chums, watching the wakes of the boats in the water. She said I couldn't understand. She said with complete conviction:

"You were never young."

MY MOTHER, a matron of fifty but for some reason shrunk to the size of an infant and wrapped in baby clothes, is lying in her cradle. Swaddled, her arms at her sides, furious. Frowning— this is no way to treat a grown woman! She is about to bawl. I could leave her there and she'd die—dirty herself, starve, become mute and apathetic—she's just a baby. Maternally I take into my arms my fifty-year-old mother because you can't leave a baby, can you? and cradling her tenderly to my breast I start dancing around the room. She hates it. Screaming and red-faced. Maybe she wants a different dance. I change into a waltz, rocking her softly, and right away, my goodness, the little baby is rocked into quiet, she's straightening her corrugated little brows, un wrapping the snaky moist curls that come finely from under her cap, smoothing her sulky little mouth. I guess she likes waltzing. If I didn't take care of her, how would she ever grow up to be my mother? It would be infanti-suicide, to say the least (if not something worse). When she stops crying I'll put her back into the cradle and sneak off, but there is command in that steely little face, those snapping little eyes, she stares up at me like a snapping turtle making plans, telling me with her expression all the terrible things she's going to do to me when I'm the baby and she's the mother and I know she did them because I was there. *You keep on rocking me!* she says.

So we keep on waltzing around the room.

When i was a child—
a child—
When I was a chidden child—
I came into my right mind at a certain age, I think I inherited it, so to speak, although they didn't allow me to use it until I was already fairly cracked. Coming home from the dentist at sixteen on winter evenings with the sky hot-pink and amber in the west and the wind going right through your coat; it's discouraging to find automata in the living room. Cars shooting by to cheery dinners, homey lights from the windows above the stoop. Mirages. Inside, a steamy kitchen, something horrible like an abstract sort of Frankenstein's monster made up of old furniture, plates, windows misted over. My mother, who is with us tonight, is also sixteen, and going this time under the name of Harriet (I think) which is a false name and no kin to the beautiful, imaginary playmate I had when I was four, who could fly and would write me letters with hand-painted stamps on them (canceled). After coming all the way in the cold, to be in a room with no living persons in it. To be distressed. To feel superior. To hold myself in good and hard, to know what's possible and what's good for me. Little Harriet Shelley watches wide-eyed the intercourse of a real human family.

AUNT LUCY: No one would tell you the truth about yourself, Harriet, unless they loved you very much. I love you and that's why you can trust me when I tell you the truth about yourself. The truth is that you are bad all through. There isn't a thing about you that's good. You are thoroughly unlovable. And only a person who loves you very much could tell you this.

UNCLE GEORGE: Tell me all your troubles, but don't say a word against your aunt. Your aunt is a saint.

My MOTHER SITS listening to the radio, learning how to sew.

She's making a patchwork quilt. Does she dislike her family? She denies it. She's not really going to grow up to be a poet. My mother has a mind like a bog; contraries meet in it and everything becomes instantly rotted away. Or her mind is a peat bog that preserves whole corpses. The truth is that I haven't the right to say what's going on in her mind because I know nothing about it.

She goes on sewing, gentle, placid, and serene, everything she should be. I told her that she could have any color car she wanted as long as it was black but even this failed to shake my soundless mother; One's Personal History Is Bunk, she might have answered me but didn't; she didn't even move away down the couch because my mother is not even mildly stubborn. Perhaps if she were not so polite she would say, "I don't know what you're talking about," but no, she's perfect, and when she raises her great, wondering, credulous, tear-filled gaze, it's not for me but on account of bad Mr. X in the kitchen, who is telling stories to Uncle George about the women who have jobs with him, for example, that their asses stick out:

MR. X: ⸺ ⸺ ⸺ ⸺ ⸺ ass.

UNCLE GEORGE: Mr. X is only joking, dear.

MR. X: That's right. Don't be so sensitive. How can you go out and get a job someday if you're so sensitive? I don't have anything against the ladies who work with me. I think they're fine. I think you're fine, even though you're so sensitive.

AUNT LUCY: See? Mr. X thinks you're fine.

MR. X: I think your aunt is fine, too.

UNCLE GEORGE: He thinks your aunt is fine, too, because he *likes* ladies.

AUNT LUCY: See? Mr. X is generous.

UNCLE GEORGE: Even though your aunt Lucy is a fool.

To cut out those noises people emit from time to time. To be hard and old. To retreat finally. To be free.

"My parents love each other," says my mother, shaking out her work, malignancy in its every fold. She's a wonder. She really believes. I used to think I knew the form of the ultimate relation between my mother and myself but now I'm not so sure; there's that unbreakable steel spring in her accepting head, no longer can I come clattering up the King's highway on my centaur/centurion's hindquarters (half Irish hunter, half plough horse, gray, fat, lazy, name: Mr. Ed) and I no longer look down from my wild, crazy, hero-assassin's eminence at the innkeeper's little daughter in her chaste yet svelte gingham (with its décolletage) and her beautiful, spiritual, dumb eyes and her crumby soul.

"Do you," I said, "do you—tell me!—oh do you—believe me!—*do you*—DO YOU—BELIEVE ALL THAT?"

"Yes," she says.

Oh if you only knew! says her face. Her hands, resting on their sewing, change their import: Life is so hard, hard, hard. An unspoken rule between us has been that I can hate her but she can't hate me; this breaks. (A day in the longed-for life: for once when my mother is carried across the crumbling battlements on the screen the audience laughs, they hoot when she wrings her hands, when she obeys her father's prohibition they howl, when she is seduced they screech, when it starts to snow and the hero walks on her face with his lovely black boots it's all over, and by the time she commits suicide, *there is nobody there*.)

"I think," says my mother thoughtfully, biting a thread, "that I'm going to get married." She looks at me, shrewdly and with considerable hatred.

"That way," she says in a low, controlled voice, *"I will be able to get away from you!"*

(When she was little my mother used to scare her relatives by asking them if they were happy; they would always answer, *"Of course* I'm happy." When I was little I once asked her if she was happy and she said "Of course I'm happy.")

SOMETHING that will never happen: my mother and I, chums, sharing secrets, giggling at the dinner table, writing in each other's slambooks, going to the movies together. Doing up each other's hair. It's not dreadful that she doesn't want me, just embarrassing, considering that I made the proposal first. She would beam, saying sentimental things about her motherhood, anxiously reaching for my hand across the table. She was not wicked, ever, or cruel, or unkind. We'll never go skating together, never make cocoa in the kitchen at midnight, snurfing in our cups and whooping it up behind the stove. I was never eight. I was never eleven. I was never thirteen. The mind I am in now came to me some time after puberty, not the initiation into sex (which is supposed to be the important thing) but the under-standing that everything I had suffered from as a child, all my queerness, all my neuroses, the awful stiffnesses, the things people scorned in me, that all these would be all right when I was an adult because when I was an adult I would have power.

And I do. I do.

Power gave me life. I like it. Here's something else I like: when I was twenty-nine and my mother—flustered and ingen-uous—told me that she'd had an embarrassing dream about me. Did she expect to be hit? It was embarrassing (she said) because it was incestuous. She dreamed we had eloped and were making love.

Don't laugh. I told it for years against her. I said all sorts of awful things. But what matters still matters, i.e. my mother's kicking a wastebasket the length of the living room in a rage (as she once bragged to me she did) or striking her breast, crying melodramatically, "Me Martian! Me good! You Jupiterian! You bad!" (as she also did). Bless you! do you think she married to get away from me, the Lesbian love-object? I wasn't born yet.

It's immensely sweet of her to offer to marry me, but what I want to know is: do you think we're suited?

DON JOSÉ, the Brazilian heiress—wait a minute, I'm getting them muddled up, that was the other one where I was the Brazilian heiress, this one's Don José and he's *Argentinian* and an *Heir*—anyway, his cruel smile undressed her with his eyes, I don't think I can go on writing like this, she said. Are you not woman enough to know? And the unfortunate sadist tossed his typewriter out the window. That is what they called working girls in those days. My mother will never forgive me. For what? cried the incautious maid with the almond-blue eyes. Thank you, sir, I shall make the bed, she sobbed. Only do not lay me in it; that will crease the counterpane and I will be fired. And your children, his mustache twitching, I have sworn to have them, have me first, no, have a shashlik; there is blood on my dress.

Blood!

I have murdered the butler.

(A lively game of bed-to-bed trash filled the evening air as the charming little summer-camp maedchen disemboweled the myth and passed it gigglingly from hand to hand. Salugi! Gesundheit. Thank you very much.)

What Every Woman Knows.

IT IS QUITE POSSIBLE that none of this happened or has value; still I wish life could have been different for my mother. But we're all in Tiamat's lap, so there's no use complaining. In the daytime we stand on Her knees, looking up at Her face, and at night She hides Her face so we get uneasy. Our Father Witch (in whom I used to believe) is very jealous of his name or it's a secret or it's too ugly (or maybe he hasn't got any) but you can call Her Nyame and Tanit, call Her 'Anat, Atea, Tabiti, Tibirra over the place and She doesn't mind kiddies pulling at her skirt call her Nyame and Tanit, call Her 'Anat, Atea, Tabiti Tibirra. This is what comes of re-meeting one's mother when she was only two—how willful she was! how charming, and how strong. I wish she had not grown up to be a doormat, but all the same what a blessing it is not to have been made by somebody's hands like a piece of clay, and then he breathed a spirit in you, etc. so you are clay and not-clay, your ingredients fighting each other like the irritable vitamin pill in the ad—what a joy and a pleasure to have been born, just ordinary born, you know, out of dirt and flesh, all of one piece and of the same stuff She is. To be my mother's child. (Your pleasures and pains are your belly-button-cord to the Great Mother; they prove you were once part of Her.)

I asked, Why couldn't my mother have been more like You? But She didn't answer. I felt something coming from Her. Times She doesn't like me—I don't always like myself—but we're still the same stuff.

Change my life! I said.

Sorry, won't. Her fog veiled Her face (that is one of Her moods) and Her towns (which are the rings on Her fingers) grew ugly. Tiamat is talking. She spoke through me as in the Bible, that is I spoke, knowing the answer:

Am I my mother's mother?

ON WINTER NIGHTS, when my mother and I were twelve, we would go out together with chocolate cigarettes and pose under street lights like little prostitutes, pretending that we were smoking. It was very glamorous. Now we do it in our cheap dresses, our tight shoes; my mother has waited for The Man all her life, that's why she had no time for me. In the beauty parlor, on the street, in the nursing home, waiting for The Man. We lean on each other, very tired, in our make-up, a sad friendship between us. We even hold hands.

Will you be my best friend? she says.

I say yes.

Will you live with me?

I say yes.

Will you sleep with me and wake with me?

I say yes.

Will you marry me?

I say yes.

ALL YOU NEED IS LOVE.

Arny Christine Straayer

High Heels
1980

Arny Christine Straayer, a Chicago-based writer and film-maker, is co-editor of Black Maria *magazine and co-founder of Metis Press, a feminist publishing company. With an M.A. in creative writing and publishing from the Goddard Feminist Studies Program, she has published stories in such periodicals as* Sinister Wisdom, Womanspirit, Sojourner, Albatross, Moving Out, *and* Black Maria. *She co-authored* A Book of One's Own: Guide to Self-Publishing, *with Christine Leslie Johnson, has written a children's book,* The Rock and Me Immediately, *and collected her short stories, of which "High Heels" is one, in* Hurtin & Healin and Talkin It Over. *In 1980, Straayer received a Literary Arts Award from the Illinois Arts Council. She has been employed by the Artists-in-Residence Program of the Chicago Council on Fine Arts.*

Many of Straayer's stories examine relationships between women with biological links, particularly adult sisters and mothers and daughters. She writes, "There are so many clichés about mother-daughter relationships. Most of them work against us, replacing our real or potential experiences with acted-out scripts that serve patriarchal society."

All forms of interaction can become clichéd, but for many people, prescribed language and the stranglehold it has on our thinking is the most difficult form of stereotypical behavior from which to free ourselves. In this story, the girl and her mother work to regain their original, authentic love and trust by using language as a pointer toward memories of other kinds of communication, earlier sharing of sensory experience.

Perhaps the final difference between stereotypes and archetypes is that the former are attributed to us by others and serve to diminish our sense of self while the latter are recognized by us and expand our sense of connection with those who have lived before us and that which lives on in us. "High Heels," an occasional story celebrating the reunion of a working-class mother and daughter, portrays two women struggling with themselves and each other for freedom from those "acted-out scripts," that is, from stereotypical behavior that has estranged them from each other. In their struggle, they reinvent "the pause" (discussed in the introduction), the archetypal ritual form of women's interactions with each other.

The thorazine girl and her mother sit on adjacent stools at a counter, facing the same direction. They have just walked here from Youtown Psychiatric Hospital. The short fat mother walked a few steps ahead, scouting out a narrow path between the dirty piles of snow and the sidewalk puddles. Her arms flapped at each side of her body for balance while only the pointed toes of her rubber boots touched the wet concrete. Her daughter followed, taller but slouchy, tennis shoes splashing through the muddy puddles, arms hugging a brown paper sack full of clothing.

Both women have cups of light coffee in front of them. They are not talking. The thorazine girl wears a lavender nylon jacket zipped up to her chin. Anchoring the pocket with one hand, she pushes the other inside for cigarettes. Her fingers do not bend well, making it difficult to flick the lighter. She holds the cigarette at the tips of her straight fingers like tweezers, touching it to the middle of her puckered lips, wetting the paper. It is a long thin menthol.

Her mother smokes a Camel, non-filter, and grips it between her teeth. She wears a turquoise plaid suit: a jacket that can no longer be buttoned, and a skirt that makes sitting on this stool difficult. Her legs want to spread under the counter but the skirt binds them. Feeling them stick to the plastic seat, she scooches her thighs to one side. The stool twirls. She pulls at the bottom ribbing of an orange shell, straightening it over her large breasts and stomach, rattling several strings of heavy green beads. A column of ashes is beginning to droop from her Camel. Cupping her whole hand over her mouth, she clasps the cigarette

deep in the web of her fingers. Nonetheless, the ashes fall, in a
stack to her lap. She tries to whisk them away, but they crumble
and smear on her skirt.

The mother is nervous. She wants to stare at her daughter,
to brush the shaggy blonde hair back behind her ears, to look
into her mouth for the color of her tongue. Her daughter's skin
is transparent. She needs sunshine. The blue veins along her
temples make her look like a fetus. In the middle of her forehead
is a scab. The mother wants to spread ointment on the scab and
cradle the pale head. If she were not afraid, she would ask about
the scab, how it happened, but perhaps her girl would get angry.

It is disheartening to be afraid of one's own daughter, to fear
her rejection. Yes, the hospital had been a mistake. But hadn't
she suffered enough during these months of longing, not being
allowed to visit. The love is throbbing inside her. How long can
her body hold still?

She slides the palm of her hand across the top of her head.
Her hand is red and tough like leather. Her hair is dyed pitch
black, is tangled and dry. She has not combed it today and the
set is nearly out. Neither has she washed her face. Last night's
lipstick has been rubbed into her thin lips, leaving them orange,
but dull. She stretches them back and forth and bites at them,
trying to contain the emotions inside her.

Yesterday, the daughter had finally accepted her phone call.
She did not say hello. She said, "Get me out of here." Her voice
was hostile. The mother answered, "Yes, yes, my darling," and
the daughter said, "Don't call me darling."

It was a second chance for the mother. She pressed a hand to
her chest as she hung up the phone. Her breathing was fast.
Tomorrow she would see her girl. They would be together
again. She would not make another bad mistake. At work that
night, she dropped a customer's roast beef dinner on the floor.
She was clumsy and giddy. She laughed about it. Later she had
cried, not sleeping at all, making her eyes puffy and red for this
morning.

The daughter's head is hanging over her coffee. She cannot
bear the thought of looking into her mother's eyes. At the
hospital, they were red and puffy. She had walked behind her
mother down the sidewalk so as not to see them again. Maybe,

under the redness, there is still a yellow bruise from where she hit her mother. Maybe there is a scar still fresh red.

The doctors thought she'd forgotten about hitting her mother, that the drugs had erased it from her brain. They said it was not wrong anyway but just the normal reaction of a girl who needed to break away from her mother and grow up. But that was not why she had hit her mother. It was because her mother betrayed her and called them to come after her. She hit her mother's eye with the telephone handle and saw it turn black while they rode to the hospital.

Her mother must not turn to face her. If she does, the daughter will close her eyes or stand up and walk out, rather than see the redness. She is guilty. She is the worst. She clubbed her own mother. She is not a darling.

For months in the hospital, she had dreamed of the old days when she sat in a booth waiting for her mother to get off work. Every evening seemed so long before they could walk home holding hands, she carrying her mother's high heels in summer, sometimes resting on some doorstep to rub her mother's sore feet. She wants to do that now. Her mother doesn't wear high heels anymore, but her feet are calloused from all the hard years. They need lotion. She wants to kiss them with her full lips, wet them with her tears. She wants to lie with her mother's feet tickling her belly again, with her mother laughing too, her loud shrill laughter. But she does not deserve it.

When those eyes are not red anymore, the daughter will be able to apologize. For now, she must not look, but keep busy instead with her cigarette and coffee. She moves her hand to the ashtray and pecks at the long thin menthol. The thorazine makes her hand far away. The cigarette rolls into the bowl of the ashtray. She reaches for her coffee cup with both hands. It is cold. When did it get cold? The thorazine makes her head sluggish. She raises the cup in slow motion. Then bracing her elbows on the counter, she bends forward until her mouth touches the edge, and drinks down all the cold coffee, so she can ask the waitress for more. She tries to wave to the waitress but cannot control her hand.

What have I done to her, the mother is thinking as the daughter uses one hand to lift the other. Her mouth opens to shriek for the waitress before she remembers the doctors' instructions to stay quiet for her daughter's sake. She is too loud and coarse for her big girl. Her shoulders hunch up around the chin. But the daughter hasn't noticed. She is staring into space again, her eyes glazed, far away.

The mother's blunt fingers thump against the counter. She cannot stand this separation. She'd been wrong. Wrong. Why had she thought her girl needed a hospital? It had only forced them apart, her daughter helpless, herself excluded. Her daughter didn't need treatment. Everyone was just trying to separate them. One way or another, those doctors were determined to force them apart. They were just jealous. What did they know? So what if she'd driven two hundred miles to the university, and her daughter wouldn't get out of the car. It was not wrong. It didn't mean she needed a hospital. Oh, what had happened to her girl in there while she was out here abandoned?

The waitress refills their cups. The coffee is too hot, and the daughter spills it on her chin. It dribbles down into the dimple below her mouth. Oh my poor damaged baby, thinks the mother, turning towards her. My poor broken baby. She looks at her daughter's fragile lips and thin eyelids closed. The dimple looks sad on her face now, as if she were crying. That cute little dimple that used to make her look so happy.

The mother is seeing her daughter at five, playing dress-up lady in mamma's high heels; at eight, sitting in the restaurant booth, her dimple filled with mamma's pink powder; at eleven, sticking out that sensitive chin and saying, "It's you and me, partner;" at sixteen, filling the pockets of mother's red blouse wih candy kisses.

"Hey, remember the candy kisses you gave me?" she blurts out unintentionally. Her daughter's head is lowered towards the counter. But from the side, the mother sees a delicate eyelash twitch, a corner of the mouth curl. "Remember the matching red blouses?"

The daughter's chin is moving tentatively. The lips begin to open. Words are coming out slowly, one by one, in a whisper. "Remember the picture of me in your high heels?"

The voice is barely her daughter's. The mother knows without looking that the tongue is too thick. "Yes . . . I do." She stubs out her Camel, tipping the ashtray and flipping ashes onto the counter. Tears are welling in her eyes. Her thin lips are stretching and jerking into a smile.

The daughter's head is lifting. She is holding one hand at the back of her neck as if to support it. Her eyelids flutter. "There was a woman in the hospital who still wore high heels." She stops for moment to rest. "Whenever the halls were mopped and slippery, she wobbled, like I used to do, in yours." The daughter glances timidly at the dimple in her mother's fat chin. "I told her, I sure wished my mom could see that."

Ann Allen Shockley

A Birthday Remembered
1980

In "Towards a Black Feminist Criticism," Barbara Smith names Ann Allen Shockley (b. 1927) as one of "a handful of Black women who have risked everything for truth" having "broken ground in the vast wilderness of works that do not exist." A librarian and professor of library science at Fisk University, Shockley has written a number of important works in the field of black librarianship, as well as the novels Loving Her *(1974) and* Say Jesus and Come to Me *(1982), and the short story collection* The Black and White of It *(1980), from which "A Birthday Remembered" is reprinted. In addition, she has published several dozen stories in such periodicals as* Negro Digest, Freedomways, Black World, Feminary, Umbra, *and* Sinister Wisdom *She writes about herself,*

> [I] was born in Louisville, Kentucky, where an eighth grade English teacher helped to give birth to my thoughts of becoming a writer. I have been writing since that time.
> I was a newspaper reporter, free-lance writer and substitute teacher before entering the field of librarianship. . . . Working as an academic librarian, I write on weekends, holidays, and summer months, with my dogs, Tiffany and Bianca, watching the birthing pains. I wish it could be different.

She is divorced and has two grown children.
Most of Shockley's short fiction deals with how the lives of individual and coupled black heterosexuals—mostly middle class—and black and racially unidentified lesbians are short-circuited by racism, sexism, and homophobia.

There is a constant interface between intracouple tensions—those that exist between the partners in every relationship who choose each other and yet need to define personal boundaries—and the tensions of shared victimization.

Shockley's work illuminates how shared oppression and, in the case of lesbians, social invisibility, make the partners in a relationship more dependent on and desperate for each other in comparison to couples for whom external validations exist. Such partners are often pushed closer together than autonomous adults can stand to be. At the same time, the shared oppression gives greater priority to their shared persecution and to those attributes for which they are victimized than to the unique personal qualities that make or break relationships undertaken in greater freedom and with social reinforcement. Shockley documents the erosions of hope, the challenges to loyalty presented by threats to survival, the insecurities of those trapped in socially devalued categories, and the poisoning of love and intimacy by invasions of bigotry. She writes poignantly of the personal and illuminates by implication the political.

"A Birthday Remembered," while it touches on all the pain and cruelty delineated in her other stories, is one of the few that ends with an affirmation, testifying that mothering is something more than a biological accident, that the spirit and the activities of nurturance equal or transcend the claims of blood. With this message, Shockley reaffirms the points made in Helen Hull's story, "The Fire," in Fannie Hurst's story, "Oats for the Woman," and in Sherley Anne Williams's story, "The Lawd Don't Like Ugly": Women give the gift of mothering to women across the generations not only as mothers, but as teachers, as step-mothers, as mentors, and as friends.

"Hello—Aunt El—?"

The familiar voice came over the telephone, young, vivacious, excited—a girlish echo reminding her of the past. "Tobie—"

"Happy birthday!"

"Thank you—" Ellen felt a rush of warmth, pleased that Tobie had remembered. But hadn't Tobie always. Besides, her birthday wasn't difficult to remember, falling on Valentine's Day. *A heart born especially for me,* Jackie used to tease.

"May I come over?"

Now Tobie's voice sounded a little strained. Ellen could visualize the puckers of thin lines forming between her wide-spaced eyes. The tightness in her throat delayed an answer. Why shouldn't she? Then again, why *should* she really want to? Tobie no longer belonged to her—*them.* When Jackie died a year ago,

Tobie had to go back to her father. A splintering separation, after all their years of living together, *belonging* together—Tobie, Jackie and herself.

The three of them had survived through the tumultuous stress of trying to make it, ever since Jackie walked out on Roger and came to live with her. Tobie was just five years old—too small and pale for her age, too nervous from the parental arguments.

Roger had been furious, appalled and angry at his wife's leaving him for a woman. Ellen knew it was more an affront to his male ego than losing Jackie. Particularly when it belonged to one who was striving ruthlessly to become a top business executive, amassing along the way all the exterior garnishments that were supposed to go along with it. He had purchased a large, two-story brick colonial house in the suburbs, replete with swimming pool and a paneled country squire station wagon for Jackie to do her errands. When she left him, he had tried to declare her temporarily insane.

Ellen thought that perhaps Jackie *had* been crazy to leave all of that and come to live with her in a cramped apartment on her salary. She wasn't making that much at the time as a staff writer for *Women's Homemaking* magazine's food section. But, somehow, they had made out, until Jackie got a job teaching in an elementary school. Jackie loved children, and had a way with them.

"Hey—Aunt El. You still with me?"

Tobie was waiting for an answer. One could get so involved in the past. "Of course, dear. Please *do* come over," she invited, thinking it wasn't until later she was to have dinner with Harriet. All she had to do was change from her jumpsuit to a dress.

"I'm bringing a friend who I want you to meet. Ok?"

Tobie never had an abundance of friends, only special ones who were close, for that was her way. At first, she and Jackie had mistakenly thought Tobie was ashamed of their relationship—what they were to each other. They knew Tobie was aware of it. How could she not have been. Real love can't be hidden. It inevitably is transmitted through a glance, affectionate touch, strong feelings that show.

Then there was the rainy, cold night in November, one month after Jackie had left him, when Roger came to the apartment, hurling threats, shouting obscenities. He was going to take them to court, declare them perverts, unfit to raise a child. Tobie must have heard the words flung out at them through the paper-thin walls.

"Wonderful, darling. I'll look forward to meeting your—friend."

The phone clicked and Tobie wasn't there anymore. Ellen remained seated on the couch, motionless, as if the remembrance of all that had gone by in ten years had risen like a mist to cover her in sadness. There had not been a divorce because of his man-stubborness and Jackie's woman-fear for Tobie. When she died, he buried her. She hadn't been allowed to do this one last thing for Jackie. To *be* with her during the last rituals, to hold a fourteen-year-old who was in all but flesh, her daughter too. The next morning after the funeral, Tobie came by to be with her, to cry her tears, sustain her grief. The sorrow shared as one was their solitary entombment for her. Through the passing days, the biting cruelty of it all slowly healed, leaving only the scar tissue. Jackie had been laid to rest in her heart.

Ellen's eyes fell on the array of birthday cards on the coffee table and the vase of red roses that Harriet had sent. Meeting Harriet had helped her to get over the travail of death's cruel separation. Incurable illnesses are like earthquakes—they swallow quickly. It wasn't too bad now. She could look back and recall without too much pain. All it takes is someone to help, someone who cares, and the eraser of time.

The living room was beginning to become shaded with dark-fingered lances of shadows. She reached over and turned on a table lamp. The day was quickly vanishing into the grayness of night. What she should do was get a drink. A good, stiff celebrating birthday martini. After all, she was forty-four years old. Six more years, if still alive, she would reach the half century mark.

She got up and went to the kitchen. There she turned on the light which brought into sharp, garish focus the ultra-modern bright chrome and copper, resembling the spacious kitchens featured in her magazine articles where various culinary talents were exhibited. Thankfully, through her writing skills, she had been able to help make their living better before Jackie passed.

She had become editor of the food section and had written a cookbook. Her publisher had assured her that cookbooks always sell, and hers had.

A martini called for gin, vermouth, lemon, and an olive. She got out a glass pitcher and stirrer. Jackie preferred sunrises. She made them for her in the evenings, after the lengthy daily struggles of climbing the ladder together. Jackie had become principal of the school, a model for those beneath her, and an in-school parent for the students. Ellen marveled at how she had blossomed, learning to become independent after being a college trained housewife to Roger. *There's so much to living that I did not know before*, Jackie had told her happily. Yes, indeed, there was a lot to living that neither had known before.

She mixed the drink in the shaker, stirred it slowly and poured some in a glass, topping it with a round green olive with a small red eye-circle. *Here's to you, Ellen Simms, on your birthday!* She lifted the glass in a toast and the drink went down smoothly. Then the doorbell rang. Tobie must have been just around the corner. As soon as she responded, Tobie sang out cheerfully: "Happy birthday to you—happy birthday to you!"

Tobie hugged her and Ellen found her nose pressed into the cold leather of her jacket. Tobie seemed taller. *They do grow*, she mockingly reminded herself, comparing her own short stockiness to Tobie's height.

"A present for you, Aunt El—"

When Tobie thrust the gift into her arms, Ellen protested: "You shouldn't have." The package was neatly store wrapped and tied with a pink ribbon holding a card.

"You know I never forget your birthday, Aunt El—"

At that moment, she saw the boy standing awkwardly behind her. He had a round, friendly face and a mass of dark brown hair parted on the side.

"Hello—" she spoke to him.

"Aunt El—this is Warrick."

"Come in and take off your coats. Would you like some hot cocoa to warm you up? I know it's cold outside." Tobie used to love hot cocoa with a marshmallow floating like a full-grown moon on top. This was her favorite on Sunday mornings when they had a leisurely breakfast together.

"Cocoa—you *know* what I like!" Tobie exclaimed, throwing off her coat and curling up on the sofa.

Ellen watched her, noting the girlishness hadn't gone yet in the transitional adolescent stage. She looked older. Her blonde hair was cut short and bangs covered her forehead. Physically, she looked more like her father with the sharp, angular face, but there was her mother where it counted most, in her warmth and quickness of smile. Did her father know that she was here— with her. Like visiting a widowed parent—eight years of child-rearing, child-caring, child-loving.

"Open your present, Aunt El—"

"All right." First she read the heart shaped card with the fringed edges about Valentine birthdays, and then the scribbled message: *To my one and only, Aunt El, with love, always.* She blinked back the tears and made a fanfare out of unwrapping the gift. It was a big, glossy, illustrated, expensive cookbook of ancient Eastern recipes.

"Thank you, my dear." She leaned over to kiss Tobie's cheek. "It's lovely."

"Tobie saved up a week's salary to buy it—" Warrick announced proudly, settling in the rocker opposite the sofa. His voice was changing, and there was an inflamed red pimple beside his nose. On the front of his red and white pullover sweater were the words Terrence Academy. The right sleeve had a large white T.

"Warrick! Shame on you giving my secrets away," Tobie laughed, playfully chastising him.

"Where are you working?" Ellen asked, hanging their coats in the closet. She couldn't imagine Roger Ewing permitting his teen-aged daughter to work.

"I'm a library page after school at the branch near home. I like to have my *own* money—" she added reflectively.

Ellen hesitated, wondering if she should ask. Don't forget the social amenities. Isn't that what they had taught Tobie throughout the years. "How is your—father?" she asked, the words sounding like cracked dry ice.

"Oh, Dad's ok," she shrugged, kicking off the high wooden wedge platforms with interlacing straps. "His main object in life seems to be to prove how much money he can make and *keep*."

Roger's a miser at heart: he wants every cent I spend accounted for, yet he'll go out and buy something outlandishly showy to prove he's got money, Jackie had commented about him.

Why was it that people happen to be in certain places at the right or wrong time? Like the dinner party she had been assigned to write up for the magazine to describe the elegance of the food, drinks and table setting. There seated next to her was Jackie, looking small, frail and lost among the spirited laughter and inane chitchat of the moneyed. Roger was on her other side, appearing to be thoroughly enjoying himself talking to the big bosomed woman with the glittering necklace and frosted white hair. There was the interest at first sight, hidden hormones clashing while a subtle intuitive knowingness flashed hidden messages above the clamor of the room. *If only we could decide our own fates, what would life then be?*

"I'll make the cocoa—" she said, retreating to the kitchen.

The martini pitcher was on the counter where she had left it. Immediately she poured another drink. She had been ruminating too much. Stop the past. Drink and be merry. Chase the haunting memories away.

"Aunt El—need any help?"

Tobie came in. She had put her shoes back on and they made a hard noise against the linoleum. The wedges looked like ancient ships, causing her to wonder if they were comfortable. The bell-bottom blue jeans billowed over them like sails. "No— nothing to making cocoa. After all the times of doing it for you—" The reminder slipped out. She wished it hadn't.

Tobie laughed, and the sound made everything all right again. "What do you think of Warrick?" she asked, reaching into the closet for cups and saucers. Everything was known to her in a place that had once been home.

"He seems like a nice—boy." Suppose it had been a girl? People choose who they want. This they had tried to instill in her in their unobtrusive way. "How does your father like him?"

"Dad hasn't met him yet," Tobie said quietly. "I wanted to get *your* opinion *first.* Anyway, Dad stays busy and away so much that we don't have much time to talk. The housekeeper takes care of the house—and me—who, I suppose, goes with the house." She gazed down at the floor, biting her lip, face clouded. "I miss Mom—don't you?"

"Yes—" she replied softly. "But we have to get used to living without loved ones. That time must inevitably come, sooner or later, for somebody."

She turned away, pretending to search the refrigerator so Tobie couldn't see her face. Do something else while waiting for the milk to warm. Prepare sandwiches. Young people were always hungry—feeding growth. She had cold chicken and potato salad left over from last night.

"I thought if *you* liked Warrick, Mom would too. He plays on the basketball team," Tobie continued, watching her slice the chicken and take out the jars of pickles and mustard from the refrigerator.

"Are you—serious, about him?" Ellen asked, praying that she wasn't. Not at this stage of youth—almost fifteen.

"Of course not! We're just friends. He's someone to go places and do things with."

"Good!" Ellen exclaimed, feeling an impending burden lifted. "There's plenty of time for the other. You have to go to college and—" she went on hurriedly about those things which normally fall in place for young lives.

Tobie smiled. "I *knew* you were going to say that, Aunt El." Then she looked directly at her, blue eyes locking Ellen's in a vise. "Anyway, someday, if I ever *do* get serious about someone, I hope it will be as wonderful and beautiful as what you and Mom had together."

God, for the first time, it was out in the open! She felt the shock of the words, unexpected, frank—a blessing. "I do too, dear. Like we had." Her hands trembled from the weight of the moment between them. A bridge had transformed Tobie from girl to woman now to her.

"Aunt El, the milk's boiling over!"

"I've lost my cocoa-making expertise," Ellen laughed, snatching the pan off the burner. The milk had boiled into a bubbling white-coated cascade of foam.

When the tray of food was ready, they went back to the living room where Warrick was watching TV. While they ate hungrily, Ellen finished her drink, feeling light, warm and happy.

When the telephone rang, it was like a rude interruption into a special cradle of time. Harriet wanted to know if she would be ready around seven-thirty for dinner. She glanced at her watch. It was just six o'clock. Besides, what was more important to her than this?

Later, Tobie said: "We'd better be going. Warrick's taking me to the movies. Thanks for the treat, Aunt El."

"And, thank *you* for the present. I'm glad you came by to make my birthday a happy one. *Both* of you."

"Nice meeting you, Miss Simms," Warrick said, extending his hand. "Tobie talks about you all the time. Now I can see why!"

She liked him. "Come back—anytime."

Tobie kissed her goodbye at the door. When they left, the tears were finally freed—in sadness and happiness too. Tobie was going to make it all right. Jackie would have been proud. They had made good parents.

We gratefully acknowledge permission to reprint the following material:

Susan Pettigru King Bowen, "A Marriage of Persuasion." First published in *Russell's Magazine*, 1857.

E. M. Broner, "Song of Purification" from "The Ceremonial Woman: The Ceremony of Cleansing One's Self of Impurities—Racism." Used with permission of the author.

Alice Brown, "The Way of Peace." First published in *Outlook*, 1898.

Caroline W. Healey Dall, "Annie Grey: A Tale." First published in *The Liberty Bell*, 1848.

Mary E. Wilkins Freeman, "Old Woman Magoun." From *The Best Stories of Mary E. Wilkins,* selected by Henry Wysham Lanier. Copyright © 1909 by Harper & Row, Publishers, Inc. By permission of Harper & Row, Publishers, Inc.

Helen Rose Hull, "The Fire." First published in *Century*, 1917. Reprinted in *The Ladder* and in *Lesbians Home Journal: Stories from the Ladder,* edited by Barbara Grier and C. Reif, Diana Press, 1976.

Fannie Hurst, "Oats for the Woman." Reprinted by permission of Curtis Brown, Ltd. Copyright © 1919 by Harper & Brothers.

Helen Reimensnyder Martin, "Mrs. Gladfelter's Revolt." Reprinted by permission of *The Nation*.

Tillie Olsen, "I Stand Here Ironing." Excerpted from the book *Tell Me a Riddle* by Tillie Olsen. Copyright © 1956 by Tillie Olsen. Reprinted by permission of Delacorte Press/Seymour Lawrence.

Elizabeth Stuart Phelps, "Old Mother Goose." First published in *The Independent*, 1873.

Joanna Russ, "Autobiography of My Mother." First published in *Epoch*, 1975. Reprinted by permission of the author.

Ann Allen Shockley, "A Birthday Remembered." Reprinted from her volume *The Black and White of It,* The Naiad Press, 1980. Copyright © 1980 by Ann Allen Shockley. Used by permission.

Tess Slesinger, "Mother to Dinner." Reprinted from her volume *Time: The Present,* 1935. Copyright renewed by Frank Davis. Used by permission.

Arny Christine Straayer, "High Heels." First published in *Hurtin &*

THE FEMINIST PRESS offers alternatives in education and in literature. Founded in 1970, this non-profit, tax-exempt educational and publishing organization works to eliminate sexual stereotypes in books and schools and to provide literature with a broad vision of human potential. The publishing program includes reprints of important works by women, feminist biographies of women, and nonsexist children's books. Curricular materials, bibliographies, directories, and a quarterly journal provide information and support for students and teachers of women's studies. In-service projects help to transform teaching methods and curricula. Through publications and projects, The Feminist Press contributes to the rediscovery of the history of women and the emergence of a more humane society.

FEMINIST CLASSICS
FROM THE FEMINIST PRESS

Antoinette Brown Blackwell: A Biography, by Elizabeth Cazden. $16.95 cloth, $9.95 paper.

Between Mothers and Daughters: Stories Across a Generation. Edited by Susan Koppelman. $8.95 paper.

Brown Girl, Brownstones, a novel by Paule Marshall. Afterword by Mary Helen Washington. $7.95 paper.

Call Home the Heart, a novel of the thirties, by Fielding Burke. Introduction by Alice Kessler-Harris and Paul Lauter and afterwords by Sylvia J. Cook and Anna W. Shannon. $8.95 paper.

Cassandra, by Florence Nightingale. Introduction by Myra Stark. Epilogue by Cynthia Macdonald. $3.50 paper.

The Convert, a novel by Elizabeth Robins. Introduction by Jane Marcus. $6.95 paper.

Daughter of Earth, a novel by Agnes Smedley. Afterword by Paul Lauter. $6.95 paper.

The Female Spectator, edited by Mary R. Mahl and Helen Koon. $8.95 paper.

Guardian Angel and Other Stories, by Margery Latimer. Afterwords by Louis Kampf, Meridel Le Sueur, and Nancy Loughridge. $8.95 paper.

I Love Myself When I Am Laughing . . . And then Again When I Am Looking Mean and Impressive, by Zora Neale Hurston. Edited by Alice Walker with an introduction by Mary Helen Washington. $9.95 paper.

Käthe Kollwitz: Woman and Artist, by Martha Kearns. $7.95 paper.

Life in the Iron Mills, by Rebecca Harding Davis. Biographical interpretation by Tillie Olsen. $4.95 paper.

The Living Is Easy, a novel by Dorothy West. Afterword by Adelaide M. Cromwell. $7.95 paper.

The Maimie Papers. Edited by Ruth Rosen and Sue Davidson. Introduction by Ruth Rosen. $11.95 paper.

Mother to Daughter, Daughter to Mother: A Daybook and Reader. Selected and shaped by Tillie Olsen. $9.95 paper.

The Other Woman: Stories of Two Women and a Man. Edited by Susan Koppelman. $8.95 paper.

OTHER TITLES
FROM THE FEMINIST PRESS

Black Foremothers: Three Lives, by Dorothy Sterling. $6.95 paper.

But Some of Us Are Brave: Black Women's Studies. Edited by Gloria T. Hull, Patricia Bell Scott, and Barbara Smith. $14.85 cloth, $9.95 paper.

Complaints and Disorders: The Sexual Politics of Sickness, by Barbara Ehrenreich and Deirdre English. $3.95 paper.

The Cross-Cultural Study of Women. Edited by Margot Duley-Morrow and Mary I. Edwards. $8.95 paper.

Household and Kin: Families in Flux, by Amy Swerdlow et al. $14.95 cloth. $6.95 paper.

How to Get Money for Research, by Mary Rubin and the Business and Professional Women's Foundation. Foreword by Mariam Chamberlain. $5.95 paper.

In Her Own Image: Women Working in the Arts. Edited with an introduction by Elaine Hedges and Ingrid Wendt. $17.95 cloth, $8.95 paper.

Las Mujeres: Conversations from a Hispanic Community, by Nan Elsasser, Kyle MacKenzie, and Yvonne Tixier y Vigil. $14.95 cloth, $6.95 paper.

Lesbian Studies: Present and Future. Edited by Margaret Cruikshank. $14.95 cloth, $7.95 paper.

Moving the Mountain: Women Working for Social Change, by Ellen Cantarow with Susan Gushee O'Malley and Sharon Hartman Strom. $6.95 paper

Out of the Bleachers: Writings on Women and Sport. Edited with an introduction by Stephanie L. Twin. $7.95 paper.

Reconstructing American Literature: Courses, Syllabi, Issues. Edited by Paul Lauter. $10.95 paper.

Salt of the Earth, screenplay by Michael Wilson with historical commentary by Deborah Silverton Rosenfelt. $5.95 paper.

The Sex-Role Cycle: Socialization from Infancy to Old Age, by Nancy Romer. $6.95 paper.

Witches, Midwives, and Nurses: A History of Women Healers, by Barbara Ehrenreich and Deirdre English. $3.95 paper.